BOUND BY DESIRE

Gabriel caught Ariana's lower lip between his teeth and sucked softly. She moaned, her desire growing.

"Tell me you are enjoying this," he whispered.

"I am enjoying this too much," she breathed.

His hands caressed her hips, gently stroking her skin. Tentatively, she touched his chest. He reminded her of a beautiful Greek statue, too perfect to be real. She skimmed the planes of his stomach with her fingers and enjoyed his sharp intake of breath. His body was wondrous, all angles and hardness, but his skin was soft as finely spun silk.

"I assure you, Ariana, when I take a woman, 'tis *very* pleasant for her."

The words echoed in her mind. She felt as if she were on the brink of some dangerous cliff, dizzy and giddy from the height but enchanted by the altitude all the same.

"Ariana," he murmured.

She shivered, entranced by the languid strokes of his fingers.

"Ariana, trust me." He continued his gentle assault, moving his hands to her back and simply touching, rubbing, stroking her skin.

"It would be pleasant for me?" she whispered at long last.

Leaning down, he kissed her cheek. "*Very* pleasant for you."

Her shoulders relaxed. Gabriel was so different than any man she'd ever known, so gentle in his seduction. She wanted to trust him. She wanted to experience this pleasantness, this heat. She wanted to be wild and free.

Slowly, she nodded . . .

Books by Jessica Trapp

MASTER OF DESIRE

MASTER OF PLEASURE

Published by Kensington Publishing Corporation

JESSICA TRAPP

Master of Desire

ZEBRA BOOKS
Kensington Publishing Corp.
www.kensingtonbooks.com

ZEBRA BOOKS are published by

Kensington Publishing Corp.
850 Third Avenue
New York, NY 10022

All Kensington titles, imprints, and distributed lines are available at special quantity discounts for bulk purchases for sales promotion, premiums, fund-raising, educational, or institutional use.

Special book excerpts or customized printings can also be created to fit specific needs. For details, write or phone the office of the Kensington Special Sales Manager: Attn. Special Sales Department. Kensington Publishing Corp., 850 Third Avenue, New York, NY 10022. Phone: 1-800-221-2647.

ISBN: 0-8217-7862-5

First Printing: May 2006
10 9 8 7 6 5 4 3 2 1

Printed in the United States of America

To my mom:
You pick me up when I fall.
You soothe me when I'm hurt.
You believe in me,
even when I don't believe in myself.

Mom, I love you.

Acknowledgments

I am grateful for the thousand helping hands that have come my way. This list barely skims the surface.

Thank you, Joe, for every dish you wash, every form you fill out, every kiss you give. You are my real-life hero.

Thank you, James, for making me smile. My world would be dull without you.

Thank you, Mom, for being there.

Thank you, Betty Pichardo, for your friendship, love, and prayers.

Thank you, Polly Williamson, Dawn Temple, and Melinda Porter, for rescuing me.

Thank you, Babette deJongh, for your faith and support.

Thank you, Paulette Heidbreder, for your help.

Thank you, Houston RWA chapters—Bay Area, West Houston, Northwest—for giving me so much.

Thank you, Terri Richardson, because you live life with an open and generous heart.

Thank you, Romance Unleashed Authors, for daily inspiration.

Thank you, Aunt Rita, for your encouragement.

Thank you, Shashana Crichton and John Scognamiglio for all you do.

Chapter I

Thornbury Abbey, England, 1487

The hard, long bulge tenting the priest's scarlet robe caught Lady Ariana's attention. The man paced near the cathedral altar lighting tall stalks of candles. Ornate silk and velvet robes swirled around him in a flurry of red and white ripples, but the projection remained. Right at hip level.

Her heart pounded, and she felt a tiny catch in her throat. Had she been the demure king's chattel she pretended to be, mayhap the stiff bulge would have escaped her attention altogether. But experience as a spy had taught her to notice such things and kneeling here at the altar, 'twas impossible to miss.

This man definitely carried a sword.

Folding her hands in prayer, she bowed her head and debated what she should do. A woman in her circumstances could not afford to make a mistake. She dared not look up lest by some flinch or eye movement, she reveal the true purpose for today's prayer vigil: placing the tiny scroll hidden in her bodice into a secret compartment under the altar. The parchment's message contained notes she had gathered about members of the king's court—immoral secrets of which lords played carnal games with whom.

If she could, she would abandon this tawdry business altogether. But too much was at stake. Her blackmailer was very clear: pass along privileged gossip, or find herself swinging from the gallows with no one to care for her son.

Determination steeled her as she thought of Jason, her seven-year-old. No priest-who-was-not-a-priest would stop her. She would do whatever she must to keep her son safe. Even commit theft. Or treason. Or murder.

Again.

A bell clanged outside the cathedral. The man in the priestly garment strode closer, smelling of outdoors, leather, and horses rather than the spicy incense of the abbey. She suppressed a shudder. He might fool men with his disguise, but to her trained eye, 'twas obvious he was no cleric.

But who was he?

He *smelled* of danger.

In front of her, a crack in the floor's mortar pointed toward the hiding place under a loose tile where she was to place the parchment. Prisms of afternoon sunlight from the stained windows danced along the jagged seam. Nervousness skittered up her spine.

Shifting her weight, she drew her veil lower over her forehead and willed the man to leave. Her silk gown gave little protection to her knees grinding into the black stones of the altar steps. The long sleeves of her blue kirtle brushed the marble tile, revealing the lighter blue of her undertunic. The embroidered gold of the dress's trim glinted in the candle glow.

Instead of obeying her unspoken command, the man paced closer. The hem of his garments rustled.

"Bless you, my child," he mumbled, then paused as if unsure of his words. His voice was deep and sensuous, unfit for a place of prayer.

Husky. Veiled. Erotic.

The tone would blend perfectly with the grunts of men and titters of prostitutes in a Rose Street bathhouse.

A flicker of longing—something she had not felt in years—ignited. Quickly, she pushed the unseemly thought aside. Definitely not a priest! No priest's voice could affect her senses in such a way.

She gathered her skirts to flee, but he moved in front of her, striding with lithe, impious grace, too physically confident for one dedicated to books and learning.

She paused, biting the inside of her cheek. A verse from Proverbs turned over and over in her mind like a coveted piece of jewelry being fondled by a thief who is debating whether the bauble is worth stealing: even a fool is thought wise if he keeps silent and discerning if he holds his tongue.

No sudden movements, she coached herself. *Wait until good opportunity. 'Twill take cunning, not strength, to overcome him.*

The man cleared his throat. "God favors the humble."

She refolded her hands into prayer position and bowed her head in what she hoped resembled a penitent pose.

Practical black boots with deep, ragged groves marring the shank peeked from beneath his rich garments. The unadorned leather contrasted with the fussy embroidered hem. A holy man would have worn sandals. Knots tensed under her shoulder blades as she regarded him beneath lowered lashes. His shoes were slightly pointed and scuffed around the heels. She surmised silver knight-spurs usually rested there.

Dear saints.

"It is good that you came," he said.

She closed her eyes to avoid revealing the apprehension that surely showed in her face. But closing her eyes focused attention on his deep, throaty voice.

A woman could wrap herself in that voice and sleep warm and comfortable through the night after satisfying forbidden fantasies. Against her will, moist heat pooled betwixt her legs.

Her eyes flew open. She had attended numerous parties—sensual affairs—to get the information her blackmailer demanded. Thrice she'd been married—she was neither young nor virginal—but ne'er had a man's voice affected her thus.

"May your petition be granted." He drew out every word.

"My petition—" Her hands slipped, suddenly slick with perspiration.

Surely he could not know her untamed thoughts. She pressed her palms together in an effort to compose herself.

"Gramercy," she said, shoving her carnal musings aside. She had Jason to protect and no reason to desire a man, even one whose voice sent hot chills through her veins.

"Why are you here?" He reached toward her with a large, callused hand. Crisp, dark hair decorated his muscular forearm.

Alarmed, she gathered her skirts to rise. "I have just

finished my prayers. I will leave you to your candle lighting."

"Stay. Allow me to bless you."

Afore she could stand, he pressed his palm atop the thin gossamer veil covering her hair and forced her back to a kneeling position. Blood pounded in her temples as she willed herself not to flinch.

Heat. Her scalp felt aflame. It did not seem possible a man's hand could be so hot. Calluses snared the delicate fabric in a way a true priest's never would.

"Why did you come here?"

Suppressing a shiver, she recited her formal excuse for coming to the abbey: "I came to pray and give alms for my deaf son. Who knows but that God might have mercy on us and reopen his ears."

"We welcome you to Thornbury Abbey. Unburden your spirit and soul." His legs, tall and sturdy, were braced wide apart as if he bestowed knighthood rather than religious blessing.

"Thank you."

It seemed that he should release her head.

He did not.

"Mayhap you should stay for a meal," he said.

Mayhap she should run. But over the last five years she'd learned the value of patience, of sizing up an opponent and knowing the players before compromising her or Jason's safety.

"I am expected home afore nightfall," she parried, in case he had any thoughts of detaining her. Her castle was only a few miles east of the abbey, an easy ride.

His hand tightened ever-so-slightly on her head. Leashed strength.

Apprehension prickled her nape. She imagined him shedding his imposter's clothes and holding a knife to her throat. Steadying her breathing, she slid her gaze across the floor to judge the distance to the nearest exit. The checkered tiles created a chessboard-like playing field. She knew herself to be a pawn, but which piece was he?

"I have not seen you afore." She slanted her head to the side in another attempt to let him know the impropriety of his continued hold on her scalp. "Are you new at the abbey?"

His fingers flinched, but they did not release. "I am here to recover something I have lost."

Determining to assess whether his quest had anything to do with her, she tilted her head back. "What is it you have lost?" She shivered as his hand followed the movement of her skull.

"Something precious to me." The veins of his brawny arm danced beneath his bronzed skin. From her kneeling position, he seemed enormous—a column of hard, warrior strength: broad shoulders and long, muscular limbs.

She glanced upward at his face, and icy terror froze her heart. 'Twas her last husband back from the grave?

Coldness balled in the pit of her stomach. For a moment she forgot to breathe. Couldn't breathe. Memories of Ivan wrapping his brutish hands around her throat crashed on her mind.

She blinked and looked again.

Nay, she had been mistaken. This man was *not* her husband. This man who now held her head had the same dark hair and green eyes. The same uncompromising jaw. The same broad, slightly crooked nose, the same widow's peak in his hairline, and the same imposing countenance. But this man had tiny laugh lines that crinkled the corners of his eyes and a puckered scar that ran from a generous lower lip to beneath his chin.

She hastily crossed herself and forced a steadying breath into her lungs. This man was *not* Ivan. That evil monster rotted in the ground, she reminded herself firmly. Buried twice.

Dead by her own hand.

"Who are you?" Her voice echoed across the empty sanctuary. Thank Mary, her words sounded strong.

The man inclined his head in a mock bow as his fingers tightened on her scalp. Rainbows of light from the stained-glass windows gave his features an austere appearance. He wore a mismatch of holy garments, as if he'd stolen various pieces from a storeroom. A tall, white mitre ornamented with heavy gold embroidery perched atop his thick, black hair. It made him seem tall enough to touch the cathedral's arched ceiling.

"Gabriel of Whitestone at your service, my lady."

She lifted a brow. "The name of an angel." The visage of a devil. She did not recognize his name although she had spent hours memorizing the key players at court and knew more about many of them than any Christian woman should know. Lascivious details about the private lives of earls and dukes who preferred the company of men instead of women.

Her ability to learn such things had been the main talent her blackmailer exploited while she'd been in London. She filed through her memories. Nothing. Who was this man? And why did he look like the ghost of a monster?

The corners of his full lips lifted. "I have ne'er been mistaken for an angel," he murmured.

Hot perspiration beaded between her breasts. Instinct

told her to flee, yet she knew from bitter experience she dared not until she had the advantage. She had no delusions about fighting him.

"Have you any sins to confess?" the man asked. The hand on her head seemed to be measuring her, fondling her like a ripe piece of fruit in the marketplace. Was he weighing her to see if he should pluck her for a taste?

"You are no priest."

He peered at her closely, his dark brows nearly touching in a deep crevice on his forehead. His mitre wobbled.

"And you, my lady, are no lady." His voice was slow, smooth, like velvet over steel.

Her legs tensed in anticipation of jumping to her feet. "Do you know me?"

"Aye. Lady Ariana of Rosebriar."

The heat of his fingers scorched her scalp. Their gazes locked in stalemate. What else did he know?

"How do you know me?" she demanded, her gaze darting to the exit.

"I was told you had an innocent face, questions too pointed for a mere lady, and"—his gaze flicked to her cheek, a slow grin crossing his face—"three tiny freckles beneath your left eye."

Panic fluttered in her chest. Betrayed by freckles!

The closest doorway stood to the left thirty paces away. Her pony waited outside, lashed to an iron post. As soon as he released his hold, she would walk to the exit as leisurely as she could, then run like a madwoman. Run from the future and from the past. Just as she had the last five years.

"Release me." Instinct for survival coursed through

her. This man's eyes told her he knew too much. She rose an inch.

"Release you?" He laughed. His long, blunt fingers flexed, grasped the silk of her blue veil, and ripped it off. Her heavy hair fell around her shoulders; the curly, red tips brushed the checkered tiles. "I came to take you to justice for your activities as The Spy of the Night."

"Nay!" Her heart lurched. Gathering her skirts, she tucked her chin and butted his legs violently as she leapt to her feet.

He jumped aside to deflect her attack. The priest's robes entangled him, and he stumbled, falling to one knee.

Heart pounding, she lunged past him and fled toward the arched doorway.

Behind her, his boots thumped and slid against the floor.

To slow his progress, she toppled an iron candle-holder as she ran. Wax splattered across oak benches. Burning candles rolled down the tiles.

"Damn these robes," he cursed. His steps made a hollow echo in the huge cathedral.

Ten feet more, and she would reach the exit. Lacey, her pony, nickered from the other side of the door.

Hearing the sound of ripping fabric, she spared a glance backward.

The man yanked off his imposter's garments even as he gained on her. His boots squished his fallen mitre. Thorns! He wore all black as if conjured from the depths of Hades.

For an instant, it registered she had been wrong: he did not have a sword at all. A crossbow nearly two and a half feet in length hung from his belt. An assassin's weapon.

Her breath came in short gasps as she closed the final steps to the church's exit. Her mare nickered again. Clutching the iron handle, she yanked the heavy wooden door open.

Freedom.

The man's large hands snared her about the waist and pulled her back. The door slammed, whooshing air around her face and blowing out nearby candles. She kicked backward and connected with something solid.

Unyielding masculine arms closed around her torso. His breath tickled her ear. He grunted and forced her forward, pushing her ribs against the door. His knee nudged her thighs apart until she straddled one of his legs and could no longer kick at him.

"Let me go!" Her throat threatened to close.

"Nay." His body pressed the length of hers, holding her captive against the dark oak. Dear sweet Jesu, he was big. Taller even than Ivan had been.

Her underarms stung, and her knees began to buckle. His muscular thigh pushed further between her legs, upsetting her balance and forcing her to totter on her tiptoes. Heat from his body filtered through her skirt. His thigh grazed the vee between her legs and pressed against her woman's core. The moisture that had gathered there with her earlier musings pushed shamefully outward.

"Leave be!" She shoved against him, trying to straighten her arms and hoist him off. Damn her own soul! Why had she not run when she'd first seen his boots?

"Surrender, lady." His arms and chest were formidable as any iron prison.

"Let me go!"

"Nay." His breath mingled with hers. It caressed her skin exactly as she had imagined only moments earlier.

"Please!"

"Nay."

Shivers ran the length of her spine. She squirmed, and his large frame pressed her harder against the cool oak door. The fine linen of his tunic brushed the bare skin of her neck. Her hair caught between them, forcing her head back and exposing her throat. From only a handbreadth away, he looked down on her with uncompromising green eyes.

"Cease your struggles, girl. You are well caught."

Mary, Jesu, please help me. "What do you want from me?"

His breath tickled her ear. "To see you punished for your rebellion."

"Punished?"

"The king has need to question you."

Ice froze her veins. King Henry beheaded those who crossed him. Enemies were slain with the regularity of chickens for a feast. 'Twas why she had retreated to Rosebriar for a time.

"Why? I have done naught." Naught save slay a man and spy against the nobles of the court. The church claimed that if a woman killed her lord, 'twas the same as slaying the king—a crime of treason. And if the nobles of London knew she was The Spy, they would likely have her burned as a witch ere she set foot inside the town gates. "Prithee, my son is deaf. He needs me."

Gabriel glanced around. "Why are you not with him then?"

"He is with his nanny. I beg you, sir, allow me to go home to him."

"His nanny will care for him. You will come with me." Holding her against the door with his body, he pulled a cord of rope from a pouch on his belt. The wool of his tunic scratched her arms.

"Nay! Release me!" She pushed against him, only to be forced motionless. The cold oak of the door cooled her cheek. Sharp, bitter anger born of frustration ate at her. "You filthy, barbaric peasant! I will not go with you!"

His body tensed, and he snagged one of her wrists. "You will."

She wrenched away. "How much were you paid to accost a lady of the realm?"

"Enough," he answered gruffly, wrapping his long fingers around her forearm.

Allowing her voice to trail to a husky whisper, she said, "I can pay you more."

He did not answer.

Ariana brought her foot up, then crunched it down upon his instep.

Grunting, he jostled his weight and pressed her further into the door. She felt cold steel against her neck. "Careful, lady."

Head back, throat exposed, she lowered her gaze. A thin dagger glistened in the flickering candle glow, its silver blade as long as a man's hand. Her throat constricted, the air too thick to breathe.

"Let me go. I will pay you handsomely."

"You are in no position to negotiate." The knife's point pressed her flesh, causing a tiny prick of pain.

His hand held steady, and time seemed to slow. The knife neither broke the skin nor eased from her neck.

"How dare you!" she gritted out, balling her fists.

"Cease. I will take you to London trussed like a May Day pheasant if need be."

Sweat beaded her brow, and the air she sucked into her burning lungs choked her throat. She tilted her head to the side, searching for an alternate escape path.

A yellow and orange glow flickered across the ceiling. She gasped. Large sheets of red and yellow flame burned in the balcony. One of the tapers had fallen against the long silk banners. Fire leapt across the linen hangings and spread from silk to silk at an alarming rate.

Merciful Mary!

Whether from God or the devil, the fire would be her salvation. Now was her chance.

"Fire!" she yelled, hoping the momentary distraction would cause an instant of surprise.

Gabriel turned as she expected. The dagger eased slightly from her throat. Rounding to the side, she forced his fingers from her torso with her momentum, then elbowed him hard in the ribs and sprang for the exit.

Unbalanced, he fell backward. The crossbow clattered against the door. "You little wench!"

Pulling the door open, she leapt forward. A surge of victory rushed through her. No common mercenary would catch The Spy of the Night today.

His hand seized her wrist. "Not so fast, girl!"

Chapter 2

"Leave be!" Ariana's red hair whipped around her as she pulled desperately against Gabriel, determined to escape from him and the burning cathedral.

A fiery mass fell from the balcony and landed with a crash atop the altar. She jumped. Smoke choked her lungs.

"Let me go afore we both are killed!"

"'Zwounds, girl." He tightened his hold on her wrist and towed her behind him through the church's open door. "Now is not the time to fight me. Come!"

Straining against him to make her way to her pony, she glanced over her shoulder. Heat waves slapped her face. Inside the church, paint peeled from a carved icon of the Virgin Mary.

Cold terror streaked through her. She had not thought it possible for her mountain of sins to grow higher. What would God's wrath be for setting a cathedral aflame?

Gabriel tugged her across the church's porch and into the courtyard. Smoke followed them outside, wafting on the late afternoon air. The crackle of burning parchment sounded behind them. Over to the side, her mare neighed, nostrils flaring.

"Water! Fetch water!" Gabriel yelled, ignoring her efforts to break free from his manacle-like hold.

The sinking sun silhouetted monks cleaning their garden hoes, readying for the close of day. Several stopped their hoeing and stared at them. They seemed frozen in their slow actions compared to the frenzied flame.

Gabriel motioned to them with his free hand. "Make haste! The cathedral is burning!"

Pitching their garden tools aside, the monks ran toward the church. Their hoods fell back, revealing tonsured hair. They pushed past Gabriel and Ariana to survey the inside of the sanctuary.

"Get water!" screamed one.

"Get help!" hollered another.

"Get the buckets!"

Their voices pierced the air like giant bell gongs. Robed men shadowed the doorways and spilled into the courtyard. The ground trembled as hundreds of sandaled feet pounded the grass.

Monks ran this way and that in a chaos of movement, much like ants from a toppled pile. Some scurried to form a line to bring water from the well to the cathedral. Others rushed in to rescue artifacts and important documents.

Ariana's stomach sank with a heavy sense of impending doom. Not Thornbury. Not *her* abbey where she'd planted flowers and come for sanctuary from the weariness of life.

She felt stiff and wooden as men jostled her as they ran past. Gabriel gripped her wrist like a tether in the storm. The tiller of his crossbow scraped her hip.

Her pony neighed again. Turning, she saw the dapple-gray horse kick against the iron post as the mare caught the scent of smoke and panicked. Her long legs fought against the air, and her eyes rolled with fear.

"Lacey!" Ariana's heart lurched into her throat. She yanked against Gabriel's hold, straining toward the frightened pony.

Gabriel's grip tightened, his calluses biting into her skin. "You cannot escape."

"My horse!" Frustration strengthened Ariana as Lacey banged one back leg on the post. Her hand slipped free for a moment before Gabriel grasped her by the upper arm. "She's going to hurt herself!"

He pulled her toward the mare.

"Sh-h-h!" he admonished the horse. It stomped its hooves and skittered left. Gabriel reached for the reins with one hand, keeping a firm grip on Ariana with the other.

The horse reared again, forcing them back.

"Let go of me, you dolt!" Ariana yelled, shrugging away.

With a quick movement, he released her, grasped Lacey's bridle with both hands, and jerked the ties loose.

She leapt to comfort her mare.

"Easy, girl," Gabriel soothed, patting Lacey's neck. "Be calm, all is well." His warm, liquid voice quieted the horse, no doubt affecting the mare as strongly as it had her.

Seeing her chance, Ariana grabbed the reins, pulled Lacey away from Gabriel, and grasped the saddle to mount and escape. Please, Mother Mary, let the horse behave just this once.

Glass crashed behind them in an explosion of sound as the lead on the upper windows melted. Lacey bucked loose, knocked aside a line of monks, and galloped across the courtyard. Ariana gasped.

"Lacey!" Hiking up her skirt, she dashed after her runaway mare. Men bumped and jostled her, making her feel like a salmon swimming upstream. Water from their buckets slopped onto the ground. Mud splattered her dress.

Confusion overtook the courtyard. Monks screamed. Dogs barked. Windows shattered. Flames shot from the upper vents of the cathedral. The air smelled of dark smoke and destruction.

"Stop, Lacey!"

The panicked mare reached a low stone wall, wheeled around, and pounded past Gabriel. She knocked him aside with her flank and galloped through the garden, upturning plants and dirt. The wooden handles of a cart snagged one of her back legs. Horse and cart fell with a loud crash. Freshly plucked weeds flew through the air.

"Lacey!" Ariana's heart pounded wildly. She reached the mare and snatched the reins just as it rose. Lacey wobbled as she stood, a slightly dazed look in her large, brown eyes. Her coat glimmered with sweat. She pranced nervously.

Gabriel bore down on them, pushing through a sea of monks carrying water buckets. His tall body formed a dark shadow in the light of the burning church behind him. The hot glow of the fire made him look like a specter. Or perhaps, a demon.

Her gut twisted. Thorns! Hastily, she grasped the saddle and swung onto her mount. Lacey pulled up short before finding her footing and allowing Ariana to turn toward the gate.

"Ariana!" Gabriel screamed over the roar of the fire. Shoving aside two monks, he ran toward her.

"Run, Lacey, run!" She sent up a prayer of thanks that the mare wasn't injured.

Jumping over a scattered pile of hoes and rakes, Lacey sped out the monastery gate. Ariana hung on for dear life, her thighs aching with exertion. Strands of her curly red hair flew into her face and stung her eyes.

"Girl!"

Glancing back, she saw flames engulfing the top of the cathedral. Heavens. A weight crushed her heart. Setting her mind to not think of it, she laid herself flat on Lacey's neck and gave the horse its head, not caring which direction they rode.

Gabriel ran into the road after them, a strong frown etched betwixt his dark brows. His crossbow banged against his hip, but he did not reach for it.

"You cannot escape!" he bellowed.

She did not look back again.

Plowing through the crowd of monks, he sped toward the stable to find his mount. Frustration pounded through him as he ran. He had released his prize to comfort a bloody horse. A horse!

He wanted to kick himself. His younger brother Eric rotted in a London prison—slated for execution on All Saint's Day—under charges that *he* was The Spy of the Night. Taking the real spy to the king was the only chance of proving his innocence.

And he let her go for a damned horse!

He burst into the barn and sprinted down the packed dirt aisle to the last stall. His black stallion snorted a greeting and stamped his feet, scattering hay and manure.

"Horse, you must run as you have ne'er run afore," he instructed, snatching the stallion's bridle from a nearby hook and quickly fastening it over the horse's head. "Eric's life depends on it."

The stallion pranced as Gabriel led him into the aisle. Not wanting to waste time with the saddle, he vaulted onto the animal's bare back, gave the reins a sharp snap, and spurred the beast out into the evening sunlight. They fled across the courtyard toward the gate.

Stones scattered under the animal's hooves as they rounded the abbey's entrance and turned down the cobbled road. Hedgerows and wattle-and-daub huts blurred into melting streaks of brown and green as he raced down the path. Peasants dodged aside as he tore past them, hastening to save their brimming vegetable carts.

Knots tensed his shoulders. Where the bloody hell was she?

"Ariana!" he called, though he had no reason to believe she would answer even if she was within shouting distance.

The road split into two smaller paths. He pulled the stallion up short and peered both directions, searching for a trace of his prize.

Naught but cobblestones and hedgerows. He sniffed the air, hoping against hope that he could catch the scent of the rosewater perfume that had filtered into his nostrils when he'd first ripped off her veil.

Nothing. He checked the urge to howl with rage.

"Damn!"

His pride stung.

He flexed and unflexed his hand against the shaft

of his crossbow as pent up fury ate at him. He should have shot her. But that would not have given him the proof he needed. He gritted his teeth. He *would* find her, the bloody little wench.

She'd already stolen too much from him. She'd been married to his half brother, Ivan, the lord of Rosebriar—the brother who had been legitimate and nobly born. Not like himself—the son of the village whore.

She lived in the castle that should have been his home and ate and drank the nourishment that belonged in his empty stomach. He and his horde of bastard siblings barely scraped by while she and Ivan lived like fat hogs.

But now . . . if he could prove Ariana's guilt, he could both save Eric and claim rights on her land.

Land!

The thought brought both a rush of appeal and a surge of repulsion. It went against the grain to sell out, to become one of the landed barons—but he had his family to support.

He would *not* lose her now.

A woman with a white cap, carrying a basket of laundry, cocked her head and stared at him. "Ye lost something, sir?" she asked in a thick accent.

"A girl! Curly, red hair on a dapple-gray pony."

"Thataway," she said, pointing down the southward path with a meaty finger.

A surge of expectation coursed through him. Ariana would be his by nightfall.

Wheeling his horse onto the cobblestone pathway, he thundered past a dilapidated farmhouse covered with thick hawthorn bushes. They dashed through a maze of peasants who had stopped to gawk at the billowing smoke issuing from the abbey. The stallion brushed against a wagon carrying a load of apples. The neatly stacked fruit clattered to the ground, rolling into the ditches like a red avalanche.

"Bloody nobles!" shouted the wagon's owner, shaking his fist. "Think they own the whole bloody country. First, the lady—"

"Sorry," Gabriel called over his shoulder. He'd return to the village later to rectify matters.

Up ahead, just past another line of hedgerows, he saw his prize. Imminent victory coursed through his veins. Her glossy hair fluttered in the air like a sunset-colored tournament banner.

"Ariana!" She was close enough he could practically taste her capture. The thought of having her bound for his pleasure ignited a hot wave of dark desire.

She glanced backward, then kneed her pony into a dead run. Its muscles danced with the speed of its racing.

Gabriel's chest tightened with the primal urge to capture and conquer. *Mine! Mine!* his instinct seemed to call. He spurred his horse onward. His mount caught the thrill of the chase and pushed forward. The crossbow at his waist slapped his thigh in a bouncing rhythm as steadily they gained on the smaller dapple-gray mare. Soon. Soon. Yes!

"Nay!" Ariana screamed as he pulled beside her. Her blue eyes widened. She cut to the side. Finding a hole in the hedgerows, she veered from the path and steered the pony through a grassy field.

Gabriel followed and pulled beside her again. He crouched low, then pounced, aiming for her mount's bridle.

She tugged her pony aside, away from his reaching hand.

He toppled sideways and grasped his stallion's neck with both hands to keep from falling.

"Stop, Ariana! You cannot escape." Gripping his mount tightly with his thighs, he lunged again. His fingertips brushed her horse's tacking. Once again, she pulled aside at the last moment, and his hand came away holding empty air. Her curly, red hair whipped around her, a few strands brushing his forearm.

"Leave me be!"

Gabriel clenched his knees, holding onto his stallion's flanks. Without stirrups to anchor his legs, his perch was, at best, precarious. His crossbow banged his leg. The two horses bumped shoulders as they galloped across the field. Plants upturned. A tree limb slapped Ariana's forehead, causing a thin trickle of blood to run down her face.

He checked an annoying twinge of guilt. *Serves her right,* he told himself firmly.

Gathering his strength, Gabriel determined to bring the pursuit to a halt before one of them or the horses was injured. He unlatched his crossbow from his belt in a quick, practiced motion and tossed it into a patch of tall grass with a silent plea that his prized weapon wouldn't be harmed.

He lunged toward Ariana. She pulled aside, but he anticipated her movement and, springing from his mount, reached for her instead of the bridle.

She jerked, fighting his hold, as they both slid off the side of her mare. He twisted in the air and landed on his back, protecting her from slamming into the ground. Breath fled from his lungs as she landed atop him.

Frustration swept through Ariana, swift and hard.

Acting purely on instinct, she balled her fists and clubbed at the man she now straddled. How dare he! Kicking wildly, she tried to rise. He brought his legs up and around her, anchoring her to him. She screamed and slammed her fists down on his torso, once, twice. Then his large hands bound her wrists in a crushing grip.

"Let me go!" She pulled backward and struggled to rise. He held her anchored to him.

Then she was on her back, straddled by Gabriel's thick, muscular thighs. Stunned, she tried to gather her scrambled thoughts, but his presence crowded out every sense of the world but him. His fingers encircled her wrists like manacles as he pressed the backs of her hands into the ground above her head. His chiseled features—the broad nose, puckered scar and slight shadow of a beard—filled her vision. His woodsman scent bit at her nostrils, earthy and warm.

"You are my prisoner." Possession blazed in his emerald eyes. Beads of sweat trickled from his widow's peak to his temple.

Her heart lurched. He was power and heat. At once both terrifying and fascinating.

Their hips bumped each other, and she felt his manhood through her silk dress—a large, thick bulge. He must be huge there to press so firmly into her. She shuddered. If he decided to take her, she had no hope of fighting him.

"Please," she begged, hating suddenly that she was a woman and he was a man. If only she had his physical strength.

"What shall I do with you?" His gaze roved her face for a moment with the intensity of a conqueror, then moved downward as if daring her to stop him.

She stilled, not wanting to incite his lust. She knew too well the ways of men. "I beg you—"

"Beg me to what?"

"Let me go." One side of her gown had ripped. It hung limply off her shoulder. Mercy, another inch and her breast would be exposed! She shivered, and her nipples puckered. Her vulnerability exposed raw emotions. "Prithee. I will pay you handsomely."

"I am not interested in your gold."

A man not interested in gold?

Gabriel shifted his weight. The gown ripped further, exposing the coral edge of her areola and the tiny bumps that puckered its surface.

Shame and fear twirled together inside her. She glared at him. "Stop goggling me!"

His gaze snapped to her face. "Goggling you?" A smile tugged at his lips, pulling on his chin's scar.

"Let me up!"

"Nay." Again, that infuriating single syllable word. It was spoken so calmly, they could have been discussing current fashions of the court.

A feeling of being flung into quicksand welled inside her. She *had* to get free. Screaming loudly, she raised her head and slammed it into his. Sharp pain flooded her forehead. He jerked back at the unexpected move, and she wrenched one of her arms away. She clawed at his face.

"God's blood!" He snatched her hand and slammed it back into the dirt. "You cannot win. 'Tis pointless to try."

Frustration churned inside her.

She spat into his face.

The green of his eyes hardened like ice on stone. "I have slain men for less."

"I—" she bit out, "—am not a man. And I am no use to you dead."

"Nay?" With slow, deliberate movements, he transferred both of her wrists to one of his large hands. Gathering a lock of her hair, he wiped the spittle off his face with it, then turned the hair over and spread it across her cheek.

She flinched. "Bastard."

"I should beat you for that."

"Do your worst, blackheart," she countered, wiggling her fingers against the hand gripping her wrists like slave bracelets. "You do not frighten me."

"Shall we test that?" Slowly, he reached down with his free hand and began unbuckling his belt. A frisson of fear streaked through her, and suddenly, it seemed foolish that she'd provoked him. His belt was a two-inch wide strap of thick, black leather, similar to the ones her husband had worn. Memories flooded her, and sweat prickled her underarms. A belt like that stung with fierce mind-numbing pain. Determined to bear up under whatever he dished out, she squeezed her eyes shut and concentrated on the lullaby her mother used to sing to her just as she'd done every time her husband had used his belt on her.

> *Sleep, my love, on my chest,*
> *'Tis but caring arms 'round you.*

Gabriel chuckled softly, pulling her back to the present. Irritation eclipsed her fear.

She narrowed her eyes. "What in God's name are you laughing at?"

"You are more than a little afraid of me," Gabriel said. The belt slipped from his waist, making a soft "shick."

Tears stung the backs of her eyes. Even after five years without a husband, she was terrified of a beating.

You can survive this, she chided as she awaited the blow to fall across her cheek. She turned her face aside, shielding it as best she could. Her bladder spasmed, and she clenched her thighs together to keep from peeing herself.

A minute ticked by.

Then another.

She opened her eyes a tiny crack and peeked through her lashes. Gabriel was staring at her, belt in hand. His brows were drawn together but without annoyance. He chewed one side of his lower lip pensively which wiggled his scar.

"I am not going to hit you," he said softly. "I was weary of you arguing with me."

She watched him, hating that he'd seen her naked panic, hating that her teeth still chattered and that she still needed to make water.

Indignant anger born of humiliation worked its way through her. How dare he frighten her just to prove he could!

"I hate you," she said, frustrated because it wasn't entirely true. She had hated Ivan for his brutality, but she did not hate this man. She could not find it in herself to hate a man who'd twisted in the air to break her fall and who had risked his life to calm her horse even though it meant she would escape—or almost escape, she corrected.

The back of Gabriel's hand grazed her cheek so softly it felt like a butterfly kiss. A moment stretched and then was gone. He wound the leather strap around her wrists and yanked it tight.

Chapter 3

Gabriel stared at his captive, who for all her bluster, reminded him of a lost kitten. Her hair clouded around her face, giving her a disheveled, just-ravished appearance. Mud and sticks clung to the gold and red curls. Long rips slashed her blue silk gown. The fancy gold embroidery hung askew in places. She looked as though a wild beast had despoiled her. He shoved aside a fleeting twinge of guilt that he was responsible for her appearance.

Eric! He must think of Eric. And *this* woman *must* go to London.

He rolled to one side, holding the strap, then rose to his feet and proffered his hand.

"Get up."

The thick leather pressed her wrists together, making her bones look brittle as insect legs. She stared at his upturned palm in a way that made him wonder if he'd just grown a handful of warts.

His guilt evaporated. Blasted noblewoman! The upper crust didn't mind living off the sweat and toil of serfs, but they considered themselves too good to actually touch a whore's son like himself.

Heaving a sigh, he grasped her hand, half expecting her to claw at him.

As he pulled her upright, she gave him a glare that would have roasted the skin off a pheasant. But she did not resist.

Good. A little intimidation would serve his purpose. While he had no doubt of her guilt—information he had gained from unsavory sources—he needed *proof* that she was The Spy of the Night. If he had to frighten the daylights out of her to get that, he would.

"Do not try to run." He leaned toward her and bared his teeth.

She whitened. Excellent.

Her slippers were missing, and her bare feet, small and dirty, peeked from under her gown. Her vulnerability brought an unbidden wave of protectiveness over his heart.

Abruptly, he pushed the thought aside. His brother lay filthy and cold in the king's prison because of this woman's foul deeds.

"What do you plan to do with me?" Her jaw was set; one stray lock curled over her cheekbone.

"That depends on you." He pondered the best way to get her talking.

She squared her shoulders—the pose of an undefeated warrior. "Meaning?"

"It depends on how much I like the answers you give me. What were you doing at the abbey?"

"Praying."

He scrutinized her face for signs of truth and saw only exotic beauty mixed with bullheaded stubbornness. Where the tree limb had smacked her, a thin line of dried blood marred her exquisite features. Its path, dark against her lily white skin, connected two of the three freckles on her cheek.

Glowering, she wiggled her hands against the belt binding her wrists. "What are you going to do with me?" Her voice was calm, but he detected an edge of fear.

"Turn you over to the king." He reached to wipe the blood from her cheek.

She turned her face aside and flinched when his fingers touched her skin as if she expected a blow.

"Why were you at the abbey? For information? Directions?"

"Who are you?" she asked, ignoring his questions.

"The king's hunter."

Her eyes widened. "The Hunter?"

"Aye." A streak of arrogant satisfaction passed through him. The Crown publicly denied his very existence, but she'd heard of him. Good. Perhaps that would temper her bad behavior. His reputation as a ruthless assassin was well known, at least among the underworld of smugglers, traitors, and rebels.

"The Hunter is just a legend."

"As is The Spy."

He watched the delicate skin of her throat quiver as she swallowed. Then a mask of practiced detachment fell over her face.

He retrieved the crossbow, and examined it. Dirt covered the tiller and prods, but the weapon was still all in one piece. Thank the stars for good English oak.

"Come." He tugged her forward by the belt strap and looked around for the horses. Sparse trees dotted the farmer's field. A line of hawthorns and oaks marked the boundaries of wild forest a stone's throw away. His horse was well trained, but likely had followed hers further than he should have. "We must find our mounts."

Ariana dug her heels into the soft grass. Her eyes blazed with bravado. "I will not go with you."

Tension knotted under his shoulder blades.

"I am staying here," she continued. Her voice was high.

He blew out a breath and stepped toward her. "Fighting is pointless. You are much smaller than me and cannot hope to win."

She jerked back, a flash of fury in her blue eyes. So he had not yet intimidated the fight out of her. A shame. Life would be easier for both of them if she complied.

"Stubborn woman. 'Tis a wonder you survived in marriage at all." Grasping her around the waist, he hoisted her onto his shoulder. Twigs fell from her fiery hair.

"Cease!" she screamed, pounding his back with her fists.

He slapped her lightly on her upturned buttocks. "Be still, girl."

She pummeled him harder.

"'Tis futile to struggle." Her ferocity amused him. As kitten or hellcat, he would take her to London. Ignoring her small blows, Gabriel carried her into the woods, determined to find the horses.

A mixture of brown and green swirled before Ariana as she stared at the ground from her position over Gabriel's shoulder. A feeling of unstoppable doom bit her mind.

"Let me down!" She beat his back with her bound hands. "Blackheart!" Her earlier fear burned into frustration at the humiliating position of being carried bottom up. How dare he manhandle her so. "Barbarian."

The blows seemed not to affect him at all as he strode

toward the forest, not even when he bent and picked up her slippers. He tucked the footwear into his belt and continued his trek.

With every step, she bounced against his body. Her stomach ground into his shoulder. "Beast!"

After he reached a clearing, he paused. Momentarily, the earth stopped whirling.

"Promise me you will not fight, and I will loose you."

A gust of annoyance swirled through her, but she stilled. "Fine!"

Slowly, he lowered her feet first to the ground. The calluses on his hands snared the blue silk of her sleeves as he gripped her upper arms and held her in place. She glared up at him, checking the urge to slap his arrogant face.

The determined set of his jaw told her she'd likely land bottom up over his shoulder or worse—his knee—should she attempt that.

His dark, shoulder-length hair twisted around his face. One silky lock curled across his angular cheekbone. His leather belt wound around her wrists and trailed on the earth between them.

"What do you want from me?" Squaring her shoulders, she planted her feet firmly, determined to not be intimidated.

"Answers."

"Answers for what?"

"Why were you at the cathedral? What did you go there to get?"

She blinked, giving herself space to evade his direct questions. "And if I tell you, you will let me go?"

"Nay."

Fresh irritation rankled her. "Take your bloody

questions and go to the devil. What were *you* doing at the cathedral?"

He stared down at her, a deep crevice forming between his brows. "I am trying to help my brother."

"Is he a priest?" she bit out sarcastically.

"Nay." A muscle in his jaw clenched, and she could have sworn a flash of pain crossed his features. Turning, he snagged the end of the leather belt and tugged her forward.

Muscles rippled beneath his sleeveless tunic. He was too large. Too arrogant. Too overtly masculine. Realizing she could not escape outright, she followed him. Her mind raced to formulate a plan. She'd wait until he was asleep.

He led her to a nearby oak and wound the belt around a low hanging limb.

Alarmed, she pulled against the leather. Nay! Not tied to a tree like a dog! "What are you about?"

Forcing her hands above her head, he secured her to a branch. His green eyes shone with resolve.

"Cease!" She pulled against the belt and kicked at him. He sidestepped her foot. She tried to hit him, but the leather caught her wrists and forced her backward. The tree bark scraped her shoulder blades. She felt as if a stone from one of the sacred circles surrounded her neck, and she had been flung into the sea. "Untie me, you bastard!"

"I am going to locate the horses and find us something to eat," he said calmly. His composed demeanor enraged her.

"Let me go!" Sweat stung her underarms. Her upstretched arms made her feel open and exposed to him. Vulnerable. Weak.

"Wiggle your hands every few minutes so they do not go to sleep."

She twisted against the belt. Had she thought his voice calming earlier? Nay, his voice irritated her more than a knife scraping across stone. A man such as he needed to be coated in rat guts and have his eyes pecked out by buzzards.

"I will not be gone long, and I will not go far," he soothed. "Relax."

She gnashed her teeth.

A limb grazed his wide shoulders as he slid silently into the trees.

"Stop!"

Glancing back, he chuckled. "Quiet, girl—you will scare away our supper." He slid like a wraith into the forest, blending all too easily.

A tremble skittered through her as she watched the place where he had gone and saw naught but trees and foliage. Green and brown leaves shivered.

"You bastard!" Her words echoed in the quiet of the woods.

He reemerged as quietly as he had disappeared, a black look on his face. A lock of hair cut a dark line across his forehead. She gasped, unable to stop the lurch in her chest. He stalked toward her, halting a dagger's width from her face. The thin scar on his chin came into prominence.

"I am hungry," he growled. "Keep quiet afore I decide 'tis your flesh and not rabbit that I desire."

Goose bumps popped up on her arms and legs. His incisors were slightly pointed. She swallowed.

"Not one word, or I'll gag you. Understand?"

The barbarian! But she only nodded.

He paced back into the trees.

Once he left, she let out a breath. Ne'er had she felt so defenseless. Alone. Tied like a trapped rabbit. At the mercy of the wild beasts of the forest.

Shadows lengthened, and a chilly breeze flitted through the oaks as the last of the evening sun shimmered across the branches.

She strained her ears to listen. Wind creaked the limbs. Crickets chirped. But there were no footsteps to indicate if Gabriel was far or near.

Her hands tingled so she wiggled them, struggling for freedom. The leather bit her skin.

Night was coming. Soon the forest would be shrouded in an inky cloak. Her insides swirled with the thought. How ironic it was that she was called The Spy of the Night. Nothing terrified her more than the dark.

She bit the insides of her cheeks and strained against the unforgiving leather. Her arms ached from being above her head.

Bastard, she thought furiously, but did not dare speak aloud. Surely she could free herself before the sun sank over the horizon. Her mind clouded with thoughts of her son. Jason would be in bed by now, tucked in by his nurse Beth. If something happened to her, he might be taken to an orphanage or, dear God, an asylum. No doubt his deafness would be used against him.

Bastard, bastard, bastard, she chanted silently, closing her eyes and trying to keep her focus on her anger instead of the growing quivers in her stomach. She worked her hands against the leather, shifting from foot to foot as her legs tired. Standing on tiptoe, she twisted her hands until the leather rubbed her skin raw. The musty scent of wild beasts and rotting foliage assailed her nostrils.

Bastard, bastard, bastard. Bastard, bastard, bastard.

An owl hooted. Her eyes flew open.

Darkness.

The forest was an ocean of swirling black ink. Shadows shifted. Frogs croaked.

Ariana's blood iced.

Nay! Nay! She squeezed her eyes shut, trying to block out the night. Even the inside of her eyelids seemed light compared to the shadows.

Fear fluttered inside her stomach with a tremor similar to the shaking of the ground when warhorses approached from a distance. Slowly, steadily, it spread until her innards all seemed aquiver—the warhorses pounding closer. Taking a deep, steadying breath, she tried to push her dread aside. But she knew—*knew*—'twas a feat as impossible as turning back a strong army.

Spies are not afraid of the dark, she told herself firmly.

Dread slid into her shoulders and neck until her torso shook. Sweat slipped down her cheeks. She yanked her chafed hands against the leather and bit her lip to choke back a scream.

There's naught to fear, naught to fear, naught to fear, she chanted, trying to keep the panic that lurked right under the surface of her skin at bay.

Where was her captor? He'd vowed to come back and gag her if she spoke. Mayhap she *should* scream. But nay. Noise would only attract predators.

Pulling against her bonds, she loathed her helplessness. Surely not even her cousin could blame her for being afraid of the night this time.

Her knees quivered, threatening to buckle. She yanked hard against the leather belt.

A twig snapped behind her. She yelped, her eyes flying open.

All at once, a tall, dark demon loomed before her. Yellow-green eyes glowed in the night like fierce stars.

Terror overtook her. Screaming, she kicked wildly, flailing her body and clawing at him with her bound hands.

"Be calm," he soothed. "'Tis only me."

'Twas Gabriel!

The blind panic drained away, but her legs still trembled. He retreated a few steps, and she noticed he carried a makeshift torch. The flame held back the darkness with a circle of dim, flickering light.

"Breathe, girl, breathe. You are safe."

She obeyed, allowing herself to be mesmerized by his deep, throaty voice. Anything, even Gabriel, was better than the dark with its weird shadows and eerie sounds.

"I found the horses."

Swallowing, she focused on the flame, allowing the light to push away her fear.

"And something for us to eat." He held up a dead rabbit by its back legs, clearly pleased with himself. The hunt seemed to have invigorated him. "Sorry about scaring you."

"You . . . you did not scare me," she lied.

He smirked, clearly not believing her.

Indignant anger rescued her pride. "How dare you leave me tied here alone!"

"I was nearby." He patted the crossbow hanging at his waist. "I need not be close to kill my quarry."

"Vagabonds roam the woods!"

"I would have heard any that approached, and they would have had a bolt through their throat afore they reached you."

She gave his crossbow a dismissive glance. "Knave! Do you even know how to use such a weapon?"

A deep line formed between Gabriel's eyes, and abruptly, Ariana realized questioning his skill had been unwise.

His hands flexed and unflexed against the tiller of his weapon, and she wondered how many men had reached an untimely death at his hand.

"Well," she huffed petulantly, "you should not have left me here. Something could have happened to you, and I could have been ravaged!"

A wicked smile tugged his lips, lifting one corner of his mouth higher than the other. "Ravaged?"

Heat spread up her cheeks, and for once in her life, she was grateful for the shadows. She calmed, refusing to continue acting like a hysterical ninny.

"If you want to be ravaged . . ." His husky voice trailed off.

"Arrogant coxcomb," she muttered. She sure as hell wasn't going to admit to Gabriel that she feared the dark. How can a spy be afraid of the dark?

Dropping the rabbit, he reached up and unbound her wrists. The leather slipped off with a slight sting of pain. Her arms swung down limply, and she toppled forward.

"Easy, girl." His arm went around her, steadying her.

She jumped back, disturbed by the unbidden consolation. She would *not* take comfort from him—'twas his fault she was here in the dark in the first place.

She gave him a sour look, latching on to her irritation to stave off the unwelcome feeling of comfort he gave her. "My name is Lady Ariana, not "girl.""

"Alright, *Ariana.* "

She frowned at the lack of title, but "Ariana" was still better than "girl."

Willing her knees to stop quivering, she forced her

mind to conjure up Jason's face—his large green eyes, gape-toothed smile, and spiky blond hair.

"You must let me go." She prayed her voice sounded steadier than she felt.

"I cannot." His dark green eyes were guarded.

"I have a son."

"And I have a brother." Turning, he gathered a few sticks and logs. "Behave yourself, and you can be unbound for a time."

"I am not some dog to be tamed," she said to his back.

He shrugged. Arrogant blackheart!

Her gaze flicked from him to the surrounding darkness. The shadows undulated, and she felt bile rise in her throat at the thought of running into the night alone. But now was her chance.

Taking a deep breath, she slid backward a few steps.

"Run from me, and you will spend the remainder of the journey tied *to* me."

Anger burned her at his highhandedness. He had no right. "Condescending peasant!"

Turning, he bent to gather sticks for the campfire. "I have as much noble blood in me as most of the king's court."

"And not a scrap of noble chivalry."

Time slowed as Gabriel turned. His eyes glittered with an unholy gleam. "I tire of your disrespect."

She grimaced. She should not be so careless with her tongue.

He stepped toward her, a black look on his face. Her fear of Gabriel overcame her fear of the dark. Without a second thought, she turned and fled.

An instant later, his arm snaked around her waist, pulling her back. "Damn, girl."

Chapter 4

A short span later, desperation bubbled in Ariana like a poisonous bog as she tried to formulate a plan of escape. She glowered at Gabriel, who knelt beside her scooping leaves for a sleeping pallet. A hempen rope, stolen from her saddlebag, ran from her captor's belt to her ankle and back again. 'Twas a fair-sized rope, but looped around as it was, she had only about six feet of leash. She frowned at the tight knot that anchored the cord around her leg. Tethered to him like a pet!

Swallowing hard, she bit back rising panic. It seemed that her whole life, she'd been tethered to one man or another, each of them progressively worse than the last. And this one the worst of all—not even a nobleman, but a rough barbarian.

The horses lingered nearby, munching on the soft forest grass. Tonight, she vowed, latching on to her only hope, tonight she *would* escape. She'd take a torch to stave off the darkness. And this time, she'd take both horses so he'd have no mount to run her down with. She would go home, see to Jason's safety and the safety of her lands.

Campfire light played across Gabriel, making shadowed hills and valleys on his tunic as his muscles rippled beneath it. Every movement proved his power, intensifying that he had the upper hand. The light glinted off his dark hair.

She wondered if she could make him topple over if she pulled hard enough on the rope.

"Do not test me." He glanced up at her, one dark brow rising as if he had somehow read her thoughts.

She narrowed her eyes at him. "I will escape."

Brush rustled and he glanced into the forest. "Mayhap. But do not be foolish. There are more than four-legged beasts who roam these woods at night." He stood, uncoiling his large body like a panther. Even his clothes were barbarous: black leather breeks instead of proper English hose and a sleeveless leather tunic that showed off tight, thick biceps. "You are safer with me than out there."

"There is no safety for a woman at the hands of a man." She kicked her foot against the forest floor. The leash rustled against the leaves.

Leaning down, he nearly touched her nose with his own. His spicy woodland scent assailed her nostrils. "Mayhap you have not met the right man."

"A woman is better alone," she scoffed.

"Some things in life are not nearly as pleasant done alone."

"Such as?"

He cocked a brow, and she felt her cheeks heat as she caught his meaning. How was it that he set her off-kilter so easily? Mayhap 'twas just that he was so *different* from the men she'd known at court. In an age where men wore frilly lace and ridiculously pointed shoes, Gabriel's wild black hair, mysterious green eyes and tall, strong form set him apart. Fierce. Primitive. Dangerous.

"Do men think of naught else but their own carnal desires?" she asked.

He held her gaze longer than was proper but had the grace to not answer her question. Tucking his thumb into his belt, he fingered the looped cord. "The rope is for your own good."

Of all the arrogant things! *"My* good!"

A long, sharp dagger pointed downward from a sheath around his calf. If only she could take it and free herself.

Following her gaze, he glanced at his knife, then back up at her face. His green eyes sparkled like poisonous emeralds. "Do you want it?"

She blinked, wary of his meaning.

He propped his boot beside her on the log. The gleaming hilt of the dagger glittered in its sheath. "Take it."

Her heart pounded. What was he about?

"I tire of fighting and chasing you. If you think you can best me, then prove it. Otherwise, learn your place."

"My place?"

"As my prisoner."

Her hand itched, longing to touch the hilt of the dagger, to pull it from the sheath and stab at Gabriel.

"Go on then," he said mildly. "Take it."

Could she do it? Her mind swirled.

He flexed his calf muscle. The dagger shifted slightly. "Take it!"

She imagined herself pulling out the knife—likely, the hilt would be warm from being near his body.

"Ariana." Gabriel's finger skimmed across her face.

Heat like she had felt in the chapel burned her skin. "I have been fighting with knives or sticks or bare hands since I was a child. 'Tis futile."

She jerked back. "Do not touch me, half-wit!" A tendril of her hair curled around his finger.

"I am weary of your acidic tongue." He gazed at her, green fire blazing in his eyes. "Either fight or behave."

Sucking in a deep breath, she steadied her mind. *If I can just get him a little off guard.* She slumped, feigning compliance.

He ran his thumb along her collarbone from her shoulder to the soft indenture in the middle of her neck. His touch was gentle, but her skin stung as if she'd been branded. Her heart beat rapidly. Could she kill a man in cold blood?

If she did not get away, she would be imprisoned and her son endangered. There was no hope for it. She had to try.

"We both know I cannot win against your strength," she said slyly as she lowered her gaze and pretended submission. As soon as she detected a lull in his attention, she'd steal his dagger.

A moment stretched as if he weighed her words, then he turned slightly, gazing into the trees. Yes! Sweat prickled her palm. Only a moment more, and she would be free—take the knife, stab her captor, and slice the rope. She steadied her breathing.

He set his foot back on the ground and turned. Leaves crunched.

Uncoiling herself, she leapt from the log and yanked the dagger from its sheath. Victory surged through her. Afore she could stand upright, he encircled her wrist with his large hand and twisted.

She yelped and dropped the knife. Leaves puffed up around it.

Slowly, he forced her back to a sitting position on the log, then released her. The blue silk of her gown snagged on the bark. Anger spiraled through her veins.

The dagger lay near one of his boots. Green and brown foliage hid part of the blade.

She glared at it, frustrated. But she could still get it. She still had a chance.

Arms akimbo, he gazed down at the blade between his legs. "Pick it up," he commanded.

She drew in a steadying breath, gathering her strength. The dagger lay between his feet. All it would take was one good upward slice to set him howling. Lunge and stab.

"Pick it up." His voice was smooth, heady in its intensity. Like the devil beguiling a sinner. He waited for what seemed like an eternity.

He shifted his gaze. She took the advantage and dove for the knife. *Please, Mother Mary, guide my aim!* Her hand closed around the hilt.

Twisting aside, Gabriel knocked the dagger from her grip afore she even began to lunge upward. Breath whooshed from her lungs, and she felt herself being turned in the air by strong male hands. The ground flew toward her and abruptly stopped as her ribcage landed across Gabriel's knees. His forearm anchored her face down.

She took a breath and his spicy scent filled her lungs. Shuddering, she cringed as she awaited what came next. From her position spread over his lap, every fiber of his thigh muscles showed through the leather of his breeks.

He held her across his legs as if willing her to test him again. His stomach and chest rose and fell against her side in a deep, even rhythm. Jesu, he was not even breathing hard!

"Again or no?" he said.

Her neck ached as she twisted her head and torso to glare at him. He allowed her to flop onto her side, but not to rise. His chest, clad in a black tunic, loomed before her. Wide. He was so damn wide. Worse, he was correct. Fighting him was futile.

Tears clouded her vision until his large form became fuzzy and indistinct.

"Are you satisfied yet that you cannot win? Or do we go again?"

She ground her teeth. "I hate you!"

"Aye. But do you yield?" His voice sounded infuriatingly calm.

Clenching her teeth, she resisted the urge to scream.

"Answer me, Ariana! I am not a harsh master. But I can be." His palm brushed the cheek of one of her buttocks through the blue silk of her gown. The touch was light, heated, and overwhelming. The threat clear: be calm or be spanked. Like a naughty child.

The beast! "Cease!"

"Do. You. Yield?" He emphasized every word like a thunderclap.

She'd suffered enough humiliation. Gritting her teeth, she nodded.

"Aloud."

Oh, if only she were a man and could fight! "I yield," she bit out.

"No more trying to stab me?"

"Nay." She shook her head, wishing for once she

had duller wits so she could damn the consequences of trying just one more time.

"Good."

He released her.

She crawled from his lap and plopped down on the log. Her face burned with humiliation. She could not even look at him.

"Pick up the dagger." He smoothed his hands over the tight leather of his breeks.

"Pardon?" Was he testing her resolve?

"I said, 'pick up the dagger.'"

"I said I would not fight," she ground out. She buried her fingers into the blue silk of her skirt and twisted, wishing it was his neck.

"So you did. But obey me, Ariana."

She twisted harder.

"Fight or submit. Next time, I'll not stay my hand from your backside."

"Your point is already made. You do not have to belabor it."

"Pick up the dagger, and put it in my sheath." His voice left no room for argument. He placed his booted foot firmly on the ground in front of her.

She gritted her teeth, realizing she had no choice but to do as he demanded. Her pride stung as she leaned to retrieve the knife. Her fingers closed around the hilt. Smooth. Tempting. Should she try again?

Gabriel stood above her, arms crossed. Contained power.

Fondling the knife hilt with her thumb, she pondered her captor. He was a commanding man, but his passions were well-leashed. Not at all like her dead husband.

Gabriel hadn't harmed, struck, raped, or abused her. She grappled to wrap her mind around the thought that a man with such dominance could also control its intensity. Ivan had lashed out at her for soup not being warm enough. She'd tried to cut off Gabriel's balls, and all he'd done was hold her over his lap.

A grudging respect came over her, and she shoved the dagger into its sheath on her captor's calf.

Sitting back on the log, she stretched out her arms and warmed her hands in the heat of the bright campfire. She would escape afore dawn.

Gabriel leaned down and tilted her chin up. "'Tis no shame for a queen to surrender to an army mightier than herself for a time," he said.

She blinked, surprised he would show her this measure of dignity.

His fingers grazed her cheek, warm and strong and rough. She marveled that she didn't flinch. But in her heart, she realized why: her body knew he wouldn't harm her. He'd threatened her, but his threats were contained—consequences for her own behavior—not wild ravings of a madman. He was a coarse, barbaric ruffian, but he showed more nobility than the lords she had been married to.

Taking a tendril of her curly hair, he twirled it around his index finger. The copper strand glowed against his tanned skin. "We can fight again tomorrow."

"Count on it," she said sweetly.

Chapter 5

He would get answers about whether or not she was The Spy of The Night if he had to pry them out of her, Gabriel thought with a trace of annoyance as he watched Ariana attempt to smooth her thick, sunset-colored hair. The strands trailed into a froth of copper curls in her lap. Her richly embroidered skirt spread across the log she sat upon, making her look regal despite her tangled hair. How could a noblewoman such as she be mixed up in a spying intrigue that involved gathering lewd tidbits about members of the king's court? Of a truth, this woman did not seem the sort.

Her red curls sprang out around her head and trailed down her neck and shoulders to her hips. Why could she not be a brooding hag instead of a siren on the edge of desperation? He could still sense how her body had felt across his lap—stiff and proud and full of anger that he'd bested her in their skirmish.

That she had chosen to fight rather than trying to weep and whine her way out of her predicament fascinated him. In his experience, noblewomen were simpering milksops cold enough to freeze a bear's arse, but Ariana was as fiery as a harlot.

He almost—*almost*—felt sorry for her that she'd attempted to contest him. But the sight of her round buttocks turned up across his thighs disallowed him from feeling remorse. They had jiggled and flinched in an erotic display that was uniquely feminine. And, damn it, she smelled good. Like roses and rain.

"As long as you behave, you need not be afraid of me, girl," he said. Mayhap if she were more relaxed, he could get the information he needed.

She hurled him a haughty glance, her jaw stiffening in displeasure. "Then you do not know what the king does to those he thinks are guilty."

Eric's face, gaunt and dirty, filtered into his mind. It felt like a knife jab in the heart. "I know all too well."

Her fingers stilled in her hair, and she raised an auburn brow. "Oh?"

"My brother is in prison."

"Why?"

He rubbed his eyes, wishing he could wipe away the weariness of his mind so easily. "The young fool thought to seek out The Spy of the Night. Somehow, he was entangled by deceitful men and taken to the king."

She blanched, and he wondered what lurked behind her clear blue eyes. Guilt? Horror? Her hands caught in a snarl of hair. The rope tying them together shimmied slightly as her slender fingers flickered through the locks to loosen the knot. There was both an inner strength and a fragility about her that called to his protective senses, a reaction that he could scarce afford to heed if he was to rescue his brother.

"It is said The Spy slips into the feasts and can remember all the people and who spoke with whom," he pressed. "The nobles claim to not know who The Spy works for, only that information about their activities seems to leak into the wrong hands. The king finds that some of his subjects are not as loyal as they should be . . . as if someone holds information over their heads."

She paled, and her hands worked faster through her hair.

He paused, waiting for her confession.

"I am not The Spy," she said after a long moment.

"No?" He scrutinized her face. "Then who is The Spy?"

She shrugged, a delicate lift of her shoulders. Her eyes shifted. "'Tis just a legend."

Her eyes held his firmly, but the freckles on her cheek flinched. No answers there. No proof of her activities.

"I am just a country noblewoman," she said.

"*Country* noblewoman?" The little lying wench! "You were in London until Henry took the throne. The Spy's activities diminished after you left."

She pressed her lips together and shuffled her feet, stirring leaves.

"Why did you leave London?"

"I needed to see to my holdings."

"What were you doing in the cathedral?"

Her nostrils flared slightly as if she breathed in some grasped for answer. A soft breeze lifted a section of her long hair. "Praying for my son."

"So you claimed earlier."

"He's deaf—" she started.

"So you also claimed."

"'Tis true."

Gabriel huffed a tense breath, wanting to slam his fist against one of the forest's trees. He needed proof if Eric was to be freed. This conversation was getting nowhere. He wished he could pace about the campfire to ease his frustration. The rope trailed between them, anchoring him to her as much as her to him.

She drew circles in the dirt with the toe of her slipper and turned pleading eyes on him. "If I am detained in London, the king will claim my land."

Blasted nobles! They cared more about land than their children. "'Tis no concern of mine if you have land or not, lady."

She shuddered. The log she was sitting on wiggled. "My son will be cast out."

An old anger kindled in his chest. "No different from many other children."

"How can you be so unfeeling?"

He picked up a stick and snapped it in half. 'Twas poor compensation for the black fury that edged his heart. "A noblewoman lectures me on feeling for others? How quaint. You wear fine silk and sit above the salt while my siblings beg for scraps."

He stood and wiped his hands on his breeks. He wanted to pace across the clearing to soothe the beast that threatened to rise inside him.

Ariana marveled at the change wrought in Gabriel. Something she had said angered him, but she could not imagine what it was. Vexing man! Surely he could not blame her for caring for her son. Even bastards and peasants cared for their children. Had he not seemed concerned about his siblings?

For a time, only the night sounds of the frogs and crickets filled the forest as she contemplated her options. She must get back to Jason and see to his safety.

Gabriel turned his back to her and threw a log onto the campfire. The orange and yellow light shimmered against his leather breeks and cast a flickering glow across his face. He had a couple of days' growth of beard, and his jaw looked scraggly. Brutal and handsome. Sparks danced into the air, and she wished one would land on the rope and burn it in two. She smoothed her skirt down out of long habit.

The horses lingered nearby tied to a low branch of an oak tree. His horse was a tall black stallion of indeterminate breed. The best way of escape would be to steal the mounts.

"Get up," Gabriel said abruptly, holding his hand out, palm up.

Ariana flinched, frowning at his highhandedness.

"I have to see to the horses." He blew out a breath. His shoulders looked tense, reminding her of a caged bear. He was a man used to moving about freely. He probably disliked being tied to her as much as she hated being leashed to him.

She checked the urge to cross her legs and sit petulantly on the log. Doubtless, that sort of behavior would earn her a place over his shoulder, carried like a sack of apples.

"Ariana," he warned.

Balling her fists, she stood.

"Your pride overrules your common sense," he said.

She smarted, but did not reply.

Turning, he stalked toward the horses. The rope thunked on the ground, and she had to step lively to keep from tripping on it. How wretched to have to follow along like some common prisoner.

A moment later, they reached the horses. When she

escaped, she must take both animals, she mused. Then Gabriel would never catch her.

Regaining control of her composure, she eyed his stallion keenly. "'Tis a beautiful horse," she said, feigning what she hoped looked like innocent interest, not a pump for information on how to steal it.

Gabriel paused, his hand on the stallion's neck, and glanced at her. If he thought her interest unusual, he did not indicate it. "The stallion is from my friend's prized horse—a smarter animal you've never seen."

"What is his name?"

Gabriel shrugged, his muscles rippling under his black tunic. "Doesn't have one."

"No name?" What sort of man did not name his horse?

"'Tis just a horse," he said flatly, but he patted the horse's flank. His actions belied his words. 'Twas almost as if he did not want to care about the animal but could not help himself.

The stallion nosed him atop the head. "We've been through many a skirmish. He does not spook easily. When he was trained, they felt he did not have enough spirit to be a warhorse, but he has proven that incorrect many a-time."

Despite herself, Ariana felt a tug of attraction. A man who saw strength where others saw fault was rare indeed.

The stallion rooted in his hand, as if the praise meant he deserved a treat.

"You know I am talking about you, do you not? Well, I have naught." The lines around Gabriel's green eyes crinkled into a smile, and Ariana was grateful the horse had somehow lightened his mood.

He turned back to Ariana. "He has one weakness."

His voice was low, tempered with amused tolerance. "The beast will do *anything* for apples."

"I see," she said noncommittally, stifling a smile. Men and pride. Men and horses. It probably never occurred to him that he'd just given her a valuable weapon. She'd pilfered an apple from a cart in her race from the abbey in case she did not get to eat that night.

An uneasy truce settled between them as Gabriel finished preparations for sleep. As she watched him spread out a blanket for the night, she pondered how she could find out what he knew without giving anything away. It was clear he did not believe her outright denial that she was The Spy, but what *did* he know? She had always been cautious in her spying, and it disturbed her greatly that she was under suspicion.

The parchment she needed to place under the altar thankfully had not fallen out of her bodice in the skirmish. She could feel the corners of the paper scrape her skin near her waist—safe from Gabriel's eyes. It contained information about Lady Buxton's private liaisons with Thomas McFey, a solicitor. Over the last few months, Ariana had gathered enough solid information to ruin them both. The countess's husband was not a forgiving man. It was this sort of tawdry tidbit that kept her blackmailer happy.

After a time, Gabriel led her back to the log, sat beside her, and unbound the crossbow from his waist.

"How is it you became the King's Hunter?" she asked without preamble.

"A man has few options in life save the ones he makes for himself."

"'Tis better than having no options at all."

"What would a noblewoman know about having

no choices? You always had clothes to wear, food to eat, yes?"

She pondered this. Yes, she had, but at what cost?

He laid the weapon across his knees and ran his hand over the highly polished wood. The crossbow was unlike any she had ever seen. The tiller spanned two feet from tip to tip and had a beautiful engraving of a Celtic dragon carved into the side. The prod was made of heavy black steel nearly two thumb's width wide.

Realizing only a man of unusual strength could bend the bow, she found herself marveling at the width of Gabriel's shoulders and the size of his upper arms.

Her husband Ivan, thank God he was dead, had been strong, too. But Ivan had worn his strength like a bull, whereas Gabriel wore his casually. Oddly, she felt safer being Gabriel's captive than she'd ever felt being Ivan's wife.

"I have had little opportunity in my life to make choices." She kicked at the rope surrounding her ankle. "It seems that every time the crown changes hands, the new king finds me a new husband."

He looked up from his work to probe her with his emerald gaze. His shoulder-length hair bobbed slightly. "How many times have you been married?"

"Thrice."

"Thrice? But you are—"

She held her hand up. "Young. Yes, I know. The first husband came when I was but twelve years of age."

His hair fell across his widow's peak as he nodded.

"Each husband was worse than the last. The first was old enough to be my father. The second, old enough to be my *grand*father. And the last—" She paused. Perhaps she should not tell him these things.

"The last?" he prompted.

She licked her lips, disconcerted with the direction of the conversation. "Ivan was slain by ruffians." She felt the rise of familiar guilt at her lie—like an old friend who did not bother knocking. Only one person knew her secret—her cousin, the bishop, who had helped her cover up the murder and now was using the information to blackmail her into finding out secrets of the nobility.

Gabriel looked at her as if trying to discern what lay beneath her forehead. She tensed, anticipating questions, but he said nothing.

After a moment, he took a cleaning cloth from his belt pouch and made long languid strokes down the length of the crossbow's tiller.

The tightness in her shoulders dropped.

An unnerving fascination with his large, callused hands tickled her senses as she watched him. His fingers traveled, searching for any nicks or dust that would betray the accuracy. Why did men ne'er caress women with as much care as they did their weapons?

"Do you enjoy your work?" she asked, seeking to change the subject from their earlier topic.

His hands paused on the crossbow. "Enjoy killing people?"

She shuddered and turned her gaze to the forest. Leaves shivered in the breeze.

"Nay, I do not enjoy killing people," he said flatly, drawing her attention back to him. "But I am good at it."

"Oh," she said, unsure what to make of that. "What made you become an . . . an . . ."

"An assassin?"

She nodded, wishing he didn't unnerve her so much. It was just that he was so direct when everyone else in her life was full of shades and subtleties. At court, every glance and shift and contact meant something other than what was on the surface.

"I do what I must to support my family." He brushed a speck of dirt from the prod of his crossbow.

"You have family?"

He smiled, and she felt even further disconcerted by him. "A passel of children."

"Your own?"

"Nay. Siblings, orphans." His tunic rippled as he shrugged. "None of them are mine. My mother was a harlot."

"Oh." She stiffened, feeling awkward that he spoke so frankly.

He gave her a look that did not invite comment.

"You spoke of a brother . . . ?" she asked.

"Eric. He's being held in the Tower. In truth, I do not believe the king thinks he is guilty; he merely seeks to secure his throne and wanted assurance that I would not rest until The Spy is found. The barons have given him an earful about how The Spy did this or that." His gaze roved her face in a way that made her stomach do a slow roll. "You are quite a legend evidently."

She shivered. "I am not The Spy."

"As you say." He went back to polishing his crossbow.

She watched his hands, unable to turn from their slow, concentrated movement. Startled, she realized that the smallest finger on his right hand and half of his ring finger were missing. How had she not noticed that before? Surely she had not been so fascinated by the slow, precise strokes of his hands that she had failed to notice something so obvious.

Unbidden, her heart reached out to him for his injury.

"What happened to your hand?" she asked, the question coming out of her mouth before she checked the need to stop it.

He looked up from his bow. "My fingers were cut off in a fight when I was a boy."

"Oh." She paused for a moment, letting this information sink in. "How old were you?"

"I was nine."

Her heart lurched. Almost the same age as Jason. She said the silent prayer that all mothers pray upon finding out a child has been injured: please, God, allow mine to grow up safely.

"What happened?" she asked.

A crevice formed between Gabriel's brows. "My older sister was hauled off by slavers. I failed to stop them."

Ariana felt her breath leave her body. Of all the horrid things. "Slavers?"

Gabriel's grip tightened on his crossbow, and a flash of pain crossed his features. "I should have stopped them."

Without thinking, Ariana reached out to soothe the tightness from his jaw. "You were but a boy."

He jumped when she touched him, and she pulled her hand away, mortified at her lapse in judgment. He was a beast, for Christ's sake! This was not some cozy chat in the dark!

Gabriel stared at Ariana, his thoughts sucked backward in time. He clutched his crossbow, wanting to stave off the memories, but that day remained fresh and clear in his mind as if it were yesterday. He may have been only a boy that day, but he could have . . . could have . . .

As a nine-year-old he watched a huge, hairy man drag his thirteen-year-old sister headlong across rocky ground toward a waiting ship. Mother of God!

"Nay! You cannot take her!" he'd yelled, grabbing for the man. His fingers had closed on empty air. Oh, God. Oh, God. Oh, God. Desperation pounded in his ears. But God didn't give a damn about bastards and whore's sons.

The barbarian grasped Eleanor's slim body, flinging her over his bull-like shoulder. Her hair matted with mud as it trailed on the ground behind him like a bridal train. She whimpered but did not awaken. Blood dripped from a large gash across her arm.

"Eleanor!" Scurrying forward, Gabriel lunged again. His small hand gripped the man's booted ankle. "Let her go!"

"You little rat! Get off!" The man kicked at him.

"I won't let you take her!" Wrapping one scrawny arm around the giant's calf, he pulled himself onto the man's leg. The man's boot smashed his cheek, and Gabriel gritted his teeth. Never show fear. Never. The stench of the barbarian's unwashed body nearly choked him.

"Cease, runt! The wench is bought and paid for!"

"Nay!" Gabriel pummeled him fiercely, his fists bouncing off the man's thick legs. Tears stung his eyes.

"Brat!" The giant glared down at him, cocking one meaty hand back.

Gabriel squeezed his eyes shut, determined to not let go until he had his sister back. A sharp crack of pain flared across his cheek. Red and gold flashes of light sparkled before his eyes, and he tumbled to the dirt. Nay!

Scrambling up, he seized his sister's arm, which hung down the giant's back. Digging his toes into the earth, he tried to drag her off the giant's back. "Eleanor! Awaken!"

The man chuckled, continuing his trek toward the ship.

"You cannot take her!" He pulled harder on his sister.

"Who's going to stop me, brat? You?"

"Please!" he screamed, hating that he was forced to beg. He yanked at Eleanor. She slipped an inch off the barbarian's shoulder.

Laughing, the man hoisted her higher. Eleanor's unconscious form bumped against his body. "What's the matter, boy? Can't hold on to 'er?" he taunted.

Her brown kirtle snagged on a bramble, ripping a long rent in the coarse homespun wool. The man squeezed her exposed thigh with one meaty hand.

"Nay!" Tears burned his eyes. He wiped them away angrily. Boys didn't cry.

Halting, the man snickered. He grinned down at him with a mouthful of crooked yellow teeth. A gold hoop earring gleamed in one ear. "Tell you what, boy. We'll play tug o' war with this here prize. You win, and I'll give her to you fair and square."

"Leave her!" Gabriel screamed, hating that he barely reached the man's belt. His arms looked like sticks compared to the giant's.

The man laughed again, his bushy mustache puffing around his lips. "I don't think I'll be aletting go of such a prize. Look at this hair, boy! It's like wheat!" He held up a handful of Eleanor's blond hair. "Your sister will fetch a fair price on the block."

White-hot anger scorched Gabriel. Spying a knife sticking out the top of the man's boot, he lunged for it.

The giant stepped back, but Gabriel grasped the hilt and yanked it from its sheath with both hands. Leaping with all his might, he swung the blade in a wild arc above his head, aiming for the man's face. Take that!

"Ho, boy!" The giant stumbled back, nearly losing his hold on Eleanor. Her eyelids fluttered.

Gabriel's breath came in short gasps as he swung wildly again. The dagger sliced across the man's hairy cheek and caught in the gold loop. Victory! The earring tore loose, flying across the rocks with a chunk of bloody flesh attached. Ha!

Bellowing, the barbarian dropped Eleanor. Her body landed on the ground with a clunk. He grabbed the short, curved sword from his belt and lunged. The blade sliced through Gabriel's fingers, completely severing the smallest digit. Agony shot up his arm, and he dropped the knife with a yelp. Warm blood ran down his palm. His teeth chattered.

"Gabriel," his sister rasped, her eyes fluttering open. "Help me."

"Run, Eleanor!" Clutching his injured hand, Gabriel saw the giant bear down on him. His vision swam, its edges black and indistinct.

Rocks and twigs scattered. Gabriel scuttled backward as the man's hamlike fist rose.

Then the world went black.

His sister was gone when he awoke.

Chapter 6

"Do you need privacy afore we sleep?"

Ariana flinched. Gabriel had been sitting so still, staring into the fire, that the question startled her. What demons lurked just behind his forehead?

He stood. The corners of his eyes were tight, and his fingers gripped the crossbow so firmly his knuckles whitened. His hands looked capable despite their odd, monstrous shape. His long legs seemed like towers of strength, and she knew already of their speed. But he was calm.

Whatever hellish memory he'd had, he still possessed control of his emotions. For a surreal moment, she wished they were not enemies. She did not press him for his thoughts. He had said his sister was stolen when he was a boy, and she did not want to care about a boy who'd had his finger cut off trying to protect his sister. It wouldn't make any difference—she would be gone afore daybreak. As soon as he went to sleep, she would begin loosening the knot by tiny increments. If she was quiet and made only small, deliberate movements, she could slip her foot free, even if he were within breathing distance. She'd take a torch to keep away the darkness.

Be patient, she told herself. 'Tis only a matter of time afore he sleeps.

Gabriel laid the crossbow on the log. "I will give you a longer leash if you need privacy, but do not attempt to leave."

She nodded, pleased with this small freedom.

Forcing herself to remain stiff as a rod, she tried not to flinch as Gabriel knelt and took her calf in his hand. His thick black hair tangled about his head. The part made an imprecise zigzagged line on his scalp. The graceful line of his back was all too masculine in its size and contours. His warm palm sent shivers up her spine. She leaned as far away from him as she could, trying to pretend his hands were not stroking her ankle and that a hidden part of her soul didn't revel in the primal earthiness of being touched by a powerful, handsome man. Shocked at the direction of her thoughts, she pulled away.

"My hand is injured, not poisonous." Bitterness laced his voice.

Shame that she'd inadvertently rubbed salt into his old wound flowed into her. That she'd felt desire in the first place. "You misunderstood. I—"

The muscles in Gabriel's shoulders knotted with tension. Should she explain 'twas her own emotions that frightened her, not his scarred hand?

Nay, she should not. It changed naught between them.

He retied the rope with quick, practiced movements, practical and cold, leaving her with a longer leash. He held the end of the cord loosely across his palms like some morbid offering to an ancient goddess. "Go. You have until I count to two hundred."

She did not have the strength to be annoyed with him. He'd offered her the dignity of privacy—that was more than any of her husbands had ever done when she'd been under their thumbs.

She scooted away into the trees. The hemp encircling her ankle nipped her skin. How awful to be on a leash like a pet, she thought, yet the rope linked them in a way that comforted more than it chafed: Gabriel's presence banished her fear of the dark.

After she had relieved herself, Ariana made her way back to the campfire. Gabriel crouched over the flame, stirring the ashes, her leash looped around his belt.

"Come," he said. Light flickered over the muscular angles and planes of his body as he rose. "'Tis time for sleep."

Heat swept through her as he gently took her by the hand and led her to the spot by the fire where he had smoothed the leaves. Her captor. Her protector.

By dawn, she would be away and ne'er have to think of him again, she told herself firmly.

Taking the free end of the rope, he wrapped it around one of her wrists.

"'Tis unnecessary," she said, drawing her hand away. The rope fell slack between them. "It is dark, and I am an unarmed woman."

"Unarmed woman, mayhap, but too stubborn to care, I'd wager." He held out his scarred hand. "Give me your wrist."

She shook her head. If her hands were tied along with her foot, she could not undo the knots! "I cannot go anywhere in the forest alone."

He waited.

"'Tis tied around my ankle already," she pleaded. "What if the camp is attacked?"

He lifted a brow as if he could see right through her thin excuse. "Now, Ariana."

Her hopes for the night shattered. She stared at his hand, wishing she did not know 'twas hopeless to fight. Silently, she surrendered her wrist.

"Gramercy," he said.

She shivered at the deep huskiness of his tone. The fingers surrounding her wrists felt warm and strong.

The rope looked very brown compared to the white skin on her arm, and the rough hemp scratched her already raw flesh as he wrapped it around her wrist. She flinched at the pain and wished for a second she had not fought so determinedly against him earlier. She should not have let her temper get the best of her. Perhaps if she had not, he would trust her more now.

"The rope hurts?" His gaze met hers.

She shrugged, feeling the scrape of the note within her bodice at the movement. "Would it make any difference?"

His hair fell over his widow's peak as he leaned closer and halted in his work. "Aye."

Blinking, she looked up at him. She had become so used to the simple word "nay" from him that for a second, she thought she'd misunderstood.

Slowly, he unwound the rope and looped it over his arm. The thrill of her easy victory floated through her. Mayhap he would be easier to manipulate than she'd thought.

In a graceful, unhurried motion, he untied the neck of his tunic and grasped its hem.

Her world tilted as the shirt lifted over his waist. Hard warrior's stomach was exposed.

Her eyes widened. He did not look like any man she'd e'er seen afore. Certainly not like any of her husbands. No wrinkly skin. No flabby belly. Angular planes and valleys covered with tanned skin and criss-crosses of old scars filled her eyesight. His upper chest was smooth, but a thin line of dark hair pointed downward from his navel and disappeared into his breeks. The soft black leather strained across his groin.

An involuntary shiver quivered through her shoulders as a mixture of emotions spiraled through her. Fear. Desire. Longing. Terror.

Mentally, she kicked herself. She was no blushing bride to go weak-kneed at the sight of such blatant masculinity. Nor was she some innocent lamb who had no knowledge of the pain that the primal urges of a man created in women.

She checked the impulse to turn away, unwilling to reveal that his naked chest affected her.

He chuckled, showing once again his attractive, pointed incisors. "Whilst you seem to mind if I goggle you, I find that I enjoy you goggling me very much, my lady."

Disgusted with herself, she turned aside. "I was not goggling you," she lied, irritated he'd thrown her own words back at her.

"You were."

"I was not!"

He laughed aloud, and she clamped her mouth shut, annoyance nearly ruining her purpose to be civil. Tonight, she told her pride. Tonight she would escape.

Wrapping the tunic around her arms for padding, he secured the rope around her wrists, then pressed her down to the ground and sat beside her.

The leaves crunched under them as they settled in to rest. Ariana flopped onto her side away from him, determined not to sleep.

Hours later, she wiggled her hands back and forth as Gabriel snored softly beside her. His jawline seemed less harsh, and she marveled that he slept so soundly. The cool air did not appear to bother him, despite being shirtless. A small y-shaped stick pressed against his thick bicep.

Having ne'er slept outside afore, she found that every sound kept her from resting, and lying on the ground was very uncomfortable. The tunic padding gave the bonds some play as she worked the rope loose. She hid her movements under the thin blanket. Time was short, but with luck, 'twould be enough to get free.

Chilly night air pushed through the forest, bringing a layer of milky fog. The mist shimmered. It swirled around trees and covered the ground with a fat, white wrapper. The full moon perched high in the bright starlit sky. At one side of the clearing, the horses dozed.

Gabriel rolled, letting out a loud snore. Pausing, she waited until he fell back into a slumber, then resumed her labor. Even through the tunic, the rope scraped against her wrist bones as she tugged. A thin layer of sweat coated her palms.

Time passed. The fog thickened, building a filmy wall between her and her sleeping captor. Pink rays tinged the horizon.

The ropes slid, biting into the backs of her hands, then with agonizing slowness, one hand slipped free. Thank Mary. She made a silent vow to double this month's alms to the church.

Her heart beat a rapid staccato. Freedom was near. She made hurried work of the rope encircling her ankle. A sense of enormous victory clutched her. For a wicked, impish moment, she longed to kick Gabriel's slumbering form.

Gabriel jerked in his sleep as if reading her thoughts; fog swirled around him like smoke from a cauldron. She caught her breath. *I didn't mean it. I didn't mean it. Go back to sleep.*

He rolled over and snored.

Biting the inside of her cheek to keep herself from thinking any other evil thoughts, she trained her mind on the task ahead. This time, she would make sure he had no mount to run her down with.

Stealthily, she moved across the grass, barely lifting her feet to avoid snapping any twigs. Her dress, damp from the fog, tangled around her thighs, making it feel as though she moved through a bog. Raising the hem slightly, she glided toward the horses.

She found her saddlebags, removed the apple, and shoved it into her bodice. With luck, he had spoken the truth when he said that his horse would do anything for apples. Reaching Lacey, she covered the mare's nostrils to keep her from nickering.

"Sh-h-h, sh-h-h," she admonished the horse, praying Gabriel would not awaken.

It had been a long time since she had ridden without either bridle or saddle, but she had no time to bother with them. She untied Lacey's rope, used it to make a set of makeshift reins, and looped it over the mare's head.

Gabriel's stallion stomped his feet, and she glanced at her captor's sleeping body. Apprehension tightened her chest. He let out a loud snore. Thank Mary.

Untying his horse's lead rope, she pulled him forward. "Come, boy," she coaxed.

He resisted and tossed his head, obviously unsure about leaving his master.

Perspiration gathered on her brow. She patted him. "'Tis alright, horse," she whispered, thinking again how odd it was that the beast had no name.

He calmed somewhat. She swung onto Lacey's back and kneed her mount into the forest.

Whickering loudly, the stallion protested being led. He stomped his hooves, bucked, then lowered his head and bit her mare on the backside. Lacey neighed and lunged forward.

Ariana jerked both the reins and the lead rope, barely keeping her hold on them. Come on. Come on.

"Hey!" Gabriel shouted, jumping to his feet. His hair stuck out at odd angles, and he swayed slightly, his body still drunk with sleep.

She started. Oh heavens, not now!

Leaping into action, he sprinted toward them.

Desperation caught in her throat. Yanking the apple from her bodice, she bit off a chunk and held it out to the stallion, allowing him to catch the scent. Please, may Gabriel have been right about the horse and the apples.

"Come on," she cooed, kneeing her mare into a trot. "Come on."

Lacey wheeled, nipping at the apple.

"Whoa!" she commanded, wrenching the reins to

press her mount forward. Coldness ran through her like victory melting.

Gabriel reached them; his hand brushed her thigh.

Gripping the stallion's lead rope, she spurred Lacey onward. "Run, girl, run!"

Gabriel leapt for her mount's halter but was thrown aside as they bolted forward. Yes! Her gut gave a little triumphant jerk.

"Stop, Ariana!" he shouted. "These woods are dangerous!"

The horses lunged into a gallop. Glancing over her shoulder, she saw Gabriel running after them. His hair was in wild disarray, his eyes wide with astonishment.

Ha! Serves him right!

"'Tis dangerous!" he yelled.

Within seconds, she'd outdistanced him. But every backward glance showed him still sprinting.

Moments later, they hurtled onto the cobblestone path. Her heart soared. She'd thwarted Gabriel's attempt to take her to London. The edge of dawn glittered over the horizon, casting a pink and gold glow on the hedgerows and huts lining the road. Home soon. She would see Jason to safety, mayhap even flee to the Continent until the rumors of spying quieted. Gabriel would come for her, but she would be ready for him then.

All at once, a mangy humpback with ragged garments and a knobby cane launched himself onto the road in front of her. He wore a short, dingy cape with a hood that covered his face. Mud caked his bare feet.

Sweat stung her underarms as he threw aside the cane and pounced at her. His dirty fingers caught the lead rope. The scent of sheep manure and rotting skin assailed her.

She gasped and felt the world spin.

"Thorns!" Ariana crouched low on her mount to stop herself from sliding. She released the lead rope on Gabriel's horse, and the stallion fled.

The beggar grasped her leg, threw his hood aside, and straightened. Instead of an old humpback man, a tall, young vagabond with greasy yellow hair and a scraggly beard emerged.

Gasping, she pulled sharply to the left. "Nay!"

"Now, men!" he yelled, his fingers biting into her calf.

The trees shivered, and she screamed. Two cutthroats ran toward her—a stocky beast with a pocked face and a lean, wiry devil who wore a gleaming sword. The scent of unwashed bodies soured the dawn as they crowded around her. Neighing loudly, Lacey reared. Ariana clamped her thighs tightly around the horse, fighting to keep her seat. Her world swirled.

Hands clasped her calves and wrenched her from her mount.

She gasped as the browns and blues of earth and sky jumbled together. Dear God! Why had she left Gabriel?

Chapter 7

She kicked at the nearest man as she fell but connected only with air. Her hip smashed into the road, and sharp pain snapped in her ankle. The mare broke toward the trees.

"Get the horses!" Yellow-hair yelled, his scraggly beard bobbing.

The stocky man latched on to Lacey's makeshift bridle with a pocked hand, wheeling the horse around.

Yellow-hair clutched her upper arm. "Gots me a noblewoman."

"Release me!" She fought to stand. A line of agony darted from her ankle to her hip. She stumbled. Mother Mary! She should not have left Gabriel's protection.

The monster grinned at her; his beard twisted.

"Nay!" Her breath came in panicked gasps. Her lungs ached.

Turning, he dragged her toward the forest. "Come, men!" he hollered at the others. "Let's see what we 'ave under these noble skirts here."

"Let go of me!" The blue silk dress ripped, and her knees scraped against the cobblestones. Hair flew around her face, temporarily blinding her. She struggled to her feet and grimaced at the agony shooting up her leg.

The man laughed and hauled her forward, lugging her off balance. A ripping sound rent the air, and chilliness brushed her bosom as the small tear in her bodice became a valley. Sweat prickled her underarms.

The vagabond's eyes widened at the sight of her naked breast. Mother Mary, have mercy.

He held her in place and reached for her exposed flesh.

Grasping her gown closed, she twisted away. Her skirt flew out around her.

His lips lifted in a snarl. Despite the grime on his body, his teeth were white and even, gruesome in their perfection. "I'll be alooking at ye if I wish."

"Get away!" Flailing her arms, she sought to claw at his bearded face. Her heart threatened to beat its way out of her chest.

He thrust her hands aside and ripped her gown to her waist.

"Nay!" Bucking wildly, she scratched her fingernails across his cheek. Strands of his blond beard tore from his face.

"Bitch!" A trickle of blood dripped down his chin. "Ye'll pay for that." He cocked his hand back.

Her teeth rattled as the blow came. Pain spread across her cheek, harsh and sharp. "Oh, Mary," she breathed. Images of Ivan flooded her mind. She squeezed her eyes shut against the vile memories.

The man wrenched her hands behind her back, his white teeth gleaming in a horrid, too perfect smile that shone against his filthy, lice-ridden beard. Her bodice flapped outward, and her breasts poked through the opening.

Crying out, she shoved as hard as she could and threw her weight backward. She slipped from his grasp. Air fled her lungs as her back thudded against the ground. Moaning, she tried to roll to the side. To get up. To run.

The man let out a snort of laughter and dove atop her. Sweet mercy. Sweet heaven. Please. "Nay," she screamed. He raked his nail across her nipple, sending a line of pain across her chest.

"Nay! Cease!"

From above her, she heard Pockface speak. "Leave some, Hugo. Brother wants her, too."

Her assailant grunted a reply and pinched her nipple, pulling viciously on the tender skin.

A streak of agony shot from her breast outward.

"Lay still," Yellow-hair ordered. His ghoulish white teeth grinned at her.

"Nay. Please."

He twisted, forcing her areola to an unnatural angle. "Lay still I say!"

Fear iced her veins. Her nipple stung with tight, throbbing agony. 'Twas like a thousand other nights. A man used a woman. 'Twas the way of the world.

She latched on to her mother's lullaby, forcing her mind to detach from what was happening with her body.

Sleep, my love, on my chest . . .

The man made a strangled gasp and collapsed against her. His blond beard scratched her neck like coarse wool. She pushed his heavy weight aside and realized he was dead. Her eyes widened. A crossbow bolt protruded from his throat, the sharp point sliced clean through his neck. Blood flowed from the wound and spilled onto the ground. His mouth hung slack, showing his weird white teeth.

Gabriel! Gabriel had found her!

"Hey!" Pockface shouted. Fear hunched his shoulders, making him appear even more bull-like as he looked this way and that at the trees. The nostrils of his broad nose flared.

"Who goes there?" demanded the third outlaw. He crouched his wiry body and pulled a sword that was the length of a short man's arm from his belt. Silence shrouded the forest as he turned from side to side, holding the weapon ready.

Ariana's heart pounded. She scrambled aside, struggling for the cover of the thicker trees. As she rose, Pockface rushed to her and grabbed one red curl.

"Show yourself!" he demanded to the unspeaking trees and bushes. His wide, flat forehead crinkled with animal wariness. He wound his hand tightly around her hair, snapping her neck backward. Her scalp smarted.

Silence. Then the crunch of leaves and the soft twang of a bolt being loosed.

"U-u-uk." The sting on her scalp ceased as the man's grip slackened. He toppled, twitched slightly, then lay still, as dead as his comrade. A crossbow quarrel jutted from his heart.

Twigs snapped, and in a blur, Gabriel emerged from the forest. He was shirtless. Sweat and dirt streaked across his face and torso. Perspiration ran down his arms in rivulets, and his face was a mask of intense hatred.

But ne'er in her life had a man looked so hand-

some, so powerful, or altogether so beautiful. She
wanted to melt into a pool of relief.

"God's toes!" said the third man, twisting his tall, sinewy
body in Gabriel's direction. Unlike his fallen comrade,
keenness glowed in this one's eyes. He gripped his sword
confidently as he held it before him.

Biting her lip, she shivered. Gabriel had no time to
reload his bow.

Without hesitation, Gabriel drew the knife from his
calf and returned the man's glare. The vagrant
glanced from his sword to Gabriel's dagger and gave
a smug smile. Ariana's heart lurched. The ruffian's
weapon easily extended thrice the length of her protector's. For several unholy moments, the two men
circled each other like angry bears.

A fleeting thought entered Ariana's mind: she
should run away—or crawl, given the state of her
ankle. Even if Gabriel won this fight, they were enemies. But to abandon her rescuer afore being assured
of his safety went against her sense of honor.

With a sudden thrust, the wiry man's weapon bit the
air. Its sharp point aimed at Gabriel's heart. He jumped
to the side, and the sword slashed his shoulder.

Ariana gasped.

Blood dripped down his arm. The vagabond
laughed. He lunged again, and a red gash appeared
on Gabriel's forearm. Then another on his leg. Bit by
bit, he was forced back—the man's longer blade a
clear advantage.

Ariana frantically scanned the ground for a stick or
rock to even the odds. She grabbed a fallen limb
about four feet in length and thick as a man's wrist.
Scrambling to her feet, she hoisted it over her head.

Her ankle stung. Ignoring the pain, she limped toward the men.

The vagabond twisted at the sound of her feet crunching leaves, his lip lifting in a snarl. Gabriel took advantage, closed the distance, and sank his dagger into the man's side with a hard thrust just as she cracked the limb down atop the man's head.

Coughing, the vagabond sank to his knees, his arms slack. Blood gushed from his side and head. He twitched twice before collapsing onto his face in a puff of leaves. His unblinking eyes stared blankly up at her.

The stench of death assaulted her nostrils. Her stomach soured, and bile rose in her throat. Covering her mouth with the back of her hand, she swallowed hard and squeezed her eyes to keep her stomach from lurching. Her teeth began to chatter uncontrollably.

"Breathe slowly, girl." Gabriel embraced her in a fierce hug, his arms strong and warm. Heat flowed off his naked torso.

Common sense begged her to resist. To flee. Naught had changed between them. She was still his captive. He was still her captor.

But she was shivering violently, and he felt hot as a campfire. She wanted to melt inside him. He'd saved her life. She'd saved his. And somehow, that changed everything.

Closing her eyes, she surrendered to his embrace, accepting and reveling in the power of his arms, in the thickness of his biceps, and in how good it felt to simply be surrounded by his controlled strength. Turning, she buried her nose in his chest. His spicy masculine scent drowned out the smell of violence. As disconcerting as it was, she wanted to remain here forever.

"I feel so dirty."

"'Tis alright, Ariana. You are safe here."

"He . . . he—"

Gabriel hugged her tighter. "He is dead. He can never harm you again."

They stood in silence for long moments. Gabriel made no move to release her. Slowly, her tremors faded. Blood flowed back into her legs, and her knees stopped knocking against each other.

Propriety dictated that Gabriel let go of her. But he made no move to do so. He was a wild thing—a bastard, a barbarian—not bound by society's rules. That thought sent a thrill up her spine.

She redirected her mind and cleared her throat. A thin red gash was on Gabriel's shoulder and another on his arm.

"You-you are bleeding," she said.

"'Tis but scratches."

When she made to leave his embrace, he released her all at once, not holding her captive as she expected. Her injured ankle gave, and she stumbled.

"Easy, Ariana." He helped her sit on a nearby stump.

Stalking back to the dead man, Gabriel pulled his dagger from the man's side. His movements were practical and efficient. No worry lines creased his brow. Red liquid dripped onto his hand as he calmly wiped the blade on the dead man's tunic. Unlike herself, he seemed unaffected by either the sight of the dead man or the metallic smell of blood.

A shiver passed through her as she stared at him. Her gaze roved over the planes of his chest. His biceps were easily the thickness of a small tree. The cuts on his arm and shoulder evidently bothered him naught.

He was an assassin. The king's hunter. A paid murderer. Killing was commonplace for him.

And she'd just luxuriated in the strength of his arms.

He gazed at her, an unyielding resolve in his green eyes. "'Twas foolhardy to leave my side."

She did not dispute his claim.

Muscles rippled under his skin. He exuded danger and power as he reached for her. "Come."

She willed herself to move from the stump, to run, but the throbbing pain in her leg disallowed it. "My ankle is injured."

"Your ankle?" Concern lined his face.

"It snapped when I fell off Lacey."

Frowning, he knelt beside her and took her foot in his hand.

She stiffened.

Gently, he probed the skin and bones of her foot and ankle with the three fingers of his right hand. "I do not think it is broken, but it needs tending."

He stood and wrapped his arm around her upper back in a possessive, claiming gesture. It should have frightened her and given her the strength she needed to stand and run. But his warmth comforted her quivering nerves, and she found she had no will to fight.

"I'm dirty," she said lamely.

"So am I." He hugged her tighter.

For a moment, she stared at him, marveling that she felt secure within his grasp. A giddy thrill tickled her stomach. Dominance radiated from him, calling to a secret female portion of her soul.

"Come. You need not be afraid of me. I know a place we can wash," he said.

'Twas as if the devil himself beguiled her. The low, soothing tones of his voice wrapped around the inner parts of her being. She shivered as forgotten desires came crashing to the surface.

"Saints help me," she muttered to herself as she wrapped her arm around him. "Lead on then."

Gabriel caught the edge of her gaping bodice between the thumb and index finger of his defaced hand and pulled the fabric together. Ariana glanced down. For the love of St. Jude, one of her nipples poked out the front of her gown! Its coral tip pointed toward heaven in the cool morning air. Heat prickled her cheeks, and she snatched the dress's edges together. Her small hands closed over his larger ones. Mortification burned inside her.

One side of Gabriel's lips lifted in a roguish half smile, then he leaned forward. "'Tis alright. You are safe." His lips brushed her cheek.

Mayhap he'd meant the kiss to be merely comforting, but as soon as his lips touched her skin, an inferno erupted. Sensation arced between them, stronger than the clang of a blacksmith's hammer striking iron. She leaned her head back. Their difference in height felt awkward for a moment, then all at once, his arms surrounded her body, and he lifted her into his embrace. His mouth trailed across her cheek and found her lips, leaving a warm, wet path in its wake. She started, feeling as though she'd been yanked from the ground and hurled upward into the sky. She clung to him, reveling in the sensation of being held in his arms. Her added weight seemed to make him little difference.

He kissed her deeply, his lips willing hers to part. She found it impossible not to submit. His tongue swept inside her mouth to caress her teeth and gums. Heat shivered through her.

Chapter 8

Gabriel frowned down at the woman in his arms. She looked . . . dazed—like a beautiful injured bird. Blast it all! He had meant to comfort her, not kiss her!

He cleared his throat. "I did not mean to do that."

Her face turned an even brighter color of red, and she ducked her head.

Bloody hell!

"I'm sorry. I . . ."

Blast. He had not meant to take advantage of her temporary fragility. This was neither the time nor place for kissing.

He whistled, and his horse poked its head from behind a large shrub. Well, at least one thing was going right. He glanced upward. 'Twas near midday, and the sun had begun to stretch the clouds. The hurly-burly had drained the life out of the morning.

He carried her toward the stallion.

Her body stiffened. "What are you about?"

"You should not walk until we tend your ankle."

She nodded, clearly relieved that they were no longer talking about kissing. She held her bodice together. "There are bandages in my pack, and a needle and thread as well."

"I had to leave the saddle and supplies where we slept last night in order to follow you."

He stared down at her as he stepped over a fallen log. Damnation, but she confused the hell out of him. His experience with noblewomen told him they were self-centered and self-preserving. Yet this lady had clobbered a man even though it meant she was, once again, captive. That she had come to his "rescue" disconcerted him. It seemed that all of his life, one person or another—be it sibling, king, or friend— needed his protection; ne'er before had *anyone* tried to save *him*. No matter what happened in the future, he'd never forget the look of fierce determination in her eyes when she'd wielded the limb at the ruffian's head.

Her weight felt good in his arms. Her gilded red hair curled around his bicep. Beneath the vagabond's stink on her bodice, he caught a whiff of roses. Devil take it, what should he do with her?

Ariana.

Ariana, the lady.

Ariana, The Spy.

None of the titles fit. All of the titles fit. He blew out a breath. He needed answers. His investigations had led to her being the one who was finding out the secret lives of the courtiers, but somehow, it just did not add up. What use would a rich lady have in finding out tawdry secrets? Based on the fineness of her clothing, she was wealthy enough not to need money. She did not strike him as the sort who would black-mail anyone. So if she wasn't doing the blackmailing, then who was? And why?

He forced himself to be patient. There would be time to talk after they had bathed and her ankle had been tended. He knew a magical place to take her after he had found the other horse and gathered their belongings.

Hours later, the sinking sun bathed the horizon red and pink when Gabriel halted the horses and swung down from his stallion. They had gone back to the camp, collected their supplies, and eaten leftover rabbit and some berries that Gabriel had foraged from nearby vines. Gabriel had put his tunic back on, but the sleeveless shirt did little to disguise his blatant masculinity.

Having always lived in a civilized town or her manor home, Ariana found his ability to find food without bakers and servants a little amazing. Most of her meals at court and at Rosebriar were prepared by French chefs and served with an elaborate feast. They were delicious and luxurious, but she found the simple fare Gabriel provided satisfying in a wholly different way that she could not explain.

The evening sun bounced across his skin, giving him an otherworldly appearance as he strode toward her and Lacey. Angel or demon? 'Twas hard to know. He had saved her life . . . but to what end if he took her to London to be tried before the king? He said he'd keep her safe, and a part of her wanted to believe it. The other part said that believing in a man was for daft fools.

His hands, firm and strong, grasped her waist and lifted her from her mount. His scarred hand made the pressure on her waist uneven. She slid against him as she dismounted, and he held her so no weight was on her ankle. He helped her hobble a few steps, then stopped. Frowning, he lifted her into his arms.

"I can walk," she protested weakly, but she knew 'twas a lost battle. He would not let her walk. And, she thought guiltily, it felt so good to be cared for. She took care of her son, her people, her land, and a thousand other things. No one ever took care of her. She allowed her head to drop onto his shoulder.

"Up ahead is a place of healing," he said.

"Of healing?"

"Aye. I came here after my fingers were severed."

"But your fingers—" Her head bumped on his chin as she lifted it.

"Are still missing. Aye. I was so ashamed of my deformed hand that I did not wish to be around anyone. I came here to be alone, and my hand healed. My pride would not allow me to beg, so I learned to steal."

Blinking, she turned this information over in her mind. "You were a thief?"

"Aye."

"You stole to stay alive."

He laughed. "I stole because I enjoyed it and was good at it."

"I see," she said, scandalized. They were both thieves—she was a stealer of secrets, but her work was about duty, ne'er about thrills.

"I stole food and baubles and whatever I needed as I searched for my sister. While in Constantinople, I stole a trinket from an Englishman named Godric." He paused as if paying respect to a hero. "Where others saw only a whore's son, Godric saw potential. He acknowledged that my grip was poor but recognized my shoulders were strong and I was able to sneak in and out of places unobserved. He gave me no choice but to be turned over to the authorities or to be his servant. He helped me find my sister and taught me to use a crossbow. It takes no gripping strength to pull the metal piece that releases the quarrel. 'Tis why it's called the tickler. I practiced long hours, and he showed me that I could use my skill of stealth to become a bounty hunter and thereby provide for my family."

"He must be quite a man."

"He is."

The leaves crunched under Gabriel's feet as he walked. Frogs and crickets sang. Owls hooted. Branches swayed. The moon hung full and bright.

Somehow, being with him comforted her fatigued spirit. She enjoyed listening to his story, and she felt safe allowing him to carry her.

After several moments of walking in silence, Gabriel went to one knee and set her on the ground. "We are almost there."

"I see no water."

"Sh-h. Trust me."

She scrambled until she was kneeling beside him. Sticks poked her knees. "Trust you?"

"Why not?" He grinned, one corner of his mouth lifting slightly higher than the other. "I am the king's hunter. I rescued you. What is not to trust?"

Her heart flipped as she looked up into his face. His teasing emerald eyes contradicted his dangerous dark looks. He was easily the most fascinating man she'd ever seen—power and softness melded together. Worse, she did not feel like his captive. She felt like she was being courted.

A large leafy bush clouded the way before them. Its dark leaves glowed silver in the moonlight. Gabriel slipped one arm around her shoulder. It occurred to her that she should be afraid. But she was not.

His gaze caressed her face. "You are safe with me," he murmured, slowly pulling a linen cloth from inside his tunic. He bent forward and kissed the bridge of her nose. She swallowed. Slowly, he dragged the cloth across her face. The linen had been next to his skin, and his spicy woodland scent filled her nostrils.

Closing her eyes, she allowed herself the guilty pleasure of simply inhaling him. Her shoulders relaxed.

She gasped as the moonlight was suddenly shut out as he covered her eyes with the cloth and pulled it tight.

Chapter 9

"Wha—"

"Sh-h," he admonished, kissing her lips.

Time pitched like a drunken ship as his lips claimed hers. With the blindfold over her eyes, all she could do was feel. His tongue swept over her teeth, licking and teasing. She sighed, surrendering to his expert lead and allowing him to kiss her.

She was too impulsive, to be sure, but Lucifer's horns, it felt *so good*.

After a moment, he pulled away and knotted the blindfold behind her head. Darkness. Pitch black. Amazingly, she felt safe—as if he had mastered the night. A thrill went through her at this new game. So long as he was near, she need not fear the dark.

"Have you ever been kissed by another man?" His voice sounded low and husky.

Heat crept up her cheeks as she realized that he must be asking because he found her kisses so lacking.

"I've been married thrice," she began.

"Nay, I speak not of a chaste kiss at the altar. I speak

of kisses that make your knees quiver and your stomach rock with anticipation."

She shivered at his words, grateful the cloth prevented her from having to look at him. Her eyelashes fluttered, stroking the linen cloth. A man such as Gabriel must have kissed many women. He would think she was naive for knowing so little about kissing.

"Well," she huffed, her embarrassment burning into annoyance. She reached up to undo the blindfold, but he caught her wrists and held her arms down. The soft leather of his breeks touched the backs of her hands, and through them, she could feel the hard sinew of his thighs.

"Unlike you, I have not kissed a thousand other people," she said irritably, no longer finding their game amusing.

He chuckled. "Ariana," he murmured, "'tis not a thousand other women I want to kiss. Only you."

Her stomach did a lazy flop. She wiggled her hands.

"I will release your wrists if you tell me you are afraid."

Her heart pounded wildly. Was she afraid? She searched her mind. Dare she admit she enjoyed his hands on her? His palms were rough, callused, so very different from the smooth, satiny feel of Ivan's or the crinkly, wrinkly feel of Raphael's. Her other husband, William, had not touched her at all.

Gabriel's mouth met hers again.

She clamped her lips, unwilling to allow such a rogue to take control of her senses again. But she wanted . . . wanted . . .

"Relax your lips, Ariana. I want to taste you."

He kissed and licked the seam of her mouth for long, languid moments. She frantically held on to her annoyance, but it seemed to float away like a dead log on a rushing river. Slowly, she allowed her lips to part. His tongue slipped inside her mouth. Wet. Hot.

Warmth pooled in her queynt.

"Good," he breathed. "Now, kiss me back. I want to feel your tongue on mine."

A surge of womanly power went through her at his wicked words. He wanted more of her, not less, she realized. Tentatively, she touched his tongue with her own. A wave of sensation tickled down her back. Heat. Desire.

When he broke the kiss, her mind reeled, befuddled. He released her wrist and ran his finger slowly across her jaw.

"Methinks you have ne'er been kissed by a real man, Ariana."

Methinks you are right, she thought, dazed.

He chuckled again, and heat flooded her cheeks.

"Did I just speak aloud?" she asked.

"Aye."

"Merciful heavens," she breathed. "I am touched by lunacy."

He kissed her lightly on the end of her nose. "Come." He slid her hands outward. She felt the leather of his breeks, then night air, then a leafy bush as he held her hand in front of her. "There is a trail beneath this bush. I will hold the branches back until you pass. Sink to all fours and crawl forward slowly, then stop. I will crawl around you and lead you the rest of the way."

"Crawl?"

"Aye." She could sense the smile in his voice.

A tremor of anticipation giggled in her stomach. "Noblewomen do not crawl."

He laughed darkly. His hand went to the top of her shoulder, and he pressed her downward. "'Twill be fun."

"Fun?" The word came out in a strangled gasp. For the last five years, she had been on many adventures, but none for fun. The thought gave her a heady thrill.

"For pleasure," he murmured. She felt his body sink down beside hers.

"Life is not about pleasure, but about duty."

"Some duties are pleasurable," he countered.

A wicked thought spiraled through her: mayhap a wife's marital duty with *this* man would be most pleasurable.

"I will ruin my dress," she protested lamely.

His hand touched the rip on her bodice that she had patched. He fondled the torn embroidery. "'Tis ruined already. Asides, you can well afford another."

She chewed her lip. He was right.

"Go on," Gabriel said. "The branches are out of the way. The path is fairly wide once we are past the first bit." She felt him move slightly away.

Dropping to all fours, she felt outward with her hand to reach for him. She heard the rustling of his breeks as he moved, and she crawled forward after the sound. Frogs croaked in the distance. Rushing water sounded nearby.

She touched his leg, and he redirected her course. "Crawl that way," he instructed, moving her hand in the direction he wished her to go. "I will come after you, but the branches must be held back."

She obeyed, feeling her way past the bush. "How far in do I go?"

A twig snapped behind her. "Enough; stop and wait."

She heard him shuffle past the branches that guarded the entrance of the bush. A giggle welled inside her, and she felt free as a child at play.

Gabriel crawled around her; the heat from his body brushed her as he passed.

"Grab hold of my ankle," he instructed. "'Tis not far from here, but we must go on hands and knees."

She stretched her fingers out, patting the ground and searching blindly for him. Her hand closed on the thick muscle of his calf. Sliding her fingers down his leg, she grasped hold of his ankle.

"Good. Follow me." Slowly, he moved forward.

She followed, curiosity burning inside her. Twigs and sticks popped as they crawled toward the unknown destination. Branches brushed her sides. The ground was cool against her knees. Her skirt wound around her legs.

After a few yards, she could no longer feel the leaves. She heard Gabriel stand. He touched her shoulder. "You can get up now."

Rising, she heard the sounds of moving water and frogs croaking. She sensed Gabriel behind her. His large body grazed her back, and his hands covered her ears loosely.

"Are you ready?" he whispered.

She nodded, feeling suspended in a dreamlike state where life was somehow both more real and less real at the same time.

Slowly, he slid the blindfold upward. She blinked, and her mouth slackened.

Water surged off a cliff in a huge waterfall and frothed in a swirling pool before them. Ferns crowded the edge of the basin. Light from the full moon silvered the plants' fingered leaves. Fireflies wove drunken trails around them. Mist rose off the water, creating ghostly strands of whiteness.

"'Tis a faerie land," Ariana breathed. A sense of magic seemed to surround the place, as if for once everything in the world was set right. "I have ne'er seen anything so beautiful in my life."

"Come." Gabriel took her hand and led her to the water's edge. His emerald eyes glowed with pleasure. Reaching the bank of the pool, he drew her forward onto a rock and sat down. "Take off your shoes."

A place of healing, he had said. Aye. 'Twas a place of magic.

Gabriel smiled at the wonderment on Ariana's face. Of a truth, she was used to silks and fine furs—he had not wanted to admit he'd harbored worry that such a pampered lady might not appreciate the wonders of nature. Her amazement washed over him, and he was glad he'd taken the chance of bringing her here. 'Twas a special place that would have been tainted if she had not been as awed as he had been upon discovering it.

He took off his boots and tossed them aside, then unlaced his tunic and slipped it over his head.

"What are you about?" She stiffened, but her gaze darted back and forth across his chest.

He grinned. "I am going to bathe. That's what we came here to do."

"In the pond? Without a bathing tub?" She looked scandalized.

"Aye. That's how we peasants get clean. No bathing tubs. No servants to heat the water."

"Yes, but—"

He waited, enjoying her obvious disconcertment. He basked in the way her gaze caressed his body and how her pulse quickened in her neck. Lady or no, she was all woman.

"You are going to be naked whilst I am here?" she blurted.

He winked at her. What a pleasant thought. "You are still my prize. You do not think I am going to let you out of my sight, do you? The grime of today's toil does not sit well. Come."

"I think not." She turned her face aside, but he saw her peek subtly through her lashes. Likely, 'twas a skill she'd perfected as a spy. He knew women too well to be fooled by such actions.

"But you said you wished to bathe."

"Not with you."

He untied the strings of his breeks and was rewarded by a soft mewl in her throat.

"Surely a woman who's been married and borne a child has seen a naked man," he teased.

She gasped and surged to her feet, wobbling as she struggled to balance on her one steady leg. "Nay!"

Reaching forward, he wrapped his arms around her. "You are safe here, Ariana. We are going to bathe, naught more."

"I am not going into that water with you."

He let out a deep breath. Noblewomen! When would he ever understand them? She'd practically jumped out of her skin with impatience for a chance to get clean and now, once she was here, she wanted a bathing tub. "Fine. Once I am finished, I will give you privacy."

She quivered, then relaxed somewhat.

"Forgive me," she said. "Your looks are similar to those of my last husband. And when you stood, my memory deceived me."

Gabriel drew in a quick breath. He should tell her his relationship to Ivan. He tipped her chin up. "Ariana—"

"Nay. Prithee, say naught. 'Tis only my overactive imagination."

Frowning, Gabriel glanced at the rippling water. If he told her of his kinship with her husband right now, he would likely have to spend half the night calming her nerves. And tonight, all he really wanted to do was bathe and enjoy her presence. Tomorrow would be soon enough for truth.

He released her, and she sat again. Turning his back to her, he slid his breeks down his hips. He glanced over his shoulder and was surprised to find her watching him intently. Her eyes dilated as her gaze wandered lazily across his body. Blood flowed into his sex.

He winked at her, and a pretty pink blush crept up her face, but she did not turn her eyes aside. His cock throbbed.

The water made a soft splash as he hopped off the rock into the waist-deep water. He reveled in the wetness for a moment, then turned toward her.

Ariana gaped at him with a look of sheer wonderment. 'Twas as if she was a child looking at all the sweetmeats in the baker's shop, but had never been allowed to have any. Beneath her blatant fascination, her eyes held a haunted look, and he realized he'd only seen her smile once. Tiny crinkles around the corners of her eyes proved that at one point in life, she'd known joy. What weighed so heavily on her?

"Ariana," he said, "when was the last time you laughed?"

"Laughed?" She spoke as if the word was foreign to her lips.

A mischievous urge kicked him. He changed his mind about allowing her privacy to bathe. Paddling over to her, he grasped her waist and pulled her into the pond, careful to keep her injured ankle from hitting the bottom.

She squealed, her hair coming undone from her messy bun, as water splashed around them.

Chapter 10

"Gabriel!" Ariana squealed, clutching his arms for balance as she slid into the pool. Of all the rotten things!

He chuckled. "I've changed my mind about giving you privacy."

The water was warm, she realized with a shock. Warm and wet and delicious on her skin. Probably fed by a hot spring somewhere deep in the ground. Her skirt floated around her. Water drenched the bodice of her gown, wrapping her in a cocoon of heated wetness. No wonder he had called it a place of healing. 'Twas wondrous.

Gabriel's biceps felt firm and strong against her fingers. Her stomach flipped as she realized she held a naked man.

He grinned at her. Moon-kissed pearls of moisture dripped from his hair onto his tanned shoulders. They combined with larger drops to form rivulets that trickled down his body onto the grooves of his hard stomach.

"Surely 'tis nice to bathe after a day like we have had," he said huskily.

Ariana swallowed, trying to gather her thoughts to comprehend what he'd just said. Everything seemed dreamlike, like the edges of reality had been blurred.

The night beckoned her inner soul with an ethereal song spun of crickets, flowing water, and moonlight. The water was refreshing and welcome.

Being touched by vagabonds had made her feel unclean, and 'twas sheer pleasure to rid herself of the stink of this day's events. This . . . this absurdity was not at all what she'd had in mind, but Gabriel was as tempting as a fallen angel.

His green eyes danced with pleasure, and she felt herself being sucked into a dream world where only the two of them existed.

"'Tis outrageous," she protested feebly, "for me to be here with you thus."

"Sh-h." He silenced her with a kiss.

She tried to herd her thoughts back into the harsh, cold reality of life. "I have a son—" she started.

"Who is perfectly safe in his nanny's arms." Gabriel kissed her on the side of her neck.

A line of white-hot desire streaked from the spot of skin his lips touched to her woman's core.

Shivering, she squished her toes into the mud and wiggled them, feeling like a naughty child.

He leaned forward, and his lips brushed hers as warm and wet as the water. Time slowed.

She sighed and sank into his arms, allowing herself the guilty pleasure of feeling instead of thinking.

Gabriel's tongue slid between her lips, licking and teasing and tasting the inside of her mouth. She relaxed, vowing that she would stop the kiss soon enough.

He pulled away from her, his lips less than a

dagger's width from hers. "Wrap your arms around my neck."

She blinked, trying to conjure up reasons to refuse. "Now, Ariana."

The intensity of his husky voice stirred forbidden longings within her.

She obeyed him, twisting her fingers into his hair. Her husband had been equally demanding, but Gabriel's appeal was in his fire and heat. She knew deep within herself if she said nay, Gabriel would not force himself on her.

Water undulated across the surface of the pond as Gabriel slid his hand across her back. He kissed her cheek and trailed kisses down her neck. With a husky chuckle, he nipped her on the top of the shoulder.

She gasped, heat rippling outward from where his teeth had grazed her skin. He slid her gown off her shoulder and stroked her upper arms softly as if she were some fragile, expensive work of art. A part of her knew she should resist, but ne'er in her life had she felt so wanted, so cherished.

Cherished.

'Twas an emotion that had been missing completely from her life's experience. Three husbands and nary a one had truly wanted her. And now this man, a rough peasant, made her feel as though she was queen of the moon.

His hands rubbed languidly up and down her back, his thumbs making tiny magic circles with each slow stroke. Just for tonight, she promised herself. Just for tonight. Tomorrow there would be time for escape and conflict and war between them.

He caught her lower lip between his teeth and sucked

softly. She moaned, her desire growing. The water lapped
around them, a gentle beckoning sound.

"Ariana," Gabriel whispered.

"Um-m-m?"

"Tell me you know what you are doing. Tell me I am
not forcing you or tricking you." A line of concern
formed between his brows. "Tell me that no matter
what happens on the morrow, this thing between us
tonight is real."

She took a deep breath, wishing she could lie to
herself and pretend she was not a willing participant.
She pulled him close.

"Gabriel, I am not a virgin."

He pushed her gown down to her hips. It floated
beneath the surface of the water in soft, mesmerizing
ripples. Her nipples puckered in the cool night air.

Lowering his head, Gabriel licked the exposed
peak. Lightning sensation arced into her sex.

"Tell me you are enjoying this."

"I am enjoying this too much," she breathed. Her
stomach prickled as she spoke. The words were true
enough, but it seemed odd to say them aloud.

His hands caressed her hips, gently kneading and
stroking her skin. Her gown sank further under the
water.

Tentatively, she touched his chest. He reminded
her of a beautiful Greek statue, too perfect to be real.
She skimmed the planes of his stomach with her fingers and enjoyed his sharp intake of breath. His body
was wondrous, all angles and hardness, but his skin
was soft as finely spun silk.

Gazing up at him, she realized he watched her with the
intensity of a hawk stalking a field mouse. He leaned forward, and his manhood grazed her stomach, then

prodded lower, bouncing against the crisp hair betwixt her thighs.

She gasped, jolted back into reality. What had she been thinking? The act of a man jabbing his penis into a woman's quim was painful and jarring.

"Gabriel, cease."

He lifted his head from where he had been kissing the crook of her neck. "Huh?"

"Cease, Gabriel. Cease. We must halt."

He kissed her eyebrow, his breath caressing her skin. "Why?"

"I did not know you were going to . . . you know," she lied, ashamed she had lost her nerve for the act.

Water splashed as he stepped back, holding her at arm's length. His fingers wrapped around her upper arms.

"What is wrong?" he whispered.

"I did not . . ." she paused, grasping for words, ". . . know you planned to . . . take me." She ducked her head to hide the lie. Her forehead bumped his chin. She had known, but until his manhood had touched her, she'd forgotten that she hated copulation.

"Did not know?" His shoulders stiffened, but his voice was soft and mesmerizing. "You are not a virgin or some blushing bride. What did you think we were doing when you kissed me thus? When you touched me thus?"

She shook her head, embarrassed. Gooseflesh popped on her arms. She had not been thinking at all. She'd been feeling. How could she tell him that he'd made her forget the pain of having a man inside her?

"A woman cannot just tease a man with mad passion and expect him to turn aside like a cold fish." Did she detect an edge of irritation in his voice?

"I was not teasing you . . ." Oh, 'twas pointless to deny it. Digging her toes in the mud, she gazed up at him. "Prithee, Gabriel. I did not know what I was doing. I have never done this afore."

"Ne'er done this afore?" He sounded cross, and she shivered.

She raised her hand to his chest to ward off his annoyance. Her fingers absently found the edge of an old scar.

"What is wrong, Ariana? You are not a virgin." His hand tightened on her upper arm; she could tell he was somewhat cross, but oddly, she did not feel afraid. "You have a child. You know what happens between a man and a woman."

"Aye. I . . ."

He took hold of her shoulders.

She looked down at the water, trying to concentrate on the tiny ripples and waves. "I, er, I forgot I do not care for it."

Suddenly, she felt very naked with her breasts exposed and her gown undulating around her ankles. She bent her knees, trying to dip into the water, wishing she could sink into the mud and disappear like a worm.

He held her upright. "How can you forget you dislike a man inside you?"

Her cheeks heated at his frank speech. "I am sorry, Gabriel. Verily, I am." She pulled back, but he held her captive. Humiliation mixed with frustration shivered through her. "Please let me go."

"Tell me what happened between you and your husbands."

"Please."

"Tell me."

Mortified, she covered her face with her hands. How could she tell him about the times Ivan had woken her from sound sleep to poke his man thing inside her and pump violently for a few moments? She squeezed her eyes shut; if she thought about it too much, she could smell the soured ale on his breath and feel his fingers twisting and pinching her breasts. One time, he'd flipped her over and forced her to lie still whilst he'd frigged her like a man.

"The usual, I suppose," she squeaked out when Gabriel showed no signs of letting her retrieve her soggy gown and wrap the shards of her dignity around her.

"The usual?" he prompted.

She bit her lower lip, again wanting to sink into the mud. "Please, Gabriel. Let us just get dressed." She reached to pull up her dress, but he held her rooted in place.

"Not until you answer my question. What happened between the two of you?"

She wiggled her toes in the mud, this time not enjoying the cool, squishy feel of it. She lifted her chin haughtily, grasping for some shred of composure. "I do not want to speak of it. Especially to a stranger."

"A stranger?" He pulled her forward and wrapped her in a tight embrace. His naked chest slid against hers. Skin on skin. His manhood pressed her belly.

She felt her cheeks prickle further, if that were possible. He was proving with his body that he was definitely more than a stranger.

Worse, it felt good to be wrapped in a man's heated embrace—*this* man's embrace, she corrected. Confusing emotions jumbled together. She wanted to run, and she wanted to stay.

"Have you e'er seen a man's cock afore?" he asked softly.

She nearly choked. "Seen a man's c-c-" She stumbled over the crude word. She'd felt one many times. Hard. Hurtful. Bruising. Only her husband had not called it a cock—he'd called it his prick. And she'd never actually seen it. Their copulation came in the dead of night: *wake up, woman; roll over; I'm going to stuff you full of prick*. Then he'd jump atop her, hike her gown up, and pump himself into her woman's place. It hurt like she'd been rammed with the devil's horn.

"'Tis the appendage betwixt his legs upon which a woman is impaled for the pleasure of both of them," Gabriel prompted when she did not answer. She detected a measure of soft teasing as he spoke. The memories of her husband's brutality fled with the soothing, erotic tone of Gabriel's voice.

"Pleasure?" she repeated dumbly.

"Aye, pleasure."

Ariana bit her lower lip. She knew much about the impaling force of a man's member. "A man's c . . . er . . . member is for a man's pleasure," she said, scarcely believing they were having a conversation about what was between a man's legs.

"And a woman's, too."

She shifted in the water, unsure what to say. For all her years of marriage, she felt ignorant of the ways between a man and a woman.

"'Tis not pleasant for a woman," she said at last. "'Tis simply something that the Church commands women to do."

"The Church? Christ, girl. Swiving has naught to do with the bloody Church." 'Twas the first time he'd raised his voice since their conversation had begun, and the sound startled her.

She stared at him, at a loss for words.

He took a deep breath and blew it out. Water trickled down his temple. "I assure you, when I take a woman, 'tis *very* pleasant for her."

Very pleasant for her. The words echoed in her mind. A long moment passed. He eased her away from him, allowing a little space between their bodies. His grip loosened on her upper arm, and he made slow circles with his thumbs. His heated gaze pierced her, beckoning to a long hidden portion of her soul.

She felt she was on the brink of some dangerous cliff, dizzy and giddy from the height but enchanted by the altitude all the same.

"Ariana," he murmured.

She shivered, entranced by the languid strokes of his fingers.

"Ariana, trust me." He continued his gentle assault, moving his hands to her back and simply touching, rubbing, stroking her skin. He made no move to jump on her or force her to his will.

"It would be pleasant for me?" she whispered at long last. Her heart pounded in her chest.

Leaning down, he kissed her cheek. *"Very* pleasant for you."

Her shoulders relaxed. Gabriel was so different from any man she'd ever known, so gentle in his seduction. She wanted to trust him. She wanted to experience this pleasure, this heat. She wanted to be wild and free, instead of knee-deep in worry and responsibility.

A thought tickled her mind—experiencing pleasure in copulation would be like driving another nail in Ivan's coffin. 'Twould be one more proof that he could not defeat her.

Slowly, she nodded.

Gabriel grinned. Moonlight danced across his jaw. "Good."

She smiled, laughing at her own folly as she realized how awkward she must seem to him. Self-consciously, she reached for her dress, which rippled around her calves.

"Nay. Leave it." He pulled her forward, leaving the dress to fend for itself on the bottom of the pond. "You are beautiful. Let me look at you."

"Beautiful?" She blinked, then glanced down at her body.

Feathering his fingers outward, he softly flicked them across her chest, then cupped a breast in each hand. He lifted first one and then the other, planting a kiss on each. "Very beautiful."

Heat flowed through her, pooling between her legs. Gabriel ran his hands down her stomach and circled her waist. She gasped as he lifted her out of the water and sat her down upon a rock.

"What are you about?" she asked. The air was slightly chilly but not cold.

"I want to look at you."

She covered herself as much as she could with her hands and arms, feeling herself blush all the way to her toes. "Heavens, Gabriel, I am naked."

"So am I." His heated gaze bore into her, and his hands trailed down her stomach to her thighs. "And you did not seem to mind being naked just moments ago."

"I was in the water."

Bending forward, he kissed her thigh. Embarrassment

burned her cheeks as she realized that Gabriel was at eye level with her sex. She clamped her legs together, but the auburn curls peeked out at the vee between her thighs. 'Twas one thing to think of committing fornication in the water but quite another in the open air.

"Sh-h," he said, kissing her leg again. His tongue licked a path from her knee to the curly hair nestled betwixt her legs.

"Gabriel," she protested, but did not resist as he pushed her thighs apart.

She glanced down, both ashamed and thrilled. Her body was open to him, her white thighs parted with his face between them. He gazed at her sex. Passion burned in his eyes, scorching her with desire.

Heat flooded her body at the wicked thought of a man looking at her *down there*. Nay, not just looking at her, but looking at her and wanting her. Not once in three marriages had a man wanted her thus. Sex had been about duty, ne'er about pleasure.

He laced his fingers through her dark, curly nether hair and parted it. She swallowed, and her heart pounded as the pink edges of her inner sex were exposed to his gaze. Gently, he tugged her quim apart. Womanly moisture glistened on her folds. Modesty dictated she turn away from the sight, but curiosity prevailed. Cool night air brushed her skin.

He touched her sex, catching her woman's moisture on his index finger. Fascinated, she watched as he slowly raised his finger to his mouth and sucked her woman's fluid from it.

Desire raced through her; liquid heat flooded between her legs. She swallowed as she saw another drop of moisture slide from her quim.

"Gabriel, I feel hot."

One side of his mouth lifted in a sexy, roguish smile. Bending, he licked down one side of her queynt, then up the other. Her legs quivered, and her hips flinched involuntarily as his tongue swirled expertly against her woman's parts.

"Dear heavens, Gabriel. Heavens."

She lifted her hips, shocked at her own wantonness. An odd tingling sensation tickled one side of her buttocks near her spine. She rubbed the twitchy spot.

He lifted his head, his lips glistening with the proof of her desire. God's wounds, he was beautiful.

"Did I harm you?" he asked.

"Nay. Oh, heavens. Nay. It feels so good it makes my fanny tingle."

He grinned, his green eyes twinkling. "There is much more to come, I assure you."

Sighing, she gave up thinking altogether and leaned back against the rock. The coolness of the stone contrasted with the heat of his tongue. Sensation built inside her like a kettle bubbling over onto the fire.

"Oh, Gabriel," she moaned.

Tension mounted. Ne'er in her life had she felt so hot. Her quim quivered. She felt as though she would fly into a thousand pieces. Then abruptly, just as she thought she could take no more, Gabriel's tongue ceased.

"Please, Gabriel. Do not stop."

Her eyes flickered open as the water made a small splash, and Gabriel hoisted himself out of the pond and onto the rock. She gasped as his naked body hovered above hers. Water dripped from his skin, splashing tiny puddles on her stomach. Desire shivered through her, and she stared up at him in amazement.

Slowly, he lowered himself. His rod grazed the edge of her sex. She flinched, her body preparing itself for the usual pain.

"Have I hurt you?" he whispered as if he could read her thoughts.

She shook her head.

"You are not a virgin. I will not hurt you now."

She relaxed a little, forcing herself to trust him. Nothing he'd done so far had hurt, and she found herself curious and wanting to know what it would feel like to be taken by a man for pleasure. His *and* hers.

He kissed her, and she tasted herself on his lips. Desire spun through her. Oh, wicked, wicked man. He entered her slowly. One inch, then two.

"Breathe," he commanded.

She obeyed.

"Are you well?"

"Aye."

He slid fully inside her. She stared up at him, a feeling of awe coming over her. A stretchy heat filled her quim.

"Does it hurt?"

"Nay. Not at all. I feel full and . . ." It was on the tip of her tongue to say *loved*, but that made no sense.

"Full and . . ." he prompted.

"Full and delicious."

He smiled his mischievous smile and pressed his hips down, stuffing himself further inside. She shifted her legs, restless now. The feeling on her sex was intense, but not quite focused now that his tongue no longer licked and stroked her nether lips. She wiggled. There was still that one place that wanted, needed rubbed. The place right above where his manhood slid into her body.

He moved inside her. Slowly, the focus rebuilt. Tingling sensation poured into that little area. She gasped and pressed her hips against his, wishing suddenly he was licking her there again. But how could she tell him?

"Gabriel?"

In answer, he rocked his hips against hers and kissed her across the bridge of her nose.

Surrendering to his expert lead, she flattened her legs on the stone so she could press herself closer to him. The hair between his legs tickled the area that burned and tingled with need. For long moments, their bodies moved in a slow rhythm.

"Oh, oh, Gabriel."

His strokes quickened, and the world shattered into an explosion of feeling. Her body quivered with ripples of sensation.

"Oh, dear heavens, Gabriel." Her limbs felt limp and wrung out.

He moved his hips in small, tight circles, allowing her to float languidly in sensation.

"Ariana," he whispered hoarsely, "wrap your legs around my waist."

Her legs weighed ten stones apiece, but she did as he asked, locking her ankles around his body. In this position, she felt stretched and anchored to him. He thrust into her, harder this time. She moaned, amazed there was no pain in their coupling. Only sensation. Only pleasure. She clung to him as he rocked, then thrust, then pounded into her body until at last, he cried out in ecstasy. In the aftermath, time floated, and they both lay still.

Staring up at the stars, she felt she was swirling a few inches from the ground, rather than lying on a cold, hard rock. "'Twas wondrous," she breathed.

He lifted himself slightly, easing partly away from her. "I have ne'er deflowered a woman who is no longer a virgin," he drawled.

"Thorns." She pushed against his chest. "You must think I am a ninny."

He chuckled softly. "Not a ninny. A hellcat. A water nymph. A wanton mayhap. But ne'er a ninny."

She warmed at Gabriel's words, pushing back an unpleasant memory of Ivan screaming at her. *You stupid cow,* he'd said one day when she'd been inept at a particular task he had given her.

Gabriel kissed her cheek. "Why the long face?"

"Sorry. An unpleasant memory." She hugged him. "It has naught to do with you."

Gabriel sucked in a breath to keep himself from blurting out his relationship to Ariana's dead husband. He rolled from atop her and stared at the stars. This was a fine muck. For Eric's sake he had no choice but to take her to London.

Ariana sighed and laid her hand atop his chest. Content. Trusting.

He stared at her fingers, slender and delicate against his tanned chest. She twirled her index finger against the edge of a long-healed scar.

What a blackheart I am. To swive her and then package her off to prison like some tawdry common whore.

He hadn't brought her here to swive her, he told himself, but it did naught to ease his conscience. Mayhap if she had been some cheap tart, he could be so callous.

But despite her marriage, despite her lack of virginity, despite her child, despite being a spy, she was an innocent. He had not intended their pleasure to turn into something so . . . pleasant.

"What are you thinking?" she asked, startling him.

He sat up, unsure what to say. Moonlight flickered over her face, making her large eyes seem luminous. Ringlets of hair fanned out around her in tumultuous disarray. Curly strands twirled over and down the rocks. She no longer seemed afeared to be naked before him, her body a lush banquet for his eyes.

He traced his hand down her throat, flicking his fingers across her breasts, which had relaxed outward. Her coral-colored nipples puckered. Her breasts were neither overly large nor small, but a nice weight that fit his palms perfectly. She sighed as he cupped his hands around them, then ran his fingers down her rib cage and stomach.

Her alabaster skin flinched at his touch. Small whitish grooves snaked across her rounded stomach, proof that she had once been with child. He slowly traced these with his finger. What would he do with her?

Just take her to London and be done with it, his mind reasoned. Spend a day or week or month in the stews, and you'll forget about her. Think of Eric. Think of the children.

His conscience roared at him. Mayhap he had no proof that Ariana was The Spy because she was not—she had not confessed to it after all. Perhaps he could find another way to get Eric out of prison. And as for food and clothing, times had occasionally been tough, but none in his care had starved or been without shoes. He'd provided for them ever since he had returned from the search for Eleanor. He had been seventeen.

Ariana giggled, drawing his attention. Giggled!

"Cease, Gabriel. It tickles!"

A low rumble started deep in his throat. He wiggled his fingers on her stomach. She jumped, then squealed. Then laughed.

"I'll get you back," she promised, lunging for him.

He jumped away, but miscalculated the length of the rock and fell backward into the pond. Water splashed, soaking them both.

Laughing, she scrambled to her knees. "Serves you right."

Latching onto her upper arm, he dragged her into the water. She smiled, wrapped her arms around his neck and her legs around his waist. He kissed her, enjoying the feel of her in his arms. Here was a woman brimming with passion waiting to be unleashed. Laughing, fighting, crying, or moaning, she felt right in his arms.

He must keep her, he realized with a start. She had given up her innocence to him, something much more precious than her virginity.

In the back of his mind, his dreams of freedom shattered, and the bands of duty cut into his soul.

For years, he'd staved off having to marry for money by hunting down criminals and taking them to justice. Now, that pathway had snared him. He could not take Ariana to London and see her rotting in prison, nor could he set her free.

He frowned, unhappy with the only option that made sense. The option that would put him in the same class as his distasteful pig of a brother. It galled him to think of selling out, but he had no choice.

"You will marry me," he said flatly, the words tasting like gall in his mouth. Duty squeezed his throat like a too tight collar. One other time he had thought to marry a noblewoman, but Fate had saved him.

Silence had never seemed so loud. It seemed even the frogs stopped croaking.

Ariana stared at him as if he'd just sprouted horns. She unwrapped her legs from his waist.

Gabriel blew out a breath, unsure what to make of her response. "'Tis the best solution."

"Solution? To what?" She lifted her chin, but its stubborn line was ruined by a trickle of water that dripped off. "I am not some puzzle to be solved, sirrah."

"I cannot let you go, Ariana. If I take you to London, your enemies will see you in prison or worse."

Ariana's mind raced, and she felt blood drain from her face. So this was what his seduction was about—a way to chain her to him.

Marriage brought evil on a woman. Her title would be retained, but a husband controlled everything— the land, the gold, the decisions. Anything she needed would be his to grant or deny at will. Even her body would no longer be hers to command.

For five years she'd worked to make Rosebriar profitable for her people. Her lands were rich. Save for her cousin's demands, she went where she wanted, did as she pleased. Wealthy widows had enormous freedom.

Gabriel was a peasant, a whore's son, a thief; he did not know how to run an estate. She had Jason and her people to think of. She *could* not submit herself again to a man's rule.

"Nay . . . I will not marry you." Nor any man.

"Why not?"

"Because 'tis lunacy!"

He took her hand, sending shivers racing up her arm. "'Tis the only way."

Outrage shot through her. "I do not even know you!"

He winked at her. "Well enough to swive me."

Heat burned her cheeks. He had turned her into a wanton, and they both knew it.

"You are in danger. Men know you are The Spy. They will not stop until they see you brought to justice."

"I am not—"

"Let me protect you. Marry me."

Her mind raced, trying to regain some composure. "Protect me? With marriage?"

"'Tis best."

"I do not love you," she protested.

"The marriage of nobles rarely has to do with love," he countered. "Were your other marriages for love?"

Her heart pounded. Of course not. And she wasn't entirely sure she was not a little in love with Gabriel. "I have a child to think of."

"All the more reason to marry me. You shall be safe from the gallows, and your boy will be safe."

"The king will not allow it," she said, feeling desperate that his offer was starting to sound a little more rational.

Bringing her hand up, he kissed her fingers gently. "The king will accept the marriage."

She eyed him warily, suddenly struck again by how much he resembled her husband when he bent forward. Ivan's hair had fallen rakishly over his forehead just as Gabriel's did. Her husband had been just as charming when he'd wanted to be.

Water glistened across his shoulders as Gabriel straightened, and she was all too aware of the strength of his body. She shivered.

"You are a peasant," she reasoned. "The king will disallow it and have the marriage annulled."

He opened her hand and laid it, palm down, across his cheek. His beard's growth pricked against her fingers. He gazed at her, his eyes guarded. "He will not."

She tried to pull back her hand, but he kept it anchored to his cheek. Annoyance worked its way through her. "You do not know that! What do you know of nobility and duty?"

Anger flashed in his eyes and then was gone. "He will allow the marriage," he insisted. "He will be glad of it, I assure you."

Gabriel's highhandedness irritated her. She blew out a breath. "Men! They think they know everything."

"Nay, not everything. But mark my words on this."

The cocky set of his shoulders gave her pause. She narrowed her eyes. "How can you be so sure? What are you not telling me?"

His dark expression softened, and he turned his head slightly to kiss her palm. She wished she could ignore the heated sensation his lips sent to her sex.

"I am your husband's brother."

Ariana felt the earth spin out of control. The water, which only moments ago seemed warm and playful, now felt like a watery grave. The moon lost its luster. The waterfall became noise instead of music.

"You can't be," she whispered. But in her heart, she knew it was true. His hair, his eyes, his shoulders had all reminded her of Ivan. She'd seen it but not seen it. She wanted to scream. She wanted to cry. She wanted to scratch his eyes out.

Gabriel caught her as her knees gave.

"But my husband had no brother," she whispered, desperate to gain a semblance of composure.

"Aye, Ariana, he did."

She looked into his eyes—green eyes with thick, black lashes. The same colors as Ivan's. Gabriel stared back at her intently. His gaze was as severe, as uncompromising as Ivan's. A tiny brown mote glittered at the lower edge of his right eye. Just like Ivan's.

"Why . . . why did you not tell me?" The fringes of panic pricked her heart.

"I was selfish and tired of our arguing." Gabriel stroked her shoulder. "I am not like him, Ariana. You must believe me. He is only my half brother."

She stared at him. A gnawing sensation bit its way into her stomach. Now that she paid close attention to his features, the resemblance was obvious. The aristocratic nose, the green eyes, the uneven part of his hair. She wanted to kick herself. Mayhap she had been right the first time she saw Gabriel—he was the incarnate of Ivan, come back from the grave to haunt her.

"You will marry me," he said at last. His tone did not invite argument. His hand gripped her upper arm in the way one would hold a prisoner.

Heart pounding, Ariana debated her options. If she told him nay outright, she'd likely end up bound to the bed for the night and in London on the morrow facing the gallows.

If he trusted her, she'd have a better chance of escape, but she did not want to sound too eager either because that might make him suspicious.

"'Tis outrageous."

"'Tis the only way," he insisted.

She glanced over his naked form, not having to fake the hungry look she wanted to give him. Despite her fear, even despite his resemblance to her dead husband, Gabriel was an attractive man.

She inhaled his sweet, spicy scent and then leaned forward to kiss him. She'd escaped once; she could do it again.

"Alright, Gabriel. I will marry you," she lied, vowing to leave as soon as he fell asleep.

Chapter 11

Gabriel was sound asleep when Ariana stole the horses and ran. Because of their marriage agreement, because of the peace that had come over them after their lovemaking, he'd let her sleep unbound. Her conscience let out a squeak of guilt, but she had already made one mistake by fornicating with him. She would not compound it with another. Being cocooned in his arms felt good. Too good. She had not wanted to leave him, but it could not be helped. Jason. Rosebriar. Duty before pleasure.

It had been relatively easy to get away. Praise the saints, this time she'd had no trouble on the road.

The scent of smoke hung in the air as she rounded the bend of the cobblestone path. Thornbury's abbey stood just ahead on the right. A charred roof peeked over the stone wall. Blackened brick lay in scattered piles. The cathedral's thick columns still stood, but soot marred the stones. If her luck held, she would be able to deliver the parchment on her way home to Rosebriar. From there, she would fortify her defenses and send a letter to her cousin the bishop to plead with him to leave her be. This spying had become too dangerous.

She brought the horses to a halt at the abbey's gate and pondered the man she'd left behind. In a different world, mayhap she would gladly have accepted an offer of marriage from him.

But this was not a different world. She had been forced to marry three times. Each time, her lot became worse.

Marriage was the equivalent of the slave market. A married woman had no choices except those her husband permitted. She could neither buy nor sell land, nor go where she wished, nor do as she pleased. Mayhap if she was more foolhardy, she could accept such a choice, but she had Jason to protect.

The corners of her mouth turned down as she stared at the abbey. Truth bit at her soul: although she had rid herself of Gabriel, she was still a man's pawn—she must go where her blackmailer demanded.

She reflected for a moment, wishing she could simply fade away and become a hermit.

Sighing at the entanglements of her life, she realized that even with the bishop's demands, her life was better than it had been as a wife. Especially as Ivan's wife.

Her cousin the bishop had helped her cover up the part she had played in her husband's death. At the time, it seemed the best thing to do, but then slowly, he began to ask for little things. A few pounds for this, a few gold pieces for that. A few parties to go to, a few people to follow.

So now, here she was, once more doing a man's bidding. Crossing herself, she prayed it would be the last time.

The edges of dawn pinkened the charred stones.

The abbey seemed deserted. Upturned grass lay in small clods around the forsaken courtyard. Likely, the monks were too weary and disheartened from fighting the fire to be up and about.

Half-burned chairs, hymnals, and ruined statuary piled on the abbey's lawn. The bishop's chair, which had once been a huge gilded throne, lay on its side in the middle of the dirt, its paint peeling and its seat burned-out. From a blackened heap of ashes, the charred head of the Virgin Mary lolled, staring up at her with blank eyes.

Guilt squeezed her heart, but she pushed it aside and focused on the mission.

For a moment, she debated the best way to enter the charred cathedral. Although the courtyard was currently empty of monks, the bells announcing Prime would ring soon. Most likely, the abbey's occupants would not feel charitable to the one who had caused such a fine disaster.

Tying the horses outside the gate, she prayed for forgiveness, then crept quietly into the courtyard. The thick stone of the church stood solid and steady, but ash hung heavily in the air, painting the bricks a dull gray. She crossed the lawn, stayed near the wall, and crept from tree to cistern to building until she made it to the burned-out door of the church.

Glancing around, she sent up another silent prayer of thanks that no monks were present. The bells tolled in the background, and her heart leapt into her throat. No time to tarry.

Slipping into the cathedral, she headed toward the burned-out altar. The vast emptiness of the room ate at her. Most of the contents had been pulled into the courtyard, and the huge room reminded her of an empty skull bone. The windows, lifeless with their missing panes, stared at her like vacant eyeholes. Charred shreds of silk hung limply from the upper floor like the last sinews of muscle. Black soot covered the floor's checkered tiles, resembling a layer of flies.

She cringed, disgusted with her role in such destruction. If only so much was not at stake, she thought, kneeling on the altar steps just as she had done before Gabriel's arrival. A surge of anger at men's rampant quest for power flowed through her.

I must find a way free from spying. I will finish the missions he has already planned for me, then tell my cousin I am done with it all, she vowed silently.

Perhaps she could hire some guards and stay close by her castle. And if Gabriel came for her . . . well, her time at court had gained her some skill in fending off men.

A fingernail broke as she grappled with the edges of the tile. She shook her hand at the biting pain and tried again. Mortar crumbled, and one of the floor pieces lifted. Good. She shoved it. The tile slipped from her fingers and fell back in place with a little puff of dust and soot. Taking a better hold, she lifted the stone again. It screeched along the floor as she pushed it aside.

A low bellow rang outside in the courtyard. "Get him!"

She jumped. Mercy, had Gabriel arrived already? If so, how? Hurriedly, she placed the parchment under the tile and raced for the door.

Monks pattered across the courtyard, their sandals flopping against the churned up earth. One carried a pitchfork, his face full of grim determination. A stone's throw away, she saw Gabriel pushed against the wall, held there by a horde of angry, brown-robed men. Garden tools had been turned into makeshift weapons. One monk held a hoe at his throat; another brandished a rake.

Dagger drawn, he fended off the first wave of attackers. Toward the side, a horse whinnied, and she reasoned he'd stolen it from one of the farmhouses in order to reach the abbey.

A monk slammed a hoe across Gabriel's temple. She recoiled, realizing that Gabriel sought only to defend himself, while the monks fought for vengeance over the cathedral. He was outnumbered and at a disadvantage.

She moved forward, thinking that she must help him.

His blade flew from his hand, knocked aside by a monk wielding a sickle. His eyes caught hers as he fell to the ground.

She moved behind a tree and peered at the sea of monks. Gabriel was hidden; he had been swallowed into the depths of flowing brown robes.

She heard him shout and knew he still lived. A tall, bony man glided toward the horde. The mob halted in their attack as the new monk, the Abbot himself, walked toward them. His brown robe dripped off his emaciated shoulders in elongated waves.

"Leave him," he said in a thin, pinched voice.

"But he burned the Lord's house!"

"We do God's work!"

"Our garden is ruined!"

"Silence!" the man commanded.

Ariana breathed a sigh of relief. She was familiar with the men of the abbey because she oft came here to pray. The Abbot was a pious man. He would not allow them to beat Gabriel to death with a garden hoe. Once he learned of Gabriel's connection with the king, Gabriel would be released.

Best that she withdraw and make herself ready for that time. She shrank into the shadows, toward the horses, comforted that she would not have Gabriel's death on her conscience.

As she exited the abbey, her imagination floated to the feel of Gabriel's tongue on her quim.

Duty before pleasure, she told herself with regret.

Quickly, she turned and left.

Chapter 12

Betrayed once more by a noblewoman and tied like a bloody hound! Anger coursed through Gabriel's veins as he stood on a makeshift wooden box, his hands bound behind him and his head nearly touching the top of a canvas tent. A rope anchored him by the neck to an iron post.

Of course she had betrayed him, he thought grimly. Ariana was a *spy*, dammit. She betrayed *everyone*. His pride stung. He had stared into her brilliant clear blue eyes and had believed her when she'd said she'd marry him. Fool! Fool! Fool! Had he not already learned that for all their moans and sighs, noblewomen did *not* marry whore's sons? Years ago, one had taught him this lesson when she had not shown up at the altar. And still he had dared to trust Ariana.

His kind were good for swiving, but ne'er to marry.

He squinted in the sunlight, the brightness stinging his eyes. Until this morning, he had been locked in the abbey's dank cellar. After three days of darkness, his eyes were unused to the light.

Bloody damn! He would find Ariana and haul her

to London trussed like a pheasant so he could get Eric back. The reward for her would keep the children in food for the winter.

Thornbury's abbot sat in a high-backed wooden chair before him, his expression dour. Deep, permanent frown lines ran from his hairline to his nose. He was a tall, skeletal man with a long, horselike face, and his plain brown robe draped over his elongated form.

The county bishop sat beside him, his plump, bejeweled hands a sharp contrast to the abbot's bony ones. The bishop's gilded mitre alone probably cost a king's ransom. His lavish red and white vestments were made of finely spun silk. Fat pink cheeks with jowls that would have made a swine envious squatted atop thick layers of chins. He looked altogether out of place in the crude tent. His squatty figure was squeezed into a narrow, high-backed chair.

Gabriel stared from one man to the other.

The Horse and the Pig.

Vastly different in their religious convictions, they both glared at him with a fervor that bespoke ill tidings. Whatever personal differences they might have, they were united in their desire to punish the sinner.

Gabriel strove to not curl his lip in distaste. He knew their type well—they claimed to be men of God but cared only for power and control.

Glancing to the side, he saw four armed knights, the bishop's personal guard, standing ready in case he was able to free himself of the biting ropes.

No jury had been selected for this "official" church meeting to determine his punishment.

Wariness and anger crept over Gabriel's shoulders as silence stretched through the tent. One guard's hand slid to his sword hilt. The abbot steepled his fingers. The bishop flicked one of his rings.

"I am on the king's business," Gabriel said at last, although he doubted it would make a difference. Likely, they intended to send him to rot in debtor's prison for the rest of his ill-cursed life.

"You will remain silent until spoken to," the abbot said.

Gabriel met the man's intense glare but remained silent. Best not to dig his own grave.

"Gabriel of Whitestone," the bishop said in a high-pitched, cranky tone, "you are hereby accused of burning property belonging to the High Church of our Lord."

"I am here on the king's business," Gabriel repeated calmly.

"And what business might that be?" the bishop asked.

"I am the King's Hunter."

The abbot coughed. "The King's Hunter is merely a legend."

Gabriel glowered at him. "I came to capture the Lady Ariana. She has been accused of spying and is wanted for questioning in London." He strained at the bonds, a surge of anger passing over him at the thought of Ariana. "Had your monks not been so intent on beating me with garden hoes, I could have taken her. She is to blame for the cathedral's burning."

"You have been charged with desecrating holy ground," the bishop continued as if Gabriel had not spoken. "It is a sin to lay your guilt at the door of the innocent."

"Innocent!" Gabriel yanked against the rope,

making the iron post quiver. "The woman is a menace to the whole country."

The abbot sniffed. "Lady Ariana has been a great benefactress of the abbey."

"The abbot tells me Lady Ariana was not in the cathedral," the bishop said. His jowls wobbled when he talked.

Anger burned in Gabriel's chest. "She was there!"

"Shirking your responsibility and blaming others is a mark of the devil," the abbot said, his voice thin and gravelly.

"I do not shirk my responsibilities!" Gabriel shouted.

The abbot blinked and pursed his nearly nonexistent lips. "Lying is a sin against heaven. It is important to God that your sins be cleansed."

"Nay!" Gabriel pulled at the ropes, rage burning him. He stepped from the wooden box, wanting to grasp the abbot by his thin neck and snap it like a twig.

"Guards!" the bishop squeaked out, much like a sow at market.

A knight stepped forward, grasped Gabriel's neck rope, and yanked him back onto the wooden box. Gabriel pulled against him, furious with the bonds biting his wrists. Unbalanced without his hands, he fell forward. The guard caught him before the rope could hang him and pushed him upright. Straightening, he glared at the churchman.

The abbot's nostrils flared. "You will have the letter D burned into your flesh as a reminder that you have *desecrated* holy ground."

Gabriel balled his fists, willing himself to remain motionless. The man seemed to relish the punishment, and any reaction he showed would only add to the abbot's perverse pleasure.

The bishop laid a fat hand on the abbot's arm. "The physical chastisement will no doubt cleanse his soul and free him from Hell's pits, but only a monetary amount will rebuild the abbey."

"You fat pig!" Gabriel said, directing a pointed look at the man's bejeweled fingers. "Don't you have enough?"

The bishop curled his lip as if he'd just tasted something rotten.

"Guard," the abbot said, addressing the closest knight. His voice was thin. "Bring me a whip. I see that this man needs to learn humility before God."

"You are not God," Gabriel said evenly.

The abbot smiled. "Nevertheless, my child, I believe I can help you."

"Be grateful I am tied, holy man," Gabriel snarled.

"Take him into the courtyard so he may see the desecration he has caused, feel sorrow for his sins, and learn respect for God."

Hands grasped him, untying the neck rope from the post and wrenching him forward. Jerking back, Gabriel pulled one of the guards to his knees. Two others clutched his shoulders and flung him away from the knight. He stood and kicked one man in the knee, sending him flying to the ground. The guards yanked the end of the rope.

His knees ground into the dirt as he fell onto his face. One man kicked him in the ribs, another on the leg.

"Crawl, dog, crawl!" one cried, tugging him by the neck.

Laughing, they slid him forward a few feet. "Crawl, cur," they taunted. "Crawl for us."

"Beg us to stop."

A knight handed the abbot a long leather whip.

Gabriel struggled to his knees, realizing the choice was either to crawl before them or be dragged by the neck. Hot hatred coursed through him. He shuffled into the courtyard, his knees burning.

"Mayhap an extra set of lashes is necessary for one as large as yourself," the abbot announced, uncurling the whip and gliding out of the tent.

"I will kill you," Gabriel promised. And see Ariana brought to justice as well—if there was anything left of her once he was finished.

The abbot snapped the whip in the air, making a loud cracking noise. The guards tugged Gabriel's rope. He struggled forward.

The whip cracked again, and a thin line of white-hot pain crossed Gabriel's back. He flinched, crying out involuntarily.

The abbot made a small sound of satisfaction. "The devil is let loose from you already." He snapped the whip across Gabriel's back again as three guards dragged him into the courtyard.

Two men grasped him under his arms and hauled him upright. For a moment, it felt as though a thousand hands grabbed at him. He struggled against them, but fighting so many while being bound was hopeless.

From the corner of his eye, he saw the bishop slide across the courtyard, his massive red vestments swirling around him. He glanced over his shoulder sheepishly, then hurried into a side building. Obviously, he had no stomach for the scene that was about to transpire.

"Coward!" Gabriel called.

The abbot made a tsking noise. The whip cracked down four times in rapid succession.

Agony laced Gabriel's back in a crisscross of stripes. He sank to one knee, then was hauled again to a standing position. Two guards held him upright between them.

The whip snapped through the air, its tip popping Gabriel's shoulder close to his neck. He felt blood trickle down his back, and he vowed he'd not give the abbot one cry of pain.

The thin leather snapped, its sound a low whistle, followed by a crack. Stinging waves slammed into Gabriel as the whip fell across his back. Gritting his teeth, he counted the strokes. One, two, three, four . . . pain ate at his back, the whip taking a little bite of flesh every time it snapped. Five, six, seven, eight. He moaned, then mentally kicked himself for breaking his vow not to cry out. Nine, ten, eleven, twelve.

A red haze clouded his vision, and through it, he saw Ariana's face in his mind—looking at him, laughing at him. The bloody bitch.

The whip bit the air again and again until Gabriel felt his knees buckle. He lost track of the strokes. Turning his head slightly, he saw the abbot give him a small, discreet smile.

"I will give you another set in a week so that you may have time to contemplate your sin." He seemed to relish the thought.

Time to heal so they would hurt more is what the man meant, Gabriel realized with a wave of anger. The abbot took no pleasure in the mere whipping; 'twas the pain of it that excited him.

Fury burned in Gabriel's belly as the guards released him and he slumped to the ground. He tasted dirt and grime on his tongue. Raising his head, he willed his body to stand. Red waves crossed his vision, and he knew he could not.

The backs of his eyes stung, and he squeezed them shut, determined not to let the men see the extent of his frustration. A tear slipped down his cheek, burning a path through the dust on his face.

The abbot tossed his whip aside and moved forward. He tipped up Gabriel's chin and wiped the moisture away.

"Not so strong then, eh?" the abbot said with a low chuckle.

Mortification melded with rage.

"Mayhap I stopped too soon. The next set will be longer. Guards, bring the branding iron." He motioned toward three men tending a fire across the courtyard.

A thin, blond man pulled the glowing red iron from the flame. His skinny arms poked out of a minstrel's tunic.

Summoning his last bit of strength, Gabriel fought the rising bile in his throat and glared at the churchman.

The abbot would pay. The bishop would pay. And most of all, the haughty Lady Ariana would pay.

Chapter 13

A fortnight later, Ariana hurried across the church grounds, determined to speak with her cousin and demand he leave her be. She had sent letters to no avail, and she had no choice but to plead her cause in person. Surely he must see 'twas too dangerous for her to continue. But she could not quit so long as he held it over her head that Ivan's murder would come to light.

After the hurly-burly with Gabriel and then a feast in London to gather information about how Lady Monning was swiving her blacksmith, she felt ill-tempered as a harpy. She'd also followed an earl into a brothel and learned he had quite a thing for young boys.

'Twas no way for a woman to live. She wanted naught more than to remain home, mending and cooking and caring for her castle. Well, she amended with a gentle laugh at her own folly, *supervising* the mending and cooking. Her stitchery, while adequate, certainly would win no prizes. And Cook Margaret did the kitchen work. But she missed her flowers, the feel of dirt on her hands, and the satisfaction of a seeing a well weeded garden.

A child ran by kicking a stick, and a wave of homesickness passed over her. Her son was home being cared for by nannies, while she was spying out tawdry secrets for her cousin. She missed everything about Jason—his smiles, his happy demeanor, his frustrated tantrums when they could not communicate. If only he weren't deaf, mayhap she would not worry so much about him.

A troublesome niggling pulled at her brain. Her menses was a week late. She pushed the worrisome thought aside. Her breasts felt tender, and her stomach swollen—sure signs that her woman's blood would come soon.

She paused outside the new hall where mass was being held until the church could be completely repaired. The abbey had been straightened, and although the cathedral was still unusable, the rest of the grounds were back to normal. Bells rang. Monks hoed in the gardens and wrote in the scriptorium.

"You!" a man's voice called. "You!"

Startled, she turned to see a man swinging from a tree in an iron cage. A tremor went though her. Nay, this was not the gentle abbey she was accustomed to. The figure inside looked ragged and filthy.

"Ariana!"

She felt as though someone had smashed her betwixt the eyes with a large rock. Saints in heaven, 'twas Gabriel!

Iron bands looped around his massive body as he swung in the cage known as iron chains. He'd lost weight, giving him a lean, strong look. His face was a mass of purple and black bruises.

She shivered, a wave of horror flowing through her. She took a step toward him before catching herself.

"Ariana! Bloody wench!"

Merciful heavens. Even bound in chains, he looked all too capable of ripping a man's throat open. Or a woman's.

What should she do? She drew the hood of her cloak closer around her face. Why was he still here? Surely his connections with the king should have seen him freed. He was the King's Hunter after all.

Aye, she and the bishop had much to talk about. She hurried inside the hall, resisting the urge to chew on a fingernail. Surely she could set this in order.

"You noble whore!" he yelled. "Come back."

She racked her brain for answers. If he were freed, he would come for her. And yet, she could not leave him here to rot. If her cousin knew of the intimacy they had shared, Gabriel's life was forfeit. But if she left him hanging in chains, he would starve to death. Questions. Questions. No answers.

She shuffled inside, heading to the wooden confessional where she and the bishop met. Seeing Gabriel abused jabbed guilt into her like a knife.

Kneeling on the padded prayer bench, she stared at the wooden panel separating her from her cousin, the bishop. She determined once and for all she would be done with this. His demands had gone on too long.

Wheezing sounds came from the other side of the panel. Likely, he was squished like a tightly packed fishmonger's basket to even fit inside the confessional. "Ariana." He paused. "My dear."

"Yes, cousin." She knocked three times softly on the side, and he answered with two taps, the signal that they were alone and free to talk.

"Did you bring it?"

"Aye, but we must talk."

"My dear."

"I cannot continue."

The wheezing turned to coughing. "You are doing a fine job for a worthy cause, my dear."

She gritted her teeth. What he meant was no. Ariana silently wished he would become too fat to squeeze inside the box at all. Greedy pig.

"I mean it, cousin. 'Tis too dangerous."

"My dear, these connections are what keeps your land safe from hostile men."

With innuendoes and veiled remarks, he threatened her. She felt panic grow inside her. She was not sly enough to play his game. She backed away from that topic. She needed to know what he knew about Gabriel.

"I saw a man outside, hanging in iron chains." She schooled her voice to sound blasé.

"Ah, my dear, that man, sadly, is a demon worshipper."

"A demon worshipper?"

"Fire flew from his eyes and consumed God's house." She heard a shuffling sound, and she supposed the bishop crossed himself. "A more unholy man I have never met. The good abbot has tried to purge him of his sin, yet still the demon resides within him. We keep him here to purify him."

She gasped, then quickly covered her mouth with her hand to muffle the sound. To hide him from the king's attention, he meant. Would the bishop guess her reasons for the questions? "Purify him?"

"My dear, you are too gentle a soul to worry about such matters."

"I have seen much," she said. Too much, she added to herself.

"Nay, my dear."

"'Tis barbaric to leave him thus," she pressed.

Her cousin's robes rustled as if he leaned closer. "What do you know of this man? Why was he here? He has a look about him."

Chewing her inner cheek, she debated her choice of words. If he became suspicious, Gabriel's life was forfeit. She couldn't allow that, but she must do something.

"I do not know him," she said. "I need a strong man to plow my fields and thought I might purchase him."

She heard the drumming of the bishop's pudgy fingers. "He spoke of you."

Her heart sank. "Of me?"

More drumming. Faster this time. "He endangers our work. Tell me, Ariana, how do you know him?"

Taking a deep breath, she pretended for a moment that she was deep in thought.

"He calls himself the King's Hunter," the bishop prompted.

To deny him outright would be disastrous. As would telling all she knew. Mayhap she could use this knowledge to her favor.

"The King's Hunter is only a legend," she whispered.

"Hm-m-m."

"If the king knows he is here, then you must release him."

More wheezing. "This man is not your concern. He is deeply in debt to the church."

"I will pay his debt."

"You would offer to pay his debt? Why?"

Christ! She'd just tipped her hand. Biting her lip, she laid her hand on the wood separating them. "I do not wish to have the gentle abbey inundated with such cruelty," she said with a silent prayer that he would believe her. "I feel certain I can rehabilitate him from his sin. I will work him in my fields with hard labor."

There was a pause where she could hear only the sound of her cousin's wheezing breath.

"Ariana, my dear cousin, think of your immortal soul. I could not allow you to be near a demon worshipper such as he."

"Surely my soul is lost already," she whispered, more to herself than to him.

"Oh, nay, my dear, nay. Do not say such things. You have done great work in the name of the Lord to recompense your sins."

She gritted her teeth. What he meant was, she had given him a lot of money and he had not forgotten that she had slain Ivan.

"Surely with such a recompense, I am in no danger from this one lowly man," she said smoothly.

"Harrumph." The bishop took a long wheezing breath and coughed on the exhalation. For a moment, she wished his breathing would stop altogether.

"I can pay well. I am sorely in need of a strong man."

"Hm-m-m . . ." He was softening, she knew. Greedy pig. She'd dangled the one thing he could never turn down. Gold.

She put her hands in prayer position and waited for him to make a decision.

"Alright, cousin. You may buy the man. But the price will be steep."

No doubt about that, she thought crossly. He'd charge her as much as he could without garnering suspicion.

"Ten pounds."

She gasped. "Ten pounds?"

She heard him rise to leave. Their conversation was done. "Bring it on the morrow afore dawn."

Then he left her alone with her thoughts.

The morning dawned pink and orange and altogether too lovely for dealing with such crude affairs as she was forced to encounter. Sunlight radiated from behind white strings of clouds. The sky burst with color, painted by a master's hand.

Leaving her friend Nigel, who had accompanied her to the abbey, at the gate, she made her way toward the hall and its confessional. She clutched her pouch for comfort. Ten pounds! An outrageous amount. Her estate was wealthy, and she could well afford the gold, but it still smarted.

Glancing up, she noted that Gabriel no longer hung from the tree. Mayhap God smiled upon them.

The door to the confessional squeaked as she made her way inside. She knelt and waited.

After what seemed like an hour, she heard the door on the other side of the booth open, then wheezing sounds, then the closing of the door.

"My child," she heard her cousin wheeze.

She knocked three times. He knocked twice. They were alone and free to talk.

"I brought it," she said without preamble.

The bishop wheezed, coughed, and wheezed again. He opened a small door in the wooden screen between them and reached a jewel-encrusted hand through the opening.

She handed over the pouch. "Where is the man?"

The screen snapped shut. "Forgive me, child. God has taken the sinner's life this night past."

Shock swept through her. She barely contained her gasp. Her cousin was a greedy man . . . but *murder?*

Her hand flew to her throat to keep from crying out. Do not show fear, she chided herself. It will only give him more of a weapon. Do not show fear.

She squeezed her eyes shut against the hot sting of tears.

"My dear," her cousin wheezed, "'tis for the best. A gentle soul such as yourself should have no part with demon worshippers."

He knew! He knew something! She choked back a strangled sound.

"I will make an offering to atone for his wrongdoing and see his soul redeemed with this gold." He clucked his tongue. "I trust you will make it to Lord Monning's banquet next week as I requested."

Her throat threatened to close as if a noose had yanked it. "Good day, cousin," she whispered, her heart pounding. He would never let her quit. Hurriedly, she opened the door, scampered for the exit, and fled out of the abbey.

Her childhood friend Nigel met her at the gate. His long arms poked from his too short sleeves. "You look vexed."

Guilt weighed on her mind. She nodded, too disconcerted to say anything.

"What happened?"

When she did not reply, Nigel nodded and helped her mount Lacey. 'Twas always thus between them. He did not press her for her thoughts.

"I will play a song for you when we get to Rosebriar."

Her hands trembled on the reins. "Aye, that would be nice," she said shakily. Nigel always accompanied her when she needed an escort, but mayhap she needed a more able guard.

She shook off the thought. Nay, she would get along as she always had—through wit and cunning and good wool trading. She did not have it in her heart to be glad of Gabriel's death, but 'twas one less complication to deal with.

Oh, God, Gabriel.

Tears stung her eyes and trickled down her face. She felt her numbed heart melting. Memories of Gabriel kissing her, tasting her, teasing her flowed through her. She should have married him.

'Tis too late for regrets, she chided herself. *Stiffen up.*

More tears. She angrily wiped them away. You have your people and Jason to think of, her logical mind argued. But her traitorous body could still feel his heat and the way he kissed her neck. *He was a peasant,* logic said. *He was noble inside,* her heart replied.

"Ariana?"

She sniffed and straightened her spine. These thoughts had no place in her life. Duty oft came with sacrifice. "Aye?"

Nigel leaned over and patted her shoulder awkwardly. "You need a strong man. All you have in your castle is women and old men."

"I have guards."

"You have a few mercenaries and a knight or two. What you *need* is a husband." His voice brought a measure of anchor back to her swimming emotions.

"I do *not* need a husband."

"You need a strong man," he repeated. "A lord to rule the defenses."

She stiffened. "I do not need a man." But her heart ached in disagreement.

Chapter 14

Six and a half months later

"Dearly beloved, we are gathered here today to join this man and this woman in holy matrimony," the clergyman mumbled, and Ariana wanted to kick herself. If she had not been so impulsive, she would not be here in the chapel, pregnant and forced to marry!

I can do this, Ariana told herself. *'Tis my duty to keep my family and the castlefolk safe.* If she were to have the baby out of wedlock, the king or church could strip her title and take her lands. She silently prayed for a miracle, but knew it was only a matter of minutes before she would be once more chained to a man.

When she looked up, she could make out the reflection of her swelled stomach in the pince-nez spectacles that perched atop the priest's huge nose. 'Twas mostly covered by her voluptuous green gown and generous cloak, but the small bump was obvious to her. Her baby. Gabriel's baby. It seemed that every morning she looked and felt larger. Even as she stood here, she felt her ankles swelling like two dead, bloating fish.

Her thoughts rested on her baby's father for a moment. Would Gabriel have made a good father? Guilt that she had been unable to save him ate at her. 'Twas for the best, she told herself, disallowing her choppy emotions to surface. With strength of will, she turned her mind to her present duty. No matter how distasteful, she would do right by her people.

She stared at the man standing beside her who would be her new husband. His skinny, white wrists poked out his sleeves. Thin blond hair formed a ring around his egg-shaped head. He stared at her doelike with large brown eyes. His fingers clamped around hers, damp and cold.

Nigel of Grosmont was everything Gabriel was not—thin, willowy, passive, dull, blond. She had chosen him for precisely those reasons. He was not the sort of man who would track mud through the kitchens or leave his tunic balled on the rug.

He'd been her childhood friend. He'd been her confidant when she'd been married to Ivan. And now he'd be her husband. Many years ago, they had met on a cold day when she'd stumbled into the library while visiting friends. She had been crying over a particularly cruel remark by one of the other children. He'd been playing his violin, a peculiar habit of his.

After their meeting, she occasionally followed the mellow sounds of the notes to seek him out. She'd been a ward of the king, passed from place to place, and they were oft at the same gatherings. His passion was his violin, and he would speak for hours about the intricacies of music, a strange and altogether too grown-up topic for a boy of his age. He nearly always had his head buried in a piece of music while other boys practiced with swords. His parents badgered him to go into the priesthood, but he wanted only to play his tunes. Likely, he would have become a wandering minstrel if his father had not opposed it so violently.

In this, they understood each other—the inward passion and the outward limitations.

Now he played private concerts for her cousin, who loved music and luxury above all else. Their marriage would not interfere with this.

"A woman's place is in the home . . ." said the priest, bringing her mind back to the present.

Nigel gave her a soft smile. Morning sun streamed through the stained glass windows, tinting his color-less hair with a rainbow of blues, greens, and yellows. He hunched over in the fashion that men too tall for their bodies often do, all men except Gabriel, she corrected. Gabriel's body language never seemed to apologize for his dominating height or relentless mas-culinity. Never *had* seemed, she amended.

Best to put Gabriel behind her. Nigel would be a good father to her baby.

The babe in her womb kicked. She patted her stom-ach absently and gazed at Nigel, trying to discern what their marriage would be like. Her offer was likely the best one he would ever get, even with her stipula-tion that there would be no marital relations in the bedroom. Perhaps a different man would have minded her terms, but Nigel had not even blinked— his only love was for his violin.

Jason, her seven-year-old, tugged on her skirt. His small fist wrapped into the green velvet. In wild ges-tures, he signaled that he needed to pee.

She shook her head at him, smiled tightly at Nigel, and turned back to the priest, who was reciting a long exhortation from Proverbs thirty-one about the qualities of a good wife.

Jason tugged at her again, this time making whimpering sounds. His normally neat hair stuck up this way and that. Thorns. She'd been so forlorn about her need to get married she'd forgotten to comb it this morning.

She frowned and shook her head, motioning him to wait.

"I do," Nigel said.

Ariana cringed. Was it already the grand finale of the ceremony?

At that moment, a loud bang sounded through the chapel. The door slammed open, and a cold, blustery wind whipped into the sanctuary. Ariana jumped, her nape prickling. She turned at the collective gasp of the wedding guests.

A warrior dressed in armor made of stiff black leather stood in the doorframe of the chapel. His dark, blunt cut hair trailed past his shoulders in disarray. Dirt smeared his face in long streaks.

Her heart leaped. 'Twas as if her thoughts had somehow conjured him from the beyond. Gabriel was alive!

"Gabriel!"

He stared at her. A few days' worth of stubble lined his hard jaw. A black smear that barely covered an angry red welt smudged his cheek. He looked so much harder and more dangerous than he had before—like he'd been cast into hell and spit up again.

"Mercy," she gasped, feeling her knees weaken.

"You!" Gabriel shouted, staring at Nigel.

Nigel wheeled to look from her to him, his eyes wide. "It's him," he whispered urgently.

Ignoring him, she stepped forward. "Gabriel, I thought you were dead."

He held a cocked crossbow at the ready as he strode into the church. A scowl pressed deep lines betwixt his brows and a snarl marred his generous lips.

Her smile faltered.

The quiet sanctuary erupted into a cacophony of chaos as a group of large, barbaric men wearing mismatched furs and leather pounded inside after him. They toppled statues and benches.

People gasped. Jason screamed. The priest stumbled back and slammed his Bible closed. His spectacles fell off his nose onto the tiles with a soft tinkle. The scent of horses, sweat, and leather shaded the chapel's air as the men fanned out and surrounded the congregation.

"Gabriel?"

"Silence!" he roared, and the chapel quieted except for the rustle of his leather breeks as he stalked closer. A black look darkened his features. He looked like a wild beast angry enough to slay them all.

Her eyes widened, and apprehension shivered through her.

Nigel grasped her arm with a trembling hand.

Old Tom stood up from midway back in the congregation. "I say, man, what are you doing? The mistress has a wedding here." His white coif jiggled as he spoke.

Gabriel swung his crossbow around to aim it at Tom.

Ariana cringed and stepped forward. "Wait! Leave him be!"

Tom's wife Margaret wheezed and rubbed her pudgy hands together. "Oh, saints. Oh, mercy."

"Sit and be silent, old man." Gabriel pierced him with a glare.

Tom made to say something else, but Ariana caught his eye. "Nay, Thomas. 'Tis between Gabriel and me." Surely she could get this under control.

"Oh, mercy." Margaret took her husband firmly by the hand and pulled him onto the bench beside her.

"Anyone else have something to say?" Gabriel swung his crossbow back and forth across the crowd. His brutes watched the congregation closely as if looking for an excuse to kill.

Beside her, Nigel shuffled his feet. "You should not bring weapons into a house of God." His hands trembled as if it had taken all his will to say anything.

A shiver ran down her spine. She shook her head at him, warning him not to fight.

Gabriel reached the front of the chapel in three strides.

"Gabriel?" She laid her hand on his chest. "I am confused."

He gazed down at her fingers as if they were pox-ridden. "Mayhap swinging from the gallows will clear your head."

Gasping, she snatched her hand away as if stung. "Have you forgotten our time together?"

A palpable wave of fury poured off him. "'Twas you who forgot mere hours after swiving me."

"Nay, Gabriel, I did not. I came for you."

"I saw how you came for me." He thrust her away as if not trusting himself to be so near. "I am taking your castle. And I'll take that stubborn pride from you as well. You'll beg at my door for food. Your people will be my slaves."

Trembling, Nigel stepped forward. "You, you canna speak to her thus."

"Stay back, dog," Gabriel warned.

"Nigel, no!"

Wide-eyed and trembling, Nigel balled his fist.

Abruptly, Gabriel cocked his arm to one side and backhanded Nigel across the cheek. A loud crack sounded in the sanctuary. "Imbecile."

Dear God!

Squealing, Nigel faltered backward. Ariana caught him before he could plunge to the tiles. The bouquet of flowers she'd been holding fluttered to the floor.

Slipping and sliding, Nigel forced himself upright.

Wrenching her would-be bridegroom away from her, Gabriel slammed his fist into Nigel's nose. Blood sprayed across his face and onto his frilly collar.

"Cease!" she gasped. Breathing seemed impossible.

Swinging his arm wildly, Nigel threw a punch at Gabriel.

Gabriel stepped aside. The muscles of his arm danced violently as he cocked his fist back again.

"Nay!" She had to stop him. Reaching forward, she grasped him by the forearm.

As if she weighed nothing, Gabriel lunged forward and dug the three fingers of his deformed hand into Nigel's neck. Her bridegroom made a strangled sound. Boots squeaked against the tiles.

"Nay," she whispered.

Gabriel's hand twisted, and Nigel's eyes rolled back, his face reddening.

"Gabriel! Listen to me! He's not a fighter."

"He was at the abbey."

"He's just a musician. Release him."

Lifting her bridegroom off the ground, Gabriel

speared her with a vindictive scowl. His lips lifted in a snarl. "Let go of my arm. Get on your knees and beg for his life if you wish him to live."

The brute! Bile rose in her throat.

While she hesitated, Gabriel shook Nigel. Nigel moaned and made a croaking sound. His fingers were white as he strained against Gabriel's hold.

Mother of God! Gabriel would kill him if she did not do as he asked. The barbarian! Releasing his forearm, she sank to her knees. Her green dress spilled across the tiles.

In the back of the church, she heard Margaret gasp and others shuffle uncomfortably on their benches.

To humiliate her in front of her people—dear Jesu, 'twas worse even than Ivan. But Nigel stood no chance against him.

A tic formed in Gabriel's jaw as he glared at her.

She cringed, knowing he was waiting for her to beg. "Please. I pray thee. He is only a violinist."

A look of arrogant satisfaction gleamed in Gabriel's eyes. He lowered Nigel, who gasped and choked as he collapsed on the floor.

"'Twas not what you thought," Nigel rasped, his throat already beginning to purple. He raised an arm toward Ariana.

Gabriel grabbed hold of Nigel's hand and twisted one of his fingers.

Ariana screamed.

Nigel gasped, his face distorted in agony. Red and purple welts were rising on his face. He opened his mouth, but only a croak sounded.

"Nay! Not his hands!" she pleaded. How could Gabriel be so cruel? Nigel's violin playing was all he had in the world. "You bully! You monster! He cannot defend himself."

With a look of disgust, Gabriel pushed him aside with one of his boots. Nigel stared at her but did not rise.

She reached for him, but Gabriel grasped her shoulders and pulled her roughly to her feet. Glancing around tensely, she tried to determine the best way to bring the situation under control.

Her mind seemed scrambled. Jason latched on to her skirt with trembling fingers. Grabbing hold of her son, she backed up a step to put distance between herself and Gabriel.

The wedding guests stared. Jason's nanny Beth chomped her fingernails. Margaret looked on the verge of hysteria. Her people were quiet country folk, not warriors or mercenaries. If Gabriel chose to beat them all, there was nothing she could do.

"What do you want?" she asked.

He latched on to her upper arm. His fingers dug into her skin with a bruising grip. "I want what is mine." His gaze burned through her dress, leaving no doubt that he meant her.

She gaped at him. All those nights, she'd wanted him, dreamed of him. It made her queasy to think of it. "I am not yours."

He laughed darkly.

The dangerous glitter in his eyes chilled her bones. His hair fell across his widow's peak just as Ivan's had.

"It would serve you well to be afraid of me."

Her heart slammed against her ribs. The babe in her womb kicked her bladder. She put her hands out to ward him off as he loomed closer.

Jason whimpered and hid his face in her skirt.

Holding her son, she willed her feet to run, but they seemed leaden and too heavy to lift.

Two of the barbarians paced forward, snatched Nigel, and dragged him toward the door.

"Help," Nigel moaned, his brown eyes wide and his blond hair mussed. "Ariana."

She struggled toward him, but Gabriel held her in place. "Go to him, and I'll break his fingers."

Shuddering, she gazed frantically around the church. The congregation stared at the scene, but no one made a move to help her. Gabriel's men guarded the doorways.

"You are mine," he said, his voice calm.

Bile rose into her throat. This was not the same man she'd known before.

One of his barbarians drew a short dirk from his belt and held it to Nigel's throat.

Nigel squealed, his voice high-pitched and girlish. His pale skin flinched.

"Quiet!" Gabriel commanded.

Ariana trembled, clutching Jason. Her womb clenched painfully. In that moment, if Gabriel had not been holding her, she would have sunk to the tiles like a rag doll. The crowd breathed in quick, nervous gasps.

"What do you want?" she repeated.

His hands tightened on her arms, biting into her skin. "Revenge."

The edges of her vision whitened, and she swallowed. 'Twas as if she had been cast into a bewildering nightmare.

Her chest ached. The cold trickle of panic iced her veins. Inside her imagination, she heard logic laugh at her. *You dreamed of him, a cruel barbaric peasant with no sense of honor.*

Jason wrapped himself further in her skirt, twisting round and round in her dress until the neckline pulled tightly on her neck and threatened to choke her. His hugging plastered the dress to her, exposing her body's outline.

Gabriel's gaze drifted over the soft swell of her stomach, which had been hidden by the overlarge green velvet kirtle.

His frown hardened. "I did not know you were with child."

She swallowed, her breath coming out short and tight. She did not want him to know how vulnerable she felt. Several wedding guests coughed politely.

"I assume it is mine." His fingers flexed on the tiller of his crossbow, which was now slung across his shoulder.

The coughing turned to small gasps of disbelief.

Hot shame worked up her spine. How could she have been intimate with this animal? Gathering her skirt in her fist, she wanted to run, to drag herself and Jason from the chapel. But her son was wrapped around her legs, his weight buried in her skirt. There was nowhere to run. No way to get away.

Handing his crossbow to one of his men, Gabriel turned her toward the altar. Keeping a biting grip on her arm, he reached down, snatched the priest who was patting the floor desperately for his spectacles, and hauled him to his feet.

"Continue the ceremony, priest. Only the name of the groom must be changed."

Ariana gasped. Dear heavens, no. If they were married, she would have no legal recourse for him taking the castle by force.

"You have the castle," she said after she was able to catch her breath. "There is no reason for us to marry."

"Selfish to the core, as all noblewomen," he snarled, his fingers pinching her skin. "I will not have my son labeled a bastard."

The babe kicked, and another pain shot through her womb.

"The bans haven't been—" the priest interjected.

Gabriel shot him a warning gaze that left the churchman gape-mouthed.

Nigel squealed again from one side.

Clutching her son, Ariana steadied herself. Even though her knees were knocking, she must stand up to this beast. To marry him would mean a lifetime of imprisonment.

"This isn't legal," she said. "I won't—"

With a mirthless grin, Gabriel bared his teeth. "Think you I care what is legal?"

She shuddered, then steadied herself. How sick she was of the arrogant ways of men! She latched firmly onto Jason and vowed to find a way free.

"No papers have been drawn—" she began, trying to reason with him.

'Twas like trying to reason with an ox. He stared at her for a moment, then turned back to the minister. "Go on, priest. Finish the ceremony."

Alarmed, she shook her head. "Nay."

"You have no choice." Gabriel nodded toward his men. A large, hairy redheaded man stepped forward and tore Jason away from her skirt. Her son's skinny legs kicked, one scraping her shin.

"Mum!" he screamed, his arms reaching frantically into the air for her. 'Twas a word he'd learned afore the deafness had closed his ears.

It tore at her heart. "Cease!" She twisted toward her son, but Gabriel's arms anchored her like iron bars.

The redheaded man dragged Jason across the tiles. "Mum!"

"Jason!" Panic clutched her throat.

Gasping for breath, she sought to worm out of Gabriel's hold.

"Marry me, and he will come to no harm." Gabriel held her in place.

Realizing the futility of her actions, she ceased her struggles. Gabriel was easily a foot and a half taller than she and strong as a mountain.

"Please! I beg of you! My child is innocent."

"Aye, but you are not."

"Surely you would not harm a child for your own gain." She searched his face, searching for signs of the Gabriel she had made love to. The tiny scar on his chin looked white against his tanned skin, and the new red welt glowed angrily.

If possible, her heart sank even further as she searched his face. His eyes were cold and hard. What had happened to his warmth?

"Prithee." She wanted desperately to touch Jason, to assure him all would be well. "Let him be. He's deaf. He cannot understand."

A flicker of softness lit Gabriel's eyes and then disappeared. "Say the wedding vows."

Despair overtook her. 'Twas the way of men to take what did not belong to them, to use those around them for their own gain. "You can take what you want!" She gave him a scathing glare. "You have no need of us!"

He pulled her forward. "Letting you go would be too kind. I plan to crush the stubborn pride from your body."

She shivered. Her gaze flicked to the angry welt marring his cheek.

The hairy man pulled Jason back, holding him in front of himself like a shield. Wild red hair puffed around his lips. Jason trembled and made grunting sounds. His large green eyes widened with terror.

"Mum," he whimpered. "Mum."

She reached for him. "'Tis all right." She struggled to soothe them both, even knowing Jason could not hear.

The air seemed thick, and sparkles of light formed around the edges of her vision. What revenge would Gabriel exact from her? She took a deep breath to steady herself. Surely, whate'er he planned, she could bear it. For Jason's sake, she *would* bear it.

Sunlight reflected off the men's naked swords, and a flicker of blues and greens flashed across the altar. Gabriel allowed her to touch her son, then hauled her back sharply.

"Now, priest!" Gabriel demanded.

"I-I-I do not believe this is quite right," the priest stammered.

Gabriel fisted his hand into the priest's robe and pulled him until their faces nearly touched. "Do it, man."

Fury spun through Ariana at Gabriel's heavy-handedness.

The priest stared at Gabriel, his jaw shaking. He pushed the pince-nez spectacles back up his large nose when Gabriel released him. "I-I-I—"

Ariana wiggled, struggling to loosen herself from Gabriel's grasp. "You do not need to hold me so tightly."

"Go on," Gabriel snarled. "You may start again at the part about 'do you take this woman . . .'"

The priest stammered and fumbled with his Bible.

Nigel, who was held at the back of the church between two large guards, screamed, "Ariana! Help!"

She turned. The two guards had messed up his thinning hair and were in the process of divesting him of his clothes. Bullies set on shaming him on what should have been his wedding day.

"Cease!" Anger clouded her vision at such a soft, gentle soul being treated so poorly.

"What should we do with him?" a tall guard wearing a brown fur jerkin asked.

Gabriel shrugged. "Find a dungeon."

"Nay!" Ariana protested. "The dampness will kill him."

Nigel shivered. He made a fearful pip over his shoulder as the two men hauled him toward the chapel's doors. "'Twasn't my idea to marry her, my lord," he squealed.

Even as her heart went out to him, her anger turned into repulsion. Poor Nigel. She had known he was not much of a fighter—indeed, that was why she'd chosen him—but his willingness to give up her and Jason was disgusting beyond anything she'd ever imagined. That he was so easily manipulated, a quality she'd thought was a strength, now seemed his greatest fault.

"Get him out of here ere I slay him in front of everyone." Gabriel turned to the priest. "Start," he prompted.

The priest's chin quivered as he tried to find the place in the Bible where he had been reading from. "W-w-what did you s-s-say your name w-w-was again?"

"Gabriel of Whitestone."

"Do you, Gabriel of W-w-whitestone take this w-woman to be your lawfully w-wedded w-w-wife to have and t-to hold, to cherish and t-to love, in sickness and in health, so help you God until death do you part?"

"I do." Gabriel's low voice sounded erotic despite the atrociousness of his words.

"A-a-and do you, Lady Ariana of Rosebriar, t-take this man to be your lawful wedded husband, to have and to hold . . ." The priest's voice was so strained she could barely understand the words. ". . . t-to love and o-obey . . ."

"Nay. Nay. Absolutely not. I will marry him, but I will never obey that man. Change the vows."

The priest pushed his pince-nez up on his nose and gazed at Gabriel for direction.

"Go on." Gabriel turned to her, his cold gaze heating for once. "You will obey me in *everything,* my lady."

"Nay." Never.

He nodded at the man holding Jason, and the guard pinched the boy on the arm. The child let out a loud squeal that seemed to flow all the way through Ariana.

Her stomach churned. Gabriel knew, *knew,* she would do anything for Jason. Him using the information so vilely sent a streak of frustrated hatred flowing through her.

Gabriel motioned to the man. "Take the boy outside until his mother calms down and speaks correctly."

The redheaded man hustled the boy out of the chapel. Jason dragged his feet against the tile making a bumping noise.

"Mum!" he screamed, but his voice was muffled as the door slammed shut behind them.

Her vision seemed foggy. She had no choice. No choice at all.

"Please," she whispered, all hatred, fury, and anger burning into fear for Jason. "He's deaf."

Gabriel took a deep breath, his face impassive and unreadable. "Swear to the priest you will obey me."

"I-I hate you!"

"So you have told me afore."

"'Tis truth!"

For a second, he seemed to soften. His hands gentled on her arms. "Nay, it is not. You are just angry with me for claiming you this way and afeard I will be like my brother."

"Well, are you not? You and your brutal, bullying barbarians."

"T-to love and obey, in s-s-s-sickness and in health, till death do you part, so help you God," the priest finished in a mumble.

"Say it," Gabriel said. "Say 'I do.'"

"I do," she choked out.

"Inowpronounceyoumanandwife," the priest rushed, wide-eyed and obviously relieved that there would soon be an end to the fiasco. "You may kiss the bride." He slammed the Bible closed and took three steps back.

Dear God, she was married again to a beast! The walls felt too close, as if the chapel had been a cunning trap set by a hunter. Her heart pounded.

Gabriel pulled her toward him. "I do not harm children," he said flatly.

She had no time to turn her face aside before his lips crashed down on hers. Time spun into a dizzy storm like untimely snowflakes in July. His mouth slanted over hers, not teasing gentle kisses like before, but bruising punishment.

She silently cursed her betraying body, which had

spent too many nights longing for him. Her furious anger made no difference to her woman's core. Moisture seeped from her queynt.

She hated him. She wanted him. Could her humiliation be any greater?

"Lady." Abruptly, he set her away from him.

She gazed at him—had he felt anything between them?

His eyes were enigmatic. "Here, take my new *wife* to the bedchamber for our wedding night."

A muddle of emotions—fear, resentment, desire, anger—swam inside her, each fighting for dominance. "You cannot be serious."

"You belong to me now," he said, pointing toward the exit. "Take her. I will come anon to complete this business between us."

Chapter 15

The march to her chamber felt solemn and frightening as a funeral procession. The world had become her casket. Tallow candles stung her eyes with their acidic vapors. Two of Gabriel's guards, a one-eyed man and a tall, lanky giant, flanked her as they walked with heavy steps down the castle's corridors to the solar. That she could count, Gabriel's men were seven in number.

Bile rose in her throat as she crossed the threshold of her chamber—'twas like crossing the gate into a cemetery. Shuddering, she vowed to endure whatever Gabriel dished out. For the sake of Jason and her unborn child, she could do it. She rubbed her arms and latched on to her mother's lullaby.

> *Sleep, my love, on my chest,*
> *'Tis but caring arms round you.*

The babe roiled in her womb, kicking and fighting. She patted her stomach, trying to calm the frenzied jumping. The maids had prepared the room for the wedding night. The frilly curtains of the four-poster bed had been tied back. A low, romantic flame burned in the hearth, and the intoxicating scent of smoke and fresh mint tinged the air. Instead of tallow, beeswax candles had been used here. Soft light reflected off her belongings.

Her belongings! Not his.

Desperation stirred in her heart. How dare he force her to marry him! She tread across the floor planks to her dressing table and plunked down in the chair beside it. A menagerie of items crowded the surface: three combs, a hairbrush, five hair baubles, two scarves, a pot of lead powder, a small looking glass, and a number of other female dressing items.

She gazed at the rest of her chamber. Frilly curtains. Feather bedding. Fancy goblets. She had spent the last few years ridding herself of every bloody reminder that a man had ever been in this room. After her husband was gone, if she could have burned the place and started over with a new castle, she would have. No man had been allowed here since Ivan had died. Not even Nigel.

If Gabriel thought he could just march in and conquer the place without a fight, he was mistaken. She'd poison him in his sleep if she had to. The baby kicked her.

Picking up an ivory comb, she felt a ripple of frustration run through her. Nay, she could not kill her baby's father. Not even after what he'd done today.

She picked absently at her long red curls with the comb. She had killed her husband—thank God he was dead—because he'd laid a hand on Jason. But despite her earlier fears, she'd known Gabriel spoke the truth when he said he did not harm children. She would have to find some way to make peace with him.

Laying the comb on the dressing table, she surveyed herself in the small mirror. Tiny lines crinkled her forehead between her eyes. She rubbed the wrinkles away, but they returned after she removed her hand. She didn't look like a blushing bride—she looked haggard. And she felt even more exhausted than she looked. The babe flopped, and she absently patted her stomach.

She reached for the comb again, then spied a tiny slip of parchment beneath a tortoiseshell comb. Curious, she slid it from under its hiding place.

In tight, precise writing, the ink read: *The poison is in the blue clay jar.*

Her hands trembled. 'Twas as if someone had known of her murderous thoughts just moments earlier. Unease quivered through her as she stared at the note. Over the past five years, she'd received many notes, many instructions to go hither and yon or do this or that, but *none* of them had been sinister. Who would leave such a note? And why?

Chewing her inner cheek, she crossed the room to pull the bellcord that summoned Francine, her chambermaid. Mayhap she had seen someone come into her room during the wedding.

Afore she could ring the bell, the door slammed open with a gusty bang, blowing out a nearby candle. Gabriel! Startled, Ariana shoved the note into a pot of white face powder. There would be no chance of peace between them if he discovered the message.

Composing her face, she looked up. He stood in the doorframe, his tall figure gilded in candlelight. His dark, curling hair hung past the top of his shoulders. He had washed his face, and the handsome planes of his harsh features stood in bold relief.

"There is unfinished business between us." His eyes flicked to the bed.

She cringed, all too familiar with the "business" of men. How many nights had she been forced by Ivan to do her wifely duty? Remembered pain and humiliation flooded her.

"This marriage will be in name only," she said, her voice stronger than she felt. "I am pregnant already. There is no need to repeat the act."

"Is that so?" Gabriel stepped over the threshold.

She scooted her chair back; its legs scraped against the stone, making a screeching noise echo off the walls.

"You cannot get away from me," he said.

She felt like a bear, caged for some brutal game for men's titillation.

"Stay back," she warned.

"Nay, *wife*. I will not." His boots thudded on the planks as he stalked toward her. "We have issues we must deal with."

Gripping the handle of the hand mirror, she prepared to hurl it at him. "I will not fornicate with you."

"Copulate," he corrected, moving steadily closer like a stalking panther, "not fornicate."

"What?"

"Fornication is what happens before a couple is married," he drawled. "We have done that already. Now we can only copulate."

His eyes held a teasing twinkle, which made him all the more irritating. He had a beautiful catlike grace when he walked. The muscles of his thighs flexed and relaxed in a show of intense masculine power as he stalked her. Unbidden, her nipples tightened. Erotic energy charged the air. *That* was nothing at all like how it had been with Ivan. The distance between them closed.

She backed away, her heart thudding in her chest. "Stay back, I say!"

He stepped forward.

Frightened, she scooted around the vanity table, her eyes darting from the bed to the dressing screen to the garderobe for a place to run. Lungs squeezing, she plastered herself against the wall. She gasped for air but couldn't seem to take a breath. Memories held her captive.

Years ago, Ivan had cornered her here. He'd been displeased that she had not complied eagerly enough for her wifely duty. He'd held her against the wall and slapped her face until she'd stumbled. *Do not defy me again, woman!* he'd yelled.

A chair scraped against the floor. Through the haze of her memories, she saw Gabriel bearing down on her, moving her dressing chair aside with casual indifference. No longer erotic, he seemed huge and monstrous. And angry. Would he beat her for defying him? Beat her, then tup her as Ivan had?

She moved her arms protectively over her womb. "Why are you doing this?"

"Because you belong to me." He took another step forward, determination in his gaze.

Merciful Mary. Her knees quivered. She *could not* bear this. Her earlier quest to make peace seemed foolish. She had gained too much independence to go back to living under a husband's rule. Not now. Not ever!

Realizing abruptly she still held the looking glass, she cocked her hand back and hurled it at him. The mirror flew over his left shoulder and smashed against the chamber's door with a crash. Rainbows bounced around the room.

Gabriel paused, looking dispassionately at the broken shards on the floor. A tic formed in his jaw, reflected twenty times over by tiny bits of looking glass.

"You will behave," he said flatly.

Panic made her reckless. No longer would she passively accept a man's rule. She searched for something else she could throw at him. Picking up a nearby vase, she cocked her arm back. "Get away!"

He reached her in two steps, his hand closing around her wrist like an iron manacle.

"Cease." His voice was calm as death.

Shivering, she swallowed a lump of dread. Slowly, he forced her arm down until the vase's bottom touched the table.

"Release the vessel," he commanded.

She strained against him, but 'twas like trying to hoist a tree.

"Release it, Ariana." His fingers tightened.

Frustration at her ineffectiveness worked through her veins. She unfurled her fingers. The vase wobbled back and forth a few times before settling on the table.

"Gramercy," he said.

She raised her chin. She wanted to curl into a ball on the bed and wail. Her insides felt squeezed and suffocated—her choices all taken from her one by one until she had no room to breathe.

"If I were a man—" she started.

"You aren't."

She glared at him, hating his strong, solid chest and his muscular arms. His unrelenting masculinity seemed to speak for itself: *I am master here.*

"I will not bow to a man."

"Mayhap not, but you will refrain from using my head as a target."

She drew in a shaking breath. "Leave me be."

"Nay."

Releasing her, he strode to her dressing table and sat in her ruffled chair. His black garments contrasted with the soft feminine colors. He picked up a scarf, his hands seeming strange and large against the delicate fabric. The material floated across his maimed finger.

She stumbled to the window seat and sat on a cushion in the embrasure. "I will not be a good wife. I will make your life a living hell."

Gabriel stared at his new wife, debating whether he should swive her or throttle her. He would see Ariana humbled and her pride broken if 'twas the last thing he did. Checked anger tensed his shoulders, forming hard, painful knots under his already raw skin. The Abbot had kept him as a toy for his sadistic pleasure—long, brutal months for a crime he had not committed. His brother had been hung for her activities.

"You have made my life a hell already, girl." He reached to pick up a wooden hairbrush from her dressing table. His unhealed back stung from the movement. "You left me to take the blame for your deeds."

"*My* deeds?"

"'Twas you who toppled the candle that burned the abbey. If you had not run—"

"If you had not given *chase.*" She lifted her chin in a show of haughty defiance and plucked dismissively at the emeralds in her necklace in a way that sent a fresh wave of annoyance through him. She had worn elaborate decorations while his family had starved. The thought of divesting her of her stubborn pride had been the motivation that had buoyed him under the Abbot's whip.

"I thought you were dead," she said at last.

He smiled grimly. "You thought wrong."

"How? What happened?"

"I slew the Abbot with my bare hands and fought my way free."

She frowned at him. "They told me you were dead."

The little wench. 'Twas she who had come to the abbey and ordered him gone.

She shivered at his glare and rubbed her arms as if cold. "What happened after you escaped?"

"I went to see the king in London."

"And he gave you leave to marry me?"

"Nay." Gabriel thought grimly about his parley with the king. He had been mild in his displeasure of the Bishop—a pox on the souls of noblemen who reward money over loyalty—but the king had granted Gabriel permission to do with Ariana whatever he saw fit. Wed her. Bed her. Or hang her. Vengeance was his so long as the Crown was no longer harassed by The Spy of the Night. "He gave me leave to do whatever I wished with you." He gave her a long leer that set her fingers atrembling. Good.

"I have done naught to deserve this," she said.

Fury pounded in his ears. In his mind, he could still see her eyes laughing at him while the monks clubbed him with hoes and rakes.

"You left me to die."

"I did not!"

"You lied to me—"

"Lied to you?"

"About marrying me."

She hurled him a contemptuous look. "No more than a blackheart like you deserves."

"You heartless, selfish wench," he said, thinking of the long months his siblings had been nigh without food to feed their bellies whilst he languished on the cellar floor of the abbey unable to provide for them. Vengeance stirred again within him—'twould be true justice for him to set her and her son out on their ear to face the harsh winter alone and penniless as his family had.

"My brother was hung for your activities as The Spy."

"Hung? But that is not possible." Her lip quivered, and she looked stricken. Good. A little fear would be good for her.

"But I saw him in London." Her eyes were wide.

"No doubt granting him the same treatment you gave me." He growled, biting back the beastly urge to upturn her vanity table and hurl all her pretty baubles in the fire just to spite her. "I should set you and your boy out to starve."

"Surely not. I am with child."

Haughty, haughty witch. To use her pregnancy as a shield to save herself was despicable, but he should have expected such. His gaze slid over her full belly. The swell of her stomach formed a gentle line in her gown. Her breasts, fuller than they had been when they had lain together, strained the fabric outward.

His baby rested inside her. The thought was almost too bewildering to comprehend. A wave of possessiveness crowded his annoyance. He fought it. To think even one kindly thought about her dishonored Eric's memory.

She fidgeted with the embroidered edge of her

sleeve, her delicate hands soft against the fabric. Well, he mused, mayhap her pregnancy prevented him from throwing her out of the keep, but he had no intention of her parading around in beauteous dress whilst his siblings wore rags. Her gowns, once hemmed, would fit his sisters nicely.

"Undress."

She flinched. "Absolutely not."

Slapping the hairbrush against his thigh, he rose and stalked toward her. Color drained from her face, and he realized at once that beneath her show of bluster, she was terrified. He slapped the brush down on his breeks again. A satisfying little gasp escaped her lips, and he smiled inwardly. Mayhap this could play to his advantage.

"Let us get this straight between us, Ariana. I did not come here to marry you. But now that the foul deed is done, there will be only one master here."

He expected her to cower, but instead, she took a deep breath and straightened her shoulders.

"Get away from me, barbarian! You will have to force me if you intend to rape me."

Towering over her, he allowed the hairbrush to drop from his hand. It landed on the floor with a clatter. He wanted her humbled, not debased. "I have no intention of raping you now or in the future. Now undress, or I will undress you myself."

Her hand flew to her throat protectively.

"Now, wife." Reaching down, he touched the gilded bone buttons on the front of her bodice. Only the very wealthy could afford such fastenings.

She shrugged him away. "You cannot be serious."

Snatching her wrist, he held her arm out to the

side. She wiggled, but he leaned forward, imprisoning her within the confines of the window ledge.

She glared at him. "Lewster!"

"Nevertheless, remove your garments."

For a long moment, their gazes wrestled. Gabriel silently counted to twenty, unsure what he would do should she resist in truth. He bared his teeth, attempting to intimidate her into submission.

Hesitation flickered in her gaze, and he felt the battle sway his direction.

"Monster!"

"Mayhap," he said mildly, feeling victory draw nigh. "Remove your clothing."

Eyes blazing with frustrated anger, she grasped the edges of her bodice and ripped it open in a deft movement. The bone buttons popped from their threads and bounced off his tunic. Her breasts sprang free from their confinement with a jiggling, chaotic motion.

By the devil's codpiece, they were huge! Much larger than they had been afore. Easily the size of melons! She wore a thin linen shift, but it did nothing to hide her enormous dark areolas.

Having never seen a pregnant woman's breasts, he found himself at a total loss for words.

He forced his gaze lower. Divested of her outer garments, she looked a lot more pregnant. Her stomach strained outward against the shift, and her belly button made a small protrusion in the white linen.

He was altogether unprepared for the throbbing blood rush to his member. His wife. His baby.

Reaching down, he laid his hand flat against her stomach.

She shivered but did not resist.

Her belly was warm and firm. A slight stir moved against his palm. A sense of amazement trickled through him.

She tried to shrug his hand away, but he kept his palm firmly on her stomach. His misshapen hand seemed monstrous against the pristine whiteness of her shift. Her delicacy emphasized his missing finger.

"Did your bridegroom know you carried my baby?"

She narrowed her eyes at him. "How arrogant to assume it is yours."

"It is."

Crossing her arms petulantly, she stared out the window and did not answer. The motion caused her enormous breasts to lift up and out. Another wave of desire swept through him. He stepped back, unsure if he could trust himself. His every instinct pushed him to take and conquer.

"You planned just to pass my child off as Nigel's to save your own noble hide."

She turned, mutiny in her gaze. "'Tis your fault a child grows in me."

"Ariana." Gabriel let out a long breath to control his pent-up fury. For six long months, he'd wanted revenge. The thought of conquering her, of forcing her to suffer the same humiliation he had suffered was what had kept him alive under the Abbot's whip. Like all noblewomen, she was a prideful, haughty witch. 'Twould do her good to be pulled down a notch. He eased his hand from her belly.

"I wish you would leave." Her voice sounded bitter.

"Nay, Ariana. I will not. The sooner you accept me as your lord and master, the easier your life will be."

A strangled sound issued from her throat. "And if I do not?"

He stalked back to her dressing table and sat in its chair. Crossing one foot over the other knee, he leaned back and contemplated their new life together. The pregnancy was a frustrating complication—he couldn't just yank her over his knee and give her the spanking she deserved. That would have to wait until after the child was born. Truth be told, he wasn't quite sure what to do with her.

She slumped on her seat within the embrasure. Her hair snagged against the stones.

In her eyes, he could see a flash of panic lurking just beneath the surface. A burst of satisfaction flared inside him. Her haughtiness was definitely slipping.

"What do you plan?" The pulse fluttered in her throat.

"I intend to train you to cater to my every whim."

She gave a little gasp of outrage, and he nearly laughed. Perhaps having her under his hand would be much more entertaining than sending her from the castle as he had first planned. Her bosom rose and fell with piqued anger.

"Mayhap," he murmured, enjoying the bouncing, feminine movement of her breasts. "I will have you tend to my personal needs. Have you clean my boots, care for my clothing as a proper wife should."

He was rewarded with another indignant breath, which made her nipples slip against her linen garment.

"Or mayhap I will have you bathe me."

Her nipples threatened to heave themselves out of her shift.

Jesu. As much as he enjoyed it, he could not keep up this game. His self-control was not that strong. "Ariana, I married you because 'tis for the best."

"Best for you, you mean." Her lips turned down at the corners. She shifted her weight on the cushion.

Briefly, his dreams of traveling to the Continent flitted through his mind. He pushed them away.

"Men forever think that what is best for them must be best for women as well," she said bitterly.

"Ariana, that is unfair. My plan was to take your castle, not to be saddled with a wife. I married you for the sake of our child."

Strands of her curly hair caught on the rough stones as she leaned her head against the sill and gazed at him. The copper strands contrasted with the gray brick. "How can you speak of what is fair after what you have done this day?"

"What *I* have done?"

"Interrupted my wedding—"

"That *wedding* with that *boy* should never have been conceived." A primal possessiveness burned inside him, and he felt fury flame.

She ran her fingers along the delicate stitches of the ivory-colored cushion she sat upon and hurled him a haughty look. "Nigel is not a boy."

"Humph. Not man enough to handle the likes of you, I'd wager."

Her back stiffened. "I do not need handling."

He lifted a brow pointedly at the shattered mirror on the floor planks. "My lady, you are a woman who needs to be handled often and handled well."

She turned away, staring out the window into the bailey, and Gabriel felt his heart tug.

"He's ill-suited to protect you," he offered. "You are better off with me."

"I do not need protection!"

"You do. A heiress alone and pregnant is a prime target."

"I was not going to be alone."

"That pale mouse you were to marry can scarcely count as protection."

"A woman can care for herself."

He gazed at the tight swell of her belly. "And her children?"

She turned, looking ready to rise from the window seat and claw his eyes out. "'Tis your fault I am in this condition."

"Another reason why I am a better suited bridegroom than he."

The ornate lace of one of the window seat's curtains drifted softly against her shoulder. She brushed it aside and hugged one of the fancy pillows to her chest like she was trying to squeeze the stuffing out of it. "I did not wish to marry at all."

"And yet, here we are."

Glaring at him, she hurled the pillow at him. It bounced off his chest and landed on the dressing table. Powder from a jar puffed into the air.

Lifting a brow, Gabriel rubbed his thumb against his forefinger. "Do you plan to spend all our married life throwing mirrors and pillows at me?"

"Nay." She stood, looking for all the world like Hera who had just caught Zeus in the arms of a human lover. "I plan to poison your food."

"Ho, wife. Remind me to keep you away from the kitchens."

"You cannot keep me away from my own house."

"I can if you plan to poison me."

Crossing her arms, she huffed.

"Ariana, I am master here now. The sooner you come to heel, the easier our life will be." He toyed with a hair bauble on the dressing table.

She reached for another pillow, then evidently

thought better of it and left it on the window seat. Her shoulders slumped, and he could not help but feel a little sorry for her. Even hellcats needed care.

After a moment, she faced him squarely. "You did not need to harm Nigel."

"He is no longer your concern."

"You must release him."

He cracked the knuckles of one of his hands, a red haze of anger clouding his vision. "His life was spared for your sake. His wounds are being cared for. Do not press me."

Standing, she took a deep breath. "I have duties to attend to."

He found himself admiring her resolve. Mayhap once she accepted her new lot, they could get along as well as any other noble couple.

"You may attend to your duties, but let this be clear, Ariana—*there will be no more spying*. Finish removing your garment. I will have the maids bring you your new clothing."

Looking disdainfully at him, she stood and allowed her outer garment to drop around her ankles.

Unease prickled Gabriel's neck. Already Ariana had had three husbands. Mayhap he should investigate their deaths.

Chapter 16

Ariana cringed at the muddy footprints running up and down the stairways as she and Gabriel made their way to the great hall a half hour later. After his declaration that he did not intend to rape her or harm Jason, she determined that somehow they would muddle through.

She wore a rough woolen garment that caused the skin around her ankles and wrists, places her linen shift did not cover, to itch unmercifully. No doubt he'd insisted on her wearing such a garment to humiliate her. Vexing knave! Ne'er in her life had she worn something so awful. The scratchy wool drove her mad.

Bear up, she told herself firmly, determined not to allow such a simple thing to break her spirit. *The dress is the least of your worries.* Husband or no, she had a household to run and servants to see to. She needed to find out who had put the sinister note in her room, and, God willing, she would determine what Gabriel had done with Nigel so she could release him. She said a silent prayer that Gabriel had told the truth when he claimed Nigel's wounds were being cared for.

She sighed. After she released her friend, she would endure this marriage as she always had. Surely this husband could be no worse than the other three. Asides, she had learned a thing or two about handling men over the years.

Balls of dirt that smelled suspiciously like horseshit lined the corridors. A wave of exasperation passed over her. She *would* get this place back under control. In the windows, her frilly curtains hung askew. Filthy handprints marred the pristine linen as if they had been used as hand wipes.

"Your animals are ransacking my castle."

"*My* castle," he corrected, taking her elbow.

Condescending beast!

The scent from the great hall wafted into the hallway even before they entered: musk and maleness and sweat. Appalled, she crossed the threshold and stared at the disaster her hall had become.

Everywhere she turned, loud, boasting soldiers lounged. Their large, sweaty bodies knelt on the floor, or leaned against the tapestries, or spilled across the tables and chairs. A maid shrieked as she passed a knot of men throwing dice and one of them reached up to slap her soundly on the bottom.

Ariana let out a disgusted huff. This would not do at all.

For five years, the castle had been pristine—the curtains washed, the floors free of dust, the air free of noise.

Since her husband had passed, no men had resided in the living quarters of the keep. They stayed only in the guardhouse or their own huts.

"Watch this, Ian," hollered a thick-waisted, black-bearded fellow.

Several men turned, and the speaker let out a loud,

echoing belch. The men guffawed and slapped him on the back. Another barbarian patted his stomach and burped even louder than the first.

Irritation ran up Ariana's spine. "Filthy, disgusting pigs."

"Mind your tongue. These are good men, all."

Afore she could respond, Jason, who sat at the fireplace, jumped up and hurled a clump of rushes into the air. The clean hose and tunic he had worn to the wedding were caked with mud. Tender pink skin showed through a hole in one of the knees. Heavens. She thought about the note she'd found. Poisoning Gabriel, as it had suggested, seemed almost sane.

"Jason!"

As if sensing her, the seven-year-old turned, a guilty look widening his blue eyes.

She gave Gabriel a pointed glower before turning back to her son and motioned for him to come. "Jason, come hither this instant!"

Looking down, the boy shuffled toward her.

"What are you doing with *those* men?" Ariana scolded, heedless that he could not hear her. She marched to him and began vigorously brushing mud from his tunic.

A few warriors stared at them, but for the most part, they ignored the exchange.

Jason's blond eyebrows lifted up and down, and he pulled a short knife from his belt and showed it to her.

"A knife!" Ariana exclaimed. She frowned and shook her finger at him.

He shrugged sheepishly and pointed at a man sitting at a trestle table. The barbarian was large, although shorter than Gabriel. He had brown, furry hair like a wild beast and wore a patch over one eye.

She turned to Gabriel. "How dare you let your monsters into my hall to give knives to children!"

Gabriel smiled tightly. "*My* hall, wife. And Rodney is completely trustworthy. He has been around my siblings for years without injuring one of them." He paused. "Well, that is, except for Sam's arm."

"Sam's arm?" she exclaimed.

The man in question turned around and squinted at her with his good eye.

Clearing his throat, Gabriel took her by the elbow and led her to the dais without answering her question. She dragged Jason by the hand as she pondered the best way to evict the men from the living quarters. No doubt they would want to move the trestle tables and sleep here in the great hall.

From the door that went into the kitchen, her cook, Margaret, gave Ariana a wide-eyed look of desperation. Her large bottom filled most of the doorframe, and her pudgy fingers gripped a flagon so tightly she could have been wringing a chicken's neck. Her mouth moved in her customary oh mercy, oh saints way, but no sound came out.

Ariana removed her arm from Gabriel's grip to head toward her chief cook. "Excuse me."

Gabriel snagged her hand. "Where do you go?"

"To see to *your* dinner, my lord," she said tightly. She pointed Jason toward a chair and headed to help Margaret.

Afore she made three steps, a huge wolfhound scrambled out from under a trestle table and knocked her to the side.

"Heavens!" Ariana righted herself and frowned at the dog. "What is that thing?"

"A dog," Gabriel drawled.

Jason patted the animal as if they had become fast friends. He grinned, his eyes lighting like stars.

"I meant"—she cast a scathing glare at Gabriel—"what is that *thing* doing in my great hall?"

Reaching down, Gabriel scratched the hound behind the ears. "Wife, meet dog."

"Dog?"

Its huge tail flipped back and forth, whacking Ariana like a broomstick. Her woolen tunic flopped to and fro.

Gabriel patted the beast lovingly with his marred hand. "Dog, meet my new wife, Lady Ariana."

"How do you . . . Oh, of all the—" Ariana found herself at a loss for what to say. She hadn't allowed dogs in the house since her husband, thank God he was dead, had passed, and she was not about to start now.

Jason twined his fingers in the animal's fur. The cur quivered with unchecked canine glee.

"Ach! Son! Away from that filthy beast!" She set him away from the dog.

White cap bobbing, Margaret lurched her way over to them. "Oh, mercy. I told them not to allow it inside, mistress."

Both Jason and the dog looked at her with pleading eyes. The animal wiggled close to him, and he patted it.

Ariana shook her head and pointed at the door. "Away! The beast likely carries the pox."

Jason pulled his small hands out of the dog's fur. His lower lip quivered, and tears hovered in the corners of his eyes as if she'd just denied him life itself instead of some awful, smelly hound.

The huge animal gazed up with sheepish eyes. He wiggled over and licked her sloppily on the arm.

"Ick!" Wiping her arm on her dress, she glared at Gabriel. "This will not do. Not do at all."

All at once, her large gray cat jumped from the windowsill onto the table by the hearth. With a bark, the dog leapt sideways and shot off after the feline. Cups, platters, and rushes flew into the air as the dog chased the cat around table legs and between the benches.

Margaret squealed.

"Cease!" shouted Ariana.

"Stop him!" Gabriel boomed.

More dishes crashed to the floor, setting off a cacophony. Maids screamed. Men laughed. The cat yowled, and Jason—Ariana shot him a sharp glare—stood up and clapped.

"Oh, saints. 'Tis been thus since the wedding, mistress," Margaret said with a pleading tone.

Swiping a spilled tray from the rushes, Ariana determined to bring order back to the household. "Out, out, you mangy beast!" she yelled, swinging the empty tray menacingly in the air.

The hound stopped and hunkered down, a look of supreme repentance in its large brown eyes.

Ariana huffed. Her red curls bounced. She pointed toward the door. "Begone!"

The cur slumped, pleading at her with his canine eyes, then rolled onto his back. Rushes flew into the air.

"Oh, mercy. Oh, saints." Margaret placed one meaty fist on her enormous hip.

"Get that animal out of here," Ariana said to Gabriel.

Gabriel cleared his throat. "He's just not used to cats."

"Out!" She slapped her thigh, shooing him away. "Out!"

Rolling over, the dog glanced back and forth at them.

Ariana caught Gabriel's gaze. "You live in a manor

home now. If you wish to be lord of the castle, then train your animals to behave in a way that suits your station."

Gabriel managed to look slightly abashed. He pointed at the door. "Begone, dog."

Tucking his tail between his legs, the hound slunk from the hall. He turned around three times in the doorway, then lay down, flopped his head onto his paws, and panted smelly doggy breath into the room.

"He will be better behaved in a few days," Gabriel said with a shrug. "'Tis a lot for him to get used to."

"He needs to be removed," Ariana insisted.

"Oh, mercy," Margaret agreed with a sharp nod. "'e's putting hair in the soup." She waved her arms frantically. "The kitchen's a jumble; the bread's being burned; the ham's still raw. We can't get a blasted thing done, mistress."

"I must see to the kitchens." Grasping the ends of her curly hair and winding them into a bun, Ariana gave Gabriel a pointed look and headed to set things aright.

As soon as Margaret and she were out of earshot, she leaned close to the cook.

"Have you seen Nigel?" she whispered.

"Nay, mistress, not since the wedding." Margaret's eyes widened, and she wrung her hands. "Ye don' think they've done away with 'im, do ye? Oh, mercy. Oh, saints. Ye're new 'usband is such a big man, and 'e didn't much seem happy about Nigel nor about the wedding. I thought he would slay us all, I did. Oh, mercy, but I was scared, mistress. What should we do?"

Ariana sighed. She should not have brought up Nigel to Margaret—the nervous woman was likely to fly into hysterics. She patted the cook on her fleshy shoulder.

"Be calm," she soothed. "I am sure Nigel is well. We will muddle through this. We just need to chop some turnips, and things will all seem normal."

"Oh, mercy. Oh, saints. Did 'e take ye already, mistress? Is that why you are wearing that peasant dress?" Margaret's gaze slid over the itchy tunic. "'e did, didn't 'e? The brute. Did 'e rip the other off ye?"

"Gabriel did not harm me. Did anyone go into my chambers after the wedding?" Ariana asked, swiftly changing the subject before Margaret began wheezing.

"Nay, mistress."

Ariana grabbed a paring knife and pressed it into Margaret's grasp. From experience, she knew her cook said a lot fewer oh mercys when she had a kitchen instrument in her hand. "Have you seen anyone sneaking about?"

Margaret glanced at the men lounging across the benches and wrung her hands. Rodney gazed back at her intently with his good eye. "You mean asides the menfolk here?"

"Aye."

"Nay. Naught. Why do ye ask, mistress? And *why* are you wearing that dress?"

Ignoring Margaret's question, Ariana took a spare apron from a hook and put it on over the peasant dress. "There was a note in my—"

"Oh, mercy. I forgot. Ye're cousin sent a missive, mistress." She handed Ariana a scroll. An impression from the bishop's ring was pressed into the wax seal.

Ariana's heart lurched. A mission. How would she accomplish such a thing while under Gabriel's watchful eye? From their last discussion, she had no doubt that Randall would make good on his promise to see her taken to justice for Ivan's murder if she did not continue spying for him.

A tendril of her hair slid down her neck. She wound it tightly back into her bun. There was no time to return to her room for pins or call for Francine.

At that moment, a flock of urchins even rowdier than the wolfhound poured into the great hall. She tucked the scroll into her belt and headed back into the main chamber to address the commotion. She would figure out how to deal with her cousin's demands later.

"We're go'st to live here?" A small boy with huge, rounded eyes and longish red hair said.

"Yuppers. That's what Gabe said."

"Look at all that food," exclaimed another, this one with bushy, dirt-colored hair and ripped hose.

Arms and legs that looked like scrawny tree branches during a winter storm blustered around the hall. They stuck out of ill-fitting tunics that were too short and too tight.

"Oh, saints, mistress. 'ere they come again." Turning, Margaret raced down the cellar steps and slammed the door as if a wild boar was on her heels.

The urchins jumped from bench to table. Blond, red, and brown hair flew in all directions as their heads bobbed across the great hall.

Horrified, Ariana marched back to Gabriel who was lounging in the lord's chair, holding a tankard of ale. "Who are these people?"

Gabriel took a long swig, then wiped his mouth with his sleeve. "Wife, meet my family."

Chapter 17

Ariana stared at the ragtag bunch of waifs who charged the length of her great hall like 'twas a practice field. Gabriel's *family*? Their dirty bare feet bore testament that none of them had had a bath in weeks, probably not in months. All of the children had such frizzed and matted hair, 'twas nigh impossible to tell the boys from the girls.

Verily, getting things back to normal and a measure of peace would be harder than just chopping turnips and chasing out dogs. She wiped her hands on her apron in preparation for the challenge.

"Ahoy," one of the younger boys shouted—at least she thought 'twas a boy. "I'll race ye to yon table and back."

"Yer on!"

"Right!"

"Go!"

Clattering over tables, not unlike the dog and cat had done, the children set off.

"Your family?"

"A finer bunch you could never imagine." Gabriel puffed out his chest. "Let me introduce you." He

pointed at the various moving bodies in the room.
"Sam, Myron, Joel . . ."

Ariana's gaze swung this way and that. 'Twas like
trying to count bees!

". . . Heather, Gareth, Oliver . . ."

One mop-headed waif used one of the curtains to
swing onto the fireplace mantel.

"Cease!" Ariana shouted to no avail. "Get your
muddy feet off the hearth."

Through the noise, she heard Jason scream.

She turned to see her son struggling as a large, bull-
like adolescent snatched a wooden duck from his hand.

Grunting, Jason reached for his toy.

"Ugha, ugha," mocked the larger boy. "Ye think yer
still lord o' the mount, eh? Well, jes' come and get it."
He held the wooden duck above his head.

Jason jumped up and down, trying to reach his
duck. "Mum!"

"Call for your mum, eh? She can't help you."

"Let him alone!" Ariana exclaimed, heading toward
Jason. The woolly peasant skirt swirled around her
ankles.

Gabriel caught her arm and pulled her back.
"They're children. Let them work it out."

"He is deaf and cannot defend himself!" Wrenching her arm away, she marched over, snatched the
wooden duck, and handed it to her son.

"Mama's boy," the bully taunted before turning
aside and joining the other heathens.

A crash sounded behind her, and she turned to see
one of the older brats leapfrogging the table. A plat-
ter of roasted pork tumbled to the floor.

The wolfhound bounded back into the great hall to
gulp it down, whacking her on the leg as he rushed by.

Rodney laughed, his one eye squinting.

"Stop them!" She waved her hands in the air frantically. "Stop them afore I have no hall left." *Or sanity either,* she added to herself. Her hair, unraveled from its bun, trailed down her neck.

More plates smashed against the floor, and then a silver trencher shot out like a weapon and slammed against the leaden glass windows with a boom. Shattered glass sprayed into the hall.

"My glass!" she gasped.

The broken window must have pulled Gabriel out of his stupor.

"Halt!" he commanded in a loud, ringing voice.

All of the children except two quieted. Those two were too busy tromping atop the tables, using dinner knives as swords in mock battle.

"Ah-ha!" one shouted, thrusting his "sword" into the other's too small tunic.

"Sam, Gareth, cease!"

At once, silence permeated the hall as the two troublemakers turned to stare at Gabriel. They dropped the eating daggers onto the table. One clattered to the rushes.

"Down at once." Gabriel pointed at the floor.

They leapt from the table, stumbling into a sleeping soldier. Sleeping! How could anyone sleep through all this? The man lurched and gave a loud snore, then his head lolled back peacefully.

Ariana counted the urchins, who gazed back at her with a mixture of curiosity, disdain, and awe. There were six of them. Six! And not one looked like the next.

"Heather, Joel, Gareth, Sam, Myron, Oliver, meet Ariana." Gabriel waved his hand her direction.

"How do you do," she said mechanically, watching one of the youngsters leap onto the lip of the fireplace.

* * *

God hated her. 'Twas the only explanation, Ariana thought as she made her way slowly back to her chamber several hours later.

That she was married to a brute with a pack of street brats while Nigel, dear, sweet Nigel, languished in the damp dungeon was too horrific to contemplate. Not to mention that her skin itched from the mangy tunic Gabriel had insisted she wear. Perhaps God was punishing her for killing Ivan and spying out lewd secrets.

Saints, *how* could she have ever thought she liked Gabriel? Mayhap she'd been blinded by moonlight. He was the most irksome, frustrating, overbearing oaf she'd ever known.

Jason had retreated to his room hours ago.

Once she entered the blessed quiet of her chamber, she barred the door and wobbled her way to her high bed. Rubbing her temples, she flopped across the mattress, exhausted.

Her stomach jumped, reminding her that the ruffian was her baby's father. Blinded by moonlight? Ha! She'd had a full-blown case of lunacy! She patted her pregnant belly, too tired to think straight.

The parchment in her belt made a crinkling noise. She rolled onto her back and dug the paper from her belt.

My dearest cousin, it began.

She sighed. What now?

You have been invited to a feast honoring the Duchess of York. Please give warm regards to my dear friends, the Countess of Carth and her husband.

The letter continued with the address and time of the banquet and his customary flowery signature. Thorns! Another dull party filled with nobles and courtiers. Countess Cyrille of Carth, a pretty blond-haired woman married to a rich lord, was the prey. Ariana would follow her and report back any odd sightings or naughty secrets. Whenever Randall sent one of these notes, he usually already had a lead on some form of debauchery or another, so even a minor flirtation could be vital.

The feast was less than a week hence. No doubt, he'd yanked a few leashes to get her invited at this late date. Ariana felt the noose around her neck tighten. Her temples throbbed. She would have to get her seamstresses started on making something appropriate to wear first thing in the morning.

She yawned. For now, sleep.

Bang! Bang! Bang!

Rolling onto her side, she stared at the oaken door.

Bang! Bang! Bang!

"Leave be!"

"Ariana!" Gabriel's deep voice boomed. "Open the bloody door."

"Nay! Leave be!" Her head throbbed.

"Now, Ariana! Defy me, and I will have Nigel's skin stripped from his very bones."

She shivered. Men such as Gabriel had a certain rough code of honor against harming children and women but no such honor about other men, even soft, gentle ones like Nigel.

Bang! Bang! Bang!

Fresh frustration pounded through her head.

She eased off the mattress, realizing there would be no rest unless she opened the door.

"Think about Nigel!" Gabriel threatened.

Bang! Bang! Bang!

"Leave off the bloody banging! I am coming!" Irritating, vexing man!

She reached the door and lifted the crossbar. Silently, she vowed to see to Nigel's safety so he could not be used against her.

"There, you bloody oaf!" she said, opening the door.

He strode inside with panther-like grace, his presence dominating the room. A wave of shock made her blink. He had bathed and changed into fresh garments—hose and a well-stitched green tunic. His dark hair was slicked away from his forehead, and water dripped onto his wide, wide shoulders. His features were too intense to be considered handsome.

She blinked. Nay, he wasn't handsome. He was magnificent. Shoving the irksome female thought aside, she closed the door behind him and leaned against it.

"Do not bar me out, wife."

Crossing her weary arms, she gathered her strength. "'Tis my chamber."

"Only because it pleases me to have it so."

Exhaustion made it impossible to think, much less bicker with him. "Fine." She dropped into an exaggerated curtsy and feared for a moment she would be unable to hoist herself back up. "Whatever pleases you, *my lord.*"

Her sarcastic tone earned her a sharp look.

She ignored it. All she wanted at this moment was a moment's peace so she could sleep. Tomorrow would be soon enough to solve the complications in her life.

Making her way back to the bed, she lay down and

rolled onto her side. The baby kicked in her womb.
Jesu! Now she needed to make water.

Forcing herself back up, she climbed off the bed
and walked to the garderobe.

Gabriel turned and frowned at Ariana as she walked
past him. Dark circles smudged the skin under her
eyes. Her stomach, which looked a lot bigger in the
simple dress, moved this way and that in an easy
rhythm. He pondered her for a moment as she closed
the door to the small garderobe.

He would have thought a creature as shallow as she
would have been livid at wearing the patched and
torn peasant's garb, but Ariana hadn't voiced one
word of complaint. It had been his experience that
costuming was one of noblewomen's great pastimes.
Odd. She'd absently scratched her wrists and belly
all night, but even doing that, he could tell she was
not humbled by the dress, merely irritated.

His plan to bring her down a notch had not worked
at all—she still looked noble, and something about
her inner strength made him feel petty for trying to
get back at her in this way. Even in peasant's garb, she
was above his station.

He gazed around the room for a moment. He had
known she was wealthy, but this was beyond his imagin-
ings. Her castle was more of a stately manor home than
a keep. In every nook and cranny, some expensive trinket or decoration lingered. Each door was beautifully
hand carved, even the ones to the garderobes. The furnishings looked to have been made by master craftsmen,
and the silks and furs cushioning the chairs and beds
were delicately and wonderfully wrought.

For a moment, his mind wandered to Cyrille whom
he had almost married. Did she live in a home with

such luxury? He found himself sympathizing with her more than he ever had in the past. She had not shown up at the altar—had sent a note instead informing him that she would be marrying the earl, but that it need not change their relationship.

He was good for a tryst or a diversion, but not for a husband. For years, he'd hated noble ladies for their spoiled selfishness, but after seeing all this wealth, he knew he could not have provided for her the way the Earl of Carth was doing. Still, it stung his pride that she'd chosen a stooped and wrinkled old man over him. None in his care had ever gone hungry, at least not until he'd been locked away by the Abbot. Year after year, one or more of the children had some ailment or another that required the services of a leech or apothecary. Always, it cost a great deal of gold. But he had always managed to provide.

Still—he looked around the gilded room—mayhap he'd judged Cyrille too harshly.

Ariana emerged, yawning, from the facilities, and all thoughts of Cyrille ceased. His wife's softly rounded belly wiggled as she moved. He could see she neared collapse. She tripped on the edge of the rug. Instinct pushed him to his feet, and he grasped her elbow, steadying her.

A flash of genuine gratitude lit in her eyes for an instant before her guarded, prickly persona slammed back into place.

"I can find my way to the bed myself." She shrugged his arm away.

"I will not have you tripping and harming my child."

"I am pregnant, not helpless," she sniffed. Her stomach bumped into the dressing table.

A strong wave of protectiveness flooded him. In a swift movement, he reached down, hoisted her into his arms, and carried her to the bed. The soft perfume of her hair teased his nostrils, an exotic scent. Rich amber. He recognized the scent from his travels in the Holy Land, searching for his sister. Only the very wealthy could afford such a precious spice for use in soap. People such as his lady.

His lady. Despite his misgivings about marriage, he liked the sound of that. He laid her gently on the bed, fully expecting her to scramble to the other side and fling another pillow at him.

Instead, she stared up at him with a look of astonishment on her face. "Why did you do that?" she asked.

"Do what?"

"Carry me."

He shrugged, unwilling to think about the things he felt. She'd thumbed her nose at him. She'd called him a barbarian. She'd left him to die. Eric was gone. His intention had been to set her out on her nose for the winter—allow her to become one of the beggars at the castle's kitchen, then use her money to tear the abbey apart brick by brick. But he found he could scarce stand the thought of her tripping, much less being cold and hungry.

She pushed herself up on one elbow, gazing at him with weary, guarded eyes.

He ran his thumb over the three freckles that caressed her cheek.

She shivered but did not turn aside.

For a frightening moment, he contemplated kissing her.

A line of anxiety knitted between her brows. He smoothed it away with his fingers.

"Gabriel?"

His name on her lips startled him. It resonated deep inside his heart. "Aye?"

"Did your men harm Nigel?"

He stifled a growl.

An image of himself on his knees, serving the Abbot bit his memories. *You have much pride, sinner.* The Abbot had thrown his food onto the floor. *Lick it up, sinner. Taste of God's provision.*

A bitter hatred ate at Gabriel—not because the Abbot had been so cruel, but because of his own weakness. Famished and weak, he'd eaten the slop directly off the tiles, heedless of his pride.

He slammed the door on his memories. He was not about to lay his weakness bare for such a heartless woman to know.

"Sleep, Ariana," he said, not bothering to answer her question. "Tomorrow is soon enough for our life together to begin."

Chapter 18

The next morning, Ariana gazed, stricken, at her ransacked great hall and determined to get a handle on things before they went any further downhill.

Trestle tables rested against the walls, and chairs lay toppled on their sides as if a pack of wild wolves had ravaged the place. At least Gabriel had allowed her to wear her deep blue gown lined with ermine instead of rags—order was so much easier to establish when the leader was clearly defined.

A silk veil shot with silver threads covered her hair, which was braided into a tail that bounced at the top of her hips. Why he had changed his mind about her clothing, she could not fathom. Years ago, she'd given up trying to understand the odd ways of husbands.

Margaret raced up to Ariana, flailing a straw broom. She seemed even more frantic and nervous than usual. "Oh, mercy, mistress. Naught but a bunch of great lazy beasts." She pointed at the remaining soldiers. "Out of 'ere, ya mangy pigs. Out!"

She smacked Rodney soundly atop the noggin with the bristles of her broom. Straw went flying.

"Away from here, I say! We can't do no cookin' as long as ya are lazin' around in the bloody way."

The man shielded his head with his arm so she couldn't get another good crack at it. "Unnatural woman," he grumbled.

"Bunch of beasts! Bunch of beasts!" She headed back to Ariana and gave her a short deferential dip. The six wiry hairs on her upper lip quivered with indignation. "Oh, saints, mistress. We must be rid of them."

Ariana breathed a frustrated sigh and dusted her hands. "Agreed, Margaret. Agreed."

"I had to run 'em out of the kitchens, and then they settled 'ere on the tables with their great mangy bodies. Oh, mercy. You must get rid of them, I say, mistress. Rid of them." Margaret gave the nearest man, a tall pointy-headed brute, a chastising look.

"We'll get a handle on it," Ariana promised. "Were you able to ask if anyone had come into my room after the wedding?"

"With these pox-ridden beasts around? Oh, saints. They've been 'ere all bloody morning, eatin' and burpin' and passin' wind and God only knows what else."

"Beg pardon, good woman." Gabriel stood in the entranceway, casually leaning against the doorframe. He smiled at her disarmingly.

She stared at him, obviously taken aback by his white teeth and interesting incisors. He had a stunning smile. "Oh, mercy," she huffed.

His eyes danced. "The men are hungry, and just looking for a little something to eat from a pretty thing like you."

Pretty thing? Of all the cheap, lowdown tricks.

Margaret's mouth opened and closed, causing her lip hairs to twitch. "Well, of course, I say," she said at last.

"That will be enough," Ariana cut in. The last thing she needed was Gabriel charming the pants off the kitchen staff with meaningless flattery. "We will set this place to rights immediately."

At that moment, four of Gabriel's siblings fell through the doorway—a redhead, two brunettes, and a blonde. Two of them landed in the rushes, screaming and punching each other like wild, primitive heathens. Both wore ragtag bits of clothing. They rolled on the floor, hitting each other. Straw flew into the air.

The other two, a shorter child and a taller, lanky one, stood on the sidelines, clapping and cheering them on.

"Go, Sam; punch him in the 'nads."

"Watch it, Myron!"

They rammed one of the tables as they tumbled forward. Dishes toppled with a loud crash.

"Halt!" Gabriel commanded, but the boys paid him no attention. "Sam! Myron!"

Heading into the hurly-burly, Gabriel yanked the smaller of the two from atop the other one. "Cease, Sam! You're going to have another tooth knocked out!"

Gabriel held Sam, a wiry urchin with wild, frizzy blond hair, while Myron, the older, fatter child, scrambled to his feet. Ariana recognized Myron as the one who had tormented Jason about his duck yesterday. Myron, even though he looked like he had a stone's weight on Sam and a couple of years' growth, had a bleeding lip and a purpling eye. Sam had a large red gash down his cheek.

"Children!" Ariana exclaimed.

"Behave!" Gabriel demanded. "Apologize to each other."

"Absolutely not!" the smaller one said. "'E deserved every punch."

"I'll ge' ye," Myron said, thrusting his pudgy arms out.

Gabriel shook him, lifting him nearly off the ground. "Cease!"

The boy stopped and glared at Gabriel.

Gabriel gave him another shake. "Clean up this mess."

Myron narrowed his eyes, but he reached to pick up some of the scattered trenchers.

Ariana breathed a sigh of relief that Gabriel had a measure of control over his pack of brats.

"Sam, go with Ariana to fetch a cloth. You'll be helping in the kitchens until you learn some manners."

"The kitchens!" Sam grimaced. "Like a girl?"

"You *are* a girl."

"A girl?" Ariana looked at the unkempt frizzy-haired child. At the torn and dirty breeches. "You are a girl?"

Sam propped a hand on her hip and jutted out her chin. Her blond hair puffed around her. "What's it to ye?"

"Oh my," Ariana said. Setting things aright was going to be nigh to impossible—Gabriel's siblings were shocking to the point of being scandalous. "Why are you wearing breeches?"

Sam's expression fell slightly. "I ain't never had a dress."

"That's not true," Myron interjected. "Ye had one, but ye got it dirty."

Sam stuck her tongue out at him.

"Did ye see that?" Myron made to lunge at her, but Gabriel restrained him.

Ariana straightened to her full height and used the most authoritarian voice she could muster: "Children, behave or there will be *no* breakfast."

Myron pivoted to face her. "But I'm hungry."

"Then mind your manners," Ariana instructed.

In the corner, Rodney let out a loud belch.

Ariana swiveled around. "That goes for the men too. Margaret is an amazing chef—she was hand-picked for me. She makes delectable pastries and mouthwatering white bread. But if she is going to fix our meals, then no men can linger in the great hall while the servants are preparing the food." She made eye contact with several of the ruffians. "Outside, all of you—children, men, and dogs. We will break our fast shortly. God willing, we will find a way to work through living together both peaceably and well-fed."

The promise of food had several of the men rising to their feet. The one they called Ian twisted a lock of his beard. Rodney squinted his one eye at her and put the knife he had been sharpening back into his belt. "Pastries and white bread ye say?"

"Aye." Ariana patted her veil. "Pastries and white bread if you go. Dried meat and rotten turnips if you stay." She lifted her brow at Gabriel. "Unless my lord knows how to run a kitchen."

The men exchanged meaningful looks. Ian cleared his throat, glanced at Gabriel, and stood.

"With respect, sir," he said, shuffling from the great hall.

The others followed.

"Oh, mercy. Bless ye, mistress," Margaret said,

wiping her hands on her apron. Her white cap hung askew on her head.

"That was quite impressive, wife," Gabriel drawled once his men had filed out. His eyes sparkled with laughter. "Mayhap you should go into battle and lead your own band of men. Did you see the look on Myron's face when you threatened his breakfast?"

His amusement at her expense earned him a sharp look.

He laughed, his wide smile dazzling. "And what would my wife, the commander, have *me* do?" he teased.

She shrugged and rolled her eyes. "Something manly," she mocked. "See to the defenses mayhap."

Moving closer, he kissed her abruptly on the cheek.

Frowning, she slapped her hand to her face as if swatting a midge. The skin where his lips had touched was heated and moist. "What was that for?" she blurted.

"You needed it." His lips quirked. "I will do it again if you ask."

Vexing, that was what he was. Simply vexing! She would never ask for his kisses.

He stared at her a moment longer than was appropriate. "I'll see to the defenses, and you see to your duties, girl." He winked at her, then turned toward the exit.

Thorns, but the man set her on edge.

She cleared her throat. Duty afore pleasure. "Sam . . . Samantha, come with me." She would have the seamstresses make the girl a dress while they worked on the clothing for the feast that her cousin wanted her to attend. Perhaps she could ask them if anyone had seen someone who could have planted the note about the poison sneak into her chamber during the wedding.

Seemingly of their own accord, her eyes lingered

on Gabriel as he headed to the exit. The muscles of his tight buttocks flinched and released in an all too masculine strut. He'd kissed her! What on earth for? It certainly was no love match between them.

Was he really going to see to the keep's defenses? She tried to ignore her little feeling of relief that someone besides herself would even take an interest in such things. In truth, 'twas a strain at times to be solely responsible for the welfare of the castle.

He paused at the doorway and gave Sam a serious look. "Do not give my new wife any trouble."

"Wouldn' dream of it, luv," Sam said cheekily.

After they broke their fast, which was every bit as delicious as Ariana had promised, Gabriel spent the better part of the day learning the layout of Rosebriar and sizing up the strength of the walls and guardhouse. The keep itself was of moderate size, but the walls sprawled across an enormous courtyard that was as elaborate as the inside of the castle. Within the yard, several well-tended gardens grew. One for herbs, one for flowers, one for roses. A large wooden chess set with pieces nigh four feet tall squatted in one corner, and an equally oversized board was set up to play Nine Man's Morris on the other side. 'Twas the most wondrous garden he'd ever seen. Of a truth, the caretaker must love his work.

He made a quick list of needed supplies for fortifying the walls. One section needed new mortar and another new lumber to replace some rotting boards. There seemed to be only a minimal number of guards, so before heading to find his new wife, he made a note to hire more men.

Afore he made it inside the keep, a lad in a billowing red cape bounded up to him and threw aside his hood. His brother Eric!

Gabriel started as if he'd seen a ghost. His breath lodged in his throat.

"Gabriel! I came as soon as I learned you were alive. We've thought you dead all these months."

Blinking, Gabriel rubbed his eyes. "Eric?"

"You look pale, brother. What ails you?"

Gabriel felt as though a crossbow quarrel had caught him full in the chest. For a long moment, he stared at his brother.

"Gabriel? Are you well?

Lunging forward, he clasped Eric in a huge bear hug.

"Damn," Eric said, nearly collapsing under the weight of the hug.

Stars, but the boy was almost as tall as him now! "I thought *you* were dead."

Eric laughed.

Setting his brother slightly away from him, Gabriel looked Eric up and down, taking in his finely stitched tunic and cape. "Where did you get those clothes?"

"Ariana."

"Ariana?"

"She came to London and found me in prison. Ransomed me and set me up with work as an apprentice at an apothecary."

"She did?"

"Aye." Eric flicked his red cape over one shoulder.

Gabriel's world rocked. "Are you sure?"

Eric touched his forehead as if to indicate Gabriel might have a touch of madness and needed to be sent to St. Mary's.

Bloody hell! He'd blamed Ariana for Eric's death, and she'd gone to London to save him.

"Have you any food in this place?" Eric asked.

Gabriel laughed. "Always thinking of your stomach. Have you seen the others?"

"Nay, not yet. I sent gold a few months past."

"Oh?"

"To get the family through the winter."

Blowing out a breath, Gabriel looped an arm across his brother's shoulders and steered him toward the great hall. He never wanted to let the lad out of sight again. A dark thought settled on his mind: he owed his new wife an apology.

"Do you know where they placed Nigel?" Ariana asked Dionne, her head seamstress, in a conspiratorial whisper while the other sewing ladies measured Samantha for her first real dress.

"Nay, me lady." Dionne's linen wimple fluttered as she shook her head. She was a tall, thin woman with twinkling blue eyes who had been a beauty in her youth. Her back humped slightly now, and liver spots marred the skin on her hands and face, but she still had most of her teeth. "I'm aworrying, I am. A new husband, and this one a tall, wide man. None o' us have seen the other one since the wedding. Edwina the ale-mistress thinks she aheard him crying one night though."

Ariana cringed. Poor Nigel. If only she knew for sure which of the dungeons he was in, mayhap there was some chance she could free him. He did not deserve to be in the cold and damp—she'd practically had to beg him to marry her.

"What are we to do, me lady? What are we to do?"

"We have to find out just where they are keeping him." Ariana patted Dionne's thin hand and gazed about the room.

In the corner, Samantha had an expression on her face that alternated between horror and exhilaration. Two seamstresses hemmed and hawed around her. She giggled as each new piece of silk or velvet was wrapped around her body and squealed whenever one of the ladies prodded or pinched her.

"Where is Edwina?" Ariana asked.

"Out swooning up and down the practice field, a-pretending to be pullin' weeds. She's been amakin' eyes at that one-eyed lout all this day."

"Rodney." Ariana huffed a deep breath. Only one day into having men around all the time, and already the women were leaving their duties to chase after them. "Have Edwina attend me at once if you see her."

"Aye, me lady."

"Now, one thing more—did anyone go near my chamber during the wedding who could have placed a note inside?"

Dionne shrugged, her bony shoulders lifting up and down.

Thorns! Frustrated, Ariana paced to an open window and stared into the courtyard. No leads on Nigel or the author of the note.

On the lawn, Jason and Gabriel's monstrous dog ran in circles. Jason's giggles reached her, and she shook her head in defeat—the cur would stay. No mother could resist the musical sound of her child's laughter. Somehow, she and the wolfhound would make friends. Jason's hose were torn, and a streak of dirt marred his cheek, but she smiled all the same. 'Twas nice to see him happy.

"Did you need aught else, me lady?" Dionne asked.

Ariana turned. "A tunic for my new husband and a gown for me. Something suitable for a large banquet. I need them by week's end."

If Dionne thought this request odd, she did not indicate it. "Aye, me lady. He would look nice in green."

A vision of Gabriel in an emerald green tunic flitted into her imagination. Nay, not nice. He would look *splendid* with his wide shoulders displayed to perfection and his eyes enhanced by the color.

After Samantha's fitting was finished, Ariana settled her into one of the rooms and gave instructions for the servants to find chambers for the other children. She spent the rest of the day being pulled this way and that by household duties as well as trying to find Edwina so she could ask for information about Nigel. Frustrated with her slow progress, she made her way into the gardens to find Edwina, pull some weeds, and have time to think.

Edwina, the ale-mistress, stood on the side of the practice field still goggling Rodney. Thorns, but the man was ugly. Ariana shook her head—when would she ever understand the fascination women had with men?

Her mind drifted to Gabriel, and she wondered if she appeared just as dreamy when she looked at him. She had been very busy, and they had not spoken since breakfast, but he seemed to have floated in and out of her thoughts all the daylong. Well, that was certainly different than the other husbands she'd had—she'd done her best to pretend they did not exist at all. But something about Gabriel made him impossible to ignore.

Perhaps 'twas the kiss he'd given her. She frowned. 'Twas wickedness of the lowest form to think only of Gabriel's kisses when her dear friend languished in the dungeon.

Edwina sighed, and Ariana walked over to ask about the sounds she had heard to ascertain whether they could have been Nigel.

"Milady!" Edwina jumped as if she'd been caught with her finger in a blackberry tart. She was a short, pear-shaped woman with thin shoulders and thick ankles. Her coif was on backward, as if she'd put it on in too much of a hurry. Likely, she had been so distracted by Rodney that she had not noticed it did not fit properly.

"Peace, Edwina." Ariana gave her a moment to compose herself. "I came to ask you something." She lifted her brow. "And to see if you need any help getting back to work making ale."

Edwina blushed. "Right, milady. Yes, of course." Her gaze flitted to Rodney and then back to Ariana.

"Dionne said you had heard sounds in the night. Mayhap from Nigel . . . ?"

Edwina's eyes widened, and she twisted her fingers in her skirt. "Right, milady. Yes, I heard something, I did. 'Twas some time after the wedding—a man crying and going on. Such noise you've never heard afore."

Ariana's stomach fluttered nervously. Information at last! She leaned closer. "Where?"

"Beneath the wine cellar."

Heavens. Rosebriar had been built nigh three hundred years ago as a lookout and a holding point for keeping rebels. It had three dungeons and a maze of catacombs beneath it, some of which contained ancient equipment for questioning prisoners, a dark reminder of the past—the castle had been in Ivan's family for generations. The dungeon beneath the wine cellar held a rack and thumbscrews.

She shuddered. Did Gabriel harbor the same sadistic tendencies as his half brother? He'd been so angry at the wedding.

"Be you well, milady?"

"Aye. Do you think the noise was Nigel?"

Edwina nodded, her coif strings fluttering against her back. "I saw them take a thin figure down those steps after the wedding."

Ariana wrapped her cloak tightly around her shoulders, trying to think of a plan. "We must find a way to release him."

"I hope he's being fed."

Ariana drummed her fingers for a moment. "Fed. That's it!"

"Right. What's it, mistress?"

"Those men." She swept her arm around, indicating the men who practiced with swords and bows on the practice field. "They are unused to nice meals. They practically scrambled out of the kitchen when I promised them white bread. We'll design an elaborate feast with plenty of ale and wine. I will send the ladies down to the meadows to collect as many valerian blossoms as possible; we can disguise the taste with that new batch of spices. That should give us a few hours of relative peace to sneak in and see Nigel off to safety."

Edwina twisted her hands in her skirt. "Right, milady. But your husband is a large man, yes? He is liable not to be too pleased."

Ariana considered this for a moment. Nay, he would not be. But there was no help for it—she had to get Nigel out of that dungeon. "I will think of some way to take care of him. How long until the next batch of ale is ready?"

"Just past a week, milady."

Nodding, Ariana turned back to survey the garden's plants. "Thank you, Edwina. Make the batch as strong as you can."

"Right, milady." Edwina gave one last longing glance at Rodney before heading back to the ale-making cellar.

Ariana drew her cloak tightly around her shoulders and plucked a nearby weed from under a bushy rosemary plant. Her pregnant belly felt heavy as she bent, but the cool soil against her fingers was heaven. At times, she thought plants were her closest friends. They had helped her through three husbands, and they would see her through the fourth. She formulated plans for the feast as she worked in the garden.

She was so lost in thought she did not hear Gabriel approach until he was nearly upon her. Startled, she jumped, then crossed her arms and gave him a sour look.

"You could have warned me," she admonished. How did such a large man move so silently?

His pirate-green eyes danced, and a lock of his hair fell across his widow's peak. "And miss the look on your face?"

She turned down one corner of her lips. "What are you doing here?" Had he been here when Edwina and she were talking?

"I've come to see if you've reconciled yourself to our union."

"It would help if you would keep your men out of the way whilst my women work."

"Come, sit with me," he said, drawing her to a low bench situated to one side of the garden.

"Have I a choice?"

He lifted an eyebrow. "Not at all."

Her stomach gave a lazy turn at the low drawl of his voice. Dusting her hands to rid her fingers of dirt, she sat beside him.

"All these plants—you care for them yourself?"

She nodded. Surely he had not come here to talk about gardening. "Pulling weeds calms me. I enjoy watching the plants grow." When he said naught to indicate his true purpose for being here, she continued. "I wish I had some purple ones to round out the pinks and whites here in the corner."

He nodded.

"You did not come here to talk about flowers," she said.

He took her hand. "I know you are afrighted of this marriage, but I believe we can make a fresh start."

Ariana blinked. "You do?" His mannerism was so much softer than it had been yestereve.

"I know about Eric." He paused, looking uncomfortable. "He came here this morning." He stared into the garden for a moment.

Was this his idea of an apology?

Tucking one leg underneath her, she shifted on the garden bench so she faced him directly. Her pregnant belly bumped him, and she scooted back a few inches. Was there yet hope for this to be a peaceful marriage? She chewed the inside of her lip. Mayhap, but not so long as her friend remained imprisoned.

"Nigel—"

Gabriel stood all at once, startling her. "Your loyalties are misplaced." He looked very tall from her position. "Do not think on him."

"But I just thought you might rel—"

His eyes narrowed, and she swallowed. 'Twas clear there would be no discussion about Nigel's release. She would have to see to his freedom herself. Taking a deep breath, she steadied her mind and reached her hand up to him. "Please, my lord, I did not mean to anger you. Sit with me again."

He scrutinized her face for a moment, then sat and stretched his legs in front of him. He wore leather breeks instead of proper English hose. His fingers drummed on the bench's edge.

She widened her eyes, hoping it made her look innocent and guileless. "Did you find your brother well?"

"Well and wearing finery." Gabriel's shoulders hunched as if he felt guilty.

Good. She knew men well enough to know now was the time to ask for a boon. "We have been invited to a feast at Baron Robert's country home at week's end. I would very much like to go."

After five years of making her own decisions, it galled her to ask permission to go to something as simple as a banquet. But Gabriel was not the sort to accept a wife making demands, so she would do what she must to attend the feast. Her cousin had clearly threatened to have her tried as a murderess if she did not do his bidding.

"Where is this feast?"

"A few miles from here. 'Tis the baron's wife's birthday. We will spend the night."

The drumming of his fingers increased. A white

blossom floated on the wind and landed on his tunic. The elegant flower looked out of place against the roughspun cloth.

She touched him on the forearm in a silent plea. "For a new start on our marriage."

He looked like he'd just swallowed a frog. "Alright. We shall go."

Pleased with both herself and Gabriel, she leaned forward and kissed him on the cheek.

Afore he could react, Heather, the dark-headed child with long, straight hair, came running toward them, waving frantically. "Gabriel! Gabriel! Come! Joel's coughing again, and he cannot breathe."

Springing to his feet, Gabriel ran toward his sister. Ariana followed, silently sighing that her life 'twould ne'er again be as it had been.

Joel was in one of the western rooms, wheezing and struggling for breath. His small face flamed nearly as red as his hair. Tears streaked down his face.

Gabriel snatched him into his arms, and the child wrapped his skinny arms and legs around him in a choking grip. "Be calm. Be calm," he said, patting the boy on the back.

One by one, the other children entered the room, clearly upset about their brother. Samantha wrung her hands, a worried look on her face. Even Myron looked disturbed. Ariana had ne'er seen the like. She was so used to being alone and fending for herself, she'd never realized how nice it must be to have such a clan caring for you.

Ariana watched, amazed as the boy slowly calmed and

began to breathe much more evenly and deeply. 'Twas as if Gabriel worked magic on the child's nerves.

"He gets choked where he cannot breathe, and then becomes frenzied. No one can calm him save Gabriel," Samantha whispered to Ariana.

"The last of the potion is gone, and we've no gold for more from the apothecary," said Myron.

"No gold," echoed Oliver.

"We tried to trade, but the chickens are not yet fat enough," another said.

Gabriel grimaced, and Ariana's heart went out to him. Based on the condition of the children's clothing, most likely, 'twas a scenario he was overly familiar with.

"What do you need?" she asked, walking across the room and placing her hand lightly on Gabriel's back.

Gabriel glanced at her, still holding tightly to Joel.

Joel sniveled. His eyes were closed, and he seemed either asleep or wrung out exhausted from the ordeal.

"The apothecary makes a special batch for him," Samantha explained. "But 'tis expensive." She wrung her hands. "I've been so selfish thinking of getting a new dress when Joel needs medicine."

"Where is the apothecary's shop?" Ariana asked, not allowing Sam to wallow in self-loathing. There was work to do.

"In the village, my lady." Samantha twisted a lock of her blond hair, which looked slightly less frizzy since Ariana had set Francine to oiling and combing it.

"And can you find this shop yourself?"

"Nay."

Myron straightened and waved his hand. "I can." His brow was wrinkled with concern.

She scrutinized him. Mayhap her first impression

had not been fully accurate. He seemed very worried for his brother.

"Fetch the steward, and tell him to come at once to the stable with coins. I will meet you there, and we will ride to the village to get the potion Joel needs."

A relieved smile broke out on Samantha's face.

"At once, my lady," Myron said, hurrying to the exit.

"We shall return as soon as possible." Blue skirt swirling, Ariana walked briskly to the door.

By the evening's meal, Joel's breathing had returned to normal. Gabriel stared at his new wife as she shared a trencher with him at the great table. Damn. Double damn. He felt like the worst sort of blackheart for forcing the marriage. 'Twas obvious from her treatment of his siblings that the woman was a bloody saint. First, she saved Eric. Then she had levelheaded concern for Joel. Furthermore, she'd set the servants to bathing and clothing the lot of them. They were well-scrubbed and well-stitched. Jason and Gareth waved back and forth at each other. Even Samantha's hair looked tamed for once, curly rather than frizzy.

Of a truth, she was a fine woman.

Ariana's eyelids drooped. She appeared tired as she lifted her eating dagger, and he resolved to march her straight to bed once the meal was done. The banquet they had been invited to filled him with dread. But 'twas the least he could do to repay what she'd done for the lot of them.

"Are you finished?" he asked abruptly.

Raising her brow at him, she set her eating dagger aside. "Yes, my lord."

"'Tis time for bed."

She paled slightly. Damn. He'd messed up again. Taking her hand in his, he kissed her palm. "I did not mean to frighten you. We go only to sleep. You look exhausted."

Relief crossed her face, and he lifted her to her feet.

Once they had settled in her chamber, she rubbed her temples and sat on the edge of the bed. Her blue skirts floated around her ankles. "Thank you."

"Nay. Thank you for what you did for Joel."

They stared at each other awkwardly for a moment.

She yawned and glanced at the bell pull. "May I call my maid? I need help with my dress."

Heat flooded his loins at the thought of her divest of her garments. "Nay," he said, "I will help you."

She stiffened but did not flee or attempt to throw anything at him when he neared her. That was progress from yesternight, he thought wryly. Placing his hands on her shoulders, he turned her so that her back was to him. He could see the pulse pounding in her throat.

"Ariana." He kissed her on the neck, enjoying the sweet roselike scent of her skin. He half-expected her to lunge for the door, but she merely shivered. "Do you remember how it was between us on the rock?"

Her sharp intake of breath told him she did. He kissed her neck again, this time near her earlobe. Slowly, he began unlacing her bodice.

"Gabriel—" Her voice was high-pitched, and he feared she was close to panic.

"Sh-h, Ariana. Whatever orders I give you, coming to my bed unwillingly will not be one of them. I will help you with your dress, and then we will sleep. I will not have you thinking I am like Ivan. There is time for pleasure when there is more trust between us."

Chapter 19

Clutching a woven basket, Ariana headed across the bailey to get started on the day's activities. She planned to check on how her ladies were doing with gathering the valerian blossoms. Glenna the midwife expected her sometime today as well to assess the progress of her pregnancy.

The walk into the village and meadows would be a nice diversion from the daily life of the castle. The air felt cool on her cheeks, and she wanted to hurry in case it rained.

On the other side of the field, Jason and the wolf-hound bounded across the green grass. Gabriel stood nearby watching him.

The old feelings of needing to protect her son caused her to halt. She drew her cloak around her shoulders.

Gabriel tossed a brown sphere into the air. A home-made leather ball.

Curious, she stepped closer and realized Gabriel was showing Jason how to throw.

Jason waved to her as Gabriel threw the toy. The

dog caught it and ran back to his master. Taking the ball from the hound's mouth, Gabriel motioned Jason to come near. He gave the toy to Jason and, with large arm signals, indicated that her son should join the game.

Odd. Very odd.

Jason threw the ball, but it did not go far. His shoulders slumped. Her heart went out to him. Being unable to communicate fully, every new skill took him thrice as long to learn as it would have with a hearing child. She could feel his frustration.

Beckoning him closer, Gabriel cocked his hand back and demonstrated the motion again.

Jason tried, and the ball went farther this time. Jumping up and down, he grinned and pulled on Gabriel's breeks.

Ariana cringed. 'Twas Jason's excitable, overenthusiastic nature that had irritated Ivan. She stepped forward to remove her son from her husband's presence.

Gabriel glanced up and waved her away. "Peace, Ariana. He's almost got it."

Leaning down, he helped Jason grasp the ball and showed him the movement several times before allowing him to try again. This time, her son made a good throw. The wolfhound nearly bounced out of his skin with wiggly canine joy as he bounded after the ball and brought it back.

Jason clapped his hands. Gabriel laughed and patted him on the back encouragingly.

Ariana's heart melted. She knew no other man who would take the time to teach such a skill to a deaf child.

Leaving Jason and the dog to their game, Gabriel walked toward her. "I think he's named dog."

"Named? But he cannot speak."

Gabriel brought his hand to his mouth and opened and closed it as if he were making a puppet talk. "I am unsure, but it seems that he does this to indicate the hound."

Cocking her head to one side, she watched Jason and the dog closely. In a few moments, she saw Jason do the motion Gabriel had shown her.

"Hm-m-m . . ." If this were true, perhaps there would be a breakthrough in being able to communicate with Jason. They stood in silence for a short time as she pondered this new development and her new husband. That such a fearsome man would take time to coach Jason and pay attention to him amazed her. Most unlike any of the other men she knew. Despite the circumstances of their wedding, she felt a surge of attraction to him.

"Where are you off to, wife?"

She indicated her basket. "To the village. Glenna the midwife expects me," she said, grateful that she had a ready excuse.

"I will go with you."

"Nay." If he went, she'd be unable to check on the ladies picking valerian blossoms. "'Tis no trouble for me to go as I've always gone. Edwina said she would accompany me."

He shrugged. "'Tis a good day for a walk."

She gazed at the overcast sky. "It's gray. Surely you have some duty you must attend to."

He smiled, and she was taken slightly aback by how boyishly charming he looked. His green eyes danced. "Pleasure afore duty, my lady."

Tilting her chin down, she gazed up at him. "The saying is 'duty afore pleasure.'"

"Mayhap we need a new saying."

"My lord," she admonished, "truly, you need not come with me."

He did not budge.

She worried her lip with her teeth for a moment. "I've ne'er had a husband go with me about my errands," she said at last.

Reaching forward, he ran a finger across her collarbone.

She shivered at his nearness.

"Ariana, you have had enough husbands you have been afeared of. 'Twould do you well to become accustomed to me." Taking her hand, he led her toward the gate.

Disconcerted, she followed. Her hand felt small and smooth within his large, callused one. His tanned skin contrasted with the lily-white of hers.

They passed a pond and an old farmhouse as they headed down the short path into the village.

How odd to have a husband accompany her. She was unsure what to make of it.

"The midwife's hut is ahead on the right," she said after a time, indicating a small cottage with clumps of dried herbs hanging on the outside down the path a ways.

"I have been here afore."

"Of a truth?"

"With my mother."

"Your mother brought you here?"

"Oft she was with child." He shrugged, his wide shoulders rippling his tunic, and Ariana found she was curious about him.

"What was it like to be the son of, of . . ." Her voice trailed off, and her cheeks heated.

"The son of a harlot?" he supplied.

Blushing, she nodded.

"There were wealthy men around, and life was always chaotic. We were required to go outside the cottage whenever one of mum's 'friends' arrived. The lords came, they brought a little gold, and sometimes planted another seed in her womb."

She turned this knowledge over in her mind. 'Twas no wonder he held a disdain for the members of the nobility. "What was her name?"

"Roselle. Do you have any siblings?"

"No, none."

"Was it dull with no brothers or sisters?"

She contemplated that. Her life had not been dull. But it had been dutiful. "Nay, not dull. I was orphaned when I was but four years of age, so I became a ward of the crown. I was first married at twelve."

"You were but a child."

Sighing, she reflected on her first husband William. "True. But my husband was not around much."

"You should have been playing with dolls, not running a household."

"I did what had to be done. Here we are." She knocked on the cottage door, and Glenna the midwife answered. She was a short, bony woman with waist-length silver hair.

Gabriel waited outside while the midwife prodded and poked and felt her enlarging belly.

"Healthy as a cow," she declared to Gabriel when they were done. "And this baby will be easier than the last, I say. You take care of her, you hear me?"

Gabriel nodded stoically. If Glenna's mannerism bothered him, he did not indicate it.

After they left the midwife, they wound their way around the cobblestone streets while Ariana bargained for fabric and supplies for the keep. They

talked about this and that, about the running of the
keep and who they should hire to repair some of the
rotting boards. Gabriel listened with interest and
made suggestions. 'Twas nice, she decided, to have
someone to talk household matters over with.

At the end of the street, she found poppy seed for
Margaret and gold thread for Dionne. The women
would be thrilled with the little bonus.

Gabriel leaned against the shop wall as she paid for
the purchases. "Have you always bought extras for
your ladies?"

"On occasion. It keeps them happy. They are good
women." Putting the supplies in her basket, she headed
back up the cobbled street. The air had grown chilly, and
'twas time to get home to Rosebriar.

He took her hand as they walked past the shops
again.

She found she enjoyed Gabriel's presence—he neither rushed nor badgered her, but seemed content
simply to be with her in the daily ebb and flow of life.
'Twas a new experience for her.

She waved to the villagers—Mrs. Brown, the cob-
bler's wife; John the smithy; and others. A few
whispered loudly, but even this did not rattle Gabriel's
composure.

As they once again passed the old farmhouse,
Gabriel squeezed her hand. "So you get things for
your servants, but who gets bonuses for you, Ariana?"

She shrugged. What need had she of extras? She
had fine clothes, jewelry, and other things suited to
her station. Her castle was cared for. Of a truth, she
was without lack. "I need naught."

Glancing around, Gabriel walked to the side of the

path. "Wait here, my lady." He bent and plucked several long, fat blades of grass.

Cocking her head to one side, she waited.

Moving the foliage round and round, he twisted the leaves together. Curious, she said naught. He glanced at her as he folded the blades, a knowing smile on his lips. A flutter formed low in her body at his wicked gaze. He was flirting with her! A husband, flirting with her! Of all the ridiculous things.

After a few moments, he proffered the plant. "A rose for my lady."

Blinking, she looked down at the twisted grass. The green edges, folded and creased, resembled a rose. It looked small and dainty against his large hand.

She stared up at her new husband, stunned. One side of his mouth lifted, but he said nothing to indicate what he was thinking.

"My mother taught me how to make them," he said with a shrug.

Their fingers skimmed each other, and heat worked through her as she took it.

She grew tons of roses. She had embroidered roses on fine clothing. She could afford precious jewelry fashioned as roses. But no one had *ever* given her a rose of any kind.

They looked at each other for an awkward moment.

Bringing it to her nose, she inhaled the earthy scent of grass. "'Tis the most beauteous blossom I've ever seen, my lord."

Taking her hand, he walked on to Rosebriar.

Chapter 20

At week's end, Ariana observed Gabriel's white-knuckled grip on the edge of the great table and wondered if coming to Baron Robert's banquet had been a poor plan after all. She intended to collect information about Cyrille, Countess of Carth, for her cousin, but her husband's tight shoulders made her feel guilty that she'd coaxed him into coming. He looked magnificent in his new green tunic, but his glower ruined the effect. She had not realized he would be so uncomfortable at the feast.

Acrobats and jugglers displayed their talents to the accompaniment of a band of loud minstrels. The scents of bread and rich foods wafted around them. Ale and wine flowed freely. Harried servants passed back and forth from the kitchens to the tables carrying ham, eels, and venison. Nobles mingled around the great hall, talking and laughing.

Gabriel and she had settled into a measure of peace, and she hated to see the progress they'd made deteriorate. He'd brought her several more twisted grass roses and some wildflower bouquets. He never explained them or asked for anything in return, but instinctively, she knew what they were. She had always taken care of others. She had gold to spare. She gave and gave and gave. No one brought presents to her.

Now that they were married, he could have emptied her coffers to buy silly trinkets, but instead he gave something more: he gave something of himself. The thought of wild, untamed Gabriel scouring the fields to bring her flowers tickled her inside.

"Are you well, my lord?" she asked, laying her fingers on his forearm.

"Fine." His jaw was clenched so tightly she feared his teeth would crack. He'd become more and more on edge since leaving Rosebriar and nearly intolerable since entering the crush of the feast.

Perhaps she should suggest they leave. But, nay. Cyrille would be here. So long as her cousin held the threat of Ivan's murder over her head, she would spy out the gossip he wanted to hold him at bay. Asides, the countess was no friend of hers—beautiful, haughty, and not particularly likeable—so she had no qualms about this mission.

Motioning a page over to refill Gabriel's goblet, she gazed about the room in search of her quarry.

Mayhap she could gather the information quickly, then Gabriel and she could head back to Rosebriar. Of a truth, she had no love for these feasts and all their chaos. She fanned her face against the sweltering heat.

Taking one of the small feasting crossbows, she speared a hunk of roasted lamb and reeled it in for herself. "Try it, my lord," she coaxed, handing him the bow. Mayhap 'twould set him in a better humor.

He took the bow, turned it over in his large hands,

and set it on the table. " 'Tis silly. Grown men playing with toys."

She sighed, disappointed he had not taken the bait. No doubt a man used to killing prey with a real weapon would take no pleasure in the puny feasting bow. Mayhap she could take him to the gardens later and coax him out of his foul mood.

The musicians started a lively tune, and several sets of nobles rose and swirled their way to the floor for one of the court dances. Others pushed back against the walls.

Gabriel's forearm stiffened against her fingers.

"My lord?"

He was staring grim-faced at her prey. Beautiful as always, Cyrille wore a finely embroidered blue gown and an elaborate hat with two tall points that vaguely reminded Ariana of devil's horns. Several rows of sapphires surrounded her neck. Her husband, a stooped, gray-haired earl, tottered against a wall behind her, holding onto a crooked cane.

The countess was laughing wide-eyed at Lord Longue, whose main sources of pride were the yards and yards of lace around his neck and his long, pointed shoes. Red strings tied the toes of his footwear to his knees so that he would not trip on them. Ridiculous. He looked like a prissy peacock. Ariana nearly rolled her eyes as Cyrille tapped him flirtatiously on the arm with her feathered fan.

"We are leaving," Gabriel announced through gritted teeth.

A streak of panic chilled her. She did not yet have any gossip to appease her cousin. "But, my lord—"

Gabriel stood, his shoulders tight with tension. "Come." He drew her to her feet.

"They will speak ill of us if we do not stay the night."
She took his arm. "Perhaps a walk in the gardens.
Lord Robert has a wondrous maze."

"I do not belong here." Gabriel's gaze flickered
back to Cyrille and the Peacock.

"Nonsense. At least finish your ale," she said, struggling for an excuse to keep him here. The crowd
clapped loudly at a backward flip done by an acrobat.

"Nay. Come now, wife." He headed toward the exit,
passing jugglers and a knife thrower so quickly they
looked like blurs.

She huffed along beside him, trying to keep up
with his long strides, but pregnancy and the ball gown
made running impossible.

"Slow down," she whispered frantically. "I cannot
match your pace." What had him so on edge?

"Gabriel," screeched a high-pitched voice across
several rows of courtiers.

Gabriel's arm stiffened. Ariana turned. Cyrille was bearing down on them like a pig running to a feeding trough.
Her hat's points bobbed as she dashed around a lord
holding a tankard of ale. The music crescendoed.

"Gabriel?"

His bicep felt like iron. "Cyrille."

Ariana gazed from Cyrille's overly bright smile to
Gabriel's taut jaw. The scar on his chin seemed particularly white. "You know each other?"

The points of her hat wavered as Cyrille glanced dismissively at Ariana. "Gabriel and I are *very* old friends."

Swallowing the shot of jealousy that catapulted through
her, Ariana forced herself to smile. "How nice to see you
again, Countess. Is your husband well?"

Cyrille lifted a powdered eyebrow, which had been
plucked down to a few strands as was fashionable. "He

coughs overly much these days. Decrepitude, you know. And how are you? Lord Robert said you were married mere days ago. 'Tis odd you would come here to celebrate your"—she paused significantly—"honeymoon."

No doubt she had heard the whole horrid story of the forced wedding and how Gabriel had thrown Nigel in the dungeon. Ariana felt her face heat.

"Mind yourself," Gabriel said. His gaze flickered to the door.

"Honestly, Gabriel." Cyrille smirked, her fan popping open and closed. "Surely you are not still angry with me over that minor misunderstanding years ago."

She gave him a long, scrutinizing stare that set Ariana's teeth on edge. She was the worst sort—an attractive woman who wielded her beauty like a magician's wand. Men fell prey to her charms like sheep to the shearers. Did Gabriel find her as appealing as the Peacock had? The hair on Ariana's neck bristled.

"So you have married well." Cyrille's gaze roved over his new tunic as if sizing up the cost of the thread, then slid down his new hose and stopped at his old boots—cleaned and polished, but shabby and worn all the same. She tittered. "Such shoes, Gabriel. And to a feast."

"We had not time—" Ariana started.

Cyrille smirked. "You needn't explain. We both know his talents lie in other directions."

Gabriel turned sharply to Ariana. His tunic pulled tight across his hunched shoulders. "Wife, fetch me a tankard of ale." His eyes seemed to plead with hers not to argue with him. In that instant, she knew whate'er had occurred betwixt Gabriel and Cyrille, she had no need for jealousy.

She gritted her teeth and stepped to do as he requested.

"How clever to send your wife away," Ariana heard Cyrille say as soon as her back was turned.

Clenching her fists, she wondered if she had been mistaken at the look Gabriel had given her.

"My dear Gabriel." Cyrille laughed loudly. "I would have taken care of you. You had no need to saddle yourself with an old maid . . ."

Ariana slowed her step.

"A castle is quite an undertaking for someone of your station. What would a whore's son know about running a keep?"

Furious, Ariana turned, not bothering to get the ale. Gabriel might think he could handle taunts alone, but this was women's war. Whate'er battles lay betwixt them, she would not have him dishonored by another, especially not a sly vixen such as Cyrille.

Marching back to them, she shook her finger at Cyrille. Her pregnant stomach bumped the shrew. "Whate'er rumors you may have heard about my new lord, he is more than capable of caring for Rosebriar. Keep a civil tongue."

Cyrille eyed her as if she were a midge to be swatted, then turned to Gabriel. Her pointed hat wobbled and the sapphires encircling her neck sparkled. She smirked. "Be careful, Lord of Rosebriar, or you may meet the same fate as Ariana's last husband. Mayhap you should ask her about the true cause of his demise."

An icy chill fingered its way through Ariana as Cyrille flounced away, her large skirt swirling.

Taking Ariana's hand, Gabriel headed toward the door. "We are leaving."

Ariana laid her fingers on his forearm. "Nay, my lord, prithee. If you do, you will never gain entrance."

"I do not need such."

"Mayhap, no. But you need their respect to manage the lands of Rosebriar and get the best price for wool."

His brows slammed together, and she knew her case was won. Of all things, Gabriel did not shirk his responsibilities. He would do right by her estate.

"Come." She led him forward, wondering about the past relationship between Cyrille and him. "I will get you a cup of ale now. Let us enjoy the labyrinth."

A short time later, they walked along the trimmed hedges of Lord Robert's outdoor maze. Gabriel had never seen the like. With its shallow, overdressed nobles and elaborate décor, the whole estate made him as uncomfortable as a bear in an underwater cage. He wanted naught more than to return to Rosebriar and see to his siblings. Ariana had said staying here was good for the sheep business so for the people of Rosebriar's sake, he would endure the next few hours. She had a good head for making the land prosperous, and he would trust her judgment. But he did not have to enjoy staying here.

Torches lit the lawn, sending smoke spiraling into the night sky. Lengths and lengths of plants swirled round and round providing private alcoves for lovers. Ariana's fingers felt warm on his bicep as they walked along the pathway. Thank the stars they were no longer in the feasting hall. He'd had enough of noblewomen who gave him sly suggestions about where they would be after midnight and noblemen who scrutinized him suspiciously behind guarded expressions. Not to mention those stupid, childish feasting bows.

That Cyrille had suggested he was an unfit lord but a fit lover galled him. Mayhap because he feared there was some truth in it.

"My lord, slow down. This is a pleasure walk, not a race to London." Ariana was panting, holding the hem of her skirt up from the grass.

Gabriel slowed. Taking her hand, he pulled her into one of the private alcoves where a flat rock had been strategically placed to make it seem accidental.

"How is it that you know Cyrille?" she asked once she'd settled on the rock. She spread her velvet skirts around her.

"She is no one."

Ariana tilted her chin down and gazed up at him, clearly waiting for an explanation.

"Did you mean it when you said I would be a worthy lord?"

"Aye. How do you know Cyrille?" she repeated.

Gabriel blew out a breath. There would be no peaceful living with her until the tale was told in all its awkward detail. "I met her long ago."

"And you were in love?" Ariana supplied when he paused.

"I thought I was." He grimaced and stared upward into the heavens. "We were to be wed."

"She was to marry you?"

He nodded, hating the story. Telling it made his mouth feel like he'd tasted rotten meat. "I waited at the altar, and she sent a message telling me whore's sons and noblewomen did not marry."

Ariana's hand on his shoulder warmed him.

"I was a fool." Thumbing his lower lip, he gazed at her. In that moment, he knew he could not bear Ariana's rejection. He had thought all noblewomen were like Cyrille, but he had been wrong. Ariana had saved Eric. Saved Joel. She'd stood up for him against Cyrille. She'd fed and clothed and bathed his siblings. He'd taken her captive, seduced her, made her pregnant, and forced her to marry him. She was used to silks and music and fine food. She deserved better than a peasant such as he. Standing abruptly, he pulled her to her feet.

"She spoke the truth, Ariana. I am a whore's son. I should not have forced you to marry me."

He watched her swallow. "My lord—"

But he was not a lord. He was the son of a harlot. The fancy feast made him uncomfortable and crowded. His newly stitched tunic scratched. The air seemed stuffy and too hot. He wanted his leather breeks, his crossbow, and a ride in the moonlight— mayhap even a chance to go to the waterfall and bathe in a pool instead of a tub. He had naught to give her but folded roses and wild flowers.

He pulled her forward, guided her quickly out of the maze, into the keep, and down the corridor, then walked her into the chamber Lord Robert had given them.

She was panting and holding her stomach by the time they made it to the room. "Goodness, Gabriel. Was the devil chasing us?"

He gazed about the furnished room. For all its richness, it made him cold. Nay, he could not give her riches like one of the nobility, but he did have something he could give her: he could erase the memory of Ivan and return her passion to her. The very thought stirred his blood, and he could scarcely wait until they were back to the privacy of Rosebriar. But for now, he wanted some time alone to think.

"Sleep. I will return soon." He slammed from the room.

Chapter 21

Two hours later, Gabriel's large, warm arm flopped across Ariana's chest, pinning her to the bed. She lurched awake to the sound of soft breathing.

All was darkness. Deep, swirling darkness.

She whimpered, biting her lip to keep from crying out. Her maids knew better than to allow the fire to die and leave her in the dark, but she was not at home.

Her heart pounded. She gazed into the blackness around her, imagining grotesque demons sliding between the bed curtains to pounce on her. She forced herself to breathe in and out. In and out. 'Tis a child's fear. 'Tis a child's fear, she chanted silently, but numbness spread through her limbs as the shadows seemed to undulate around her.

Rustling noises sounded. The headboard clattered against the stone wall. She screamed and lurched upright, jiggling the bed.

A hand clamped across her mouth. "Quiet, girl; 'tis me."

Gasping for air, she pushed blindly against her captor. His body hovered above hers. She opened her mouth to scream against his palm. The smell of spices and virile male filled her senses.

"Peace, Ariana." Gabriel's husky voice calmed her frayed nerves, and her fear began to trickle away.

For a heart-stopping second, a wild internal desire urged her to lick his palm to see if he tasted as masculine as he smelled. He released her mouth afore her nitwitted impulses could be enacted.

"Get off me," she gasped.

"Be calm, girl. You are safe." His composed tone soothed her.

She drew in a deep breath as she turned his words over in her mind. Safe. She had never felt safe being married. And now?

She swallowed, not trusting the direction of her thoughts.

"When did you come to bed?" she asked.

"Only a bit ago."

He eased away, but she could still feel his body's warmth. The mattress shook, and the heat lessened. She felt him shift into a sitting position and then heard him shuffle with the tinderbox and candle that lay beside the bed.

Sparks flickered. A candle flame rushed away the darkness. She stared at him. Shirtless, his chest was a landscape of magnificent valleys and hills. The shadow caressing the midst of his torso magnified his masculinity. A shiver went through her.

He was strong. She didn't like strong men, she reminded herself firmly.

But mayhap he was strong enough to chase away the night demons, her body argued.

She should have felt afraid of him as she had of Ivan. She searched her mind. She was afraid of the dark, afraid of her nightmares, afraid of this marriage, afraid of the future. But she was not afraid of Gabriel.

Except for Nigel, she had never known a man she wasn't a little afraid of. She even kept her guards at bay.

Fascinated with this new line of thought, she reached out and touched him. Warm, firm muscles flinched under her fingers. She drew her hand back as if burned. What was she thinking?

He chuckled, grasped her wrist, pulled her hand back to his chest, and laid her palm flat against him. "I like you touching me."

A thrill of womanly heat went through her veins. "I should not," she protested.

"Why?"

She sputtered for a moment, unable to think of an answer.

He cocked his head to one side. His dark, shoulder-length hair stuck out at odd angles. "Why did you scream?" he asked, changing the subject.

She cringed. How could she tell him her ridiculous childish fear? He'd probably never been afraid of anything in his life. "I had a bad dream," she lied.

Holding the candle aloft, he scrutinized her face with an intense gaze. The low light made his eyes look black instead of green.

She smiled tightly, waiting for him to finish his gawking.

"You are lying," he said.

"Of course I am not."

"You are." He cupped her face with his misshapen hand. Tenderness and strength melded together in his touch. "Tell me your fear."

"I told you already. 'Twas a bad dream."

He eased back from his looming position, grabbed a couple of pillows and stuffed them beneath her head and upper back so that she sat up slightly.

"There was no dream," he said calmly. "There was only the two of us. Am I so frightening?"

"Nay. Aye. Nay." She crossed her arms and stared at the swinging bed curtains.

"Ariana." His voice was husky, bordering on erotic. "'Tis twice you have shown this blind fear, yet you show uncommon courage in other situations such as when those men attacked me. Not to mention standing up to Cyrille. Come. Tell me."

She shifted her eyes.

He intertwined his fingers in hers. His missing finger made her ring finger and small digit smash together, but it did not distract from the strength radiating from his hand. She ran her finger along the scar. "You said your finger was cut off by slavers. What else happened?"

He tightened his grip on her hand, which pressed her fingers even closer together. "If I tell you, will you confess your fear to me?"

"Why should I care?" she said churlishly, not wanting to tell him anything.

At once, he released her hand, withdrawing its heat from hers. He held his hand up in the candlelight. The twisted form made a gruesome shadow on the bed curtains.

"Ivan paid for someone to steal my sister," he said, flexing his hand. "The damn greedy pig. Serfs are like property, not even considered human. I tried to fight. They cut off my fingers."

All surliness left her in a whoosh. "Ivan did this?" Her voice sounded small and far away. "Dear God."

In a terse voice, Gabriel reiterated the horrors of that night his sister was stolen.

Ariana shivered. "What did you do afterward?"

"I searched for her. I spent my boyhood on ships and in alleys, stealing what food I could as I searched. I tracked down numerous villains and highwaymen and became good at tracking."

"But your sister?"

"I found her in a harem." His erotic voice took on a flat, bleak tone. "I brought her home, but she ne'er truly recovered. She lives in our old hut and does not greet outsiders." He turned, his green eyes glittering like emeralds.

"It was not your fault."

"What are you afraid of, Ariana?" he asked, turning the conversation back to its earlier topic.

"Me?"

"Aye."

Taking a deep breath, she squeezed her eyes shut. "I am afraid of the dark."

Silence. Then, "The dark?" He chuckled.

Anger shot through her. What a fool she had been to think she could trust him with her fear.

Sitting up, she grabbed a pillow and walloped him in the chest with it. The motion blew out the candle, shrouding them in darkness. She was too angry to care. She smacked him with the pillow again.

He laughed harder.

A pop sounded, and feathers tickled her nose as the pillow burst. "'Tis not funny!"

The pillow was yanked from her hands, and strong fingers latched on to her wrists. Gabriel pressed her to the mattress, careful to avoid squeezing her pregnant belly.

Instinct told her to fight, but unbidden, feminine craving wiggled through her. Be soft, it urged.

"Surrender, girl. If I planned to harm you, I would have done so already. Surely you know this."

Slowly, she relaxed, her body buzzing with restless energy. His calves paralleled her legs as he sat atop her thighs, anchoring her to the mattress. She took a shallow breath; the weight of her pregnant stomach pressed down on her lungs, disallowing the luxury of deep breathing.

Through her shift, something prodded her between her legs. Abruptly, she realized he was naked. His manhood pressed into the vee between her legs just below her rounded stomach. Her shift had scrunched up her thighs. Moonlight trailed across his skin. She shivered.

"Are you afraid now?" he asked, releasing one of her wrists to trail his fingers gently down the length of her forearm.

She should be. There was no doubt about that. In the dark, under the hand of a huge, dominating man, she should be terrified. But was she?

She could have sworn she heard him smile. "I will release your hands, but leave them as they are. Do not move."

An erotic hum buzzed the air as he released both wrists. The backs of her hands pressed against the mattress.

"Focus on my voice. Just on my voice."

She did not move her hand. It seemed very important to obey him. This new game had a daring thrill. Oh, so different than it had ever been with Ivan.

"Breathe deeply, Ariana."

"I cannot."

"You can't?"

"The baby."

He rolled her slightly on her side. The weight on her lungs lessened so that she could take a deep breath.

"Are you afraid?"

"Nay." She shook her head, amazed she spoke the truth.

"Good. Leave your hands thus." He spread her hands out on the sheet. "Nothing will happen here that you do not wish. Can you trust me?"

Slowly, he ran his finger down the length of her index finger and the seam between it and her next digit. "Turn your palms up for me."

"Why?"

"Because it makes you more vulnerable." She heard a catch of desire in his voice when she complied. "And I want you to trust me that you are alright."

He drew soft circles with his fingertips in the palm of her hand. A shiver of delight went through her. Wicked. This man was wicked.

"Why are you afraid of the dark?"

"I—" An evil image of Ivan flickered into her mind and then was gone as Gabriel drew a little circle in her palm with his finger.

"I want you to pretend this is the most intimate part of your sex," he whispered, changing the subject.

The area between her legs felt hot, flushed with blood.

He touched the place where her thumb pad connected with the muscle to her smallest digit. "The ancient texts say a woman's secret parts are linked to this place in her palm."

Disconcerted, she blinked.

More tiny circles.

"Have you always feared the dark?" he asked, changing the subject yet again.

"Nay," she whispered.

His hand paused. "Tell me."

She bit her lip. "Ivan would come to me in the night. Sometimes alone, sometimes not." A shiver ran through her.

"And?" His finger drew another circle, replacing her fear with desire.

Her brain felt cloudy, befuddled. She tried to fight away the cobwebs and think clearly.

"Relax, girl. Cease trying to logic it out and just feel."

His deep voice resonated around her, conjuring up images of sandy beaches and warm sunlight.

"He enjoyed startling me, I think. Whenever I had the candle lit, he could not do that. He would just come in and start pounding away inside me."

Gabriel kissed her forehead. "He is gone. There is only you and I."

She blinked, trying to get a handle on her feelings, but, oh, dear, sweet, merciful heavens, he began to sing.

"Sleep, my lov—"

She gasped. "Gabriel! I used to sing that song to myself when he came. 'Twas something my mother sang to me!"

"What happened to her?"

"She died when I was young. 'Tis all I remember of her."

"Hm-m-m." He kissed her again, this time on the cheek. "And your father?"

"I do not remember him at all. I have been a ward of the king most of my life."

"I'll tell you what, Ariana. Whenever you are afraid of the dark, tell me, and I'll sing it to you."

A lump formed in her throat. Ne'er in her life had someone offered to sing for her. No wonder Joel had calmed when he was held in Gabriel's arms. No wonder all his siblings depended on him. He was the sort of man who could chase away nightmares with a word.

"*Sleep, my love,*" he sang the soft lullaby. Haunting. Husky. His song was low in pitch, and seemed to come from deep inside himself. Not at all how her mother used to sing it. Or how it had sounded when she sung it to herself. She was unsure if he spoke in actual words or simply in tones and syllables.

The melody called to her, beckoning, promising. Erotic.

She felt dizzy, intoxicated by his voice.

With a sigh, she surrendered, relaxing her body so it sank into the mattress. All the while, he made circles the size of a coin on her palm.

"You need never fear the dark, Ariana," he murmured, stopping the song for a moment. "The dark is made for feeling. Feel this." He drew his finger up one side of her palm and then the other. "Pretend 'tis your queynt, my lady. And this is one side of your quim, and here is your other."

"Gabriel," she whispered, "'tis not." But she felt blood rushing to her nether lips. Her sex felt swollen. Surely he didn't know though. Surely.

But he kept drawing circles. And he kept humming.

"And here, pretend 'tis that most sensitive spot, the one above your queynt where your pleasure culminates," he said, pressing lightly on the pad beneath her middle finger. "Some call it a woman's jewel."

She nearly gasped, for it felt as though he had just touched her sex on that tender bud, the place where he'd licked and teased on the rock.

He drew his hand back to the middle of her palm and continued with the tight circles, pressing more firmly now.

She licked her lips. Her sex burned. The place on her lower back just above her hip tingled. Shifting on the mattress, she felt herself floating in a dreamlike state. Abruptly, she caught herself. Her body urged her to surrender, but her conscience pricked her. This was not right so long as Nigel rotted in a cell.

"My lord?" She closed her hand around Gabriel's fingers, stilling them.

Heat poured off his skin, and she could tell he wanted her as much as she wanted him. Mayhap she could negotiate for Nigel's release.

"Aye?"

"A bargain?"

"Of what sort?"

"Release Nigel, and I will willingly be a true wife."

Gabriel growled and rolled from atop her. "You will have sex with me in trade for Nigel?"

"Prithee, I cannot bear for him to rot in the dungeon."

The bed jiggled as he sat up. "Enough about Nigel."

"But Nigel is my dear friend."

"No longer."

"You cannot choose my friends." Withdrawing her hand from his, she laced her fingers together. She resisted the urge to wipe her palm on her shift, as she did not want Gabriel to know how much he affected her. Her palm still burned where he had touched her.

So did her sex.

"Nigel stays as a hostage against your good behavior," Gabriel said. She shuddered at the black tone that had entered his voice.

Frustrated with the turn of the conversation, she rolled onto her side and stared at the door.

The mattress shifted, and his large body spooned her smaller one, his heat pressed against her back.

She stiffened as his hand traced a fiery line from her shoulder to her hip, then back up, and down the length of her arm to her hand. She raised her head to protest.

"Sh-h," he admonished, taking her hand in his.

When he did not move or try to jump atop her, she relaxed slightly. He did naught. Only lay behind her, holding her hand, his thumb pressing gently into her palm. But in her mind, she could hear his voice. *Pretend this is your queynt. And here is your quim. A woman's jewel.*

She tried to conjure Nigel's face in her mind, but could not see him at all. How wicked she was to betray her friend so quickly. She vowed to go through with her plans for a feast as soon as they returned.

The vee betwixt her legs felt hot. And wet. Every now and again, Gabriel's fingers twitched, but she had no idea if 'twas accidental or apurpose. She clenched her hand, not wanting to feel the desire pulsing through her as his thumb moved ever so slightly. 'Twas as if all the sensation in her palm was directly linked to the nerves on that place—her woman's jewel—between her thighs. Just as he had said.

She tried to think of the dungeon where Nigel slept to give her strength to shake him off.

"Be still," Gabriel commanded. "Or we will finish what we have begun."

Closing her eyes, she feigned sleep. But he did not release her hand.

Chapter 22

A short time later, Ariana was positive Gabriel slept. She slowly removed her hand from his and sat up on the bed. Thorns. How could she betray Nigel so swiftly?

She pushed the thought aside and rubbed her forehead. Her life felt like uncultivated vines, the strands tightly woven into a miserable tangle. Ivan. Randall. Nigel. Gabriel.

Blowing out a breath, she reached for her wrapper and rose to complete her spying duties for Randall. 'Twas well after midnight now, and no doubt, the more vulgar activities would have begun.

"Ariana?" Gabriel asked, his voice gravelly with slumber.

She laid her hand across his cheek. "Sh-h. Do not awaken. I go to check on Francine, my maid. She is uncomfortable in new places."

"Be back soon."

"Aye."

Rolling over, he let out a moan, and his breathing deepened.

Leaving, she allowed herself a small smile. Getting past Gabriel had been simpler than expected. If the rest of the mission went as well, she would be back afore he awoke again. And if this was usual, then mayhap she could satisfy both Randall as a spy and Gabriel as a wife.

She dressed, crept from the room, and made her way toward the lords and ladies still in the feasting hall. Likely they would drink wine until dawn.

When Cyrille was not in the great hall, she turned to explore the other hallways of the keep. She came upon pairs of drunken lovers and was forced to hide several times. Lord Robert's door hung partially open. Quietly pushing it open an inch further, she saw him mounting Lord Seymour's wife.

Further down, another lord gave drunken instructions for one of the kitchen boys to undress him. The boy was trying, with minimal success, to explain that this was not his duty. Behind another door, Lady Hamptom moaned across her mattress while Lord Grinnway and his wife frigged her roughly with a carrot.

Ariana shook her head and snuck further down the hall. An overly high-pitched titter caught her attention: Cyrille. At last.

Making her way quietly to Cyrille's door, she bent to spy into the crack between the doorframe and the wooden panel. She heard moans and giggles, but the tightly fitted door prevented her from seeing whom the woman coupled with. Thorns! She would be forced to use the window. Turning, she tiptoed to the manor's exit, taking careful note of how many doors she passed as she made her way into the gardens.

Carefully picking her way around the flowers, she

positioned herself behind a rosebush and peered through the window. 'Twas getting more arduous as her stomach increased in size. But luckily, she was not clumsy in pregnancy or overly large as some women were apt to be. Glenna had spoken the truth when she'd said she was hale.

Cyrille, wearing her pointed hat and naught much else, knelt on the mattress, buttocks high in the air. The Peacock tickled her sex with the elongated points of his footwear, which had been untied from his knees. The countess moaned and flopped and ground her hips into the air as if she had paroxysm. Of all the weird things.

After a bit, Cyrille slid partway off the bed with a moan. One point of her hat crumpled against the mattress, and the Peacock began stuffing his shoe inside her. Ariana cringed and turned aside. She'd seen enough. A woman should not have to live with that sort of picture floating around in her head.

Shuddering, she picked her way back around the rosebush. A curly strand of her hair caught on one of the thorns and pulled against her scalp.

Afore she could get free, a thick hand covered her mouth, and a brawny arm encircled her waist. She gasped and tried to scream, but no sound passed the harsh grip of the man's palm. The babe in her womb kicked.

"Checking on your maid, wife?" Gabriel whispered.

Thorns! A tremor worked through her shoulders.

He pulled her from behind the rosebushes, scooped her in his arms, and headed back to their chamber.

"I can explain," she started. "I—"

"Not one word until we reach our room, wife, or I

will march you to Rosebriar wearing a scold's bridle."
She had not seen him so furious since the wedding.
The scar on his chin glowed white in the moonlight.

She bit her tongue.

Once in their chamber, he deposited her unceremoniously on the bed. Her hair flew into her face, and her skirts wound about her legs. She scrambled to untangle herself as Gabriel lit a candle.

"I—"

He pinned her with a dark gaze and lifted an eyebrow.

Shuddering, she decided the wisest course was to clamp her lips together and wait for his anger to cool. The scold's bridle was a thick iron cage that surrounded a woman's head and held her tongue down. Most considered their use archaic, but John the smithy frequently used one on his wife, not that it helped her gossiping habit much. Ariana had no desire to test whether Gabriel thought the device was antiquated or not. He flexed and unflexed his fist in a manner that made her wonder if he wished he had his crossbow.

"This was the true reason for us to go to this feast, was it not?" He stated it in a way that told her it was not a question.

Wary of his mood, she nodded.

He sat in a chair by the hearth and crossed one booted foot over the other knee. "I was very clear that there would be no more spying."

Licking her lips, she debated how to answer. Or even if she should.

"I had thought you were not as treacherous as other noblewomen. But now I find you would trade your body for Nigel and have no qualms about being a Peeping Tom."

Guilt cut through her. She opened her mouth to speak, but he quelled her with a glance.

Candleglow flickered across his strong jaw. "I warned you after the wedding that all spy activity must cease."

Dear heavens, if only it were as simple as ceasing. But Randall would have her convicted of murder if she did not bring him the gossip he wanted.

The bed ropes creaked as she scooted to the edge of the mattress and stood.

Gabriel thumbed his lower lip and seemed to be scrutinizing her.

Encouraged that he said naught, she glided across the room to stand before him.

"My lord," she ventured. Then waited. When he did not silence her, she held her hand out to him, palm up. "May I speak?"

His fingers flinched on the arms of the chair, but he did not take her outstretched hand. "Ariana, how often do you do this sort of activity?"

She deliberated the best way to talk her way out of this. "Not oft."

Taking her hand, which was still outstretched, he drew a slow circle within her palm.

She shivered as heat flowed unbidden to her sex and tried to draw her hand away.

"Do not play games, Ariana. You cannot win." He drew another circle in her palm.

The edges of the room tilted as if reality was a little out of line. Heavens! What had he done to her this night? In her mind she heard him say, *pretend this is your quim.*

"The truth now. How often?"

More circles, until she felt dizzy, hot, disconcerted. She licked her lips, unsure how much of the gentle pressure she could take on her palm before she melted straightaway into the floor. He spoke the truth: she did not know how to play this game at all. "Mayhap once every two or three weeks."

"Was the truth so difficult?" He released her hand, and she wiped her fingers against her palm. The skin burned and itched. How did he do such things to her senses?

He ran his hand across the back of his neck as if rubbing away a thick knot. "Is this the first time since we have been wed?"

"Yes."

"On my honor, I have assured the king that he will have no more trouble from The Spy of the Night."

For a second, her gaze flickered to the door, and she wished she could run as she had so many times. Her breath felt squeezed, shallow. If she continued, Gabriel would take her to the king as a spy. If she did not, Randall would take her to the church to be tried as a murderess.

She shuddered. There was nowhere to run. Six months earlier, she'd chosen to remain a spy instead of trusting Gabriel. She glanced down at his hand with the three fingers. It had been cut while defending his sister. She remembered how it looked patting Joel on the back and how it looked when he twisted grass roses for her.

He was a barbarian, a ruffian. But he was also a man who took care of his own. She would have to trust him this time.

"Gabriel." She reached for his hand and knelt in front of him so they were nearer in height.

His face was impassive, and he remained stock-still. Remembering how he had been with his horse, she threaded her fingers into his. He had not wanted to care for the stallion either, had not even given it a name, but he was not the type of man who could disregard others. He'd been so gentle in teaching Jason how to throw a ball.

"Gabriel, I need help."

She saw the anger drain from his eyes.

"I do not want to spy. My cousin. Jason. Ivan." Thorns. It all seemed so tangled. So complicated to explain. Licking her lips, she prayed for the right words. When none came, she took a deep breath. "I killed Ivan," she blurted.

He leaned closer to her, taking a tight grip on her hand.

Her heart pounded, and she held her breath. The church viewed murdering one's husband a crime against God. Would Gabriel see it as such?

"What happened?" he said calmly. He uncrossed his legs and pulled her closer so she knelt within the circle of his body. His cheek nuzzled the top of her head.

Relieved that he had not yanked her to her feet and hauled her straight to London, she let out her breath and shuffled closer. He felt warm.

"I had to. To protect Jason." She allowed her thoughts to drift until she felt that only Gabriel anchored her to the ground. "He had no patience for children, certainly none for precocious two-year-olds. He boxed his ears, and they began to bleed. I tried to run, to take the baby."

Gabriel hugged her as if he were trying to shoulder some of her burden.

"He attacked us in the forest." Shuddering, she gripped his hand more tightly.

"You did what had to be done."

She tilted her head to look at him and bumped him on the chin with her forehead. "My cousin took Ivan's body and told everyone ruffians had killed him. No one dared question him because he's the bishop. He began to ask for things—for me to go hither and yon to collect information. Of a truth, I am unsure what he does with it. He has contacts all over England."

Gabriel drew her to her feet and settled her into his lap. His hair fell across his jaw, creating an interesting line on his cheek.

She rested her head on his chest, inhaling the spicy outdoorsman's scent that lingered on him despite his new clothes and him spending the day indoors. Her red hair spilled over her shoulder and trailed into her lap.

"At first, it seemed simple—entertaining even— to sneak around daringly learning the naughty secrets of the peers. But soon I came to realize he had no intention of ever letting me stop." Leaning away, she stared into the hearth. "He will have me tried as a murderess."

"You should have told me sooner." Gabriel pressed his hand to her cheek, his fingers warm against her skin. "I will protect you."

Whether truth or no, it felt good to have someone promise such. She sighed.

"You must trust me with all of it." He took her hand in one of his and drew a small circle. "Just as you trusted me with the dark."

Closing her eyes, she felt herself being sucked into a world where only the two of them existed. With his other hand, he tilted her chin up so he could kiss her. The area betwixt her legs felt slick already. His thumb pressed her palm. *Pretend this is your quim, your woman's jewel.*

"I cannot give you riches, Ariana. But I can give you strength if you will allow me to."

Her heart quickened, and she latched on to his shoulders, pulling him closer. The room spun as he stood and carried her to the bed. She kissed him urgently, her mouth devouring his. Her body felt alive and hungry for him. Starved. In quick movements, he stripped the garments from her body.

"Stars." His voice was rough with wonderment as his hands slid possessively across her tight, rounded stomach. Ne'er in her life had a man ever looked at her with such desire. Rapidly, he shucked both his boots and hose.

Heavens. He was huge. Just as she remembered. The edge of his tunic bobbed across the top of his member, hiding and revealing it in a provocative dance. But she had no patience for such. She reached for him, sliding his garment to one side, wanting to touch his maleness. She remembered he'd called it his cock and felt her face heat at the crude word even as she felt her queynt moisten.

He growled softly. Flipping onto his back, he pulled her atop him so she straddled his hips. The mattress jiggled. The curly ends of her hair glittered across the emerald of his tunic. Saints, he was beautiful—large and dangerous. She moved her head to take in the expanse of his chest. One tendril of her hair tangled with his nether hair and wrapped around his member.

The red-gold lock contrasted with the nearly purple skin of his cock.

He sucked in a breath as she unwound it. "Christ, girl, climb atop me."

She blushed. "I've ne'er done it like this afore."

"Lift your hips, and pretend I am a maypole."

His solemnity struck her as hilarious, and unable to help herself, she giggled. He chuckled too. The tiny lines around his eyes crinkled, and his dashing smile flashed in the candlelight.

Taking one of her hips in each hand, he guided her atop him. The wet folds of her sex parted easily, and she gasped as she was fully impaled on his member.

"Dear heavens, Gabriel." With the babe in her womb and his member in her queynt, she'd ne'er felt so full in her life. "'Tis been too long."

"Aye. Too long."

"I missed you. I wanted you all those months I thought you were dead. I should have married you just as you wanted."

"We are married now." His hands slid up her belly to rest on her nipples.

Lightning sensation spread through her. "They are so sensitive," she gasped.

He spread his hands flat and gently pressed outward, then ran his palms across her stomach. The babe roiled. He smiled, a look of complete male satisfaction quirking his lips.

Closing her eyes, she placed her hands on his shoulders and rocked back and forth. She felt as if she were floating. Ne'er before had she been able to control the depth or speed during coitus, and she found the sensation wondrous.

She leaned forward, then back, exploring how the subtle change in position affected the feel on her quim.

Gabriel ran his fingers softly down her arm and took her hand in his. He pressed his thumb into her palm, and she gasped as hot wetness flooded her sex.

Pretend this is your quim.

Her eyes flew open. How was it he had so much control over her body when all he was doing was lying there stroking her hand?

"Do not try to logic it out," he murmured. "Just feel."

Giving fully into her desire, she sped up her movements so that his member slid in and out her. She curled forward so she could see past her rounded belly. Amazed, she watched his manhood—his cock, she corrected herself—betwixt the pink nether lips of her sex.

She slowed. She sped up. She slowed again. She sighed; each sensation was more riveting than the last. She shifted to the left, then to the right.

"Christ, girl," Gabriel moaned. "Enough experimenting. We have our whole lives to enjoy this."

Her gaze jolted to his face. He seemed strained on the edge of something beautiful. His fists twisted in the linen sheet, and his jaw clenched. A surge of sheer feminine power shivered through her.

Abandoning propriety, she bucked her hips wildly, letting herself ride him without restraint.

He moaned and grasped her hips, guiding them both into heightened ecstasy. For long moments, they took pleasure in each other's bodies.

The place he'd called her woman's jewel tingled. She widened the position of her knees so she could press it closer. Ripples of sensation skipped through her. She quivered and cried out.

He moaned, his large body arching slightly off the mattress, and she felt his hot liquid surge inside her.

Wrung out, they floated. She sat atop him, eyes closed, feeling the sensations wave through her body. After a time, his member softened and eased from her sex. Even that feeling was warm and delicious.

Still in his arms, she lay beside him on the bed and placed her head on his chest.

'Twas hours later afore Ariana even remembered Nigel.

Chapter 23

"Where are we going?" Ariana giggled as Gabriel covered her eyes with his hands and led her out of the keep.

"I have a gift for you."

He'd brought her another bouquet of wildflowers this morning, and she'd remembered his words at Lord Robert's: *I cannot give you riches, but I can give you strength.*

His strength was worth more than riches.

Guilt over Nigel skipped through her, but she quelled it with the thought that soon she would be able to release him. 'Twas best to tend to her and Gabriel's relationship in the meantime.

Jason ran up to them, and Gabriel was forced to remove his hands from her eyes. He swung the boy into his arms. Jason laughed, hugged him, then made his motion for dog. Gabriel let him down, and he went to play with the hound.

Slipping a hand in his, she raised an eyebrow. "So this gift?"

"'Tis at the waterfall."

Heat spread through her as she thought of their time at the waterfall.

"Come, my lady."

With a smile, she followed him.

A short time later, Gabriel reined his stallion in by the bush they would have to crawl under. They ducked under the shrub and headed toward the sound of rushing water. Thankfully, her growing stomach did not impede her way. 'Twas thus with her first child as well—fit and hale and unencumbered until well into her eighth month.

She stood and looked at the pool and the water pouring off the cliff. 'Twas not as she remembered. Purple foxgloves grew all along the water's edge. Tube-shaped lavender blooms framed the basin.

She gasped. 'Twas even more magical and beautiful than it had been afore. The water rippled in peaceful waves, and the ferns undulated in the breeze. The earthy scent of moss tinged the air.

Gabriel smiled. "I am glad you like it. I saved some for your garden." He pointed to one side of the clearing.

Turning, she saw a hoe and several small jars filled with foxgloves.

Her jaw slackened as realization dawned. "You *planted* these here?"

She stared from him to the flowers and back again. He would have had to take them from the meadows and then crawled on his hands and knees to bring them here.

"Why?"

"You said you liked purple flowers, that you wanted some for your garden. I wanted you to think of this place, of the pleasure we shared, every time you saw them."

A lump formed in her throat. "You did this for me?"

"Only for you."

Throwing her arms around him, she kissed him. With Gabriel, life was grass roses, purple flowers, and waterfalls. Warmth and passion and cherishing. The men and children brought lots of noise and chaos, but lots of laughter, too. Before he'd come, her life had been peaceful but dull. She had not realized how dull it was. She'd had all the gold she could want but no joy. 'Twas as if she had not even truly been alive.

"I love you." The words fell out of her mouth before she could stop them.

Laughing, he kissed her back. "Truly?"

She swallowed. If only they did not have Nigel's imprisonment between them.

Chapter 24

Two days later, Margaret stopped stirring a pot of stew long enough to hand Ariana a missive from Randall as she walked into the kitchen. Cringing, Ariana opened the wax seal on the letter.

My dear cousin,
I have not yet received word on how you enjoyed Lord Robert's banquet. I hope you are well. I would not wish for anything untoward to happen to you.

A hard lump formed in her throat. Her cousin expected answers. Would he come here when she failed to send anything? Mayhap she could scribble out a few notes from the banquet and take them to the abbey.

But, nay. Since the feast, the relationship between Gabriel and herself had blossomed, and she did not wish to break their peace. Her life was more chaotic, but more interesting, too. Laughter rang out all over the keep.

Of a truth, she enjoyed having someone about to shoulder some of the burdens of running a keep, especially since his men stayed out of the kitchens and the great hall during the day now. He had no training in taking care of a castle, but had taken a great interest in the defenses. He asked so many questions of the guards and elderly men that his willingness to learn had quickly gained their respect.

And yet, despite their peace and despite spending the last few nights in heated embrace, he had not released Nigel. She had assumed he kept Nigel as assurance for her good behavior. But surely he could see that his imprisonment was no longer necessary.

Biting her lip, she decided to give her cousin's missive to Gabriel regardless. She would not risk their fragile relationship over Randall. Already she fretted over how releasing Nigel would affect their marriage.

Edwina entered the kitchen, giggling as she did every time Rodney looked at her with his one eye. If her giddiness was any indication, the next batch of ale would be divine.

"The ale, Edwina?" Ariana asked.

"Almost ready, me lady. Right."

Good. The valerian blossoms had been gathered, and Margaret had been wringing and plucking chickens for hours on end.

A few days more, and she could set Nigel free. Then Gabriel and she could truly have a marriage. *If* her cousin did not see her hung for murder in the meantime.

"Oh, mercy, mistress. Be you well?" Margaret laid aside her wooden spoon and wiped her hands on her apron. "You looked distressed."

Ariana tucked Randall's missive into her girdle. "Just tired." She patted her stomach. "The babe grows heavier. I am going to the garden for a while." She wanted to gaze on her purple flowers once more.

Margaret wrung her hands in her apron. "There is something I must confess. Oh, mercy, mistress."

"Yes, Margaret?" Likely, she'd overcooked the peas. She took any minor mishap in the kitchens to heart.

"I . . . Oh, saints. Oh, mercy."

Ariana leaned closer and patted Margaret's fleshy arm.

"I was worried about your marriage. I did not know Lord Gabriel at the time. 'Twas I who put the note about the poison in your chamber."

"What is this about poison?" Gabriel said, striding into the kitchens.

Both Ariana and Margaret jumped.

"Oh, saints. Oh, mercy." Margaret looked paler than fog.

He reached them in four strides and kissed Ariana on the forehead. "Were you planning to poison me, Margaret?"

"Oh, mercy. Oh, saints."

Ariana glanced upward and caught the teasing gleam in his eye. He was joking! He did not suspect a thing. Chances were all he'd heard was the word "poison."

"I-I-I—" Margaret started.

"Oh for the love of Saint Jude, Gabriel," Ariana cut in, quickly turning and kissing him on the lips. Gabriel might be teasing now, but he would *not* be if he learned of the poison note or the drugged meal they planned. "You will give her the dropsy with that glower."

His eyes twinkled, clearly pleased that she'd kissed him in the midst of the kitchen. He put his arm around her waist and regarded her rounded belly possessively.

She shot a glance at Margaret, who was still wringing her hands. Taking the hint, the cook went back to stirring her pot.

Ariana pulled her cousin's letter from her girdle. "My lord, the bishop sent a missive."

Frowning, Gabriel took the parchment and steered her into the herb garden situated outside the kitchen doors. The fresh rosemary teased her nostrils.

"Would you like me to read the letter?" she asked.

He opened the parchment. "I can read."

"Oh." She had no idea why this pleased her so much. Most nobles considered reading to be beneath them, the work of scribes and solicitors. Of the three husbands she'd had before him, William had been the only one who knew how to read.

A deep line formed on his forehead as he scanned her cousin's missive. He tucked the note into his belt. "I will take care of it."

She chewed her lip. "What do you plan?"

"Have you any other missives?" he asked, not answering her question. "Some with more suspicious wording?"

"Nay. Always they are thus—sly and veiled. He knows I cannot confess what I know of him without also incriminating myself."

"I will go to the abbey and speak with him."

It felt as though a weight had been dropped on her chest. If something happened to him because of her, she could not bear it. Last time he'd gone to the abbey, he'd been bound in iron chains.

"Nay, Gabriel. You mustn't."

"He will listen to me. He must be at Thornbury now for you to have received this so quickly after Robert's banquet."

"Nay. 'Tis a poor plan." She shook her head and

plucked a sprig of rosemary off the nearby bush to calm her worries. "He is too powerful."

"I will not have him bothering you."

Turning, she laid her fingers on his chest. His chest felt warm and firm against her fingers, and a frisson of desire flicked through her. The scent of rosemary wafted around them. "Prithee. 'Tis unwise."

"What would you have me do?"

"Just wait," she pleaded. "I will send him a letter."

He looked like he'd just eaten a bug. "'Tis a woman's way. I will speak with him and insist he leave us be."

She cringed. 'Twas too dangerous. "Please, Gabriel. Sending a letter would be the best choice. Then we can see how he reacts and prepare accordingly."

Frowning at her, he pressed his hand over hers. "I do not like this."

"'Tis dangerous to go to the abbey."

"Bah. A bunch of monks."

"They certainly had you down before."

He growled. "I was unarmed and trying not to harm anyone. This time, the monks will have no quarter from me should they attack."

"I know my cousin," she insisted, unsure if she spoke the truth. Whatever happened, she did _not_ want Gabriel rashly heading to speak with Randall. 'Twould be like sending him into the lion's den.

She plucked the pointed spines off the rosemary sprig so Margaret could use them to disguise the valerian taste in the meal they planned. Why must keeping the peace be so difficult? "Just give me a chance, Gabriel."

Blowing out a breath, he gave a short nod. "Alright. But I like it not. You will inform me of any other missives."

"Yes, my lord." Not a chance. Not if it meant he

would be going to the abbey with only a handful of men to face down the bishop.

Over the next few days, Ariana received four more messages from her cousin, which she burned. She composed a letter to her cousin, informing him that her new marriage did not permit her the same privileges she had enjoyed afore and asking him to understand her new status. With luck, 'twould be enough, and he would simply leave her be.

The week was a blur. Margaret was a jumble of "oh, mercy, oh, saints" as she prepared the meal to drug the men. Ariana had her hands full keeping her calm. Edwina, on the other hand, seemed to delight in the idea of getting the men—or at least, Rodney—soused. Dionne could hardly wait for Ariana to give Gabriel the new tunic she and the other ladies had made. Ariana had embroidered the collar herself. Through it all, Gabriel brought her flowers.

Jason happily played with the wolfhound, and Gabriel took a little time each day to play with him. It seemed that each day, the other children moved somewhat closer to making friends with him.

Ariana had tried, to no avail, to talk to Gabriel about Nigel. If he would just let him go, they would not be forced to administer a meal laced with herbs for sleep. Why did men always choose the hardest course? Each time she broached the subject, however, Gabriel's mood darkened.

The feast day arrived with chaos and revelry. Ignoring the trembling in her stomach, Ariana watched the men drink and eat. The tables were set with pewter trenchers and platters of Margaret's valerian-laced meat. Minstrels and jugglers performed. Men laughed. Servants scurried hither and yon. With luck, all would be fast asleep by midnight, and she could release Nigel.

"I tell ye, miss, 'twas a fine meal," Rodney said, letting out a large belch. His one eye looked slightly glazed over.

Gabriel gazed at Ariana and smiled dreamily. It seemed to her that his eyelids drooped. "Splendid, wife. Shplendid."

She noted the slight slur of his speech, glad that he was at last succumbing to the combination of drugged meat and ale.

"Have another cup, my lord. 'Tis a fine batch Edwina made, is it not?"

"Aye. Fine." He nodded as she refilled his goblet.

A serving wench offered more food to the already stuffed men.

"You have barely touched your trencher, Ariana," Gabriel said.

She patted her rounded stomach. "Of a truth, it settles not well with me some nights. Tomorrow I will likely be starving."

He nodded and sipped his ale. His head wobbled.

Taking her goblet in hand, she pretended to drink. She eyed the scene over the edge of her cup. The serving maids had been instructed to keep refilling goblets and trenchers for as long as the men would eat and drink. Thus far, it seemed to be working.

Gabriel yawned. "'Tis been a long day."

She laid her hand on his arm. "Mayhap we should retire early?" The sooner she got this over with, the better.

"My wife"—snatching her hand, Gabriel tugged her toward him—"kiss me."

She glanced around uneasily. "We are in the great hall, my lord. 'Tisn't proper."

"Come now, girl. Kiss me." He gazed at her so dunderheadedly she nearly rolled her eyes. What was it about men and ale?

"My lord," she admonished.

Rising from the table, he drew her to her feet. He wobbled a little. "My wife tells me she will not kish me here, so I'm taking her to bed for a proper bedding," he announced so loudly the sound seemed to bounce off the stones.

Rodney guffawed.

Ian slapped his thigh.

Heat rose in her face. She latched on to Gabriel's hand and began dragging him from the great hall. Best to get him out of here afore he did something stupid.

"In a hurry, she is." Rodney laughed.

"A-swiving we will go. A-swiving we will go," Gabriel sang, wobbling his way after her.

"Come on," she whispered, wishing she could slap her hand over his mouth. Evidently, he was much more foxed than he'd seemed just sitting at the table. 'Twas not his fault, she reminded herself.

By the time they made it into the hallway, Ariana felt as though she led a cluster of eels. Gabriel was all arms, trying to hug and kiss her. She kissed him back, finding his drunken kisses a cross between humorous and exasperating.

He stripped off his belt before they reached their chamber and left it in the hallway under one of the sconces. Leading him into their room, she tugged him toward the bed. His mouth crashed down upon hers, hot and wet, as he fell onto the bed, pulling her with him. He tasted of ale.

"Ariana. Ariana. My love." He wound his fingers into her hair. "I love you, my wife. You are a good wife."

Ariana stiffened, unsure what to say. She lifted her head to look at him, but he pulled her close and planted tiny kisses on her face and cheeks and neck.

"Ariana, my love. Say you have forgiven me for forcing you to marry me. I want a marriage built on trust."

His words, even spoken drunkenly, sent a surge of guilt that she would betray the trust that had been between them these last few days. "I-I forgive you, Gabriel."

He trailed kisses down her neck and stomach, sliding her out of her dress as he went. His hands spanned her rounded belly, rubbing it gently. "I will ne'er tire looking at you, my love. I love that my baby grows inside you."

Inside, she quivered, unable to resist. As always, her body felt warm and tingly as he touched her.

"I want you," he murmured, unlacing his breeks so that his member sprang free. "I want you so much."

She sighed. Naught to do but enjoy tonight. Tomorrow there would be the devil to pay.

"I want you too, Gabriel." She rounded her fingers over his buttocks, enjoying their sweet, tight form. Ne'er would she tire of this secret time between them. Moisture gathered in her woman's core. She found herself hungry for him. Wanting him.

"Gabriel?"

His lips trailed against her neck, suddenly still. "Um-m-m-m," he murmured and smacked his lips.

"Gabriel?"

Asleep!

Slowly, he slid down onto the mattress. Her body tingled with unquenched desire. She laid her hand on his cheek, feeling the rough stubble of a beard, then trailed her finger down the bumpy scar on his chin.

He drew in a deep, contented breath and released it.

She kissed his cheek, lay beside him, and interlaced her fingers with his. "I hope you will still love me in the morning."

Chapter 25

Ariana waited until Gabriel snored softly afore attempting to rise from the bed to release Nigel from the dungeon. His big body spooned hers, and his hand was latched firmly around hers, his fingers pressing gently into her palm. It felt good to sleep in his arms—safe and warm. The room was dark, but he had chased away the demons of the night, and she no longer felt afraid.

His fingers twitched against her palm, and the area betwixt her legs tingled. *Pretend this is your queynt.* Saints, she would ne'er be able to hold his hand again without heat flowing into her sex.

The sooner she released Nigel, the better. Then she would no longer have to feel the rousing guilt that accompanied her obsession with her new husband. Of a truth, she rarely even thought of Nigel, and that frightened her. 'Twas unseemly for her to experience such pleasure whilst he pined away beneath the castle.

She wiggled a fraction of an inch, then waited, afraid the slight rustling of the sheets might arouse Gabriel. He did not move, so she slowly lifted his arm away from its possessive grasp on her waist. His fingers spanned her rounded belly.

She had insisted on releasing Nigel herself because she could not bear the thought of one of the other women being punished. God only knew what Gabriel would do once he discovered Nigel's absence. She expected he would be angry, but surely over the past days, he had seen her commitment to making this a true marriage. She loved him. He loved her. For certes, he would listen to reason once he cooled down. He was, after all, a logical man.

His arm was dead weight as she placed it on top of his slumbering form. She paused, watching him for a moment. He was beautiful in sleep, softer somehow. The lines that fanned out around his eyes proved his love for laughter. Pleasure afore duty, he teased whenever she became too focused on the day's worries.

Marveling that he was so still, she reached a finger toward him to determine that he hadn't somehow died. Margaret *had* been careful with the amount of valerian she'd used in the meal.

Waves of heat radiated from him, fascinating in their intensity. His chest rose and fell in a deep, even rhythm.

Not dead. Just dead asleep. Good.

She slid slowly off the bed, careful not to jiggle the mattress. The sheets flittered, the noise unnaturally loud. She paused. He snored. She breathed in relief, then shivered as her feet touched the planks. Away from Gabriel's heated body, the night's chill seeped through her.

With any luck, she would be able to sneak to the dungeon and release Nigel in less than a turn of the hourglass.

The bed ropes creaked. Her heart leapt into her throat as Gabriel rolled in his sleep. She dressed rapidly and snatched a candle, tinderbox, and a ring of keys from a nearby table. Worry grew in her mind as she tiptoed to the exit. 'Twas too easy.

With one last glance at his sleeping form, she pushed the door open slowly and peered into the hallway. She tucked the keys into her belt to keep them from jingling as she crept through her chamber's door and made her way through the castle's labyrinth of hallways. Several men dozed on makeshift pallets, but none awoke.

A short time later, she stood by the dungeon's door, pleased the halls had been so quiet. Margaret and Edwina had done well with the food and drink, and she would see that they were rewarded.

A twinge of guilt bit at her because 'twas Gabriel's gentle touch that had helped her overcome her fear of the dark and allowed her to come into a place as dark as the dungeon.

Niggling unease ran up her spine at the silence. Nerves buzzing, she glanced around, then stared at the iron door. The candle's flame illuminated the heavy lock.

"Nigel!" she called in a loud whisper, refusing to give in to her discomfiture. She should be grateful for her fortune, instead of seeing doom in every blessing. "Nigel!"

A low moan sounded behind the thick iron panel.

Fumbling with the keys on her girdle, she found the one for the lock. It clanked against the metal.

The dungeon door squeaked open. Damp, stale air drifted into the hallway. She shivered and wished she'd thought to grab a cloak.

"Nigel!" she called softly.

A thin, dirty figure, barely discernable in the dim light, stirred on musty straw. A rat-bitten blanket slid from his shoulders.

"Ariana?" His voice was a low moan.

"Nigel!" She scurried over to him and knelt. The scent of fetid rushes and urine crowded the air. "Hasten, Nigel! We must hurry. The men are asleep."

He wobbled to his feet. His thin hair stuck out this way and that. A large purple bruise marred the fair skin of his cheek. Its twin colored his forehead.

"Mercy, what have they done to you?"

"I tried to fight," he explained.

"Oh, heavens." A wave of indignant anger that Gabriel's animals would harm such a gentle man as Nigel passed over her. "Hasten."

Holding her nose, she piled up rushes and threw the mangy blanket atop it. Mayhap in the dark, 'twould look like a person.

Nigel leaned on her for support as they left the darkness of the cell. Scrambling from shadow to shadow, she showed him to the passage at the back of the castle. Dawn's light rose on the horizon, painting the sky orange.

"Go!" she instructed. "Time is short."

"But, Ariana, what about you?"

"I shall be fine."

"Nay." He took her hand with his cold, soft fingers. "Come with me."

"I cannot. Jason is here." *I love Gabriel.*

He tugged her into the secret passageway. "We will come back for him."

"Nay." She shivered, the thought too horrific to contemplate. "Never will I leave my son."

"But—"

"Go!"

His blond hair gleamed in the moonlight. "I will write to you."

"Fine. Now hasten!"

He ducked his head and hurried into the secret passage. Breathing a sigh of relief, she closed the door. Her mind whirled with possibilities.

Releasing Nigel had been easy, but if Gabriel had awoken and was looking for her, she would need an excuse for being out roaming the halls.

She headed to her son's room, planning to claim she'd gotten up to check on Jason.

She cringed as she saw Ian outside Jason's room. He stood as she approached, wiping sleep from his eyes. He was at least a head taller than Gabriel, and sported a monstrous mustache that made his lips look permanently down turned in a frown.

"Why are you here, my lady?" he asked in a low, gravelly voice as if he had just awoken.

"I have come to check on my son." She straightened her shoulders and spoke as calmly as she could manage. "Please step aside."

He blocked her path with his oversized stomach. "Nay. Gabriel's orders. He said no one was to pass."

"But surely he did not mean Jason's own mother. 'Tis but for a moment, sir." She put a worried look on her face that she did not have to fake. "A mother's concern."

The guard hemmed and hawed for a moment, his mustache twitching hither and yon. His kind brown eyes made sport of his girth and height.

"Please, sir." She touched his arm.

"Ariana!" A voice boomed from down the hallway.

She jumped, an instinctive wariness coming over her.

"Ariana! Where are you, girl?"

Gabriel! Had he discovered Nigel's absence already?

"I am hither," she said in what she hoped was a slow, controlled tone. The more time she delayed Gabriel, the more time Nigel would have to free himself.

The guard snatched her upper arm. "Here, sir!"

Her pulse leapt as Gabriel rounded the corner and stalked toward her. Not wanting to show weakness in front of him, she checked the urge to turn and run.

"Good morning, Gabriel," she forced herself to say calmly as she kissed him on the cheek.

A tendril of dark hair fell over his forehead, and his green gaze probed hers. Did he suspect?

She smiled blandly, ignoring her erratic heartbeat. "I trust you slept well."

"Very well. Of a truth, I do not think I moved at all last night. Nor did the others—it seems that most of the men are still asleep."

She made a mental note that the valerian blossoms and ale had worked even better than expected.

"What are you doing here?" He trailed one finger down the length of her arm.

She sniffed. "Checking on my son."

"And did you find him well?"

"I have not yet seen him."

With a flick of his hand, Gabriel waved Ian aside. He leaned over, pushed the door open, took her hand, and led her inside Jason's chamber.

An erotic impulse flickered through her as he touched her palm, and she squeezed his hand. If it were only the two of them in the world, life would not be so complex. She sent up a silent prayer of thanks that he had not yet discovered Nigel was missing.

Embers burned in a fireplace, lighting the chamber with a soft glow. She stepped over the threshold and dodged a wooden duck, a small pile of rocks, and other children's toys as she made her way across the Oriental carpet.

Taking a deep breath, she shoved all thoughts of her almost-bridegroom aside. His absence would be discovered soon enough, and then she would worry what to do about that.

Jason lay peacefully atop the bed, curled on his side with one hand tucked under his chin. His eyelashes fanned across his pink cheeks. With a soft sigh, she glided over to touch him.

Flattening her hand against his face, she smiled down at his sleeping form. Gabriel followed. His dominating presence prickled the hairs on her neck. His large body cupped her back, and his hand spanned her rounded belly as he leaned down to whisper in her ear, "Children are beautiful when they are sleeping, are they not?"

A giggle sounded from the other side of the bed. A redheaded lad of about eight jumped from behind the mattress. She racked her mind to remember what this one's name was. Thorns, there were so many of them, and they scuttled around like stray cats.

"Gareth!" Gabriel exclaimed, supplying her with a name.

"Gareth," she repeated.

Jason awoke all at once, his wide eyes popping open. Unlike herself, he was pleasant on first awakening, and nearly always awoke cheerful. He smiled up at them.

"Oh, you are awake," she said, waving at him.

He waved back, indicating "hello."

"Come on. Get up. Let's play," the redheaded child said, jumping onto the bed and grabbing Jason's hand. The mattress ropes groaned.

Jason grinned and made a high-pitched, excited sound.

"'Tis gonna be real fun today. I'll take you out, and we'll play leapfrog, and then we'll climb trees, and then we'll sword fight, an' I know it's gonna be a good time an' . . ." Gareth rambled.

Jason nodded as if he understood the whole conversation.

Ariana wrung her hands. "Gareth, dear, you will have to be gentle. Jason is deaf."

Gareth grinned up at her. "Don't ye worry none, m'lady. Me an' him understands each other just fine, we do. We played last night, we did, whilst the adults were busy at sup. Today, we want to play in the meadow an' chase butterflies an' climb haystacks an'—"

Jason nodded eagerly, and Gareth laughed.

"Well," Ariana said, "I am not so sure that is quite a good idea."

Jason put his hands in prayer position and pleaded with his eyes.

"Oh, please, m'lady, please, you must let us," Gareth chattered. "All will be well. We'll just play a few games, and then we'll go and steal a sweetmeat from the kitchen, an' then we'll—"

Gabriel shifted behind her. "Let the boys play, Ariana. 'Twill do them good."

Jason's wide, excited eyes met hers.

Despite her misgivings, she found she didn't have the heart to stop her son from having a playmate. His deafness shut him off from most children. Even the ones who did not shun him had parents who were suspicious that closed up ears might somehow rub off on their own children.

Mayhap this was a new start. Or mayhap when Gabriel discovered Nigel's absence, he would send her and Jason away and Jason would be lonelier than ever. She caught herself. Nay, Gabriel was a reasonable man—he would not send them away.

"Alright. But stay close so I can see you," she directed Gareth.

Wiping her teeth with a finger, she mimed to Jason that he was to use a hazel stick to clean his teeth.

He nodded and scampered off the bed.

Gareth followed, chattering.

"They will be safe, won't they?" she asked Gabriel, resisting the urge to wring her hands.

Gabriel smiled, showing his charming white teeth and boyish incisors. "They'll make a grand team. Jason cannot talk, and Gareth cannot cease."

Ariana watched the boys scuttle off together, unsure what to make of this new wrinkle. She heard them clatter down the hallway stairs. "I will send Beth to oversee them."

All at once, Gabriel turned to her and placed his hands on her shoulders. "Your son is not helpless."

"He cannot hear."

His fingers gently massaged her arms. "He gets along well. But we have other matters between us."

Ariana's heart lurched. "Gabriel, I—"

"I found this in your dressing chamber." Gabriel pulled a small scrap of parchment from his belt. 'Twas the note Margaret had placed in her room on the wedding night. In all the bustle of preparing for the banquet, she'd forgotten to remove it from its hiding place in her pot of face powder!

Thank Mary, she had not just blurted something about Nigel.

Her fingers quivered as she took the paper. She opened it, pretending she had not seen it afore.

The poison is in the blue clay jar.

Forcing her features into a mask of blandness, she gazed at him.

"Margaret wrote this," he said as if suddenly remembering how the cook had spoken about poison a few days ago.

Ariana swallowed. "She did not mean it."

"I will speak with her."

Heavens, the cook would have an apoplexy. "She was trying to help me," Ariana protested. "There is no need to talk to her. The matter has been taken care of already."

Gabriel lifted an eyebrow. Taking her hand, which tingled when he touched it, he tugged her toward the kitchens.

Chapter 26

Margaret fumbled and dropped her rolling pin onto the floor when she saw Gabriel stride into the kitchen. It landed with a loud kerplunk near a mixing bowl.

"Margaret," he said.

"Oh, mercy. Oh, saints."

Heavens, Ariana thought. She had to get this situation under control quickly afore Margaret confessed the whole drug-laced meal. She moved forward to pat her cook on the arm and give her a warning look.

"Oh, dear saints," Margaret wailed, wringing her hands in her apron. "I did not want to do it, but it was the only way to keep all of ye asleep yesternight. I was careful about how much I put in the dishes. No one was harmed, eh? Oh, saints. Oh, mercy."

A look of confusion crossed Gabriel's face. His jaw wiggled back and forth as if he were deep in thought.

Thorns! Turning quickly, Ariana kissed him on the lips, hoping to distract him. Unlike other times, he did not respond. He just stood there.

"The deep sleeping men. The meal last night—" he started.

"Master, master!" Rodney huffed into the kitchen, his one eye wide open. "Master! The prisoner is missing!"

"The prisoner?"

"Nigel." He squinted at Margaret and Ariana.

"Oh, saints. Oh, mercy."

"Ni—" Gabriel grasped Ariana's shoulders, his hands like iron claws. "This is your doing."

Her stomach sank, seemingly all the way to the floor to rest with Margaret's rolling pin. Whatever trust they'd had between them had been instantaneously shattered. Just as she'd feared.

One of his hands slid behind her neck. "You defy me?"

Blood drained from her face. She tried to back away, but he anchored her in place. Her pregnant belly bumped him.

"Gabriel, prithee. I know you are angry, but I can explain."

"You drugged us."

"I could not leave him there."

In an instant, Gabriel scooped her in his arms. The kitchen swirled. The babe in her womb kicked.

Margaret shifted from foot to foot, her huge hips lurching.

Gabriel gave her a stern look. The scar on his chin whitened. "I will be back for you."

She looked near the edge of hysteria.

Ariana struggled to get out of his arms. Her dress slipped against his black tunic. "My lord! Nay. Leave her be."

"Be still, girl. 'Tis only your pregnancy that keeps

me from slinging you over my shoulder and carrying you upstairs for the punishment you deserve."

Moments later, Ariana stiffened as Gabriel lowered her onto their feather mattress and stepped away from the bed. His hand clenched and unclenched with checked anger.

She cringed, an age-old fear coming back to her. But Gabriel was not the sort of man to beat her. Was he?

"What am I going to do with you?" He backed away as if he were afraid of being too close.

She ran her hand along the feather coverlet, giving herself time to think.

"I told you afore I am not a harsh master, but I can be. I cannot have you releasing important hostages."

"Nigel is not important! He's just a musician."

"A musician who wanted to marry you."

"Gabriel"—she scrambled to her knees on the bed—"your quarrel is with me, not with Nigel. He did not want to marry me—I practically had to beg him to do so."

Gabriel leaned against the bedpost. "You will forget about him."

Cocking her head sideways, she searched his enigmatic face. Did she detect . . . jealousy?

"Gabriel, Nigel and I were—"

He cut her off sharply with a wave of his hand. "I am not interested in your relationship with Nigel. The sooner you forget about him and accept me as your husband, the easier things will be between us."

"Truly, you should see that I already have."

"Enough."

She sank back onto the mattress. "Gabriel, I want us to have a true marriage. I love you."

"Enough!" Her proclamation seemed to anger him further. "Noblewomen speak of love and pretty things when it suits their purpose."

Letting out a long breath, he crossed his arms over his chest. "You push me too far, Ariana. My men are good men, but they are not trained soldiers. My authority over them is not by sworn oath but by the rules of the pack."

"The rules of the pack?"

"What is the usual thing a man would do should his wife defy him thus?" he asked, not bothering to answer her question.

Blood drained from her face. She knew only too well the lot of women who displeased their husbands. Even pious men who never touched their wife fervently argued for the right to discipline them if needs be.

"Ariana, a commander cannot afford for his men to see that he is weak-willed toward his captives and those under him. 'Tis a sure formula for mutiny."

A quiver ran through her. "But surely they can see that our marriage is well-matched."

His brow furrowed, and a tight tic formed in his jaw.

"You take advantage of my leniency."

"Leniency?" Fear made her reckless. "You interrupted the wedding and threw him into a damp cell. How can you call taking over my castle *leniency?*"

Gabriel growled low in his throat. "Have you been harmed?" he demanded.

She frowned.

"Have you?"

"Nay," she bit out angrily.

"Has your son been harmed? Or your people?"

She leaned back, wary.

"You have not been harmed. Your son has not been harmed. Your people have not been harmed. The women have been safe. Answer me this, Ariana: how many *noblemen* would have assured such things?"

Biting her lip, Ariana realized he spoke the truth. How many nobles had she known who would have acted the part of prissy suitor but harmed her people. She'd been married to three of them.

She also knew in that instant whatever he planned, beating her was not a part of it.

"Let me show you a nobleman's leniency," he said. His voice was angry, bitter.

Slowly, he uncrossed his arms and lowered them. Reaching down, he grasped the lower hem of his tunic and slid the garment over his head. He turned to one side, exposing his back.

Bumpy red welts crisscrossed the skin. The angry lines zigzagged down from his shoulders and disappeared into his breeks. One raised line stood out. It ran from his hip to mid-back. Angry scarring formed a large letter "D," which had been burned into his shoulder blade. A streak of revulsion slid through her.

Her eyes widened as she realized she had ne'er seen his back since their marriage. She thought over the past week. Because of her pregnancy, she'd been on top when they copulated. He'd never taken his shirt off.

"Heavens," she gasped.

"Mayhap you should speak to your noble cousin and Nigel about leniency?"

"My cousin did this?" A bubble of horror rose in her throat, thick and unswallowable.

"Nay, *Nigel* did."

"I . . ." Her jaw worked up and down for a moment. "I do not believe you. Nigel is a musician. A gentle man."

Turning his bruised back on her, he walked across the room to a trunk and bent to open it. She watched in morbid fascination as the stripes undulated across his skin. A purple spot low on his back moved up and down with every movement of his hip.

Horrified, she slid off the bed. "Gabriel—"

He straightened; his muscles rippled under his blemished skin. "Nigel is your cousin's lover."

Her knees began to shake. "That's—that's—that is not possible," she whispered.

His gaze pierced her, and he held a chain he had removed from the trunk out to her. Its iron links clanked on the floor. "They made me crawl for their pleasure."

"Nay," she breathed. The thought of seeing such a proud man so debased brought on a wave of nausea.

"Aye!" he said, shaking his fist. The chain rattled in his hand.

She shook her head, not wanting to believe. "Nigel would not have done such a thing."

"Your Nigel is a damn coward, but he has no qualms about using the branding iron."

Coldness ran up Ariana's spine, as if an icicle had touched her. "Gabriel, I swear to you by all that's holy, whatever you think you saw, Nigel did not do this. He could not have."

His green eyes blazed with rekindled anger. "He was there."

"It is not possible." She reached for him and touched his arm, wanting him to somehow understand.

Shifting the chain to one hand, he placed his other

hand atop hers, capturing it. The heat of his fingers bore into her skin, pressing her hand into his forearm.

"I am sorry for your pain, Gabriel. Truly, I am. But Nigel would not have done such a thing." A wave of anguish crossed her.

"He *did* do it." He stared at her for a moment, then at the tapestry on the wall, and then back at her. "You leave me in a dilemma, girl. I cannot effectively lead my men with them thinking I cannot control my own wife. Moreover, you have defied me by releasing an important prisoner who could possibly prove the bishop's guilt in this spying business. You said you would trust me to take care of your cousin for you."

She tried to remove her hand from his arm, but he held it captive beneath his own. Their conversation had taken an odd turn that made her uneasy.

"What should I do, Ariana?"

She gaped at him.

A lock of dark hair fell across his forehead, making him look roguish. "Ariana, come. Do not fight." His voice was low and husky. He pulled her forward. "You have caused me enough pain already."

Guilt weighed on her heart. She followed, unsure what he planned.

He paused near the edge of the bed. "Get on the bed."

She cringed.

He sounded like a man who neared the edges of his patience. The chain clanked on the floor. "I will not hurt you, though we both know I am in my rights to do so." He motioned her to the bed.

Her stomach cramped anxiously. Chewing her inner lip, she climbed atop the mattress.

"Good. Now lie back."

She did so, feeling the coolness of the coverlet against her back. "Gabriel?"

He grasped her ankle.

Startled, she sat up.

He placed his hand gently against her chest. "Do not pick battles you cannot win. I have no desire to force you to obey me, but I will if I must."

She shivered at the finality of his tone. He gazed at her, his green eyes holding hers captive. She tried to gage what she saw in his smoldering gaze. Intensity, passion, determination, fury.

Slowly, she lowered herself until her back was flat against the mattress. The baby within her quickened, causing one side of her stomach to jump.

Gabriel's hand slid against her leg, his fingers warm and strong against her ankle. The chain rattled, then he held it out like a morbid gift.

She furrowed her brow.

Cold, heavy iron grazed her ankle. Gabriel said nothing; instead, he held her ankle firmly.

"What are you about?" She jerked her leg back, trying to yank it from his hold.

"These are the chains they used to tie me to a stake while they lashed my back. I used them to fight my way free and kept them as a reminder so I would not weaken in my resolve for revenge." He kept hold of her leg and glanced at her. "I am going to keep you here."

Her eyes widened. "You mean to keep me prisoner of my own room?"

"Of *my* bed," he corrected. "'Tis more than your cousin offered me." One of the angry red scars on his shoulder jumped with the movement. Guilt skipped through her.

"Gabriel, I swear by all that is holy, I did not know you were alive. I came for you—"

Gabriel growled. "I have no use for the things you consider holy. I give you the choice: be my prisoner here on my bed, or take Nigel's place in the dungeon."

"The dungeon?" She shivered. The dungeon was dark. Very dark. Without Gabriel there to comfort her, the darkness seemed very frightening. "I cannot go to the dungeon," she whispered.

He grasped her ankle, his hands hot against her skin. "Choose now," he ground out.

She stared at him for a moment, wishing she could soothe the fury inside him. Wishing somehow she could change what had happened. "And if I do this without arguing, will it abate your anger?"

He inclined his head toward her.

"Mayhap," he said, blowing out a long breath.

"How long will you keep me here?"

He lifted a brow. "As long as it pleases me."

"Gabriel—"

"The bed or the dungeon?"

"The bed," she said slowly.

"Good." One side of his mouth lifted.

Squeezing her eyes shut and ignoring the pounding of her heart, she allowed him to snap the iron manacle around her ankle.

Chapter 27

Five days later, Ariana pulled against the chain and flopped on the bed, wishing she could get downstairs and see to the day's events. To pull weeds, to chop turnips. Anything to keep her from feeling the bone-gnawing guilt that Gabriel had been beaten and branded at the abbey. She was the one who was at fault for the fire, not him.

He was so sure that Nigel had branded him. Nigel who supposedly spent his time playing his violin for the bishop's amusement. She could scarcely fathom it.

Her physical needs had been cared for, but restless energy buzzed in her body. Servants brought her food and water, emptied the chamber pot, and carried in a tub for bathing. Twice a day, Rodney came and took her for a walk. He never spoke, no matter how much she implored him. The servants gave her a wide berth when they went out. 'Twas as if she were a dog on its daily walk.

On occasion, she saw Jason playing either with the hound or with Gareth. He was always laughing and happy. He ran to her and hugged her every day while she was out with Rodney. At least, she had no worries about his safety and health.

Thrice, she'd seen Gabriel across the field, and all three times, he'd turned his back on her. He went shirtless most days now—as if he'd reverted back to the wild. The jagged scar of the letter D glowed against his tanned skin. The red and white edges were welted and uneven, and she could imagine the agony he'd suffered.

If only she could speak with him, so she could apologize again or tell him she loved him!

Not that he would believe her. Before, her declaration of love had infuriated him. She sighed. Naught to do but wait. He could scarcely stay angry forever.

Light streamed in from the nearby window, creating a large, flickering pool of sunshine on the half of the mattress where the curtains were pulled back.

The chain clanked as she stood beside the bed and strained to look out the window into the bailey where the men practiced. Her bonds were long enough that she had some freedom to pace around the room, but not to reach the door. Swords clanged together as Gabriel's warriors sparred in mock battle. Ian and Rodney circled around each other.

Her gaze flitted to Gabriel, towering a head taller than most of the men on the practice field. She waved to him, hoping to get his attention. If he saw her, he did not indicate it. Vexing man!

He stood, slightly crouched, with the crossbow propped atop one of his massive shoulders. For a moment, she wondered why he had hidden the scars until now. The fact that he wore no shirt seemed to be an act of scorn and contention, as if he wanted to remind all of the pain she had given him.

She cringed. If his intent was to make her feel guilt, he had succeeded. Every flinch and movement undulated his markings. While the letter D was somewhat healed, the whip slashes were fairly fresh.

He brought the crossbow to the ready. His back must surely burn, but he did not shrink from the pain. A stack of hay with a painted wooden target attached stood several yards in front of him. He pulled the crossbow up, aimed it, then loosed the bolt.

She flinched at his deadly aim, sank back on the mattress, and stared up at the tapestries that canopied the bed.

A soft knock sounded, the door opened, and Margaret entered. "Mistress. Oh, mercy."

"Margaret, what do you here?"

"Master Gabriel will not allow me in the kitchens. Oh, saints. The food be awful, mistress."

Ariana sighed.

Margaret eyed the manacle encircling her ankle and threw her hands into the air. *"Oh, mercy, mistress. 'E's bound you to the bed?"* she said in a high-pitched screech.

"Peace, Margaret. Gabriel has not harmed me."

"But you are chained to the bed! We thought you were only locked in your chamber. If I could get into me kitchen, the poison is still in the blue pot."

"Cease, Margaret. Cease. Gabriel will calm." Surely, she thought, biting the inside of her cheek. She would *have* to talk sense into him . . . *if* she could ever get him to speak with her. Margaret being out of the kitchen was like setting wild rabbits loose in the garden. The woman would wreak havoc on the castle-folk. "How is Jason?"

"'E's well. 'E plays with the other children now.

Beth and I have been helping them understand him."
Margaret dug a scroll from her apron pocket. "'Tis
from the bishop."

Ariana's heart sank. Not another note from Randall.

Footsteps sounded in the hallway. Margaret scrambled to hide behind the dressing curtain. "Oh, mercy.
Oh, saints. 'E told me I wasn't to see you. That none
of us were to see you." When the footsteps passed and
went further down the hallway, she hurried to the
door. "I must hasten. G'day, mistress."

After Margaret left, Ariana broke the wax seal and
unrolled the scroll.

> *Blessed Cousin,*
> *I have not heard from you and I fear for your safety.*
> *I will come visit you soon.*

Merciful Mary! Her cousin coming here? Likely,
'twould be a bloodbath betwixt him and Gabriel.

Her hand trembled, and she quickly scanned the
rest of the missive. It ended with *All the best, Your
Loving Cousin.* The paper weighed heavily in her fingers as if it were a stone rather than a tiny scrap of
parchment.

She folded the paper and turned it over and over
in her fingers. Biting her lower lip, she debated her
options—she needed to do *something* to stave him off.
'Twas clear Gabriel was in no mood to listen to
reason.

The chain pulled tight against her ankle as she
reached for a quill and ink. Ripping a small piece
from the corner of the parchment, she wrote a few
notes about Cyrille in tiny handwriting.

Since Margaret was no longer serving in the

kitchens, mayhap she could get her to take it . . . if she ever had enough nerve to visit again. The abbey was not far, and perhaps her husband would go with her.

The door banged open, and Gabriel strode into the room. Ariana jumped and hurriedly shoved the note beneath her pillow.

"Gabriel." She sat up and stared at him.

His crossbow was propped on his shoulder. A thin glaze of sweat beaded his brow, and he was still shirtless. His tanned skin glistened.

"How are you?" she said evenly. How odd to speak niceties as if they were any other married pair, as if there was no note under the pillow, as if she was not chained to the bed.

The dangling strings of his unevenly tied leather breeks caught her attention. Her gaze lingered, and her thoughts flitted unbidden to the sex they'd had before she'd released Nigel and earned his disdain.

He cleared his throat, and she felt her face heat. Heavens, he'd caught her staring at his crotch. She raised her gaze to meet his, praying her blush did not show.

"I trust you've slept well," he said.

"Aye." She tucked her legs beneath her, and the chain clanked against the bedpost. "Did you come to release me?"

"Nay." He stepped toward her, his big body blocking the light streaming in from the window. "I came to tell you that I am leaving to hunt down Nigel."

"Gabriel"—she shivered at his black tone—"hear me out. No matter what you believe, Nigel could not have done such a thing."

He growled, the scar on his chin whitening. "Do not speak of him, wife. I will return within a fortnight."

Alarm ran through her. "You plan to leave me here chained?"

"Aye. A servant will bring food."

"Like a pet!" she exclaimed.

"Nay, like a poorly behaved wife."

"Gabriel, I swear there is no need for this."

"You stay here."

"And when you return, will you let me go?"

"Nay."

Worry traveled through her. She had thought his anger would have abated somewhat, but apparently, it had not. "But you cannot mean to keep me here on the bed all of our life."

"I can if it pleases me."

She shuddered. "Gabriel, prithee."

"I will not have you putting my child in danger by running around with men such as Nigel."

The mattress dipped as he sat beside her, laid the crossbow at the foot of the bed, and reached for her ankle. His dark presence crowded her space, filling her vision and nostrils until all of her senses focused on him. He smelled of outdoors, leather, and horses.

His hand brushed her collarbone, sliding along the ridge and down her arm.

Fluttering started low in her stomach.

His fingers grazed her wrist, trailed over the pad of her thumb, and touched her palm. Like a jolt of lightning, sensation arced through her, tingling burning her from the tips of her toes to the top of her scalp.

He drew a small circle. *Pretend this is your queynt.* The place on her hip twitched. Heated wetness formed betwixt her legs.

"My lord Gabriel." She reached for him.

Abruptly, he stopped and removed his hand.

"Whatever your feelings for Nigel, your body belongs to me."

She pressed her lips tightly together and straightened her spine, not wanting to feel the desire pulsing through her. Her body was like a doll being played by a master puppeteer. All he had to do was wiggle his fingers. And they both knew it.

"My body belongs to myself."

He smirked.

Grasping her leg firmly, he brought her ankle upward. Because of her stiffened position, the motion off-balanced her and she toppled over. The mattress made a soft "poof" as she landed on her back with her leg up in the air in Gabriel's hand.

"Well," she huffed, crossing her arms over her chest. Her stomach looked very pregnant from this angle. 'Twas impossible to act indignant when one was chained to the bed. She would settle for petulant. The baby in her womb felt like a lead brick atop her lungs. She turned slightly onto her side, her arms still crossed.

He held her ankle steady in his hand, placed her foot atop his shoulder, and ran his hand up the inside of her leg until his fingers rested much too high on her inner thigh for propriety.

"Cease!" The fluttering in her stomach built into a quiver. The heat blazed into an inferno.

He would only have to flex his fingers, and their tips would brush the lower curves of her sex. She stilled, willing herself not to move and wishing desperately she had bothered to wear some sort of undergarment. But all she'd done for the last five days was lie here on the mattress feeling her pregnant belly grow. Every twitch of skin had seemed heightened. Her undergarments had been uncomfortable and itchy, so she'd removed them. If he wiggled his hand only a fraction, he would know her naughty secret.

His hand pressed into her skin, his fingertips a parchment width from her labia. She sucked in a breath.

Merciful heavens, 'twas hard to think or even breathe with Gabriel so close. Low on the left side of her hip, her bottom tingled, just as it had when they had copulated on the rock.

"Perhaps we should discuss the state of our marriage," he drawled. His hand did not inch upward, but it did not move away either.

"I am shackled to the bed, my lord." She licked her dry lips, wishing she could deny the heat trickling to the vee betwixt her legs. "That cannot be a way to have a marriage."

He smiled the way a pirate would afore he stole a guarded jewel. More heat. Keeping her foot on his shoulder, he turned his head to gaze fixedly at the iron shackle encircling her ankle. "On the contrary, 'tis a fine way to have a marriage with you. I have you where you cannot escape."

His husky words brought blood rushing to her sex. She gasped afore she could stop herself and stared at him. Moisture beaded inside her queynt. While her mind reasoned that she should not enjoy being bound for pleasure, her body had no such qualms.

She squeezed her woman parts together, trying to hold back the damning flow of feminine desire. If only his hand were not so close to her sex.

A lock of dark hair fell across his widow's peak, wicked and beautiful.

"Even through all, there is heat between us, Ariana," he murmured.

She squeezed herself harder, fighting the moisture she knew was only too close to sliding from within her.

His fingers flexed ever so slightly. Wetness trickled from her quim, sliding down her thigh. Nay, nay!

"Ah." He smiled. Smug. Knowing.

Mortification burned her cheeks. She turned her face away from his arrogant smirk. It should not be like this. He'd scorned her for five days. She should be angry, *not* enjoying being tied to the bed at his mercy!

"My lady." He slid his hand from betwixt her thighs; ran his fingers leisurely up the length of her leg, and took her foot off his shoulder, setting it so that her calf nestled near his hip.

She sucked in a sharp breath. 'Twas as if he'd raked her leg with a candle's flame. The skin burned where his fingers had touched.

Leaning forward, he caught her chin between two of his fingers and turned her gaze back to his. His fingers were moist, and her own spicy woman scent drifted to her nostrils.

"Gabriel"—she cleared her throat to emphasize the seriousness of the matter—"we cannot continue like this."

He traced his wet fingers over her lips. She blinked and forced herself not to react, but her insides quivered.

"Yes, we can," he said. "You belong to me." His gaze raked over her body, hot and covetous.

She breathed a frustrated sigh. Her nipples tightened of their own accord as if her body already hailed him as master. A wickedly arrogant smile that showed off his pointed incisors curved his lips. The brief impression of a hungry wolf flitted into her thoughts.

She slid her hand downward and pushed against his

chest. His muscles were solid and warm under her fingers. She shoved, but he did not move. She shoved harder. He glanced down at her hand impassively and leaned closer, forcing her to bend her elbow.

Leaning forward, he cupped her head in his hands and kissed her. God help her, she kissed him back. Desire ignited like a fueled flame, hungry and consuming.

Mayhap she could prove to him that she wanted a real marriage. Prove it, and then they could go on as they had afore. She twined her fingers into his hair, pulling him close.

He shifted his weight, trailed his fingers down her neck, and cupped one of her breasts. With a moan, she closed her eyes.

Suddenly, he stopped and lifted himself. A dark shadow passed over his face. "What is this?"

Saints! The letter she planned to have Margaret deliver to the abbey.

She yanked it out of his hand. "Naught!"

Lifting an eyebrow, he plucked it from her fingers, rolled beside her, propped himself up on the headboard, and unfolded the parchment.

She wanted to scream.

"'Tis to your cousin about Cyrille!" he accused, squinting at the words.

She moved her mouth up and down, trying to formulate an excuse, but no sound came out.

"You said you were done with this!"

She shivered at the coldness that came over him. The manacle around her ankle seemed painfully heavy. Her thin hopes for reconciliation shattered. "Gabriel."

Swinging his legs over the side of the bed, he stood. The mattress quivered. He looked at her intensely as if deciding which part to bite first. "Once the baby is born, you will be moved to a convent."

"Gabriel!" She sat up, alarmed.

He held up the damning paper. Sunlight flickered across the yellow scrap.

"Dear God, Gabriel, Randall plans to come here. I know you are angry with me, but you must listen!"

For an instant, an edge of vulnerability flickered in his gaze, then, just as suddenly, dark fury took its place.

"Prithee! My cousin has sent many notes." She touched Gabriel's forearm. "I did not know what to do."

"Your cousin sends letters oft? Why was I not informed of this?"

Ignoring the clanking chain, she scrambled to her knees on the bed. "You would not talk to me."

"How long has he been sending notes?"

She shuddered. Longer than he had not been talking to her.

He twisted the note back and forth with precise little strokes like a cat twitching its tail as it waited for a mouse. The parchment made tiny crinkling sounds. Its edge skimmed the scar where his finger would have been.

Hot tears of frustration stung the backs of her eyes. How could she explain?

"I should have told you," she said.

He seemed to soften a tiny bit, although he still glowered at her.

"I was terrified you would go to the abbey alone and be harmed. I thought I could deliver something to my cousin so that he would leave us alone for a time."

Pausing, she folded her arms and stared at the bed curtains. "Asides, I do not like Cyrille."

One corner of Gabriel's frown twitched. "You do not?"

"Nay."

"Why?"

"Only a fool would leave you at the altar, my lord."

It seemed to her that his eyes lightened somewhat from their black storminess. He paced to the hearth and back.

"Give me the letters."

"I burned them."

"I see. What do you usually do with the messages that you give to Randall?"

"There is a loose tile beneath the altar. I place them there, then put an egg-sized rock by the well as a signal that information has been delivered."

He gave her a pensive look, picked up the crossbow from the foot of the bed, and stalked to the door. "I have given Rodney instructions to release you if I do not return within a fortnight."

Her heart lurched. "Nay, Gabriel. Please! 'Tis too dangerous."

"Do not vex yourself with this matter. I am your husband, and 'tis my concern now."

"Gabriel, nay! 'Tis not your concern."

"It is."

"You know naught of this. Of what he might do. He has so many under his thumb."

"I know much about getting quietly into and out of places and handling people who would bully others. You must trust me." He patted the tiller of his crossbow.

She shivered.

"I will release you when I return."

A streak of panic pierced her heart as the door slammed shut.

An hour later, Ian entered, his huge mustache drooping even more than usual. "Master Gabriel sent me to give this to you." He pitched a grass rose on the mattress as if it stung his hands. "Thinks I'm a messenger boy," he grumbled as he turned and rushed out.

She smiled. Gabriel had not given up on their relationship after all. Bringing the little flower to her nostrils, she inhaled its grassy scent.

Chapter 28

Gabriel grasped Ariana's missive as he scanned the abbey's grounds from behind a narrow wall and waited for an opening to drop the scroll beneath the loose tile undetected. He missed her already, his unruly, high-spirited wife. He shoved aside a niggling shred of guilt about leaving her chained. 'Twas for her own good. He could not trust her not to come racing across the countryside to try and stop him.

The morning was cold and slightly misty. He blew on his hands and rubbed them together. Remembering the look on Ariana's face when she had said she did not like Cyrille warmed his heart.

The sounds of shovels picking the earth and hammers clapping the air resonated across the churchyard. Workmen ran this way and that, measuring and rebuilding the abbey.

A black mood descended on him as he surveyed their progress. Primitive urgings beckoned him to race headlong into the abbey, to tear it apart brick by brick as recompense for the humiliation he'd suffered. With strength of will, he forced himself to be patient. Revenge takes time, he said to soothe the angry beast within. The ones who were responsible would pay.

For now, he would drop the note as bait, then watch and wait. When the bishop came to retrieve it, he would have him alone and caught. 'Twas better than trying to get into the bishop's heavily guarded quarters unprotected.

Slowly, the sun completed its trek across the sky. As twilight gathered, the workmen collected their hammers and axes, preparing to leave until the morrow. From his hiding place, he could see the stone altar where he had first met Ariana. She had been beautiful, kneeling there in her blue velvets and smelling like fresh summer roses. The memory of his first glance of her sunset-colored hair flitted into his mind. 'Twas a glorious sight, and he was glad he'd ripped off her veil and set the gilded mass free. He mused that her hair was a lot like her: wild and untamed at heart, but too tightly contained.

Turning his mind back to the mission at hand, he mentally clicked off the paces to the altar. 'Twould take him less than two minutes to run, slide the tile back, drop the message, and return to his hiding place to wait for the bishop to take the bait.

He studied the men who wandered about the area. A sloped-skull dunderheaded brute lumbered back and forth carting rocks in a wheeled carriage. On one side of the worksite, a brown-robed monk instructed a group of peasants. A tallish man carried a scroll, ink, and a measuring tape about the perimeter, marking notes as he went.

But naught seemed amiss.

An hour later, darkness fell, and nary a man hung

around the cathedral. Gabriel cocked his crossbow. Best to take no chances on his two minute trek. Crouching low, he bolted across the grounds, dropped the missive in its hiding place, placed a rock by the well, and returned to his position behind the wall.

He inhaled deeply to steady his breathing and waited.

Rains came in the night, filling the forest with mud and dampness. Water seeped through Gabriel's boots and dripped down his collar. He imagined Ariana sleeping peacefully in his bed, warm and dry.

By sunrise, Gabriel neared the end of his patience. Most of the day and night, his mind had danced around the woman chained to his bed. A slow wave of dark desire gripped him as he pondered what to do with her. Guilt niggled at him that he'd left her bound. But she'd betrayed his trust too many times.

For certes, he was too easy with his hellcat wife. She needed to be tamed. And trained to his hand. Ne'er in his life had he known a woman so brimming with passion and so uncertain about what to do with it. So imprisoned by responsibility. She was good at running the keep. At getting the children, the kitchens, and the garden in order. Indeed, on that account, she did not need him at all.

But no one took care of *her.* She'd been afraid of the dark, afraid of her cousin, afraid of her own feminine desires. She did not want to continue spying, yet was too afraid of Randall to stop. If he could get her to trust him to shoulder some of her burden, to take away some of her fears, their life could be good indeed.

Slowly, he turned his thoughts from her as he watched a tall, lanky man saunter onto the abbey's grounds. A wide-brimmed hat shadowed his face. He ambled to the well, glanced back and forth three or four times, then slipped into the cathedral.

All Gabriel's senses went on alert.

Not the bishop, but this man was out of place.

A few moments later, the man emerged from the shadowed sanctuary. He stopped by the well, then casually meandered toward a well-lit room at the back of the abbey. The rock was now missing. Gabriel's nape tingled.

Hoisting his crossbow, he followed, keeping to the trees as the man made his way across the abbey. Something about him seemed familiar. He tried to catch a glimpse of his face, and after a few moments, he was rewarded when the man stopped to mop his brow.

The devil's toes! 'Twas Nigel!

So that priss had returned to his lover. He would have thought a coward such as he would have chosen a much further place to hide. Of a truth, Nigel's part in this made no sense. And Ariana had vehemently defended him.

From here, the man seemed too soft and doelike to have wielded the iron as he had first thought. Gabriel tried to conjure up the day he'd been branded. 'Twas fuzzy in his mind. For certes, Nigel had been there. He'd seen him touch the rod of the branding iron.

Afore Nigel reached the safety of the low door, Gabriel overtook him and jerked him into the shadows.

Nigel gasped like a girl. "You!"

Gabriel pulled him behind a large bush.

Nigel squealed.

"Hush, you blasted priss, or I'll be forced to kill you."

"Gabriel! My lord." Stark terror shone in Nigel's wide eyes. "I meant no harm. Ariana released me."

How cowardly of him to blame his escape on her. "Where is your lover, the bishop?"

Nigel flinched. "He isn't my lover."

"Nay?"

"Nay."

"You were there the day the D was burned into my back." Fury twisted Gabriel's gut, driving him to crush Nigel's fingers in his fist. He would ne'er play the violin again if Gabriel did. Last time, Ariana's pleas had stopped him, but she was not here. He squeezed.

The man's shoulders began to shake, and he made a sobbing noise. "My lord, prithee, not my hands. I have no love for Ariana's cousin, I swear it. I am as caught in this as she. I have no means of support, and the bishop pays for me to play the violin for him."

"I saw you there the day I was burned. I saw you take the iron."

Nigel paled, his blond hair waving. "I-I was there. I came to play for the bishop. The abbot is a horrid man, I swear it. I tried to take the iron from the fire so it would not be so hot. Of a truth, I care not for this place."

Between Ariana's staunch defense and Nigel's quivering lips, a seed of doubt formed in Gabriel's mind.

"Why did you return here?"

"My violin is here. I came to collect it, then find work elsewhere, but the bishop caught me. He told me I must get the message under the altar first, and then he would release me from his service. Otherwise, he would declare my violin an instrument of the devil and have it burned. I could not bear it. 'Tis all I have."

Saints help him, Gabriel believed him.

"You are not the bishop's lover?"

Nigel shivered. "Nay."

Slowly, Gabriel released him. "Randall is blackmailing Ariana."

Nigel gasped. "Nay! Not Lady Ariana."

Gabriel looked over Nigel's quivering form. Of a truth, he still had no love for soft men such as he, but he needed his help.

"You must tell the king what you have seen concerning the bishop."

Nigel paled and shook his head.

Gabriel squeezed his fingers again.

Yelping, Nigel slumped. "Prithee, nay. I will do it. But the man will have my head."

"You will come back with me."

"Please, nay. I cannot face the dungeon again. I swear I had no part in the scenes you speak of."

"And in loving Ariana? How is it you wanted to marry her?"

Nigel swallowed. "My lord, 'twas not my idea."

"So you said afore."

Trembling, Nigel bit his lip. "I did not agree to it until she explained there would be no intimacy between us."

"No intimacy! What husband would agree to such?"

Taking a deep breath, Nigel flushed so red his face glowed. "I am a eunuch," he said in a quivering voice.

"A eunuch?" Shocked, Gabriel nearly lost his hold on him.

"I have no lovers, male or female, my lord. My joy is in my music." His eyes pleaded with Gabriel. "Prithee, do not tell Ariana. She is a passionate, hot-blooded one. She would not understand."

"How?"

"My father hated my love for the violin. He became increasingly angry with me when I refused to take up playing with swords and fighting. One night, he ordered his men to jump on me. 'If the boy refuses to fight like a man, then he can be a girl.'" Deep sobs racked Nigel's body. "My family disowned me after that. Ariana has been my only friend."

All anger and disgust of Nigel left Gabriel's body in a rush.

"I—" Words seemed inadequate. Gabriel had not known his own father, but he was told that he resembled the late Lord of Rosebriar enough that he must be his son. But not knowing a father was better than this. What sort of horrid beasts were nobles to treat their children such? Awkwardly, he patted Nigel on the shoulder, and a long moment passed.

"You must testify against the bishop to save Ariana," Gabriel ventured when Nigel seemed in control of himself once again.

"I have nowhere to go, my lord, if I testify against my employer."

Gabriel took a deep breath. "I am sure Rosebriar could use a musician."

For the first time since their talk had begun, Nigel looked hopeful. "Of a truth? You would offer me work?"

"Aye."

Nigel sank into a position of fealty before Gabriel. "I swear by all that is holy, I will serve you well if you can release me from this place. I have no care for the abbey. None at all."

Awkwardly, Gabriel lifted Nigel to his feet. "You must get away from here. There is a cabin by the stream. My sister Eleanor lives there alone now. She would not move to Rosebriar." He pulled a dagger from his belt. "Give her this, and tell her I sent you for shelter. She does not speak, but with this token, she will accept you nonetheless."

"Does not speak?"

"'Tis awkward. I will explain later."

"I cannot leave without my violin."

Gabriel snarled. "I will get your violin for you."

"'Tis in the bishop's secret chamber."

"Good. That is where I am going. The bishop and I have much to parlay about."

Chapter 29

"Babe killer!" A white-haired crone stopped weeding her garden and hurled Gabriel a contemptuous look as he rode through Rosebriar's gates three days later. She spat on the ground. "Bloody barbarian!"

Startled, he frowned down at her.

"I'm not afeared of ye, Gabriel the Bastard." The sun's midmorning rays reflected off the woman's stringy gray hair. She was an old hunchback, but her eyes blazed bright blue and her jaw jutted out defiantly. "They say ye chained her to the bed. 'Tis no way to keep a wife. 'Twould serve ye right if the babe dies!"

"Whoa, horse." He pulled back on the reins, drawing the stallion to a halt, and regarded the woman. "What mean you, woman? My babe has come?" His heart sped.

"Born at midnight. 'Twas too soon."

A sinking feeling pitted his stomach. It was too early. Ariana had been hearty and hale when he'd left. Her time was not close. "My child was born dead?"

"Nay, but one so small won't live long! Hark, a dirge already plays." She bent, pulled up a weed, and for an instant, Gabriel thought she meant to throw it at him. The mournful sounds of a bagpipe keened in the distance.

Not bothering to gather any more details, he wheeled his horse around, spurred it into a run, and galloped for the keep. The babe dead? Dear God, nay! Mentally, he kicked himself—God didn't listen to bastards. Had he not already learned that?

"Gabriel!" Rodney met him at the portcullis. Lines of worry creased his forehead, and his one eye looked bloodshot and strained.

Hastily swinging off his mount, Gabriel tossed the reins to a nearby servant. "My child?"

"Ariana went into labor two nights past." Rodney hurried after Gabriel as he crossed the bailey and took the steps toward Ariana's chamber two at a time.

"Why was I not sent for?"

"We sent three messengers for you. Two could not find you; the third ne'er returned."

"My child is dead?"

"There has been a lot of blood," Rodney hedged.

"And my wife?"

"Is resting." Rodney glanced at the floor, his ears reddening.

Dark guilt crushed his chest. How could he have left her? And chained to the bed?

Rodney thumbed the dagger hilt at his belt. "The priest has been called."

Within moments, Gabriel reached her room. He tried the door. Locked. He rattled it loudly.

"Ariana!"

She screamed, the sound slightly muffled by the oak.

Frustrated, he banged on the door. "Open this door this instant, or I'll break it down."

"Of all things," he heard someone speak. Glenna, the midwife. He recognized her voice.

Hunching down like a bull, he slammed the door with his shoulder. It shuddered but remained closed.

Ariana yelped. "Cease!"

He rammed the door again. It creaked on its hinges.

"Of all things, I say," he heard Glenna fume from the other side.

Letting out a loud holler, he hit the door as hard as he could. It gave with a tremendous boom, slamming against the floor.

Glenna glared at him, frozen two feet away from the entrance, one bony hand reaching for it. "What the 'ell, I say. I was coming."

"Gabriel!" Ariana stared at him from the bed, wide-eyed and frowning. She clutched a tiny wrapped bundle to her chest. "That was most unnecessary!"

Her hair looked as though rats had slept in it, and her skin was blotchy as though she hadn't rested in days. The mountain of pillows, usually arranged so neatly on her bed, was scattered haphazardly across the coverlet. Piles of stained cloths crowded the top of the dressing table.

"I told you ne'er to lock me out." Frantic with concern, he stalked across the room, stopping just at the edge of the bed. Dark circles surrounded her eyes, and fine lines wrinkled her skin. She looked exhausted. Too exhausted to be caring for a baby. "Where is my child?"

"You did *not* need to break down the door."

He opened his mouth to say something, but the swaddling blanket slid aside, revealing a hideous red, wrinkly infant. The child was so small it would easily fit in one of his palms.

Christ! How could he have left her? Several heart-beats passed as shock worked its way through Gabriel. "The child lives?"

At that moment, the babe opened its eyes and stared up at him cross-eyed. Alive! The baby was alive! He wanted to raise his hands in victory and roar. Instead, he just stood rooted in place and stared down at his child.

Its face resembled a misshapen prune. 'Twas purplish red with a slight yellow cast and more wrinkled than an old knotted tree. Its egg-shaped head elongated out to one side.

Beyond a doubt, 'twas the most beautiful, perfect, wondrous thing he'd ever seen.

"Bloody hell," he said at last, not knowing what else to say.

The bundle gave a slight wiggle, but it looked limp and very yellow. Ariana hurled Gabriel an aggrieved look. "Must you be so loud?" she said crossly.

He reached for the babe, but Glenna stepped between them and slapped his hand aside. "Wash your hands," she admonished, "I say."

Glancing down at his hands, dirty from travel, Gabriel felt like an ox. He gave her a sharp look, not wanting to admit she was correct about his need to clean up.

Straightening, he stalked to the door and strutted into the hallway. "Rodney! Hither! Tell the bagpiper to cease the blasted dirge and send away the damned priest. My child lives!"

"But, sir, a child so tiny will not live past the day."

"I've seen a many like this, I say. None live. Best to let the priest come," Glenna said.

"My child will *not* die." Not without a fighting chance at life, Gabriel vowed.

Rodney squinted his one eye. "Best to baptize it and allow its soul into heaven."

"You keep the damned clergy away from my child. The babe needs food and warmth, not baptism. Go now! Call off the funeral."

Shrugging, Rodney turned and clomped down the hallway.

Gabriel paced across the room, wrapped his fingers around the bedpost, and squatted to get a good look at the child. It would live. It had to. One of the pillows tumbled off the bed as he leaned forward. The babe gasped for breath.

"Aren't you going to feed it?" He clutched the bedpost to prevent himself from reaching for the child. He shot a glance at Glenna, who hovered nearby.

"She can't breathe; how can she eat?" Ariana looked down at the child, lines of worry betwixt her brow.

Leaving his crossbow on the bed, he stalked to the washstand and poured water from a silver pitcher to cleanse his hands. He dried his hands on a cloth and turned back toward Ariana and his daughter. "Give the babe to me."

Glenna stepped between him and the bed. "Leave us in peace. 'Tis no man's place here. Allow her to enjoy the child for the few moments it has on this earth."

An old wound opened.

"You are not welcome here," Glenna said. "What sort of monster leaves his wife chained to the bed?" She turned her back to him, picked up a damp cloth, and wiped Ariana's forehead. "Be easy, my lady."

Ariana looked pale. She had slumped back on the

pillow and was gently rocking the baby. "Breathe, baby, breathe," she murmured.

"Chained to the bed," he repeated numbly. "But Rodney had the key."

"Lot of good that did, with orders not to release her until a fortnight had passed." She gave him a sour look.

"Rodney did not—" The chain clanked, cutting off his question.

"He's a damn hardheaded, one-eyed fool, I say. 'E said 'e had to stay right beside her in order to release her. 'Twould have been worse with that hairy lout a-lumberin' around in the way." Muttering and fuming, the midwife flitted around the bed, picking up cloths.

Bone-grinding guilt weighted Gabriel's heart.

"Best ye just leave." She pointed to the door. "We've no use fur ye here."

"I am not leaving."

The babe opened its mouth. She needed milk!

"Feed her," Gabriel commanded.

Ariana glared at him and gave another pointed look at the entranceway. "Gabriel, leave us. Go find someone to fix the door."

A surge of frustration coursed through him. Lifting Glenna by her thin shoulders, he set her aside.

She harrumphed. He scowled at her and she backed away.

"Gabriel, cease!" Ariana pushed a wayward curl of hair behind her ear. "Now is not the time for your male arrogance."

"If you would just leave, I say," interjected Glenna, who was flitting around the room again.

The baby wiggled, its gasping increasing.

Laying his crossbow on the sheet, Gabriel reached for her.

Ariana elbowed him aside. "Cease!"

At that moment, Margaret burst into the room. "Oh, mercy," she said, wadding her fists in her skirts. "Ye're cousin, the bishop, has just arrived. I told him you were upstairs 'aving a baby, and 'e said 'e'd come to bless the child and bring you good tidings."

"My cousin!" she exclaimed.

"Randall!" echoed Gabriel.

The baby went limp.

"Saints," Ariana gasped, desperately rubbing the infant's chest.

"I told him to wait downstairs," Margaret interjected as if to get her mind spoken quickly so that she could leave. "Oh, saints. I tell you, I have never seen quite so much of a procession as all that he has. Horses and trunks and jewels and servants. 'E must be richer than the king."

Ariana drew in a sharp breath and clung tightly to her newborn child, who just had started breathing again. Her cousin's arrival could not be good news. She glanced at Gabriel, fear streaking through her. "Where's Jason?"

Loud scuffling sounded in the hallway. Rodney fell into the chamber. "I am sorry. I tried to prevent—" He stopped mid-sentence as Gabriel gave him a black look.

Behind him, the bishop with an army of guards and servants spilled into the chamber, taking up the nooks and crannies of her frilly room.

She sat up, clutching her child. If she could have, she would have jumped and run. "Cousin!"

Ariana's insides quivered. Dear Mary, they would all

be killed if a bloodbath erupted in her chamber. Sitting up, she glared at the men, who all looked like growling bears.

"Cease, all of you!"

Gabriel spared her a glance. "Stay out of this, wife. 'Tis men's business."

"Nay, *husband*. 'Tis woman's business when her child is involved." She drew the sheet over the bed, covering the baby's face. No point in showing exactly how vulnerable she was. She made to sit up a little straighter. "Begone, all of you!"

The chain encircling her ankle clanked against the footboard.

"Gabriel—" she started.

He shot her a warning look.

Closing her mouth, she bit the inside of her cheek. Tied to the bed or no, she would not dishonor him by arguing in front of the bishop's men.

"Lady Ariana of Rosebriar," Randall said, pacing toward her, "I am here on behalf of the Holy Church of Rome. You have been charged with the murder of your lord Ivan of Rosebriar. This is Robert of Lionsgate, the bailiff of the shire, come here to take you into custody."

A tall man with a large, bulbous nose stepped forward, flanked by two heavily armed guardsmen.

She gasped.

Afore they reached her, Gabriel blocked their pathway.

The hem of Randall's garment swished against the Oriental carpet, filling the room with the scent of incense.

"Gabriel," Randall purred, extending his hands outward, "step aside. We have orders. And we have need to question you concerning the death of the Abbot of Thornbury."

Gabriel snatched the dagger from his calf and held it in front of him. "Leave ere I carve your heart out."

The bishop glanced at the man standing close by wearing scholar's robes. "Blasphemy against a servant of the church. Did you write that down?" His chins wobbled as he spoke.

"Out!" Gabriel roared. "I will tear you apart with my bare hands."

The bishop's guards drew their swords.

Ariana cringed. Saints, Gabriel looked angry enough to kill them all, but there were too many.

Randall smirked. "Surrender. You are much outnumbered."

Sliding the dagger blade down to the ends of his fingertips, Gabriel cocked his arm back. "I need only kill you."

Two guards stepped in front of the bishop, swords at the ready. Gabriel stepped to one side to get a clear shot. Two more flanked him.

Ariana gasped as the men closed in. The babe squirmed, breathing more strongly now.

Gabriel threw the dagger just as one of the guards lunged. It shot across the room, burying hilt-deep in Randall's shoulder.

He squealed like a pig, holding his bleeding flesh. "Kill him!"

Ariana screamed as one of the men lunged at Gabriel and pushed him against the wall. Grasping the man by the shoulders, Gabriel threw him aside. He spun, deflecting a second guard's sword with his hand.

The babe at her breast wiggled.

Gabriel slammed another man against the wall. He bounced off and hit the foot of the bed, jostling her and the baby.

Across the room, Randall held his shoulder. A snarl curled his lips. Blood leaked down his arm.

Panicked, Ariana watched the fray and scanned the nearby area for something to even the odds. The babe cried softly. Gabriel grunted, throwing off another attacker.

Beneath the edge of the sheet, the tiller of the crossbow poked out. Her heart pounded. The weapon had been covered when she'd frantically pulled the sheet up to hide the baby.

Shifting the child to one hand, Ariana grasped the crossbow. But if she killed one, there were others to take his place. Her fingers shook. And what if she accidentally shot Gabriel?

Saints. She eyed Randall who avidly watched the hurly-burly. No one paid her any attention. Now was her chance. If he was gone, there would be no one to lead his guards, and mayhap Gabriel could fight free in the confusion. Making an instantaneous decision, she pulled the bow from under the sheet, swung it around, and aimed it at Randall's chest. She would fear him no longer.

He turned as if suspecting something. "Cousin—"

Taking a steadying breath, she squeezed the tickler.

Chapter 30

The bolt struck with a thick thud. Randall bellowed. Gabriel's attackers turned, stunned for an instant, giving Gabriel a chance to break free, just as she had hoped. The bishop stared, wide-eyed, at Ariana for a moment before falling to his knees. She moaned, her hands beginning to shake. She'd killed a man again.

The babe gasped for breath. She clutched her tightly and rubbed her tiny chest, trying to help her breathe.

Gabriel clobbered the nearest guard atop the head. Two others went to help their fallen master. Another simply put down his weapon and gave the bishop a look of disdain as if he was glad to see him gone. The others just stood there, staring from Ariana to the fallen churchman as if stunned.

Her stomach churned. The edges of the room clouded, and she felt that she would fall asleep. She forced herself to stay awake so she could rub the baby's belly.

Loud clomping footsteps sounded in the hallway,

but as they got closer, they seemed to fade rather than grow louder. She felt weak and dizzy.

Rodney and the rest of Gabriel's band of men crowded into the chamber. Rodney's one eye blazed with anger as he held his sword aloft. "Master! They surrounded us. We had to break free, but we did."

The rest of the bishop's guards exchanged vexed looks and put down their weapons.

"Never cared much for the fat pig anyway," one muttered.

"Blast it to hell!" Gabriel cursed, staring at Rodney and the rest of his men. "Thank the stars, you are good fighters. There has been no time to hire the amount of guards we need."

The men's voices waned. It seemed impossible to hold her head up. Her eyelids felt coated in dust.

"Get this monster out of here." Gabriel shoved the bishop's dead form with his boot. "Hold his men in the great hall."

Ariana's stomach spasmed again. The bed felt wet and sticky around her. Glancing down, she saw a large red stain on the sheet beneath her hips. Blood seemed to be gushing from inside her.

Her head lolled to one side, her stomach lurched, and she vomited on the bedsheet.

"My lady!" Glenna snatched the babe.

Ariana moaned, and her eyes fluttered closed. Arms went around her, and she felt someone wipe her face with a cool rag.

The world went dark.

Three weeks later, Gabriel stared at the simple stone pile that marked the grave. Worry for Ariana, who still lay sick in bed, had driven him from the keep, and he'd come here to think.

No cross or marble headstone marked the plot. 'Twas just a simple pile of stones under an old oak.

His mother's final resting place.

She had died young, having made her living on her back and birthing a baby every year or two before succumbing to a disease of the blood after the last childbirth. No house of worship would allow a harlot to be buried in their graveyard. But despite the church's proclamation that she was not a good woman, she had not been a bad woman either. Oft the children had been nigh to starving, and oft she'd gone without food or taken extra patrons even when she neared death so her children could be fed.

Gabriel knelt, his heart weary. Ne'er in his life had he felt his roots so keenly as he had this past while.

Ariana lay in bed, weak, with blood trickling off and on from her woman's parts. She moaned and flailed in a state of neither sleep nor wakefulness. Guilt crushed him as he watched her fade, growing paler and feebler by the day. How could he have left her chained to the bed while he went to hunt Randall?

Staring at his mother's pile of rocks, he was reminded again that he was the son of a harlot. Not a nobleman. Not a lord. It struck him that Cyrille had been correct in saying that he was not a worthy husband. That Glenna had been correct when she said he did not belong.

In his mind, he could see Ariana, angry and proud at the altar as he'd forced her to marry him. *I hate you*, she'd said then. When he had come into the room after the babe was born, she'd told him to leave.

His shoulders shook, and he suddenly wanted to

pray. He knew no formal prayers. He had been told that God did not listen to those born in sin.

But mayhap God would hear his plea just this one time.

Interlacing his fingers, he bowed his head. *Please, God, let her live. Do not let her suffer for my deeds.* 'Twas the first prayer he had said in years, and he was unsure if he had done it correctly. Mayhap one was supposed to do more than merely beg. The babe was stronger now—she would live.

There were no more reasons he should interfere with Ariana's life. Bowing his head again, he added: *I will leave and bother her no more.*

Chapter 31

Ariana's eyes fluttered open. She felt thin as mist. Her curls stuck to her forehead. Lifting her arm to wipe the hair aside was like picking up a stone.

"Oh, mercy, mistress," she heard Margaret fret. "Be you awake?"

Struggling to open her eyes, she turned her head in the direction of her cook's voice. She winced at the pain in her temples.

"Margaret?" Her voice sounded croaky.

"Oh, saints. We were so worried about ye, mistress."

The room spun, and she took a few breaths before opening her eyes again. Margaret, Dionne, and Edwina hovered around the bed.

"The baby?" Her mouth felt dry as a desert.

"With Beth."

"She lives?"

"Aye. Glenna thought the babe was to die as did we all. She was so tiny. Master Gabriel would hear none of it. He kept her night and day, warming her with his own body and making sure she had milk. Of a truth,

I have ne'er seen a man so insistent to have a child so weak and puny live. Especially a girl."

Ariana smiled weakly. 'Twas characteristic for Gabriel to worry so deeply for those in his care.

"Where is my lord?"

"'E's gone, miss. Gone three weeks past."

"Gone?" She struggled to sit up. Sitting up made her sick to her stomach, and she sank back to the pillow. "Where? How long have I been asleep?"

"Weeks, mistress. Over a month."

"Weeks?" Amazed, she stared at Margaret, who was wringing her hands.

"Oh, mercy. Oh, saints."

"We've been a-feeding you broth and water. Only sometimes did ye open your eyes," Dionne said.

"Right. Francine has been bathing you and brushing your hair," Edwina said.

"But—" But it seemed as though she'd only been asleep for a few moments. And still, she felt exhausted.

"Right, me lady," echoed Edwina.

"Gabriel?"

"'E took his passel of brats and left. Said you'd been right about him not being a fit lord."

"Not being a fit lord?"

"Because he failed to protect ye. Because he chained you to the bed. Because—"

Gabriel had left her? "Cease," she moaned. "Where did he go?"

Edwina looked at Dionne, who looked at Margaret, who looked back at Edwina.

"No one knows, me lady. 'E left men to guard the castle, but not a one knows where 'e's gone."

"Samantha? Myron?"

"Gone as well."

A heavy weight settled on Ariana's heart. "Surely, someone—"

"He's a man of the outdoors, my lady. Rodney says if Gabriel does not want to be found, he cannot be. He blends with trees and nature as does a wild beast."

"I must go look for him."

"Oh, saints. 'Tis no use, mistress. All of us have looked already. His siblings be at their old cabin."

Ignoring her churning stomach, Ariana sat up. In her mind she heard Gabriel say, *'Tis a place of magic. I came here when my fingers were cut off.*

The waterfall!

"Edwina, help me rise."

"Right, my lady. I think you should stay in bed."

"Oh, saints. Oh, mercy. Do not rise, mistress."

"I say, 'tisn't wise."

Ariana looked from one woman to the next, her heart warming at their concern. "Help me up," she insisted.

She swung her legs over the side of the bed.

Edwina leapt to help her, as did Dionne.

"I need food."

"Oh, saints, mistress. Right away." Margaret looked relieved. She hurried out, her wide bottom lurching as she went.

Legs trembling, Ariana stood. Gabriel gone nigh on a month already? It made no sense that he would have left. Equal amounts of annoyance and despair worked through her. The man had forced his way into her castle and now, just to leave? Vexing! Frowning, she tried balancing without holding onto the bed. Her knees wobbled, but her legs held.

"Should I call for a bathing tub, me lady?" Edwina reached for the bell cord.

"Aye."

The more she began to move, the heartier she felt. Margaret brought broth, cheese, and bread, and the food restored a portion of Ariana's strength. She changed clothes, and had Francine comb and braid her hair.

Three weeks later, she finally had enough strength to make her way to the stables so she could go to the waterfall.

The days were quiet. Too quiet. Life seemed flat and colorless without the rambunctious children or Gabriel's men's laughter. She missed Gabriel's simple gifts of wildflowers and folded roses. Those were things all her gold could not buy.

"My lady, ye've been ill," Tom said, making to stop her.

"Nonsense. I feel fit as ever."

'Twas true. After the first groggy days, she felt as rested as if she'd slept for months. She allowed herself a small smile. She *had* slept for months.

Jason was well, but he seemed sad without Gareth. The dog had stayed, and oft, the two played with the leather ball in the bailey.

Each night without Gabriel seemed more excruciating than the next. Slowly, her nightmares returned, and she went back to leaving a candle lit in the room while she slept. How nice it had been when his presence had banished her fear of the dark.

Tom saddled Lacey for her and helped her mount. "Mayhap someone should accompany you."

She shook her head. "Nay. I go alone."

* * *

The sounds of splashing water lifted her spirits as Ariana sank to her knees and crawled under the bush toward the waterfall. She sent up a silent prayer that she had not been wrong.

Wrens and robins chirped. The place was as magical as she remembered. Sunlight bounced off the falling water, making a small rainbow in the frothy stream.

Ferns, trees, shrubs, birds, dragonflies. And the beautiful purple foxglove. But no sign of a man. Not even a scrap of food or a piece of cloth.

Her heart sank. "Gabriel?"

Naught.

She had been so sure. So positive he would be here.

Drawing closer to the water, she took off her slippers and climbed atop the rock where she and Gabriel had first made love. She stared forlornly into the water, watching the tiny ripples become wider and wider.

He'd been gone a month. Of a truth, a man could go a long distance in a month. She dangled her feet off the rock and stirred the warm water with her toes.

So much had happened betwixt her and Gabriel. Mayhap he had not left because he felt he was an unfit lord at all. Mayhap he'd left because he did not want to belong at Rosebriar.

She remembered how out of place he had seemed at Lord Robert's feast. Perhaps after the baby's birth and weeks of caring for it, he had decided he did not want to be tied so tightly after all.

Slowly, she unfastened her bodice. The water looked inviting and warm. Mayhap it would chase away the chill of her thoughts.

Divest of her garments, she sank into the pond, lay

back, and gazed upward at the canopy of leaves. Gabriel. Gabriel. Once before, she'd thought she had lost him. How could she bear it again? Closing her eyes, she allowed the water to float away her sad thoughts.

"Ariana?"

Gasping, her eyes flew open, and she sank into the water with a splash.

Gabriel stood on the rock, shirtless and wearing leather breeks. His feet were bare, and, saints above, he had a short beard. Her heart leapt.

"My lord!"

"What are you doing here?"

Rising from the water, she padded toward him. "I came for you."

Gabriel stared at his naked wife. The weight of the water straightened her red curls, and they hung in dark waves down her back. One lock lay across her breast. Her alabaster skin glowed in the tree-filtered sunlight.

"Go back where you came, Ariana. This is my world. You do not belong here."

She emerged out of the water like the lady rising from the lake. "I came for you," she repeated.

"I am not a nobleman."

"You are the Lord of Rosebriar."

"You deserve better."

She climbed onto the rock. The skin on her stomach was no longer tight as it had been when she was pregnant. Moisture ran down her lily-white body in rivulets. God, she was beautiful.

"I need you," she said, reaching toward him.

"You do not need me. You have wealth and brains enough to care for yourself."

"I have had three husbands afore you. I think I know what I need better than you." She touched him. Water dripped off her fingers. "I sleep better when you are there. The night demons no longer exist."

"Ariana"—he shrugged aside—"I almost killed you and our baby because of my anger. I refused to listen about Nigel. I am an unfit husband."

"You came here to punish yourself?"

How could he explain the biting guilt he'd felt? Or his prayer and promise to God? Frowning, he gazed into the softly rippling water so he would not be so affected by her nakedness. Seeing her thus was like a feast for a starved man.

"I heard what you did for the baby, how you kept her near and cared for her. 'Tis how you care for all who are your responsibility. How can you say you are not a good lord?"

He shook his head. He'd done too much wrong and the guilt of it weighed on him like quarry stone. "You were nearly lost."

"Look at me, Gabriel." She laid her fingers on his forearm. "I'm not lost. I'm here."

He wanted to take her in his arms, but he dared not. How could he keep his promise then? He remembered how desperate he'd been. "You were so ill. I was afraid."

Propping a hand on her naked hip, she gazed at him intensely. "Once you told me we had our whole lives to explore the sensations of our bodies. Do you intend to break that promise already?"

Her words brought a rush of blood into his cock. He groaned, knowing his flesh was not strong enough to resist her, to not bother her as he had promised. She looked warrior strong despite her nudity.

"How can you still want me?" he asked.

"When I'm with you, I no longer have nightmares. My fear of the dark is gone. My fear of men is gone."

Reaching for her, he slid a hand down the soft skin of her torso. A red lock of her hair curled around his wrist. I'll just touch her a little, he promised himself. His rough, tanned skin contrasted sharply with the smooth alabaster of hers. 'Twas as if she were made of fragile porcelain.

She smiled, wrapped her arm around his neck, and pulled him close. Tendrils of her hair made long spirals down her back and curled around her hips.

"I've missed you," she said.

'Twas his undoing. He could no more resist her than he could resist breathing. He kissed her, enjoying the sweet surrender of her mouth and the little mewl of pleasure that came from her throat.

"I've missed you, too," he murmured when the kiss was broken. "My dear, sweet Ariana." He ran his hands languidly over her back, wanting to give her all the pleasure he could. To show her how much he cared for her.

Smiling, she pulled the ties on his breeks. "I want you. I was afraid of the ways between a man and a woman until you showed me there could be pleasure for both of us."

If 'twas possible, his sex swelled harder. It felt tight and hungry. But he did not want to rush their time together.

Mine! a primitive urge beckoned, although he knew it was not right. He'd made a promise to God.

Tamping down his conscience, he determined he would give her pleasure, but he would still keep his promise to not bother her. He would let her go after

their lovemaking was over. Trailing his fingers over
the soft skin of her back, he nuzzled her neck. He
fanned his hands and ran them down her body to cup
the rounded globes of her buttocks.

She sighed.

His cock pushed outward, further loosening the ties
of his breeks until the morning air brushed across the
skin of his member.

She kissed him and ran her hands across his stomach, pushing urgently down on his breeks until his
cock sprang free. He licked water off her skin, trailing
from her neck to the peak of one of her breasts. Her
nipple puckered, and she moaned softly as he flicked
a finger across it.

"Are you well, Ariana?"

Laughing, she pulled him closer until her breasts
skimmed across his chest. "Very well, my lord."

"There is no more blood? You were very ill."

"No more blood."

"Good. Wrap your legs around my waist."

Her eyes dilated as she did as he asked. Lifting her,
he slowly guided his member into her quim. Her
queynt felt heated and creamy surrounding his sex.
He closed his eyes, wanting this time to last forever.
'Twas all he had to give her.

"Oh, Gabriel!" She clung to him, obviously as hungry
for him as he was for her.

Desire thumped through his veins. For long moments, they rocked together, luxuriating in the
throbbing heat of each other's bodies and lost in
desire. Closing her eyes, Ariana moaned and pumped
her hips. His legs quivered with exertion as his manhood slid back and forth inside her, but he did not
want the sensation to end. Not now. Not ever.

She cried out in pleasure, then clung limply to him as he climaxed. He held her to him for a few minutes. She was so soft, so beautiful.

Slowly, she unwound her legs from his waist and slid down his body until her feet touched the rock. She stood on tiptoes, his softening cock pressing against the auburn curls of her sex.

"Let us go home now," she whispered, trailing her fingers along the edge of an old scar.

"Ariana." His heart felt as though it were breaking. Swallowing, he gazed at the purple foxgloves. "I cannot."

Placing her hand on his cheek, she turned his face back to hers. "Why in the devil's name not?"

"'Tis complicated."

She tilted her chin down and stared up at him. "You have another woman?"

"Nay." Dear saints, how could one even think of another woman with a lady like Ariana around?

"Then?" she prompted.

"I made a promise to God," he murmured, cringing at how odd it sounded on his lips. A whore's son praying? He half-expected her to laugh aloud.

"You made a promise to God to not see me?" She sounded confused. Sunlight glittered off her hair, gilding it into a copper color.

"I promised not to bother you if He would heal your body." Not wanting to talk about something so intimate, he hitched up his breeks and set her slightly away from him. "You were very sick."

"Oh." She smiled. The three freckles on her cheek lifted slightly. "But surely you can come home now."

He hesitated. He'd only just found out that God answered the prayers of whore's sons, and he was unsure how this worked. What if he went to Rosebriar, and she fell sick again? He stared at the water rushing off the cliff as he debated. A soft breeze ruffled the leaves of the foliage.

"How is our baby?"

"She is well."

"And you are well?"

"Aye."

He pondered this. "I cannot come to Rosebriar," he said. He could not risk their welfare.

"But, Gabriel, you are my husband."

"I do not wish to bother you."

Cocking her head to one side, she frowned. "'Twould not be bothering me for you to live at Rosebriar."

He drew in a breath. As much as he wished to deny it, Cyrille was right: his talents did lie in other directions asides being lord of a castle.

"Mayhap we could meet here at the waterfall," he hedged.

A flash of anger lit her eyes. "You are being stubborn!"

"I am not."

"You are! I miss you."

"I will meet you here whenever you wish."

"Jason misses you. The baby—"

He set his jaw. 'Twas for her sake and the sake of the child he could not. "I cannot go to Rosebriar. Do not press me. 'Tis best for you."

"You do not know what is best for me!" She bent and gathered her clothing.

"Ariana, my love, please. We can meet here. I can make your body sing with desire."

She glared at him, and for a moment, he thought she would raise her hand to strike his cheek.

"I am not Cyrille," she said, pulling her dress over her head. "You will not get away from me so easily."

He reached for her, but she ignored his hand. Tugging her dress into place, she turned her back on him. Water dripped from her long red hair onto her skirt.

A weight seemed to crush his chest as he watched her leave the magical dreamlike world of the waterfall.

Chapter 32

Gabriel felt as though his world had turned upside down as he walked to his family's cottage a fortnight later. Since Ariana's appearance at the waterfall, he could scarcely look at the pool without remembering how she'd been when she rose out of the water.

He'd hermited himself away long enough. 'Twas time to get on with living, with hunting traitors and rebels. Mayhap then, the urge to ride in and declare himself lord of her castle would disappear.

Ne'er in his life would he have thought that she would reject his proposition to meet him on occasion for a few moments of bliss. The pleasure they took in each other's arms was one of the few things he could truly gift her with. But verily, the mention of it had made her angry.

He had hoped she might return, but after days of waiting, he knew she would not.

He blew out a frustrated breath. Wealthy beyond imagining, she had no need for a man to earn her keep for her. And now with Randall gone and Henry firmly on the throne, no need for protection beyond what her guards could give her.

Damn.

Several of the children played outside the two-room cottage. Myron and Heather sparred with sticks, pretending they were knights.

"Gabriel!"

"Gabriel!"

"You've grown a beard!"

He paused to greet his family and give each one a hug. He'd seen them all from a distance, but 'twas good to be home at last.

Dog lounged on the doorstep, his large tail flopping against the rough stones. That Ariana had returned the cur saddened him. But what need would she have of an overgrown hound? Likely she'd bought Jason a small, fluffy dog to play with.

Ah. Best to put it behind him.

He entered the cottage, then stopped, stunned. Did his eyes deceive him?

Ariana hovered over the kitchen fire, her back to the door.

He wiped his eyes.

She was still there, wearing a plain brown dress and an apron. Her hair was twisted into a simple bun, the curly strands sticking out of the messy updo.

She looked as out of place as a princess in the stews of London.

His shoulders tightened, and he cleared his throat.

Turning, she brandished a wooden soupspoon as one would a drawn sword. Her eyes widened, then she smiled. "Gabriel!"

He gripped the doorframe to hold himself up. "What do you do here?"

"I said you would not be rid of me so easily."

The scent of smoke and fresh stew hung in the air. "But—"

"You said you vowed not to bother me, but I made no such promise. If you will not live with me at Rosebriar, then we will stay here."

Gabriel scowled. What trick was this? "You would stay here?"

"I want to be with you." Smoke from the cooking fire curled around her in thin waves. A tendril of her red hair trailed down her neck.

Striding around his family's roughhewn table, he made his way toward her. "You can be with me any time you wish at the waterfall."

She pointed the spoon at him. "Gabriel, you dunderhead, I want more from you than copulation."

"But your castle? Your furnishings? Your fine clothing?"

"Cannot warm my bed. Cannot chase away my fear of the night."

Her vehemence gave him pause. He glanced around at the shabby interior of the cottage. 'Twas only two rooms, this room and the bedroom. The walls were in good repair, but no tapestries or decorations covered the rough wood. For furniture, they had one table without enough chairs for all of the children. The bed had been sold last winter while he was imprisoned. Everyone slept together piled in quilts. 'Twas a happy place, but not wealthy.

"How long have you been here?" he asked.

"Since leaving the waterfall."

A fortnight past.

"How did you know I would come home?"

She shrugged. Her brown skirt rippled. "You take

care of the ones you are responsible for. You are not the sort of man to mope your life away."

Gabriel chewed his lower lip. This was not right. She was a lady. A noblewoman. She deserved finery and jewelry. "You should not be here."

Lifting an eyebrow, she turned back and stirred the pot of stew. "I'm not leaving."

Vexing woman! He found himself admiring the stubborn set of her shoulders. The hem of her dress skimmed the cottage floor, which he noticed was freshly swept. 'Twas like her to bring a measure of order into chaos. Likely, the children had been bathed daily as well.

"Ariana—"

"If living in this cabin means having you, then so be it. My steward and ladies can certainly take care of Rosebriar without me. They have proved such these past weeks."

"But Jason? The baby?"

"Jason is playing with Gareth. Sam has Roselle."

A knot formed in his throat. "You named our baby after my mother?"

"She was part of what made you who you are."

Stalking forward, he reached for her, wanting to touch her. "Ariana, my love."

She smiled as he ran his fingers gently along her collarbone. "Gabriel, your vow was not to bother me. 'Twas not that we would not be together. If I cannot have you as a noblewoman, then I will become a peasant."

Frowning, he ran his hand down her arm. "One cannot become a peasant."

She held the wooden spoon up. It looked out of place against her lily-white hands. "Yes, I can, and I will. I have been married to three lords, and not a one of them brought me flowers or would have taught my son to throw a ball. Not a one would have cared for a tiny infant as you did. Especially a girl. Jason is lonely without Gareth. And I am lonely without you."

She looked like a pagan goddess set on conquering the world. For a second, his mind floated to Cyrille, who had thought marrying an old man was better than being a peasant's bride.

"Sometimes the winters are hard," he hedged. "But I've always provided."

"Fine."

She was serious. Dead serious. Leaning forward, he grasped her around the waist. He liked the feel of her in his arms. He liked the way she moved and the way she smelled. He liked how she cared for her son and her plants and her ladies. He liked everything about her.

"I love you," he said.

Smiling, she stood on tiptoes to kiss him. "I love you, too." The spoon clattered onto the table, and her hands wound into his hair.

He pulled her closer, enjoying how their bodies fit together.

Leaning down, he pressed his lips onto Ariana's.

Sticky fingers tugged on the back of his tunic. "Gabriel, Gabriel, will you help me fix this?"

He raised his head from Ariana and looked around. Joel stood behind him holding a wooden duck with a broken bill. "Yes, Joel. Later."

He kissed Ariana's cheek. She smelled faintly of roses. Another tug.

"I said later, Joel."

"'Snot Joel. 'Tis me, Gareth. We need you to find

the arrows for Myron's bow an' then to play leap frog an' then . . ."

Tightening his hold on Ariana, Gabriel took a deep breath and let it out. He fluffed Gareth's unruly red hair. "I am busy at the moment."

Ariana giggled. "Best you help them. I will be right here." She picked up the spoon from the table.

A few moments later, Gabriel had tied Joel's duck with string and found Myron's arrows. He slid his hands around Ariana's waist and pulled her close. As his lips touched hers, another child pulled on the leg of his breeks.

He spun. 'Twas Heather.

"My comb is missing. I think Oliver took it."

Gabriel stared at her for a moment, then glanced about the cottage for one square inch of privacy so that he could kiss or swive Ariana. Children scampered around the room, laughing and playing with each other. They climbed over and under the sparse furnishings. Jason came over and hugged him on the leg before scampering off with Gareth.

The door opened and Sam entered, holding Roselle and looking more grown-up than ever. Evidently, she'd taken well to her growing womanhood. She wore a dress, and her frizzy hair had been tamed. The bundle in her arms squirmed, then let out a soft cry.

Inside, he nearly burst with joy. Walking to her, he took the baby, wanting to hold her close again and see how she fared. He'd been so worried about her. She weighed more than she had afore—growing ever healthier, thank God.

"Beautiful, isn't she?" Ariana said, touching his arm.

Gabriel smiled, admiring the infant's rosy cheeks and pale skin. "As beautiful as her mother."

Closing her eyes, Roselle snuggled into his chest. Holding his own baby was a feeling like no other. Thank God Ariana had brought her here.

Nigel and Eleanor entered, holding hands and staring dreamily at each other. Her wheat-colored hair was braided, and she wore a plain brown dress.

Although Gabriel had not been living at the cottage, he had seen them from afar from time to time. Since Nigel had arrived, Eleanor had been different. She would sit for hours listening to him play his violin, for once at peace with her past. Two abused souls had found each other and started on their road to healing. Not so different from Ariana and himself, he mused.

He smiled at Ariana, who was poking at the cooking fire with a long stick. "I'm glad you are here."

"Gabriel?" Eleanor ventured.

He started, shocked. Eleanor had spoken! 'Twas the first time she'd done so since coming back to England. Her voice was timid, but by God, she'd spoken!

"Eleanor?"

"I think you should move to Rosebriar," she said shyly, clutching Nigel's hand. Well. Thank God he hadn't broken the man's fingers as he'd almost done. His sister needed a hand to hold.

"My lord, we wish to marry." Nigel brought Eleanor's hand to his lips and kissed it softly.

"You do?"

"Aye."

For a moment, Gabriel wondered what a sexless marriage would be like.

"We love each other." Nigel stared at Eleanor, and she gazed back at him.

Gabriel smiled. They had found love even without passion. He pondered this for a moment. Even without the passion, he would still want Ariana. He loved her kindness, her concern for the children, her ability to thrive despite three awful marriages. He loved her. Just as she was. As a noblewoman.

He watched her stir the pot of stew. "You should not be doing the cooking. We will return to Rosebriar."

"I am content here."

He handed Roselle to Sam, strode back to Ariana, and kissed her on the cheek. Heather pushed her way between them. "Gabriel?"

Glowering at his sister, he said to Ariana, "We need our own chamber."

Heather scampered off.

Ariana laughed.

Taking her hand, he gazed down at her. She was such a fine woman. Doing what he had once vowed ne'er to do again, he knelt before her on one knee. "Will you marry me, Lady Ariana?"

"Marry you?" She tried to pull him to his feet, but he remained where he was. "We are married already."

"I want a real wedding. One where I know you are marrying me because you wish to, not because you are forced to."

"Oh."

"Why the sudden frown?"

"Ne'er in my life have I been offered that choice."

"So, will you marry me?"

"Yes, Gabriel! Yes!" She threw her arms around his neck. Their bodies pressed each other. As he rose to his feet, he picked her up and swung her around.

She laughed, her simple dress flying out.

The children erupted in a cacophony of whoops and cheers.

He glanced around at his family who were all staring at the two of them. Christ! He wanted to kiss Ariana. To swive her. To hold her and ne'er let go.

Hoisting her higher in his arms, he carried her toward the door. No privacy here, but plenty at the waterfall.

Sighing, she leaned into him and wrapped her arms around his neck. Tendrils of her red hair curled against his tunic, smelling faintly of roses.

"Sam, take over the cooking," he called over one shoulder as he crossed the threshold. "We will return."

"My lord," Ariana protested, but her tone was mild, "the children need to be fed."

Nuzzling her cheek, he took her into the forest. His body was aflame for her, and he could scarcely wait to build her desire. Already she clung to him tightly. "My lady, pleasure afore duty."

About the Author

Award-winning author Jessica Trapp believes a dynamic romance is one where two opposing characters are transformed into two people who share love and passion. Despite reading gobs of romance and science fiction instead of studying for biochemistry exams in college, she is a registered pharmacist. She fell in love at first sight with her husband Joe and married him eighteen years ago on her lunch break. She believes the key to a happy marriage is to never stop having fun together. They now live in Houston, Texas, and have an eight-year-old son. When she is not reading or writing, she bellydances, putters in the garden, plays chess, and drinks copious amounts of hot tea. For excerpts of her novels, contests, and more, please visit her on the web at www.jessicatrapp.com.

Discover the Romances of
Hannah Howell

BOOK YOUR PLACE ON OUR WEBSITE AND MAKE THE READING CONNECTION!

We've created a customized website just for our very special readers, where you can get the inside scoop on everything that's going on with Zebra, Pinnacle and Kensington books.

When you come online, you'll have the exciting opportunity to:

- View covers of upcoming books

- Read sample chapters

- Learn about our future publishing schedule (listed by publication month *and author*)

- Find out when your favorite authors will be visiting a city near you

- Search for and order backlist books from our online catalog

- Check out author bios and background information

- Send e-mail to your favorite authors

- Meet the Kensington staff online

- Join us in weekly chats with authors, readers and other guests

- Get writing guidelines

- AND MUCH MORE!

Visit our website at
http://www.kensingtonbooks.com